UPRISING

MARGARET PETERSON HADDIX

UPRISING

SIMON & SCHUSTER BFYR

NEW YORK · LONDON · TORONTO · SYDNEY

SIMON & SCHUSTER BFYR An imprint of Simon & Schuster Children's Publishing Division 1230 Avenue of the Americas, New York, New York 10020 · This book is a work of fiction. Any references to historical events, real people, or real locales are used fictitiously. Other names, characters, places, and incidents are products of the author's imagination, and any resemblance to actual events or locales or persons, living or dead, is entirely coincidental. · Copyright © 2007 by Margaret Peterson Haddix · All rights reserved, including the right of reproduction in whole or in part in any form. SIMON & SCHUSTER BFYR is a trademark of Simon & Schuster, Inc. · For information about special discounts for bulk purchases, please contact Simon & Schuster Special Sales at 1-866-506-1949 or business@simonandschuster.com. The Simon & Schuster Speakers Bureau can bring authors to your live event. For more information or to book an event, contact the Simon & Schuster Speakers Bureau at 1-866-248-3049 or visit our website at www.simonspeakers.com • Also available in a SIMON & SCHUSTER BFYR hardcover edition · Book design by Alicia Mikles · The text for this book is set in MBell. · Manufactured in the United States of America · First SIMON & SCHUSTER BFYR paperback edition February 2011 · 11 · The Library of Congress has cataloged the hardcover edition as follows: Haddix, Margaret Peterson. · Uprising / Margaret Peterson Haddix. · 1st ed. · Summary: In 1927, at the urging of twenty-one-year-old Harriet, Mrs. Livingston reluctantly recalls her experiences at the Triangle Shirtwaist factory, including miserable working conditions that led to a strike, then the fire that took the lives of her two best friends, when Harriet, the boss's daughter, was only five years old. Includes historical notes. · ISBN 978-1-4169-1171-5 (hc) · 1. Triangle Shirtwaist Company—Juvenile fiction. [1. Triangle Shirtwaist Company—Fiction. 2. Immigrants—New York (N.Y.)—Fiction. 3. Factories—Fiction. 4. Labor disputes—Fiction. 5. Strikes and lockouts—Fiction. 6. Triangle Shirtwaist Company—Fire, 1911—Fiction. 7. New York (N.Y.)—History—1898–1951—Fiction. I. Title. · PZ7.H1164 Upr 2007 · [Fic]—dc22 · 2006034870 · ISBN 978-1-4169-1172-2 (pbk) · ISBN 978-1-4424-1956-8 (eBook)

In memory of the 20,000 and the 146

*T*ell me about the fire."

Mrs. Livingston stares at the young woman standing before her—the young woman who has barged into her house uninvited, unannounced. Mrs. Livingston is known for her kindness and charity; her friends say that Mrs. Livingston will listen to anyone who is troubled or lonely or sad. Even beggars in the street. Even women of ill repute.

But Mrs. Livingston cannot hide her disgust at the sight of this young woman with the dark bobbed hair, her trim body swathed in a fine fur coat.

"You're one of the daughters," Mrs. Livingston finally says. "Harriet?"

Harriet nods. Slowly.

"Then you were there," Mrs. Livingston says. "You saw what happened."

"I was five years old," Harriet says. "All I remember is smoke and flames and people screaming. And being carried to safety."

"Yes, *you* got out safely," Mrs. Livingston says. "Unharmed."

"So did you."

Mrs. Livingston does not disagree. What good does it do to speak of scars no one can see, of grief that never lifts? What would Harriet know of harm?

"Ask your father about the fire," she says harshly. Then she considers this, curious in spite of herself. "What does he say? The same things he said in court, when he had a lawyer feeding him lines?"

"He won't talk about the fire," Harriet says. "He'd like to pretend it never happened."

Mrs. Livingston can believe this.

"Read the newspapers, then," Mrs. Livingston says. "There were plenty of stories written at the time."

Mrs. Livingston herself has not read any of them. She couldn't, back then. But she is always amazed at how much other people know, because of the papers: girls who were away at Vassar or Bryn Mawr or Smith in 1911, who can recite the exact number of the dead; women who spent their 1911 all but chained to sewing machines in other factories in the city, who can describe exactly how the flames leaped from table to table, from floor to floor.

"I've already read the papers," Harriet says. "In English and Yiddish, what little I can read of Yiddish. But it's not enough. The newspaper stories are just paper and ink. It's easy to think it's not real. I want . . . flesh and blood."

Charred flesh, Mrs. Livingston thinks. *Spilled blood.*

Her legs tremble; she leans against the balustrade of the hallway stairs for support. But she does not really want to stay standing. She thinks there is sense in the ancient customs of grief—rending one's clothes, throwing oneself to the ground, and wailing to the heavens. Even now, all these years later, she is not above longing for that.

"Why do you want to know about the fire?" she whispers.

Harriet does not answer right away. She stares past Mrs. Livingston's shoulder for a moment, then brings her gaze back to Mrs. Livingston's face.

"I'm twenty-one now," she says. "I can vote. Do you remember talking with me about women getting to vote?"

Mrs. Livingston remembers three young girls taking a five-year-old to a suffrage parade. She remembers the three girls being mad for suffrage, each one topping the other marveling at the glories that would come when women had a voice in government. Who would have guessed that the five-year-old was paying such close attention?

"And," Harriet says, "my father is not a young man. Someday I will inherit . . . ."

"Blood money," Mrs. Livingston spits out.

"Is it?" Harriet asks.

The question lies between them. It is amazing how two words can fill a room. *Why do I have to be the one who tells her?* Mrs. Livingston wonders. But she knows. Of the three girls who took the five-year-old to the parade, she is the only one still alive.

"How did you find me?" she asks, which is not quite answering the question, not quite agreeing to talk.

"I hired detectives," Harriet says. When Mrs. Livingston raises her eyebrow doubtfully, Harriet adds, "My father gives me a generous clothing allowance. But I will not be wearing new clothes this year."

"So it was shirtwaist money that found me," Mrs. Livingston says bitterly.

"Nobody wears shirtwaists anymore," Harriet protests, then seems to realize what Mrs. Livingston means. "Oh. Er—Ye-es. Shirtwaist money. Insurance money. Investments."

Mrs. Livingston hears the waver in Harriet's voice, the shame and guilt. *The sins of the fathers . . .* , she thinks. But something has changed; she is no longer capable of turning Harriet away. She no longer sees Harriet as just one of the daughters, a formerly pesky five-year-old. She sees her as a twenty-one-year-old who would rather know the truth than have new clothes.

Mrs. Livingston sighs.

"The fire is not the beginning of the story," she says.

"What is?" Harriet asks. "The strike? I read about the strike, too."

She is so young, Mrs. Livingston thinks. But Mrs. Livingston had been young once too. Before the fire. Before . . .

"You wouldn't have seen any of our names in those newspaper stories," Mrs. Livingston says.

"Bella and Yetta and Jane," Harriet chants, her voice taking on the cadence of a five-year-old again. "Bella and Yetta and Jane."

Mrs. Livingston closes her eyes, and for a second she can almost feel her two friends on either side of her, the way they used to walk, their arms intertwined. Then she opens her eyes, and it is only a balustrade she is clutching.

"We did not know one another for long," Mrs. Livingston says. "We had so little time." This is both a lament and an accusation. After all these years, she still wants the story to end differently. Three girls meet, become friends, struggle, find happiness, and have their lives go on and on and on until they are three old ladies in rocking chairs.

It just didn't happen that way.

Mrs. Livingston stares off into the distance, off into the past, off into a time when she didn't know the fire was coming.

"The story begins like so much else," she says slowly. "With hope. Hope and dreams and daring . . ."

Bella

A job. Pietro had found her a job.

"*Grazie,*" Bella murmured, keeping her eyes downcast like a proper, obedient Italian girl. Which was funny, because she had been neither proper nor obedient back home in her village, Calia. She'd been the girl whose braids were always coming undone, who ran through the men's bocce games, who hitched up her skirts to chase after the goats.

But since she'd left for America, sometimes she felt like she'd left that girl behind just as completely as she'd left Mama and the little ones. This was a new Bella in the New World—a new Bella who didn't even dare to look Pietro in the eye.

"Don't you want to know what the job is?" Pietro asked, a mocking tone in his voice that seemed to say, behind the words, *Stupid girl. No more brains than a mule. And she actually thinks she'll be capable of doing some big job in New York City?*

"*Si,*" Bella said, so softly he probably couldn't hear her over the noise from the streets. There was always noise from the streets: voices calling out, "Apples! Apples! Get your apples here!" mixing with odd music and the clatter of a monstrous elevated train whizzing past just the other side of the wall. This morning, coming from Ellis Island, Bella had been terrified, clutching Pietro's arm as they fought their way through the crowd. She was afraid that she'd be trampled; she was even a little afraid that the American officials might change their minds and hunt her down and send her back. That had already happened to the family she'd come over with on the boat. The *paesani* Bella had planned to live with, the ones who'd dreamed of gold and assured Bella, again and again, "Anything is possible in America"—they hadn't even been allowed off Ellis Island. It was because of something about their eyes. Bella was just lucky her eyes were different, lucky she'd remembered her distant cousin Pietro, lucky he'd come and agreed to take her on in to America.

She'd even felt lucky when he ordered her to stay inside, sheltered from all the bustle and noise, while he went away. But after hours of sitting alone in an airless room, waiting, Bella's restlessness had begun to outweigh her fear.

The old Bella would have gone back out and found out who was making that music, she told herself. *She would have examined the apples and imagined which one she'd buy, if she had the money. She would have watched that marvel, the train, so that someday she could tell Ricardo just how it worked* . . . . Ricardo was her middle brother, the one who asked the most questions. Though Giovanni asked a lot of questions too, and—

"Bella?" Pietro said, as if to remind her that he was back now, that he was trying to tell her about her job. Maybe he could see that her mind had just traveled back to Italy, back to the family she hadn't seen in three weeks. Maybe he even noticed the tears threatening at the corners of her eyes, because his voice softened a little. "You'll be working at the Triangle Shirtwaist Factory. It's a good job."

A factory. Triangle Shirtwaist Factory. Bella turned the words over in her head, hoping to make sense of them so she wouldn't look stupid again. But it was useless.

"What's a shirtwaist?" she asked.

Pietro's face turned slightly red.

"It's what girls and women wear here. Like a blouse. Except different. With a tight neck and—" He cupped his work-roughened hands above his shoulders, maybe to indicate puffs of fabric. "And it's really pinched in at the waist. . . ." He blushed even more furiously.

The old Bella would have laughed at his embarrassment. Pietro was a boy and older than her—and she barely knew him—but she still would have dared to make fun of him. Now, though, she felt her own face growing hot.

"I think I saw someone wearing one of those, out in the street," she said quickly. "She looked like a princess." Indeed, Bella had stared after the girl in the delicately embroidered, high-necked, puff-sleeved blouse as though she'd come out of a fairy tale. Bella had done her share of laundry back home— surely only a fairy-tale princess could keep her clothes so perfectly white and clean.

The door swung open just then, slamming against the wall. A stout woman in a black dress stood in the doorway, with a dirty baby in one arm and three equally dirty children clinging to her skirt.

Pietro took a step back.

"Signora Luciano," he began, and Bella braced for the introductions. *"Buon giorno,"* she would say. "Thank you for taking me into your home. It is so kind of you to have Pietro and me as boarders." Bella knew how to be polite. She just hadn't had much practice.

But Signora Luciano was glaring at Pietro.

"You talk so loud, everyone can hear," she shouted at him. "Are you crazy? You got her a job at the Triangle factory? You stupid, ignorant boy. This girl is just off the boat, and you think she can work in a place like that? She'll be fired inside of a day, and then she'll be charged for the thread and the needles and the chair and, I don't know, the electricity. . . ."

It was hard to understand Signora Luciano, partly because she was screaming so loudly and partly because her words sounded garbled—too stretched out, with the accents coming down in the wrong places. Bella remembered that Pietro had said that the Lucianos came from another part of Italy. Was this still Italian she was speaking?

It had to be, because otherwise Bella wouldn't have been able to understand her at all.

"Bella will start as a learner," Pietro said. "She'll do fine."

Bella was glad to hear that, glad that Pietro was standing up for her.

"Pah!" Signora Luciano exploded. She looked Bella up and down, in a way that made Bella feel that her own face was dirty, and that Signora Luciano knew that Bella hadn't been able to wash her under-things since she'd left home. "You watch out, she'll end up on the streets. Who sends a girl alone to this country?"

Bella wanted to protest—she hadn't been sent alone. It wasn't her fault the officials on Ellis Island were so picky about who they let in. But Signora Luciano was still talking.

"I tell you and tell you, she can work for me, making the flowers." Signora Luciano gestured toward the table, which was strewn with bits and pieces of fabric. Bella had wondered about all that fabric from the time she'd walked in the door: The whole scene made her think of the time back home when her family's goats had gotten into the garden and left behind half-eaten zucchini vines, half-eaten tomato blossoms. But now Bella realized that the flowers on the Luciano table had been abandoned partly created, not partly destroyed.

"Get to work, lazybones," Signora Luciano hissed, and her three dirty children detached themselves from her skirt and rushed to the table.

"For hats. Beautiful, yes?" Signora Luciano said to Bella, and even through the strange accent Bella could hear the craftiness in her voice. "You work for me, you get up in the morning, you're already at your job. You never have to leave the apartment. And if you work fast, I'll pay you lots of money."

The three dirty children were twisting wires and fabric together with dizzying speed. Bella felt a little sick to her stomach.

"Bella can make more money in the factory," Pietro said. "Four dollars a week. Can you pay four dollars a week?"

Bella didn't know if that was a little or a lot; her mind still worked in lire. But she didn't want Signora Luciano to think she was just greedy.

"I have to make as much money as I can, to send home to my family," she said, though the words "my family" stuck a little in her throat. *Oh, Mama*, she thought. *Oh, Giovanni and Ricardo and Guilia and Dominic . . .*

Signora Luciano narrowed her eyes, like a bocce player studying the arrangement of the balls, planning the next throw.

"Then you work for me in the evenings, after the factory," she said. "Earn extra money."

Bella was about to say "Oh, yes, oh, anything to buy food for my family"—but Pietro stomped his foot. He laid his hands protectively on Bella's shoulders.

"Bella will not work for you," he said. "We are boarders here and nothing else. Bella will not work for you during the day or in the evenings or on Sundays. And neither will I."

He was being so disrespectful—and yet Bella felt proud of him, her tall, handsome cousin, who was only seventeen but could stand up to this frightening woman, could survive in America on his own.

Now Pietro was leaning in close, whispering in Bella's ear.

"She would cheat you," he said. "Every week, there would be a reason she wouldn't pay. She is not an honest woman, Signora Luciano."

Then why are we living with her? Bella wanted to ask. But her heart was pounding too hard, she was too aware of his breath against her skin. And Signora Luciano was glaring at them both now, a clear enemy.

"I have strict rules for my boarders," she said harshly as she thumped a sack of onions down on the only clear space on the table. "No mixing between male and female boarders. No touching our food—if I find anything missing between meals, that's it, you're out in the streets. No bringing friends here. No using our soap. If you want your sheets clean, you use your own soap, you wash them yourselves. But not too much, because I won't have you making my linens threadbare, using them up. No taking our candles—buy your own if you need them. No . . ."

Bella barely listened.

None of this matters, she told herself. *Pietro will take care of me.*

"You should probably tell them you're fifteen," Pietro said the next morning as he walked Bella to her first day at her new job.

"I am fifteen," Bella said.

"Really?" Pietro said, looking at her sideways in a way that made Bella notice his eyelashes, as long as a girl's, curving up from his dark eyes.

"Well, I *think* so," Bella said. "As near as Mama can figure. Of course, it's written down at the church, back home, but it's not like we could have bothered the priest to look up the baptism records for someone like me. . . ."

She was babbling. She stopped talking and clenched her teeth firmly together, because she didn't want Pietro to think she was foolish. She concentrated on dodging a peddler who seemed intent on shoving his cart right into her path. She narrowly missed stepping out in front of a huge horse pulling a wagon full of—was that ice? *Ice* in the summertime, glistening between layers of straw?

"Careful," Pietro said, because while she was gawking at the ice, another peddler *had* rammed his cart into her leg. Pietro jerked her away at the last minute, so it was only a glancing blow. But now he was leading her through an impossibly narrow gap between a man puffing on a cigar and a lady with a towering hat.

"Is it—always—this—crowded?" Bella managed to pant.

"Crowded?" Pietro glanced around as if he'd just noticed the cigar man and the hat lady. "This is nothing. On Saturdays, a lot of people don't come out until later in the day."

Bella didn't even want to think about what the sidewalk would be like later in the day. Already, there were probably more people crammed in around her than lived in her entire village of Calia. Even on saints days back home, when everyone marched up to the church, nobody packed together this tightly. And those were people she knew. These were total strangers jostling against her, their elbows brushing hers, their packages jabbing against her chest.

Bella longed to clutch Pietro's arm as she had yesterday, to cling to him for protection. But somehow she couldn't. Touching him would mean something different today. She'd lain awake last night trying to remember how close a cousin Pietro was—was her grandfather his grandmother's brother? Or was the connection her father and Pietro's mother? It hadn't mattered, back in Italy. Pietro had grown up in another village. She remembered seeing him only once, at a funeral. But now . . . what were the rules in America about cousins getting married?

Even in the dark, her back against the wall, two of Signora Luciano's filthy children snoring beside her, just thinking that question had made her blush. She felt the heat rising in her cheeks now, in the daylight. She tilted her head back, hoping for a cool breeze on her face. But the air around her was hot and still and stale. In America, it seemed, even air got trapped in the crowd.

Bella gasped.

"What's that?" she asked, pointing upward.

"Just more tenement buildings," Pietro said, shrugging.

"No, *there*," she said. "Those metal things, running down the side of the building like caterpillars. There's one there— and there and—" She narrowly missed poking a man in the eye. He scowled at her, spat, and rushed on.

"You mean the fire escapes—the stairs on the outsides of the buildings?" Pietro asked. "The Lucianos' building has some, didn't you notice? They're so people can climb down from the higher floors if there's a fire."

Bella counted windows. One, two, three, four . . . All the apartment buildings were five stories high. Back home, except for the priest and the one or two families who actually owned land, everyone lived in one-story, one-room mud houses. The women did their cooking in the doorways; most nights, no one bothered lighting a lamp or a candle before going to bed on the dirt floor. Fire wasn't a problem.

Bella tried to imagine living on the fifth story of some wood-framed apartment building. She imagined flames licking up through the wooden floor. She shivered despite the heat.

Pietro was chuckling.

"I forgot how strange everything seemed when I got here last year," he said. "The littlest things. Engraved buttons. Food in boxes. Bridges. Doorknobs. Traffic cops. Now I don't give any of it a second thought. Don't worry—you'll stop noticing things after a while too."

Bella wasn't sure she wanted to stop noticing. She was thinking how grateful she would be for a fire escape, if she ever needed one.

"Now, remember, at work today, don't let them see how

much you don't know," Pietro said. "Just do what they tell you. And it's payday—Saturdays are when they give out the money for the whole week. But they won't give you anything, because this is just a practice day, a tryout. They want to see if you can do the work."

"What do you mean, they won't give me anything?" Bella asked, horrified. "Pietro, I have to make money, for my family, for Mama, for . . ."

She wondered how he could have misunderstood so completely, how he could have agreed to such a ridiculous thing on her behalf. Didn't he know how close her family was to starving? Couldn't he tell by looking at her, Bella, with the bones of her face jutting out in hard knobs, her skin stretched tight, her eyes sunken in? The thin stew Signora Luciano had fed them for dinner, the slice of hard bread she'd given Bella for breakfast—that would have been three days' worth of food back home. They'd had bad harvest after bad harvest, ever since Papa died.

Why else would Bella have come halfway around the world, to this strange place, except that her family was desperate?

"They have to pay me," Bella said. "And if they won't, I'll work somewhere else."

"Calm down," Pietro said. He looked around, as if worried that someone else in the crowd would overhear. "This is just how they do things here. Any other place in New York City, it'd be the same. I got you the best job I could find for a girl. You work hard today, next week they'll pay you. And then I'll send the money to your mama, right away."

"You will?" Bella asked. "Oh, thank you!"

She walked on, not minding how thick the crowd was she

had to plow through. As far as she was concerned, she would walk over burning coals if it meant help for her family.

The Triangle Shirtwaist Factory was at the top of a ten-story building. Bella froze on the sidewalk for a moment, looking up and up and up. It made her dizzy to bend her head back so far. This was like staring at the mountains back home, except the mountains sloped down gradually, and the Triangle building shot up straight from the ground to the sky, its sheer, steep walls blocking out the sun.

Something like terror gripped Bella, and her thoughts tangled: *I can't work in a big fancy place like that . . . I'll starve and so will Mama and the little ones. . . . Oh, how far away the ground must look from those windows up there. . . .*

She swallowed hard, and the only words that slipped out were a question: "No fire escapes?"

"Not *here*," Pietro said. "Not in this part of the city. There are hoity-toity rich people just around the corner. They think fire escapes are ugly."

"But if there's a fire . . ." Bella wasn't really thinking about fire. She was thinking about falling, or failing, or being fired.

"There's probably a fire escape at the back, I guess. Or they have extra stairways inside. This is New York City. They have rules about things like that. Now come on. You can't be late your first day."

They went inside and stepped into a marvel called an elevator—a little box that whisked them up to the ninth floor. Other girls were crowded into the box with them, girls in fancy hats and elegant skirts and those shining white shirtwaists. Bella guessed these girls were royalty of some sort. She might have been brave enough to ask them who they were except that they all seemed to be speaking in other languages. Even one girl who looked Italian was chattering away in a strange tongue that Bella couldn't understand at all.

The box stopped and the doors opened. The other girls streamed out, rushing toward rows of machines on long tables. Pietro led Bella to a man standing at the end of one of the tables.

"This is Signor Carlotti," Pietro said. "Signor Carlotti, this is Bella."

"Scissors," Signor Carlotti said, handing her a pair. "When the shirtwaists come to you, cut the loose threads."

Actually, that wasn't exactly what he said. Bella couldn't quite make sense of any of his words—his accent was even murkier than Signora Luciano's. But he demonstrated as he talked, lifting a shirtwaist from the table, snipping threads, dropping the finished shirtwaist into a basket. Another girl sat nearby, already slicing threads with her own pair of scissors with such reckless speed that Bella feared that the blades would slip through the cloth as well.

"*Buon giorno,*" Bella started to say to the girl. "My name is—"

"No talking," Signor Carlotti said. "Work." At least, that's what Bella guessed he said, because he held his finger to his lips and glared.

Bella picked up her first shirtwaist. The garment was delicate and fine, with frills around the collar and gathers at the waist. It was like holding stitched air. Bella turned it over carefully, searching for hanging threads. *Ah, there's one.* She lifted her scissors, angled the blades just so, gently pulled the handles together.

"Faster," Signor Carlotti said. "You take that long over every thread, you will never earn a cent in the factory. You will be out on the streets and even Pietro won't be able to save you. Your family will starve."

It was amazing that Bella could understand what he was saying, without comprehending a single word.

Bella glanced up and saw that the other girl had whipped through three shirtwaists in the time it had taken Bella to cut one thread. Bella decided that if the other girl wasn't afraid of ripping the shirtwaists to shreds, Bella shouldn't worry either. She sliced through the rest of the threads, dropped the shirtwaist in the basket, and picked up a new one.

"That's better," Signor Carlotti grunted, or something like it.

"You're set then," Pietro said. "Good-bye. I've got to get to my job. I'll meet you on the sidewalk outside, after work."

"Okay," Bella said. She wanted to flash him a big smile, to tell him how grateful she was that he'd be waiting for her, that she wouldn't have to find her way back to the Lucianos' alone. But Signor Carlotti was glaring again, so she dipped her head down over the shirtwaist. She resisted the impulse to watch Pietro walking back to the elevator.

Pietro, Bella thought. *Such a nice name. Such a handsome man. And so kind to me . . .*

"Faster!" Signor Carlotti said.

Bella forced herself to stop thinking about Pietro. Cut, cut, cut, drop. Pick up a new shirtwaist. Cut, cut, cut . . . drop. Pick up a new shirtwaist. This was not a difficult job. Bella's little sister Guilia, who still sucked her thumb and clung to Mama's skirt most of the time, would have been capable of doing it. But Bella found herself having to concentrate hard, especially with Signor Carlotti hovering over her, watching her every move, yelling "Faster!" every time she so much as hesitated picking up the next shirtwaist. The pile of shirtwaists with hanging threads kept growing, and Bella couldn't even stop long enough to look up and see where they were coming from, who was bringing them over. Her neck grew stiff, but she didn't dare tilt her head back to relax it, even for a second.

Suddenly Signor Carlotti grabbed up one of the shirtwaists Bella had just dropped into the basket.

"You idiot girl!" he screamed, shaking the shirtwaist in her face. "Can't even handle a simple job like this! Look at the thread you missed!" The offending thread unfurled from a hiding place in the sleeve. It dangled in front of Bella's eyes, a mark of shame. "I'll fire you if I find another one of these! The Triangle label stands for quality and pride! Not dangling threads! Not shoddy work by useless girls like you!"

Maybe what he actually said was that she was being fired, right then and there. But Bella was determined not to hear that.

"I'm sorry! I'm sorry!" she said, snatching the shirtwaist from his hands, slicing through the thread. "I'll never make another mistake again. I promise!"

Her hands were shaking when she turned her attention to the next shirtwaist.

I can't be fired, she told herself. *I cannot lose this job.*

"*Tu es ale mol inem zelbikn seyder,*" the other girl said, which was totally incomprehensible. But it made Bella look up. She saw that the other girl was showing her something, turning the shirtwaist in her own lap this way and that.

Ooohhh, Bella thought. The other girl meant that she'd found a pattern to her work. The hanging threads were in pretty much the same places on every shirtwaist, so the girl cut them in the same order each time. That way, she never missed any.

"*Grazie*," Bella said. "I understand."

"Back to work!" Signor Carlotti screamed. "No chitchat!"

Bella settled into a pattern of her own. Front, right side, back, left side. Then a quick once-over just to make sure she hadn't missed anything.

Cut, cut, cut . . . drop. Cut, cut, cut . . . drop.

Something shifted in Bella's brain. She was still whipping through the shirtwaists as fast as she could, and she didn't dare look away from her work, even for a second. But she found that every now and then she could allow herself the luxury of thinking about something besides shirtwaists and scissors and hanging threads. She let herself notice the glorious rumble of the rows and rows of sewing machines, all racing together. She'd gotten a quick glimpse of them before she sat down and started cutting. How Mama would have stared, to see such a thing! Sewing was Mama's least favorite chore; when the news had come to Calia that they had machines to do such things, out in the rest of the world, Mama had talked about it for days.

"Wouldn't it be nice to be that free?" she'd asked Bella wistfully. "Just tell a machine, 'This is your job now,' and you can go out and enjoy the sunshine? No hunching over a needle all the time, no worrying about mending and patching?"

Signor Carlotti bent over in front of Bella, screaming right into her face.

"You're slowing down again! The shirtwaists are piling up! Work faster!" Spittle flew out of his mouth and landed on Bella's eyebrow, but she didn't dare take her hands off the shirtwaist to wipe it away.

Oh, Mama, Bella thought, with an ache in her heart. *You didn't know the sewing machines still left some work for girls to do! And the machines are so fast I can never keep up....*

But she had to try.

Bella worked for hours, the shirtwaists flying through her hands. About noon, the machines suddenly lapsed into silence.

Grazie, grazie, Madonna mia, Bella thought. *They're going to give us a break for lunch.*

The other girl put her scissors down, stood up, and stretched. Bella smiled at her. She dropped one last shirtwaist into the basket, and reached out to place her scissors on the table too. But Signor Carlotti shoved the scissors back at her, back into her hand.

"Oh, no, no, no, no, no! *You* do not get a lunch break, you lazy girl! You've done nothing all morning! Look at all these shirtwaists you haven't finished! You sit right there and keep working until they're done!"

Bella was pretty sure that was what he was saying, because he gestured at the pile of shirtwaists as he pushed Bella back into her chair. Bella wanted to fire back angry words of her own: "But you are not even paying me today! I'm just learning—how can you expect me to keep up? This isn't right! I'm not a machine! Even back in Calia, the landowners give the laborers a chance to eat lunch!"

But Bella remembered Pietro saying this was the best job he could find for her; she remembered him saying that it would be the same anywhere else in New York. She remembered that Guilia, her little sister, had had so little food lately that sometimes she didn't have enough energy to play, she just lay on her blanket staring up at nothing.

I can skip lunch today if it means that next week Mama will have money for food for Guilia, Bella told herself. *I can bear anything for Guilia.*

Bella picked up the next shirtwaist.

The rest of the day passed in a blur. The factory became stiflingly hot by early afternoon, and sweat poured down Bella's face, but she forced herself to ignore it. A blister rose on her thumb where the scissors rubbed, but she just shifted positions, sliding the scissors handles further up on her hand. Her back ached, her head ached, her neck ached, her hand ached—she didn't let herself care.

Bella was so dizzy, light-headed, and hungry by late in the day that she was back to needing to concentrate intensely on each shirtwaist, to focus precisely on each snip of her scissors. So she didn't notice the screaming across the room right away. The girl sitting beside her had to nudge Bella's arm.

"Ze nor!" the girl said, and pointed.

Bella looked up.

Two tables away, a red-faced man was screaming while two other men stood on either side of him, tugging on his arms. The screaming man was thin and stooped over; the men pulling at him were big and beefy and mean-looking.

They were screaming too, but their voices didn't carry. Bella could only hear what the thin man said. Of course, Bella couldn't understand any of his words, but she could tell he was very mad. And he wasn't giving up, no matter how much the other men tugged at him. The men knocked his glasses from his face; they ripped his shirt; they slapped him and lifted him and carried him out. But still the man kept screaming, kept kicking and pulling back.

Suddenly, all around Bella, the other workers stood up. It was like watching a dance, everyone making the same movement at once, except for one or two laggards who were out of step. Bella was one of the laggards, but she sprang up only a split second after the other learner girl. Bella didn't know why, but obviously everyone was supposed to stand.

The wheels of the sewing machines kept turning for a few moments, as if, being machines, they were left out of the dance. Bella could see fabric bunching, thread snagging.

Oh, no, those shirtwaists will be ruined, Bella fretted. But no one else seemed to care. People were streaming past her, rushing for the elevator. The girls Bella had thought were royalty, some women with matronly faces, the few men and boys who worked on this floor—all of them were rushing for the exit at once. They knocked over baskets of shirtwaists; they trampled the shirtwaists underfoot.

And they were all yelling and talking—even laughing— at once.

Is this how they always act at the end of the day? Bella wondered. *Or just Saturdays, when they've been paid and they know they'll have the next day off?*

In the confusion of strange languages Bella didn't understand, she started noticing that one word was being repeated over and over again: "Strike." Boys and girls yelled it; women murmured it wonderingly; men whispered it in hushed tones.

"What's a 'strike'?" Bella asked, but in the hubbub, nobody seemed to hear her.

Bella let the crowd carry her into the elevator, out of the building. On the sidewalk below, she resisted the urge to bend down and kiss the ground—*Oh, thank you, God, I was so high up in the sky, but I made it back down safely.* The sidewalk wasn't exactly "ground," anyway—not dirt, but pavement.

The rest of the workers scattered, but Bella leaned against the building, waiting for Pietro. He appeared around the corner, his dark hair curling at his temples, his dark eyes flashing, his lips pursed into an *O*—he was whistling. Bella forgot her aching back, neck, head, and hands; she forgot the throbbing blister on her thumb; she forgot her empty stomach.

Does whistling mean he's happy to see me? she wondered.

"Did Signor Carlotti say to come back on Monday?" Pietro asked.

Bella had forgotten Signor Carlotti too.

"He didn't really say anything at the end of the day," Bella said. She decided not to mention how much he'd yelled at her all day long. "Everyone just stood up to go. It was very dramatic. All the workers rushed out at once, laughing and shouting. They kept saying 'Strike! Strike!' And a bunch of other words I couldn't figure out. But that one word they kept saying, 'strike'—what does that mean?"

Pietro instantly turned three shades paler.

"*O, Madonna mia!*" he cried. "*O, San Antonio!*"

Bella wasn't sure if he was praying or swearing.

"Are you sure that was what they were saying?" he asked. "And you stood up and walked out with all the people yelling 'Strike!'?"

"Everybody did," Bella said, defensively. But she wasn't so sure of that now. Her memory seemed to be a tricky thing. Had Signor Carlotti still been standing there—still sputtering and screaming about unfinished shirtwaists, uncut threads? "I think everybody did," she added.

"Oh, for the love of God," Pietro said. "You just lost your job!"

"But why?" Bella said. "I worked so hard!"

"But a strike, see—that's when workers walk out because they want to get paid more or treated better, or something like that. And usually what happens is that they just all get fired, and the company hires somebody else, who isn't so picky."

"I didn't say I was doing a strike," Bella argued.

"But you walked out!" Pietro said. "You walked out with all the strikers! Think how it must have looked to Signor Carlotti!"

Bella felt her knees crumble. She lurched toward the ground, and would have fallen hard if Pietro hadn't grabbed her.

"I didn't mean it," Bella whimpered. "I didn't know. . . ."

Pietro looked down at her with utter contempt. He had his arms around her, but it was completely wrong. Bella jerked away from him.

"I'll find Signor Carlotti," she said. "I'll tell him I'm not making this 'strike.' I'll tell him I'll work all night if I have to—"

She whirled back toward the door, but now there was a

huge man in an official-looking uniform standing there. He held his arms out to bar the door and said something incomprehensible.

"Oh, please," Bella begged. "You've got to let me in!"

The man was shaking his head, pushing Bella away. She landed sprawled on the ground. The other people on the sidewalk had to walk around her.

"Stop it!" Pietro said, pulling her up. "Signor Carlotti's probably already gone, anyway. I'll go find him myself. I'll take you home and then I'll talk to him—it's not like he'd listen to a girl."

Heartsick, Bella trudged along behind Pietro. The jabs and jostling of the crowd seemed like a fit punishment. The faces leered around her; the foreign jabbering hurt her ears. For all she knew, the entire crowd was laughing at her. *What did you expect, you foolish girl? You're just an ignorant peasant! You don't belong here! Go home! Go starve! We don't care!*

At the Lucianos', Pietro let her in the door.

"I'll be back as soon as I can," he said.

And then he was gone.

Bella stumbled on in to the apartment. Signora Luciano and her dirty children were clustered around the table, their hands flying through the bits and pieces of artificial flowers. Bella remembered Signora Luciano's prediction from the night before—"You watch out, she'll end up on the streets"— and that made it so that Bella couldn't even look at Signora Luciano, couldn't squeeze out the barest of greetings.

"Well, there's the grand working girl," Signora Luciano snorted. "Too good for our business, of course. Has to work in a *factory*."

Tears stung in Bella's eyes, but she wasn't going to let Signora Luciano see her cry. She tried to brush past the table, to go into the other room, but Signora Luciano slapped her hand away from the doorknob.

"Oh, no, you're not going in there. Our day boarders are sleeping."

"*Day* boarders?" Bella repeated, certain she'd heard wrong.

"Mario and Antonio work nights," Signora Luciano said. "So they use Pietro's and Nico's beds in the daytime."

Bella closed her eyes weakly. What kind of place had she come to? It had seemed so simple, back home: She had to go to America to find work or else her family would starve. Period. But this was too much to think about, day boarders and night boarders, crowded streets, fire escapes, sewing machines, strikes.

"Oh, don't pull that high and mighty act on me, young lady," Signora Luciano snapped. "You're no better than us. I bet back home your family slept with goats and chickens in the house."

They had, actually, back when they'd still had goats and chickens. Pretty much everyone did: animals on one side of the room, people on the other, although Guilia was awful about toddling over in the middle of the night and curling up beside a goat for warmth. She'd cried so hard when the last one died.

Why did Signora Luciano make it sound like it was something to be ashamed of, owning animals? Bella wished that they'd had hundreds of goats and chickens—hundreds of goats and chickens and acres and acres of land for growing beans and wheat.

Because then Bella could have just stayed home.

Bella leaned back against the wall, because there was nowhere to sit. Signora Luciano was still talking, but it was harder and harder to make sense of her strange accent. One of the children said something, and Bella couldn't understand him at all. And then Bella must have fallen asleep standing up, because the next thing Bella knew, Pietro was shaking her awake.

Bella stared at him in confusion for a moment—who was this handsome man touching her?—then she remembered and burst out, "Did you find Signor Carlotti? Did you talk to him? Did—"

"Ssh," Pietro said. "Not here."

He led her through the back room, and, strangely, out the window.

"Oh!" Bella exclaimed, because now they were standing on a metal landing—the fire escape. They were at the back of the building, looking out onto a tiny courtyard and the fire escapes of the buildings behind them. Ropes hung between the buildings, and clothing hung from all the ropes, draped over and attached with wooden pins. *Do people here have so many clothes they have to store everything outside?* Bella wondered, but then one of the shirts on the line flapped droplets of water onto Bella's face, and she realized: *No, it's laundry! Drying on the ropes instead of on rocks along the river . . .* In spite of herself, Bella found this enchanting. The Lucianos' apartment was on the second floor of a five-story building, so she could look up into three more rows of hanging laundry.

It looks like angels, she thought. *Angels fluttering down from the sky . . .*

"You still have a job," Pietro said.

This was news that only angels could have brought her—perhaps Pietro was an angel too.

"*Grazie, grazie, Madonna mia,*" Bella murmured.

"Signor Carlotti says there isn't going to be a strike, people were just acting crazy," Pietro said. "But if anything like that ever happens again, anybody starts talking about a strike, you just stay put! Strikes are nothing but trouble."

"I will," Bella said. "I promise."

She kept her head bowed, meekly, feeling the last rays of the sunset on her head.

"The only thing is," Pietro continued, "I had to bargain a little to talk Signor Carlotti into keeping you on. You have to prove that you're not a radical or an anarchist or anything like that."

Bella didn't even know what those words meant.

"How do I prove that?" she asked.

"You have to work four more days as a learner. Without pay."

Bella gasped. The old Bella, the half-wild girl from Calia who'd slept in the same room with goats and chickens, wanted to reach out and slap Pietro. Maybe Signor Carlotti, too, for good measure. *But that's not fair!* She wanted to scream. *That's cheating! How can they expect me to work for nothing? How is that any better than working for Signora Luciano—at least she says she'll pay! Why is my work worth so little that I'm supposed to give it away for four more days? Four more days that Mama and the little ones will go without eating . . .*

"But, see, then they'll pay you," Pietro said quickly. "For Friday and Saturday next week—you'll get two days pay."

He was begging her not to scream. He was telling her with his dark eyes, *This is a scary place, America. You have to go along with what you're told. I can only protect you so much.*

"And then you'll send everything I earn to Mama?" Bella asked tentatively.

"You'll have to keep some money out for the rent, and to pay back the padrone for your steamer ticket, but then, yes, everything else," Pietro said. "I'm sorry, Bella. If I weren't sending money back to my own mama, I'd—"

"I know," Bella said.

She looked up again, wanting one more vision of angels. But the sky was dark now; the sun had dipped out of sight. And the hanging laundry was just dim shadows in the dark night.

Oh, Mama-across-the-ocean, she thought. *Go out into the fields and find a few more grains of wheat. Look in the garden and see if there isn't one more shriveled tomato, hiding in the dried-up leaves. I'm doing all I can but you'll have to wait. Oh, please, Mama, I hope you can wait. . . .*

Yetta

*W*hy isn't it time yet?" Yetta demanded. "Why not now?"

"Oh, Yetta, *because*," Rahel snapped back, shoving open the door of their apartment and reaching up to turn on the gaslights.

"What are you waiting for?" Yetta asked. "The Messiah?"

"Yetta!" Rahel cried, horrified. "If Papa heard you talking like that!"

"Papa's thousands of miles away," Yetta retorted, but she felt shame coursing through her. She and Rahel had just worked a full day on the Sabbath; they'd long since given up any concerns about keeping kosher or lighting Sabbath candles. If asked, Yetta would have said she was a socialist rather than a Jew.

But joking about the Messiah was going too far.

"I thought you were a revolutionary," she complained to Rahel, to cover her shame.

"I was a revolutionary in Russia," Rahel said. "And you see where it got me." She bent down and lit the stove. "America."

"Because you ran away," Yetta said, reaching into the cupboard for potatoes and carrots they'd bought the night before.

"Because," Rahel said, beginning to chop the potatoes while Yetta chopped carrots, "I could see when a fight was hopeless and I chose to escape with my life."

This was an argument they'd been having ever since Yetta joined her older sister in America. Yetta had been ten when Rahel left their shtetl and went to work in the big city, Bialystok. She'd been eleven when Rahel had come back, pounding on the door in the middle of the night, full of stories about plots against the Czar and false accusations and the city in flames. Papa had scraped together every ruble he could to send Rahel to safety. So Yetta had had three years—ages twelve, thirteen, and fourteen—to spend admiring her brave, glamorous, absent sister. When Yetta herself arrived in New York two months ago, it had been a jolt to discover that Rahel didn't walk around in a blaze of glory. In fact, Rahel looked like a completely ordinary nineteen-year-old girl: dark hair piled on top of her head, squashed hat that was a poor knockoff of Fifth Avenue fashion, threadbare shirtwaist and skirt that had definitely seen better days. And yet, Yetta couldn't scoff too much at Rahel; without Rahel, Yetta would still be sitting back in the shtetl, milking cows and daydreaming about revolution.

"You think all fights are hopeless," Yetta muttered. "And maybe they were in Russia"—this was a major concession—"but *here!* Now! There must have been four hundred workers who walked out today, all yelling for a strike. Even that new Italian girl who sat there looking terrified all day—even *she* stood up and walked out!"

It had been one of the most exciting moments of Yetta's

life. She'd been living for years on the stories of Rahel's days as a revolutionary—most of them pieced together from over-hearing Mama and Papa's worried whispers. Now, finally, at the end of another long, boring day of cutting threads, she'd had her own glorious moment of rebellion. It'd been even more incredible than she'd imagined: the surge of solidarity she felt with her fellow workers, the dizzying relief of finally saying out loud, in a way the bosses couldn't ignore, "This isn't fair! You can't cheat us and lie to us and overwork us anymore!"

Rahel snorted.

"Maybe four hundred workers walked out," she said, set-ting a pot of water to boil on the stove. "But how many actu-ally went to the union headquarters to plan for a strike?"

Yetta didn't answer that, because it had been just her and Rahel and three or four others. They'd stood outside the locked door, their excitement plummeting into something more like embarrassment, until Rahel finally said they should just give up and go home."Maybe everyone else gathered somewhere else," Yetta said.

Rahel took the knife from Yetta's hand and laid it down on the table. She slid the carrots and potatoes into the water.

"There isn't anywhere else to gather," Rahel said. "Yetta, you have to face facts. Nobody's ready for a strike. The union barely has any members. We have four dollars in the treas-ury. Even if we managed to organize, we couldn't sustain a strike. Everyone would starve. And Mr. Harris and Mr. Blanck know that!"

Mr. Harris and Mr. Blanck were the owners of the Triangle factory—the "Shirtwaist Kings," they liked to be called. They had offices on the tenth floor, and Yetta had heard the other girls whispering about seeing the men arriving or departing in their limousines. Yetta had never caught so much as a glimpse of either man.

"But it wasn't just girls who walked out calling for a strike," Yetta protested. "It was a contractor who started the whole thing. It was a man!"

Even Yetta had to admit, four hundred girls would have little more power than four hundred fleas. But men were more important; the contractors were practically on the same level as Mr. Harris and Mr. Blanck.

"Mr. Kline was incredibly brave," Rahel agreed.

Yetta let herself relive the drama she'd witnessed earlier that day. She'd just been sitting there, her hands racing through the shirtwaists, her mind counting down the minutes to the end of the day. She'd seen the contractors getting their pay envelopes, and had begun calculating: if Mr. Carlotti gave her a full four dollars, like he was supposed to, how much would be left over after Rahel took out the money for rent and for food and for sending back to Papa in Russia?

It was amazing that she'd been able to hear Mr. Kline over the clatter of the sewing machines, but he'd been awfully loud.

"I'm sick of this slave driving!" he'd screamed, throwing his pay envelope down on the table. "If I pay my girls enough to live on, there's no money left over for me! I shouldn't have to choose between starving my workers and starving my family!"

Mr. Bernstein, the factory manager, had answered in a low, hissing voice. Yetta knew what he said only because she'd asked the girls sitting nearby.

"If you don't like the way we do business here, get out!" He pointed to the shirtwaist still crammed beneath the needle of

Mr. Kline's sewing machine. "Finish up that waist and get out!"

And then Mr. Bernstein had turned on his heel and walked away. It was that motion that brought the anger surging up inside Yetta. Mr. Bernstein didn't care if everyone starved. He cared only about finishing shirtwaists.

Girls were gasping all around Mr. Kline, but he made no move to sit back down at the sewing machine. He made no move to leave. Another contractor, Mr. Elfuzin, jumped up and stood beside him.

"He's right!" Mr. Elfuzin exploded. "You're starving us all! Blanck and Harris are making millions but they're bleeding us to death!"

Mr. Bernstein narrowed his eyes and glared. Then he left.

For a moment, there was a feeling in the room as if anything could happen. Yetta heard one girl whisper, "Is he going to get more money?" Mr. Bernstein reappeared only seconds later from the stairway, but he wasn't carrying cash. He wasn't alone, either. He was accompanied by two workers from another floor—cutters, by the look of them. They each had more muscles than the strong man Yetta had seen at Coney Island.

"I said, get out!" Mr. Bernstein yelled.

One cutter shoved Mr. Elfuzin out the door; the other grabbed Mr. Kline. Mr. Bernstein slapped Mr. Kline's face, knocking his glasses to the floor. He and the cutter jerked on Mr. Kline's arms, dragging him away. Still, Mr. Kline kept fighting and yelling.

"Will you sit at your machines and watch a fellow worker treated this way?" Mr. Kline screamed out to everyone else.

Yetta was up on her feet before she had a chance to notice

that others were standing too. The shirtwaist in her lap tumbled to the floor. She cheered, "Not me!" and then that became, "Not us!" The word "Strike!" seemed to come out of nowhere, a wave of whispers and shouts flowing through the crowd, a wave carrying everyone out the door. . . .

"Eat," Rahel said, sliding a plate of potatoes and carrots in front of Yetta, bringing her back to their sad, dark apartment—and to the sad, dark fact that there wasn't going to be a strike. Monday morning, everyone would creep back to work just like always.

Which is worse? Yetta wondered. *To be a girl in a* shtetl *in Russia, milking cows and daydreaming about revolution? Or to be a girl in a factory in America, sewing shirtwaists and daydreaming about a strike that's never going to happen?* It sounded a little like the questions Papa quoted from the Talmud.

"Isn't there anything we can do?" Yetta moaned. "Anything to make the time for a strike come faster?"

Rahel surprised her by nodding.

"Yes," she said. "There is. We're going to get ready. So next time something like this flares up—"

"Next time, we'll stay strong," Yetta said. "Next time no one will give up."

"Exactly," Rahel said.

She was already reaching for pen and paper, already making plans.

Yetta loved having a sister who was a revolutionary.

Jane

Jane Wellington was on her way to tea in Washington Square. She was late, because the traffic was abominable, and because Miss Milhouse had found fault with Jane's grooming.

"Sally, those tendrils are going flat already," Miss Milhouse sniffed. "And is that a tangle I see hiding at the back? You simply must do a better job with her hair."

"Yes, miss. Yes, miss." Sally bowed and scraped and did everything but throw herself on the floor and beg for mercy, like a repentant criminal in one of the novels Jane wasn't supposed to read.

Miss Milhouse was Jane's chaperon, and had been ever since Jane's mother died seven years earlier, when Jane was nine. Sally was Jane's new Irish maid. Jane had a feeling that Sally wouldn't last long.

It took forever for Sally to take all the pins out of Jane's lank, dark hair and recomb, recurl, recrimp, and repile the entire mass back on top of Jane's head. It took forever for Miss Milhouse to inspect the new hairstyle and pronounce it "adequate." The chauffeur was waiting at the door, fortunately, but then he drove down Fifth Avenue, where the cars inched along as slowly as horses.

"Remember," Miss Milhouse lectured, "Miss Aberfoyle's brother has just married Sylvia Van Rensselaer, whose family is quite prominent. Why, the Van Rensselaers were part of Mrs. Astor's Four Hundred from the very beginning. . . ."

It was a source of great anxiety to Miss Milhouse that Jane's family was not one of the old New York society families. The Wellington name had not been on the list of those who truly mattered when it was leaked to the society press in the 1890s. In the 1890s, Jane's father was only beginning to accumulate his fortune.

"But I could buy and sell most of those families now," Jane had heard her father brag once when he'd had too much port to drink.

Sometimes that was enough in society, to have that much money. Sometimes it wasn't. Miss Milhouse was very eager for Jane to understand all the rules and unspoken rules of society. But the rules mostly made Jane feel like she was about to break out in hives.

"If you could perhaps contrive to sit next to Miss Aberfoyle, that would be most wise," Miss Milhouse was saying now.

"Perhaps I shall," Jane said, though she was thinking, *Oh, please, anyone but Lilly Aberfoyle.* Lilly Aberfoyle was a prissy, brainless bore. Lilly Aberfoyle also made Jane feel like breaking out in hives.

Barely listening as Miss Milhouse droned on, Jane peered out the window. They were almost to Washington Square now, and the sidewalks were packed. Suddenly a great crowd of girls about Jane's age piled out of one of the buildings. Their cheeks were rosy and their eyes bright, and they were

chattering away excitedly. They looked like they were having a lot more fun than Jane had ever had going to tea.

"Is that a school?" Jane asked, pressing her face close
against the glass. "Meeting in the summertime?"

"It's not a very good one, if their clothes are any indica-
tion," Miss Milhouse said scornfully.

For the first time, Jane noticed that some of the girls'
skirts were ragged; the flowers and feathers on many of their
hats were limp and bedraggled.

"Can you see a sign anywhere?" she persisted. "I just
want to know. . . ."

"It's a factory, miss," the chauffeur said from the front
seat. "Triangle Waist Company. Sign's up there, at the top
of the building."

"Oh." Jane leaned back against her seat but kept watching. "Girls work in factories?"

"Yes, miss," the chauffeur said. "My niece started in a factory when she was twelve, sewing buttons on coats, and now
she makes—"

"Mr. Corrigan!" Miss Milhouse scolded. "I'm certain that
Miss Wellington doesn't care to hear the particulars of your
niece's employment!"

Jane didn't, not really. But there was something about
those girls spilling out from the Triangle Waist Factory.
Something she couldn't quite name but almost envied.

They arrived at the tea party and made their apologies
for being late. All the usual girls were there: Lilly Aberfoyle
and Mary Stewart and Iris Ferrier and Pearl Kensington and
Daisy Cornell . . . Jane had known these girls all her life; they
all went to the same finishing school, where they learned

how to curtsy properly and select the proper utensils at fancy dinner parties and write proper thank-you notes afterward. The conversation today centered on dresses and dances and the details of Lilly's brother's wedding. Somehow, today, Jane wasn't interested. She stared down at her delicate bone china cup and thought she could see the rest of her life, all those afternoons spent drinking tea with these same girls, every one of them so carefully obeying all the society rules. Of course, there'd be a flurry of excitement when they all got married and had children. But husbands went off to work every day—or to yacht or hunt or play polo or golf—and there would be servants for raising the children. And that would leave Jane with her tepid tea and her bone china and these girls who could make an hour's conversation out of nothing.

"I saw some factory girls on the way here," Jane blurted suddenly, rudely interrupting Lilly's description of the gold crest on the dinner plates at the wedding.

The other girls stared at Jane as if she'd suggested they discuss water closets or head colds or something else equally unpleasant and unmentionable.

After a moment, Daisy Cornell, the hostess of the party, replied, "Oh, yes, they've put factories in some of the lofts near Washington Square. My father says it's simply appalling, to have that kind so close by."

The other girls tsk-tsk-ed or murmured "What a pity!" and "Such a shame!" Jane saw that they'd completely misunderstood her.

"I don't know," Jane said. "These girls looked rather . . . interesting." She shifted in her chair a bit, rustling the layers of her skirts. "I wonder what they think about, girls like that?"

"Oh, please," Lilly said, tossing her head and shaking the perfectly curled tendrils that dangled from her coiffure. "I'm sure they don't think, not exactly, not like us. They're more like servants, who aren't capable of thinking about anything more advanced than dusting and polishing and washing dirty dishes. And sometimes"—she giggled prettily—"my mama says they're not even capable of *that*."

Jane watched the servant girl who was refilling Lilly's teacup at that very moment. She had the red hair and the pale, freckled skin that were so common among the Irish servants; she might well be the twin of Jane's maid Sally. An angry blush crept up the girl's cheeks; Jane could tell she was biting the inside of her lip the same way Jane did when she was trying not to cry.

If I were that servant, Jane thought, strangely, *I'd make sure I spilled that whole pot of tea all over Lilly's white dress.*

The servant did nothing of the sort, only finished up pouring and walked briskly back to the kitchen.

"You sound just like my cousin Eleanor, wondering about such curious things as what factory girls think," Pearl said to Jane. "Ever since Eleanor went to Vassar, she's had the oddest ideas."

"Vassar?" Lilly said. "Your cousin Eleanor is attending college? My father says college is too taxing for a girl's delicate constitution. Not to mention that education would be completely wasted on a female."

It probably would be, on you, Jane thought bitterly. And then she felt guilty. How was she so much better than Lilly?

What did she know about, besides curtsying and dinner parties and prim, proper thank-you notes?

Daisy cleared her throat, somehow managing to make it a delicate, feminine sound.

"Oh, Lilly, I did so want to hear the rest of your description of the dinner plates at the wedding," she said.

I need new friends, Jane thought, and the force of her conviction surprised her. These had been her best friends all her life. If they were a little tiresome today—well, weren't they always?

At her earliest opportunity, Jane leaned over to Pearl and said quietly, "Would it be possible for me to meet your cousin Eleanor?"

Bella

Bella snipped another thread, imagining that, as it fell, it turned into a grain of wheat pouring into a bucket in Mama's hands. The next thread became a grape, one of a huge bunch of grapes that Bella's brothers were cramming into their mouths—cramming, because now they had so much food that they didn't have to eat slowly or savor each bite.

It'd been three months since Bella had left home, nearly three months of working and sending money back. She was good enough at her job now that while her hands raced through the shirtwaists, her mind could travel anywhere she wanted to go. She'd mentally returned to Calia a million times, watching her family go about their improved lives— eating feasts three times a day, buying a new hoe to replace their rusty one, maybe even splurging on a bit of ribbon for Guilia's hair. She loved to imagine Mama's reaction every time more money arrived from America: Probably Mama would throw her hands up in the air, crying out, *"O, grazie, Madonna mia. Grazie, Dio mio. Grazie per la mia figlia Bella!"* Probably she'd weep tears of joy.

Bella had no way of knowing what was actually happening in Calia. Neither she nor Mama could read or write, of course. The priest in Calia was grouchy about writing letters for villagers; even if Mama talked him into sending one, Bella knew no one in America who could read it for her. So Bella's daydreams about home didn't change much—it was the wheat, the boys with the grapes, Guilia's ribbon, Mama weeping for joy, over and over and over again.

More and more, as she sat hunched over the shirtwaists, Bella found her mind traveling in other directions. She tried to puzzle out the words she heard the other girls using— when they called Signor Carlotti an "allrightnik," their eyes rolling and their noses scrunched up, that was an insult, wasn't it? And what was this "union" they kept whispering about?

Mostly, though, Bella thought about Pietro. *Pietro . . .* Just the thought of his name was enough to cheer her up when her back ached and her eyes blurred and her fingers throbbed from her grip on the scissors. In real life, she barely saw him. He walked her to and from work, before and after his own job digging ditches. In the evenings he went out. Just about every conversation they had was in the midst of dodging peddlers, pickpockets, and horse droppings, or in the midst of the Luciano baby crying, Signor and Signora Luciano screaming at each other, the dirty Luciano children punching each other in the stomach.

But in her daydreams, Bella and Pietro sat on the fire escape together, just the two of them. The laundry fluttered and the stars twinkled above them. They gazed into each other's eyes. They—*oh, please, don't even imagine this! It will make your hands tremble, you'll cut the shirtwaist! Oh, all right, go ahead. Just be careful*—they leaned in together for a kiss.

Oh, be still, my heart. . . .

Bella had heard the other girls talk about going out with boyfriends to dances, or to the movies—she knew what they were saying because they demonstrated bits and pieces of the dance steps, they gestured the scope of a huge movie screen. So she tried to imagine that, too. The dances made for dizzying daydreams, but she'd never been to a movie, so she couldn't picture that at all. She planned to ask Pietro this very evening if he'd ever gone. And if he thought she was hinting at anything, if he thought she was flirting . . .

So be it, Bella thought, blushing in spite of herself.

"Bella?" It was Signor Carlotti, not screaming at her for once. "A girl is sick. We need you to operate one of the machines."

"Me?" Bella squeaked out. "At the machines?"

She could understand Signor Carlotti better now, though she still thought he was speaking some other language besides Italian.

"We'll pay you more. We'll pay . . . four dollars and twenty-five cents a week."

Twenty-five cents more a week? That was hundreds more grains of wheat for Mama, dozens more grapes for Bella's brothers. And a ribbon for Guilia for sure.

"*Si*," Bella said, jumping up. "I'll do it."

Signor Carlotti showed her to the vacant machine. He showed her how to make the needle go up and down, how to feed the material through. All she had to do was sew one straight seam up the side of a half-sewn shirtwaist, and then pass the shirtwaist to the next girl in line.

"You try," Signor Carlotti said.

Bella wasn't prepared for how hungrily the machine gobbled

at the material. The thread snarled; the delicate shirtwaist tore.

Signor Carlotti snarled and swore.

"That's a shirtwaist ruined," he said. "That'll come out of your salary, young lady!"

Twenty-five cents extra minus the cost of every shirtwaist I ruin? Bella wondered. *I could end up losing money on my new job!*

"But it's my first time!" Bella protested.

"And it will be your last if you don't do better," Signor Carlotti growled.

Bella bit her lip. This time, she fed the shirtwaist through the machine more carefully, pumping the needle as slowly as possible.

"All right," Signor Carlotti said. "But if you don't get faster soon, you'll be back cutting threads."

For the rest of the day, Bella worked steadily. Her palms were sweaty and her stomach twisted in knots, and she stopped every few seconds to pray for the strength to go on. The sewing machine was a gleaming, glossy black that reminded her of the landowner's horse back in Italy; sewing, Bella felt like she was holding on to the reins of a wild stallion. She couldn't risk even a single second of thinking about Pietro or Calia or anything else. But by the end of the day, she'd managed to sew dozens of shirtwaists without ruining a single other one.

Proudly, she stood up to take her pay for the week from Signor Carlotti. He counted out three dollars and one thin dime into her hand. Bella stood there waiting for the other dollar, the other fifteen cents. But Signor Carlotti had already moved on to the next girl.

"Wait," Bella said. "You said you'd pay me four dollars and twenty-five cents."

"You ruined a shirtwaist," Signor Carlotti said.

"Only one!"

"And you were a learner on the machine today. Remember, learners don't get paid. So that's only five days of work, minus twenty cents for the ruined shirtwaist—yep, three-ten."

Bella gasped.

"You tricked me!" she said. "You promised me four twenty-five! You told me I'd make more money on the machine!"

"I don't understand what you're saying," Signor Carlotti said. "If you're too stupid to learn English, at least learn proper Italian."

Bella glared at him. She knew he knew what she was saying. But how could she defend herself if he wouldn't even listen? Desperately, she glanced at the other girls around her. None of them were Italian, but *they* seemed to understand. They peered at her with sympathy in their eyes, but they were shaking their heads fearfully.

"Don't fight—he'll fire you," one girl whispered. Bella could figure out what she was saying just by the resignation in her voice.

"I'm telling Pietro," Bella said. "*He'll* make you give me my money!"

She stalked toward the elevators, but there was a huge crush of workers all wanting to leave at once. Bella was too angry to wait. Wasn't there any other way out? For the first time, she noticed a door at the other end of the building; she rushed over to it and peeked through the glass pane in the door—stairs! She turned the knob and shoved against the door, but it was locked.

"Oh, no, you don't," a man said angrily. He jerked her away from the door, then shoved her back toward the crowd again.

Bella circled the sewing machine tables widely so she didn't have to go right past Signor Carlotti again. This time, passing a row of windows, she looked out and noticed that there was a small, rickety fire escape leading down toward the ground in the narrow space between buildings. Fine. She'd go out that way. Bella was just beginning to tug on the window, trying to push it up, when she heard the man yelling at her again.

This time, he clamped his hand around her arm and pulled her through the crowd until they reached the guard who always watched the girls leave, inspecting their purses and their hair, sometimes even patting down their blouses or skirts. Bella had never understood what he was doing, and he'd never bothered her much, since she didn't have a purse or a fancy hairdo. But now the man shoved her toward the guard and said something like, "Search this one very thoroughly"— Bella guessed that was what he said, because the guard began sliding his hands along her sleeves, then reaching for her waist, even her breasts . . .

"How dare you!" Bella screamed, pulling away.

"Where'd you hide the shirtwaists?" the guard muttered, Bella understanding the word "shirtwaists" and figuring out the rest. And then, with a searing shame, she realized: They thought she was stealing shirtwaists. That's what the guard was looking for every afternoon when he peered into purses, when he curled his fingers into girls' puffs of hair, when he felt under their waistbands. And Bella, by trying to leave without going past the guard, had looked particularly suspicious.

This is what they think of me? Bella wondered. *They think I would actually do that?*

The shame of being seen as a thief mixed with the shame of being groped by a total stranger, and rooted Bella to the spot.

"Go on, then," the guard said, shoving her forward. "She's got nothing."

Nobody apologized. Bella whirled around, past the elevators, just wanting to hide her shame. She stepped through another doorway—oh, *here* were stairs she could use. She didn't care if she was supposed to or not; she just took off running down the steps. It was nine flights of stairs down to the ground floor, and she raced down them two at a time. Bursting out into the crisp autumn air, she let the door bang shut behind her.

I'll tell Pietro about this, too—he'll want to defend my honor! He'll tell them that I'm not a thief, they have no right to treat me like that, to touch me, to cheat me out of the money I earned . . .

The sidewalk outside was crowded, but she was too angry to care about how many people shoved against her. She scanned the crowd for Pietro, but he wasn't there yet. She paced.

It's so unfair! That Signor Carlotti! That guard! I can't wait for Pietro to tell them off!

The other workers streamed out of the building, in festive moods because it was Saturday night and they'd just gotten paid and they were probably all going to movies and dances. Bella crossed her arms and leaned back against the building, just so the force of the crowd didn't carry her away. The tide of workers coming out of the building slowed to a trickle, and then stopped. Pietro still wasn't there.

What if he thinks I'm to blame somehow for the guard groping me? And then he might think I am bad, like damaged goods. . . . Maybe I shouldn't tell him about that, just about the money.

To distract herself, she told herself maybe *he'd* gotten paid extra today—maybe he was right this minute buying movie tickets and planning to ask Bella to go with him. Bella had never heard of an unmarried boy and girl doing something like that back in Italy, but that was just because Calia didn't have a movie theater, right?

Bella couldn't trick herself into believing her fantasy at all. The wind whipped around the corner, and she shivered. It was going to be dark soon, and the sidewalks were emptying out. Where was Pietro? He'd never been this late before—never.

The tall buildings cast huge shadows. The wind blew more fiercely. Bella's thin cotton dress was meant for the heat of southern Italy; it was no match for this cold wind. She was shaking now, huddled against the cold wall of the factory building. She wanted to bargain with God: *Oh, per favore, per favore, I don't need to have the rest of my payment, I don't need to have my honor defended, I don't need to go to a dance or the movies, just please send Pietro. . . .*

"*Epes felt dir?*" someone said.

Bella looked up. It was a girl from the factory, the girl who had cut threads with Bella the first day. This girl had moved on to running a sewing machine a long, long time ago, so Bella had barely seen her since that first day. She was with another girl with equally dark eyes and lustrous hair— Bella thought maybe the other girl was her sister.

"I'm waiting for my cousin," Bella said, pantomiming her hand over her brow, looking around searchingly.

"Doesn't your brother usually walk you home?" the girl said, and somehow Bella understood this, even though it wasn't in Italian.

"Cousin," Bella said. "Cousin, not brother. But he didn't come tonight. . . ." She swallowed hard. She wasn't going to cry in front of strangers.

"Do you want us to take you home?" the sister said.

And let Pietro wonder what happened to me? Sure. Let him be the one worrying. Because now she was nearly as mad at Pietro as she was at Signor Carlotti or the guard. Better to be mad than to worry—what had happened to Pietro?

Bella and the two sisters set off walking, but every time they reached a corner, the sisters looked questioningly at Bella, pointing—right? Left? Straight? Which was it? Everything looked different in the dark, without the crowds, without Pietro leading the way. Sometimes Bella could remember—*Oh, yes, this is where the pigeons always roost on the light posts*—go that way—other times she had to guess and, as often as not, backtrack when nothing looked familiar. But somehow, finally, they reached the front of the Lucianos' tenement building.

"I live here," Bella said. "*Grazie.* Thank you."

"I'm Yetta and she's Rahel," the girl said, and she pointed and gestured so Bella understood this as well. "If we can do anything else to help . . ."

"I'm fine," Bella said stiffly. "Thank you."

The hallway and the stairs were dark; Bella stumbled climbing up. She shoved her way into the Lucianos' apartment, where the entire family and a few of the boarders were crowded around the table making flowers.

"You missed supper," Signora Luciano said. "It's all gone."

"Pietro—" Bella said. "Is Pietro here? Did he come home after work?"

"Haven't seen him," Signora Luciano said. Even in the dim light, Bella could see the malice gleaming in her eyes. "What's wrong—is he two-timing you? Did he take it into his head to move somewhere else without you? Or—was he too stupid to get out of the way when they dropped a pipe in that ditch he was digging?"

Bella gasped.

"Where would they take him if he got hurt?" she asked, reaching back for the door. "I have to find him. Who would know where he is? The places he goes at night—the, the bars . . ."

Signora Luciano laughed.

"No respectable female would go into places like that," she said. "You go there, I'd be forced to kick you out. Can't have you making a bad influence on my girls." She patted the nearest dirty head, though Bella wasn't sure that that particular Luciano child was a girl.

"But, about Pietro—" Bella pleaded.

The oldest Luciano boy, Rocco, stood up. He was perhaps nine or ten—Bella had barely seen him before, because he was almost always out on the streets selling newspapers or shining shoes.

"I'll go look for him," Rocco said.

"You haven't done your share of the flowers," Signora Luciano growled.

"I sold extra newspapers today," Rocco said. "The swells always feel sorry for the newsboys when it gets cold."

Rocco brushed past his mother.

At the door, he told Bella, "I'll be back as soon as I can."

Bella sank down on the edge of the bed, even though two of the children and one of the male boarders, Nico, were already sitting there, their hands twisting flowers. Nico leaned over and whispered something to Signor Luciano, and they both laughed. Bella knew they were talking about her, something crude and nasty. Something that made her feel the same kind of shame she'd felt that afternoon, with the guard touching her. Her face flamed, and she focused on praying.

Please let Rocco come back quickly, with Pietro. Or at least with news that he's fine, that the only reason he didn't meet me after work was . . .

Bella couldn't think of any good reason that Pietro hadn't met her.

The fire in the stove threw scary shadows; the baby whined, then howled, then cried itself to sleep; Signora Luciano woke it up again shouting at everyone to work faster. Bella waited.

When Rocco returned, he was alone.

Everyone stared at him, but he looked only at Bella.

"They're saying"—he panted, as if he'd run all the way from the bar, all the way up the stairs—"they're saying the padrone took him to South Carolina."

"South Carolina?" Bella repeated, having trouble pronouncing the unfamiliar words. "Where's that?"

She hoped it was just a street or two over. No matter what Signora Luciano said, Bella wanted to go find Pietro for herself and make sure he was all right.

"It's another state, hundreds of miles away," Rocco said. "The padrone took his entire work crew. He thought he could make more money there."

"And Pietro didn't even tell me?" Bella cried out, in a strangled voice. "Didn't even ask if I wanted to go with him?"

She felt betrayed, injured down to her very core.

"The girl *wants* to go off with a bunch of men?" Nico whispered, and that hurt too, what he was implying. Bella tried to ignore him.

"Pietro probably didn't even know what was going on, until the padrone had him on the train," Rocco said. "He left all his things here. It's like . . . like he was kidnapped."

Bella didn't understand. Bandits kidnapped people—bandits were the ones who kidnapped and robbed and murdered. Padroni were powerful; they wouldn't have to stoop to such things.

"But, but—the padrone gave us the money to come here," Bella said. "Pietro first, then me. The padrone helped us."

Signor Luciano laughed harshly.

"Padroni don't give anyone anything," he said. "They *loan* the money, and expect a lot of money back in return. Pietro probably wasn't paying fast enough."

My three dollars and ten cents today, instead of four or four-twenty-five, Bella thought, stricken. *Pietro was paying back my share too. Maybe it's because of me?*

But the padrone wouldn't know that she got less money today. By the time Bella got paid, he'd already kidnapped Pietro.

"That reminds me," Signora Luciano said. "Your rent is due today. And because I lost a boarder, and Pietro skipped out without paying, I'll have to raise my rates. It's . . . three-fifty now."

She held out her hand, waiting. Bella could see the dirt under her long, scraggly fingernails. Dirt as black as night, as black as Signora Luciano's soul.

"But—I only made three-ten this week," Bella protested. "I don't have that much money. I can't pay. Please, I beg of you—"

"Then you'll have to help us with the flowers, won't you?" Signora Luciano said. "Here. Get to work."

She held out wires, leaves, and petals, cheerful-looking things meant for grand ladies' hats. But Bella knew they were really chains, handcuffs, shackles. If Bella so much as touched one of those wires, she'd be chained to the sewing machine all day at the factory, chained to the flowers every evening.

"No, please," Bella moaned, but she was only a girl, alone—what could she do? Pietro was gone. No one was there to protect her anymore.

She gazed beseechingly at Signor Luciano, at Nico, at Rocco, but the men kept their heads down, carefully ignoring her. And the boy just shrugged, helplessly. Only he had the grace to look ashamed.

"Take it!" Signora Luciano ordered.

Bella took the wires, the leaves, the petals. She let Signora Luciano show her how to wrap everything together, creating the illusion of a flower. She let Signora Luciano scream at her when her fingers fumbled with the wires, when she dropped the leaves, when she accidentally smashed the petals.

The old Bella wouldn't have stood for this, Bella told herself. *She wouldn't have let anyone yell at her like that, not without yelling back. She wouldn't have let Signor Carlotti cheat her, either. And she would have found some way to save Pietro from the padrone. . . .*

But she knew none of that was true. The old Bella was courageous and daring and fierce only because she hadn't known any better. She hadn't known any better than to come to America.

That was worth it, she thought, blinking away tears. *It's worth it to work so hard, to be so hungry and tired and cold. Everything's worth it as long as my family has food.*

But that was hard to believe when the wires squirmed in her hands, when Signor Luciano and Nico leered at her, when Signora Luciano yelled at her, when everyone she loved was so far away.

When she felt so completely and utterly alone.

Yetta

We should have asked her about joining the union," Yetta said.

Rahel gave her a sidelong glance.

"That girl was worried sick over her boyfriend—couldn't you see?" Rahel said. "She was in no frame of mind to hear about her rights as a worker, her importance to the union. And I don't think she understands English."

"It was her brother she was waiting for—brother or cousin or something like that," Yetta said.

"Oh, Yetta, didn't you see the look on her face? That girl's in love."

Yetta hated this, when Rahel made her feel like a little child who knew nothing of the world.

"The union's more important than love," Yetta said stubbornly.

"Yetta, Yetta, Yetta," Rahel said in a singsongy voice, playfully swinging around a lamppost. "Let's see what you say when you fall in love."

"Won't happen," Yetta said.

Rahel snickered in response and skipped ahead. It was a cold night, but they were both in high spirits because they'd just come from a lecture by a famous socialist. They'd heard how the workers really had all the power, so much more than the bosses—all they had to do was unite. Several other girls from Triangle had been in the audience, girls who nodded and clapped at all the same moments that Rahel and Yetta nodded and clapped. They'd felt united, there.

"If the Italian girls knew what was good for them, they'd want to join the union too," Yetta said. "I think that was the girl who got cheated today."

"Who hasn't been cheated?" Rahel said, spinning back around to face Yetta. "Who hasn't had their pay docked for being a minute late? Who hasn't had the clock set back on them, so you work and work and work and quitting time never comes? Who hasn't been forced to work overtime for no pay, and been told, 'Oh, here, you can have an apple turnover for your supper—aren't we generous?' Three hours overtime, and all you get is a measly turnover! Who hasn't had a supervisor follow them to the bathroom and say, 'You're taking too long in there! You're stealing time from the company!' Who hasn't been charged for the electricity, for thread, for needles? Who hasn't been charged for torn shirtwaists that the contractor himself ripped?"

"Rahel for union leader!" Yetta cheered, her voice echoing slightly off the tenements around them.

Rahel laughed.

"Oh, you know they'd never let a girl be in charge," she said. "Those big union men, they look at us like we've got fluff for brains, and they pat our heads and say, 'Now, now, you know it's impossible to organize girls. They're just working for pin money, just working until they get married. Girls can't be depended on in a union.'"

"Then fight the union men," Yetta said. "Fight the union

men, fight the bosses—fight the world!"

Rahel looped her arm through her sister's.

"You would, wouldn't you?" she said, laughing again.

They'd crossed over now from the section where mostly Italian people lived, to an area where it was all Jews. They passed a Yiddish theater, and Yetta heard a burst of laughter when someone opened the door. The streets were crowded with people going to the theater or dances or movies or lectures or night school. In fact, there were more people out walking in this one block than had lived in Yetta's entire shtetl back home. She remembered how shocked she'd been when she'd first got to America, by the noise and lights, the beardless men, the giggling girls who didn't seem to know any of the rules about how females were supposed to behave. Now it all delighted her. In spite of her empty stomach, her aching feet, her threadbare clothes, her lousy job—in spite of everything, Yetta could still feel a burst of love for America, for New York, for the Lower East Side.

Back in the shtetl, she'd faced such a narrow future. Her parents and the matchmaker would have married her off to someone just for the status he could bring her family. If her father had had his way, it would have been a scholar, someone who'd spend his days with his head bent over the Torah while Yetta milked the cows and baked the bread, birthed the babies, and squeezed a living out of every little coin. No— that wouldn't have been a living. This wasn't quite living either—spending her life hunched over a machine, a supervisor always yelling at her, the work always piling up. In the factory, she was little more than a machine herself. But so much more was possible here. She was taking night-school English lessons and going to lectures and classes, and she could feel her mind opening up, her dreams opening up, her future opening up.

Maybe she and Rahel would be union leaders together.

"That Italian girl," Rahel said, staring off into the distance, past the throngs on the sidewalk. "I suppose she will get married. She'll get married and have babies and quit the factory. Maybe the union men have a point. How can we ask her to fight and struggle and suffer when she's just going to quit? When she won't benefit from anything we're fighting for?"

"Because maybe she'll have daughters," Yetta said fiercely. "And maybe her daughters will work in the factory. She wouldn't want her daughters being tricked and cheated. She wouldn't want her daughters to work a full week and have nothing to show for it. She wouldn't want her daughters to starve."

"Oh, Yetta, you have all the answers, don't you?" Rahel said. But she didn't sound proud or impressed. She sounded wistful, the same way she sounded sometimes when they whispered together in the night. Remember how Mama used to tuck us into bed when we were little? *Remember how she polished the Sabbath candlesticks until they gleamed? Remember how Papa would lift us up on his shoulders and cry out, "The richest man in town can only wish to have so fine a family as ours!"*

Yetta didn't have an answer for that. It didn't matter, though, because Rahel had turned away from her.

"Oh!" she cried out, her cheeks suddenly coloring up. "Mr. Cohen!"

A tall, well-dressed young man was coming toward them. On a sidewalk full of couples and clusters of friends, he was walking alone.

"Miss Rahel!" he said, then said something in English that Yetta didn't quite understand. What did "It's such a treasure to see you" mean? No, wait. "Pleasure"? He thought it was a pleasure to see Rahel?

"Your English is perfect," Rahel said, with a trilling kind of laugh that Yetta had never heard Rahel use before.

"Thank you so much. Thank you," Mr. Cohen said with a little bow, then he walked on.

Rahel stood still, watching him. Yetta watched Rahel.

"Who was that?" Yetta demanded.

"Mr. Cohen," Rahel said. "He's in my English class."

Rahel was in a different English class than Yetta, a more advanced one, because she'd been in America longer. That was something else that made Yetta feel like Rahel would always be far ahead, that Yetta could never catch up.

Rahel sighed, as Mr. Cohen disappeared into the crowd. "He's so . . . don't you think he's handsome?" she asked.

Handsome? Back home in the shtetl, it wasn't much worth noticing who was handsome and who wasn't. Girls didn't have a choice. They just married the man their parents told them to marry, and hoped he wasn't too hideous. But in America . . . what was Rahel thinking?

"About the Italian girls," Yetta said, her voice sounding rough and unnatural. "I think the bosses are trying to make us hate them. You know how they alternate us at the sewing machines so you have to lean past someone Italian if you want to speak Yiddish? And I think it's the bosses who start all those rumors about how the Italians hate *us*. That girl didn't seem to mind at all that we were Jewish. . . ."

Yetta waited for Rahel to correct her, to say they weren't Jewish anymore, they were socialists, unionists, revolutionaries.

But Rahel wasn't even listening.

Jane

Jane eased the heavy front door shut and tiptoed across the marble foyer. It was late—all the servants had gone to bed hours ago. She could see a thin strip of light on the floor, the only thing that showed under the door of Father's study. It would be nothing to tiptoe past that door. Jane inhaled deeply, just in case she'd have to hold her breath. But the inhalation brought with it a huge whiff of cigar smoke—also coming from Father's study—and Jane began to choke and cough.

The door sprang open, and Father stood there brandishing a fireplace poker over his head. He lowered it, a bit sheepishly, when he saw that it was only Jane.

"Young lady!" he said gruffly. "Where have you been? Why isn't Miss Milhouse accompanying you?"

Jane finished coughing. She backed away from the larger billow of cigar smoke that had appeared when Father opened the study door.

"I was . . . I'm returning from an educational lecture," Jane said. "I went with Eleanor Kensington, who's a Vassar student and very mature, and so Miss Milhouse's presence wasn't required."

Very innocent, Jane told herself, and it was. She was telling the truth. But she felt guilty, as if Father wouldn't approve if he knew the whole truth. If he knew how Jane had finagled to avoid taking Miss Milhouse along. (None of the college girls had chaperons constantly babysitting them—why should Jane?) If he knew that Eleanor swore sometimes—she said "Dash it all" just like a boy—and maybe wasn't as reputable as Jane implied. If he knew that the lecturer tonight had talked about women's rights. (What did Father think of women's rights?) Or if he knew that she and Eleanor and Eleanor's friends had gone to an ice cream parlor afterward that maybe wasn't perfectly clean and maybe wasn't perfectly socially acceptable.

Jane's friend Pearl had introduced her to Eleanor Kensington three months ago, and it had become common for Eleanor to invite Jane along for lectures and symposiums, academic talks and social commentaries. At first, Pearl had gone too, but Pearl yawned and squirmed and elbowed Jane to whisper, "Would it be rude to leave early? This is *so* boring. . . ."

Jane thought a lot of it was boring too. But a lot of it was fascinating, and had set Jane to wondering about everything. Was the speaker right, the one who claimed that there was enough wealth in America that *no one* should have to live in poverty? (Who would care to work as servants, then?) How about the speaker who said that alcohol was the root of all evil? (Jane had thought it was supposedly money—though Eleanor and her friends had looked the quotation up in the Bible and said it was actually the *want* of money that was evil, which wasn't exactly the same thing. Jane was still thinking about that one.) And then there were all those women's rights lectures. Would the United States be a better place if women could vote?

Jane favored her father with what she hoped was her most innocent-looking smile.

"And really," she said, trying to sound nonchalant. "I'm coming home much earlier than if I'd been to a dance."

Father scowled at her anyway, his thick black eyebrows beetling together. Jane had seen pictures of her father when he was young and handsome—she could understand why her mother stared at him so dreamily in their wedding pictures. They'd been a lovely couple, Jane's parents, back before Mother had taken sick and faded away. Now Father was pot-bellied and balding and fierce, and Jane was more than a little afraid of him.

"You were with Eleanor Kensington?" he muttered. "Of the shipping-interest Kensingtons?"

"I suppose," Jane said. "She's Pearl Kensington's cousin."

"Ah," Father said, and Jane understood that he had just begun a calculation in his head, judging the Kensington family's financial and social status relative to his own.

"They live near the Vanderbilts," Jane said.

"I see," Father said. Eleanor had been judged acceptable. "Does she perhaps have a brother?"

Jane blushed. This was new, Father asking about eligible males, instead of simply counting on Miss Milhouse to shepherd Jane through the complexities of courtship. Jane felt a sudden pang of missing her mother. Surely, even as an invalid, Jane's mother would have cared enough to ask, "Was that boy kind enough when he asked you to dance? Did his eyes sparkle when you said 'yes,' or was he just playing his role?" and even, "Do you think you could love him?"—rather than treating the whole marriage campaign like a military maneuver, a series of battles to be won or lost based on flounced dresses, tasteful décolletage and discreet flirting (but not too much! Oh, no, not too much!).

"Eh? Is there a brother?" Father repeated awkwardly. Maybe he was blushing too.

"Eleanor's brothers are older, and already married," Jane said, trying to keep her voice steady.

"Ah," Father said again.

Jane wondered what would happen if she told him what the lecturer had said tonight about marriage.

"Women are not chattel, to be traded off like cattle or hogs!" she'd thundered out. "We're not trophies, to be placed in glass cases! We're human beings, and we deserve to be treated as such. We, like our husbands, should be allowed to own property. We, like our husbands, should have a say over the money we earn. We, like our husbands, should have a determining voice in the guardianship of our children. And we, like our husbands, should have the right to vote!"

Afterward, in the ice cream parlor, Jane had spooned butterscotch sundae into her mouth and listened to the debate swirling around her. Eleanor said the speaker had been particularly brave to take on the issue of marriage, since Mrs. Belmont, who'd just donated a new headquarters for the suffrage movement, had forced her own daughter to marry against her will.

"Just because *she* wanted a royal title in the family, she made Consuelo marry that horrid duke, who just wanted her money," Eleanor had said. "Even though Consuelo was in love with someone else, and sobbed all the way to the wedding. That's the worst fad, rich Americans marrying off their daughters to dusty old counts and such. It's barbaric, I say!"

Jane hadn't heard of anyone objecting before. Her old friends thought royalty was romantic.

"Wouldn't you want to be a duchess?" she'd ventured timidly to Eleanor.

"Not unless I loved the duke. Not unless I loved him, regardless of whether he was a duke or a prince or an industrialist or a common old Joe."

"In other words, no," one of Eleanor's friends joked.

And then they'd been off on another topic. The ideas flew by so quickly, Jane felt like she was watching a tennis match. Her head swam, but it was wonderful. Who'd known there were so many things to think about?

Now Father cleared his throat.

"We'll have to be very careful with this matter," Father said. "It will be important for you to make a good match. Something like that could make a big difference in my business."

A year ago, a month ago—maybe even a day ago—Jane would have been flattered that he thought *anything* about her was important. That he noticed her at all. But with the women's rights lecture still echoing in her ears, she heard him differently now.

So—marrying me off could make a big difference in his business? Jane thought. *What about the difference it would make in my life? He does think I'm chattel—just something to trade for something else he wants more!*

Jane tried to ignore the ache in her heart. She stared past him into his study, with its dark wood, its leather chairs, its cloud of cigar smoke. The whole room reeked of power and masculinity. Once, when she was four or five, she'd tried to hide under his desk during a birthday party game of hide-and-seek. Father had come in unexpectedly and scolded, "Now, now, this is no place for a little girl! Out!" Perhaps he'd only meant that he didn't want children ruffling through his business papers, that he didn't want party games interrupting his work. But Jane had understood him to mean much, much more. She'd looked down at her lacy white party dress with the pink-ribbon sash and felt ashamed, as if she'd been trying to pass herself off as a boy. As if she'd been trying to pass herself off as important.

Jane had mostly done everything she could to avoid his study ever since.

But she wasn't a little girl anymore. And what use was it to go to women's rights lectures if she just stood there, silently, while her father decided her entire life?

"But, Father," she said slowly, trying to keep the tremble out of her voice. "Maybe I'm not really ready yet to think about . . . any of that. Maybe I won't be ready for years. Maybe I'd like to . . . to go to college first."

"College?" Father growled, as though he'd never heard of such a thing, even though he had his own Yale diploma hanging on his study wall.

"A college for women," Jane said hastily. "They have lots of them now—Vassar, Smith, Barnard. . . ."

Father was scowling and shaking his head.

"Why, that's preposterous," he said. "Almost as preposterous as women wanting to vote."

Well. So that was what he thought of women's rights. A year ago, a month ago, maybe even a day ago, it wouldn't have mattered. But now, somehow, it did. Somehow it made

Jane feel that he'd always see her as he saw her when she was five: a frilly, useless, annoying girl in a frilly, useless, annoying dress.

Jane had just finished hearing dozens of reasons why women should be allowed to vote, dozens of reasons why women should be allowed to go to college. But right now she wasn't capable of telling her father any of them. She could only swallow hard and tiptoe away and hope she made it to her room before she began to cry.

Bella

 ella trudged along listlessly behind Signor Luciano. She'd lost track of how much time had passed since Pietro disappeared—weeks? Months? Years? It was hard to keep track of anything when her life was just one constant, exhausting blur of work—making shirtwaists all day in the factory, making flowers at the Lucianos' table all night and on Sundays. She was so used to being yelled at that her ears seemed to ring constantly with angry voices. Signora Luciano: "Surely you can make more flowers than that! If you don't, I'll throw you out in the streets. Don't think I wouldn't do that." Signor Carlotti: "Faster! Faster! Faster! Don't you know there are hundreds of girls arriving at Ellis Island right this minute, who'd love taking your job? And they'd do it cheaper, too, I'd wager." Signor Luciano: "Hurry up! You make me late for my job, I'll be fired."

Oops. Signor Luciano was yelling that right this minute. Bella forced herself to step a little faster, before he followed up his words with a slap or a punch. She'd loved walking to and from work with Pietro—it'd been the best part of her days. But now Signor Luciano and the boarder Nico took turns escorting her. Nico was actually worse to walk with, because he was always leering at her and trying to touch her; at least Signor Luciano only hit her.

Don't think about any of that, Bella told herself. *Think about the money.*

This was the only part of Bella's life that gave her any joy anymore: the moment on Saturday afternoon when she carried a handful of coins and bills home from work. Sometimes it added up to four dollars, sometimes it was three—in bad weeks, when there wasn't much work or Signor Carlotti blamed her for a lot of ruined shirtwaists, it was only one or two. But she placed all that she could into Signor Luciano's rough hands: "For sending to my family. Back home. In Calia. You'll send it for me?"

"Oh, yes," Signor Luciano always said. "Of course. I'll go to the Banco di Napoli right now."

It was the only moment all week when she actually liked Signor Luciano. Suddenly his moustache didn't seem so scraggly; his eyes didn't seem so beady; she forgot all the slaps and punches, pinches and pokes he'd given her throughout the week. Sometimes he even patted her head in a grandfatherly way, murmuring, "Such a good girl, sending money home to her mama . . ."

Bella wished she could take the money to the bank herself, that she could watch the bank officials writing out the directions for where the money should go. She even wished she could write out her own directions: *For my mama, Angelina Rossetti, and Giovanni and Ricardo and Guilia and Dominic, in Italy in the village of Calia. It's such a small place you can't miss them— they're in the last house in the last piazza. . . . I am sending money and love and I miss you. . . .* But she couldn't do that. Even if she knew how to write, they'd never let a girl in a bank. She had to trust Signor Luciano.

He jerked on her arm and slapped her—she'd gotten lost in her thoughts and was lagging again.

"You make me late, so help me, I'll . . ."

Signor Luciano broke off. They were nearly to the Triangle factory, but the crowd around them had closed in tight. No one was moving now.

"Out of the way! Let us through!" Signor Luciano snarled, shoving forward. When that didn't work, he began pounding on the coat-covered backs in front of him.

One of the men turned around, his own fists bared.

"Quit it! We can't get anywhere either! It's the factory!"

"What about the factory?" Signor Luciano growled.

"It's closed down!"

Bella gasped. Signor Luciano let out of string of swear words.

"It can't be," Bella protested. "I was just there yesterday. Nobody said anything about closing down!"

She thought about yesterday—yesterday's misery as opposed to all the miserable yesterdays that came before it. There had been one odd event. In the middle of the afternoon, a man had stalked into the room and ordered them to stop their work. He screamed for a few minutes in a language Bella couldn't understand, then ordered them to start sewing again. Once upon a time, Bella would have longed for someone else who spoke her language, someone she could lean over and joke with: "What do you bet they dock our pay for all the time that took? Think they'll cut out fifty cents or a dollar?" But Bella was long past jokes. She just felt a stab of fear—what if they did dock her pay?

She was frantically cramming another shirtwaist through her sewing machine when Signor Carlotti leaned down close.

"Did you understand that, what Mr. Blanck said?" he asked, speaking slowly and loudly as if, for once, he really wanted to make sure Bella understood. "If you want to join a union, join the Triangle Employees Benevolent Association. You join any other union, you're gone."

He made a motion with his forefinger across his neck, like someone slashing a throat.

Bella shivered and nodded, though she still didn't know what a union was; she certainly didn't know what an employees benevolent association was. She understood that what she was supposed to do—what she was always supposed to do— was to keep the shirtwaists moving through her machine. What else did she need to know?

But now, if the factory were closed . . .

Signor Luciano was still swearing.

"Now I'll have to walk you back, I'll really be late to my job. . . . And how are you going to pay the rent? The signora and I can't afford to run a charity, you know."

"The—the flowers," Bella said. "If the factory's closed, I can make flowers all day long. All day, all night . . ."

She could barely choke out the words. It was like volunteering for a death sentence. And if she worked at nothing but the flowers, how would there ever be any more money to send home to Mama?

She is not an honest woman, Signora Luciano, Pietro had said, that very first day. *She would cheat you. Every week, there would be a reason she wouldn't pay. . . .*

Ever since Pietro vanished, Bella had tried not to think of those words, tried not to calculate how many thousands and thousands of flowers she'd already made without receiving a cent, always being told, "If you work a little faster, maybe, just maybe, you'll make enough to cover your rent. . . ."

Bella pressed forward, wanting to see for herself if the factory really was shut down. She managed to slip between two men's elbows and come up for air beneath the ostrich feather of some woman's hat. Now she could see the factory doors at least. There were indeed chains linked around the door handles, below a sign she couldn't read. The crowd around her was growing more and more unruly, people talking in louder and louder voices. Bella could figure out only a few of the words, mostly the ones that were repeated over and over again: "union . . . strike . . . union . . . strike . . ." She saw Yetta and Rahel, those girls who had walked her home the day Pietro vanished. What was Rahel saying?

Now. It is time now. . . .

Signor Luciano jerked Bella back by the hair.

"Come along," he said. "If I lose my job because I'm late from walking you home, I'll, I'll . . ."

"Mi scusi," a voice said behind them. Bella whirled around—it was Signor Carlotti.

"I couldn't help overhearing," he said. "If you think it's proper, *I* could escort Signorina Rossetti back to her abode."

Bella had never heard Signor Carlotti call her a signorina; she'd never heard him use words like "escort" and "abode."

"Who are you?" Signor Luciano growled.

Signor Carlotti bowed slightly, tilting the brim of his top hat.

"I am Signorina Rossetti's employer," he said. "She's one of my best workers."

He'd never said anything like that before, either.

"Fine," Signor Luciano spat out. He shoved Bella toward Signor Carlotti. With narrowed eyes, he muttered, "She'd better be there when I get home." He turned his glare on Bella. "And you better finish a lot of flowers!"

Signor Carlotti ignored Signor Luciano. He tipped his hat again, this time directly to Bella. He offered her his arm, but Bella only regarded it suspiciously. What was he doing, being nice to her? What did he want?

After a moment, Signor Carlotti dropped his arm, but he put his hand on her back, gently guiding her through the crowd.

Bella pulled away, and would have run if she hadn't been so tightly hemmed in by the crowd.

Signor Carlotti leaned in close, whispering in her ear.

"This must be very frightening for you, the factory closing down. And you so newly arrived from Italy . . . Poor little one."

If Bella had been frightened before, she was terrified now. She dived between a group of girls in lacy shirtwaists and skirts, all of them laughing as though the factory closing were a picnic. Signor Carlotti followed her, scattering the girls like geese.

"You are sending money home for your family, no?" he asked.

This slowed Bella down.

"Yes," she whispered.

"Your mother?" he asked. "Brothers and sisters?"

"My mama," Bella said. "Three brothers. One sister."

"Ah," Signor Carlotti said. "And they have no one but you to depend on?"

Bella was glad that he put it delicately, that he didn't ask, "So, is your father dead, or did he just run off?" But she wanted to defend her mother. *Mama tries,* she wanted to say. She remembered Mama marching off to the marketplace, trying to be hired as a farm laborer in Papa's place after Papa died. But there wasn't even enough work for the men; no landowner wanted to hire a woman still suckling a baby. She remembered her brother Giovanni, all of seven years old, saying, "You can't go off to America, Bella-Bella. You're a girl. *I'll* go. I'm the man of the family."

"What will your family do if you have no job?" Signor Carlotti asked.

Starve. Die.

Bella could not bring herself to say these words. Tears stung at her eyes, and she angrily brushed them away. She walked more briskly again, as if she could run away from Signor Carlotti's questions. In no time at all they were back in Bella's neighborhood, where the voices on the street all carried the rhythm of Italian, even if she couldn't understand each and every word. She saw the ragged urchins sitting on the curb, holding their hands out for pennies, begging, *"Per favore, per favore"*; the peddlers calling out "Peaches! Pears! Walnuts! Buy here!" Suddenly it seemed that they were all saying the same thing.

Please don't let us starve. Please, please. We don't want to die. Please. A whole neighborhood, hundreds and hundreds of people, all desperate to live.

Signor Carlotti touched Bella's cheek, and Bella let him.

"You are a good worker," he said. "Don't worry. The Triangle company will always have a place for workers like you. There are just some . . . troublemakers we need to get rid of. Rabblerousers. Come back to the factory tomorrow. We will be open again then. You still have a job."

Bella turned to Signor Carlotti, stared up at him through eyelashes heavy with tears.

"Really?" she said. "In truth? You are not just saying this, not just making up a story?"

"In truth," Signor Carlotti said. He chuckled a little and reached into his pocket. He pulled out a dollar bill, crisp and clean and new, not bedraggled and limp like most of the money that came Bella's way. He placed the money in Bella's hand.

"Proof," he said. "Let's say I'm paying you for today's work, and you don't even have to work!"

Bella let him press her fingers around the dollar, to hold it tight. But she squinted at him suspiciously. She was confused.

"I don't make a dollar a day," she said.

Signor Carlotti laughed again.

"Ah, but maybe you will soon," he said. "Let's say . . . let's say we raise your pay to five dollars a week. Deal?"

Bella almost dropped the money, she was that amazed.

"Deal," she said quickly, before he could change his mind.

They were in front of the Lucianos' apartment now. Signor Carlotti tipped his hat to her one final time.

"See you tomorrow," he said. Bella could have sworn he winked as well.

Signor Carlotti faded back into the crowd, but Bella didn't climb the stairs yet. When the peddler called out "Peaches! Pears! Walnuts!" behind her, it didn't sound like a desperate cry for help anymore. It just reminded her there was food she could buy.

Five dollars a week, she thought. *I could send money home and save up to bring my family here. . . . Or save up to buy land there . . .*

These were such daring thoughts that Bella laughed out loud.

The door to the tenement building creaked open, sending out puffs of foul, fetid air. The small form of Rocco Luciano appeared in the doorway.

"You're laughing," he said, the same stunned way he might have announced "It's snowing in July" or "Some swell gave me fifty dollars for shining his shoes today."

"The factory closed," Bella said, grinning ridiculously. "But it's all right—they'll be open tomorrow and Signor Carlotti paid me anyhow, a whole dollar, and I still have a job and I'm going to make more money now. And I'm just . . . just . . . happy."

Rocco kept staring at her. Bella could see the darkness behind him—the dark hallway, the dark stairway that led to the Lucianos' dark apartment, where Bella was supposed to spend the whole day hunched over a table making fake flowers. Her grin faded.

"I should—your father sent me back here to work," she said. "Signor Carlotti walked me home. I'm supposed to be making flowers right now."

She put her hand on the railing, because suddenly it seemed that she needed that to hold herself up. She pulled herself up the first step.

Rocco put his hand over hers.

"Don't," he said. His dark eyes blazed. "Don't go in there."

"What else can I do?" Bella asked, shrugging helplessly.

"What would I tell your parents? They'll know if I don't make the flowers. . . ."

"Come with me," Rocco said. "I'll show you the city. You can tell Mama and Papa . . . uh, we'll tell them I needed help with the papers, or I had so many shoes to shine, I gave you some of my business—it might be true! It's a lucky day! You can help me and then it won't be a total lie. . . ."

Bella considered. The soft autumn breeze tugged at her hair, the sunshine seemed to tease at her back. She reached behind Rocco to pull the tenement door firmly shut.

"I will," she said.

It was exactly what the old Bella would have done.

Yetta

Yetta held the sign high over her head. TRIANGLE WORKERS ON STRIKE, it said, in Yiddish and English. She'd lettered the sign herself, carefully copying the English from a sheet of paper another girl gave her. She'd dressed with extra care that morning, even borrowing Rahel's fancy hat.

"You'll be the public face of the strike," Rahel had said, placing the hat at precisely the right angle, to ride the swell of Yetta's thick hair. "I'm just going to be in the union office."

"That's important too," Yetta said loyally, but secretly she was glad that she wasn't quite as good at English as Rahel, wasn't quite old enough to be trusted with coordinating picketers and registration and funds for strikers who were already beginning to worry where their next meal would come from. They'd been on strike for exactly one week now, and Yetta had signed up for all the picketing time she could.

Now, in the light of an early October dawn, she paced outside the Triangle factory doors with a dozen other girls who held their signs equally high, kept their backs equally straight. She remembered all the men back in her shtetl who prayed each day, "Thank you, God, for not making me a woman."

They're wrong, she thought. If she was still Jewish, she

would be thanking God *because* he'd made her female. The strike leaders had decided that it was best to have the girls picket, because they would attract the most sympathy. And Yetta had seen how the bypassers looked at her and the other strikers. She'd heard them murmuring "Those poor things," and "But they're so pretty. . . ."

She saw a group of young men stop on the sidewalk, watching. Yetta lowered her gaze demurely, but she made sure that her sign was turned so they could read it. One of the young men detached himself from the group and strolled over to her.

"What's your gripe?" he asked, in English.

"Gripe?" Yetta repeated uncertainly. This young man had chestnut hair and brilliant blue eyes, and it was so clear that he was rich, with that good wool coat and those perfectly shined shoes. If she weren't so blinded by the whiteness of his teeth, maybe she could remember her English a little better.

"Yeah," the man said, gesturing up at her sign. "Why are you on strike? Do you have some reason, or do you just not feel like working today?"

"We want"—Yetta struggled to pronounce the English words correctly—"we want union recognition. We have that right! We were forming a union, we had one hundred and fifty workers go to a secret meeting, but there were spies there, and our bosses said we couldn't have our own union, we could only join this fake union the bosses made up, the Triangle Employees Benevolent Association. All the officers of that union were related to the bosses! I ask you, what kind of union is that? And then they locked us out, everyone who was trying to make a real union. They said there was no more work, but the next day they advertised for more workers in the papers! They say they just got a big order, unexpectedly, but if that were true, why wouldn't they just hire us back?"

The young man shrugged.

"So, what good's a union?" he asked. "Sounds to me like it just lost you your job."

"That's not how it's supposed to work!" Yetta said indignantly. "If everyone unites, all the workers together, a union can . . . can protect everyone. If there's a union, the whole shop all together, then the bosses cannot cheat you anymore. It's not just one girl, standing alone, saying, 'Why did you only pay me three dollars this week? Why did you lie to me? Why did you cheat me?' It is everyone saying, 'This isn't fair! You can't do this to us!'"

The young man stroked his moustache thoughtfully.

"You make three dollars a week?"

"No, but some girls—"

"Ah-ha!" the man said. "Who's lying now?"

"I have worked my way up," Yetta said, trying to keep proper dignity. "But even so, some weeks the bosses only pay—"

"You probably have a boyfriend, anyhow, to give you your finery," the man interrupted, actually reaching out to touch the feather on Yetta's hat. "And I'm sure your parents are still supporting you, so it's just funny money you're earning, just for the little luxuries every girl craves—"

"No! My parents, they—"

"Come on, Harry," one of the other men called from the corner in a bored voice. "Quit flirting. We're going to be late for class."

"Nice talking to you," Harry said, turning to go.

"My parents are not supporting me! I am supporting them!" Yetta yelled after him, but she was so upset that she accidentally yelled it in Yiddish.

"I couldn't understand a word she said," she heard Harry tell the rest of his friends when he rejoined them. "But those are the prettiest strikers I've ever seen."

Yetta was furious. He *had* understood her, she was sure of it.

Anna, the girl picketing behind her, leaned forward.

"Those were law students," she said, in an awestruck voice. "Law students, actually paying attention to us. To our strike."

"What?"

Anna pointed.

"There's a law school right behind the factory building. New York University School of Law. Haven't you seen the sign?"

Yetta hadn't. Before the strike, she'd barely seen any of the city by daylight.

Law students . . . Some of Yetta's anger drained away into pride. She'd just explained the strike to a law student. Maybe he hadn't really listened closely enough, maybe she'd have to work on her arguments for the next time, but still . . . law students!

"Watch out," Anna called out. "The scabs are coming."

Yetta tightened her grip on her sign. Policemen barreled through the strikers.

"Make way! You're blocking the sidewalks!"

Remember. Stay calm. Just tell them the truth. . . .

"Please!" Yetta called out to the scabs. "Please don't cross our picket line! We're striking for you, too, so we all have rights as workers! Don't go in to work today—go sign up at the union office! Join us!"

She was careful to speak in her best English, because most of the scabs were Americans or Italians. She was glad to hear one Italian striker, Rosaria, calling out in her language too, the words strangely musical.

The scabs pretended not to hear. They mostly cowered, keeping their eyes on the ground. They were so rabbity, Yetta could almost feel sorry for them.

Then Yetta noticed a different group of women behind the police and scabs. These women wore stoles of fur or feathers; their dresses were tawdry colors—reds and oranges and yellows. The dresses were also oddly shaped: slit up the sides, with plunging necklines in the front and back. And the women's faces were heavily painted, every pockmark and blemish coated, every cheek and lip unnaturally reddened. Yetta had never seen anyone like this before. She'd only heard stories.

Are they . . . prostitutes? Yetta wondered. What are prostitutes doing here?

"Leave the workers alone!" one of the women screamed, slamming her fist directly into Yetta's jaw.

Yetta's brain was still trying to make sense of what she was seeing: She was working on a theory that maybe these women were apparitions, hallucinations brought on by her having skipped breakfast. So it took her even longer to accept that this woman was actually *touching* her—punching, more precisely. Punching and kicking and yanking at her hair . . . Yetta fell to the ground, her sign cracking on the pavement.

"Stop!" she cried, trying to push the woman off her.

But the woman pulled out Yetta's own hat pin, from Rahel's beautiful hat, and stabbed it into Yetta's arm. Yetta squirmed away and struggled to stand up, but another woman shoved her down again.

"Help!" Yetta screamed, but all the other strikers were suffering punches and kicks and pinches too. Yetta had seen plenty of little boys fighting in the street—even men throwing punches. But she'd never been in a fight like this herself, never known how much it would hurt. Her eyes stung, and she wasn't sure if it was from tears or blood. She kept trying to push the women away, but they were right back at her, right away, punch after punch after punch. . . .

"That's enough!"

It was a policeman, pulling the women off Yetta.

"I should say so!" Yetta said indignantly. "Thank you for finally—"

But the policeman was clamping handcuffs onto Yetta's wrists, growling into her bloody face, "You're under arrest."

With his beefy hand wrapped tightly around Yetta's arm, holding her still, he turned toward the prostitutes.

"You're free to go," he told them. The prostitutes straightened their dresses, patted their hair back into place. One of them blew a kiss to the policeman.

"Wait a minute! That's not fair!" Yetta complained. "They attacked me! I didn't do anything to them! Look—which of us is bleeding?"

The policeman jerked on the handcuffs, making them rub against Yetta's sore wrists.

"You're a striker, aren't you?" He asked.

"Yes, but—"

The policeman looked back and forth between Yetta and the prostitutes.

"Then I can't see much difference."

Yetta pushed a blood-soaked strand of hair out of her eyes. She bent down and retrieved Rahel's formerly fine hat, now mashed beyond recognition. The ostrich feather was nowhere to be seen.

"We have a right to strike!" she protested. "I haven't committed a single illegal act! Tell me—what am I under arrest for?"

The policeman yanked her toward the police wagon.

"Disorderly conduct. Now, shut up, or you'll be charged with being rude to a police officer too," he said. He lifted the club he'd used to break up the fight. "*And* I'll beat you myself!"

So you're admitting those women beat me! Yetta wanted to say. But she clamped her lips together. That hurt too, because they were bloody and already beginning to swell.

Yetta's fellow strikers stood in sad little clumps by the police wagon. Anna's skirt was in shreds; Rosaria's right eye was swollen shut. Policemen were shoving the girls into the wagon without regard to their injuries. Yetta fought against the policeman holding her arm; she struggled to turn back toward the prostitutes.

"Why?" she yelled at the heavily painted women. "Why do you care about our strike?"

One woman began to laugh, revealing the toothless mouth behind her too-red lips.

"Money, of course," she cackled. "Don't you know anything? In America, money is God."

The policeman slammed his club against Yetta's head, and everything went dark.

Iron bars.

That was the first thing Yetta saw when she opened her eyes. Someone was dabbing at the wound on the side of her head with a cloth. Someone was whispering, "Yetta, oh, please, Yetta, wake up. . . ." But there were iron bars in front of her and a filthy stone floor and dark shapes moving across the floor. . . . Were those rats?

Yetta struggled to sit up. The iron bars wavered; she was about to black out again.

"Shh, shh," a soft voice said. "Take it easy. Just rest."

Yetta put her head back down, and her view steadied again. She was lying on a bare wood plank, but one of the other girls had stuffed her jacket under Yetta's head. Anna and Rosaria and a few of the others were crouched around her. Gradually, Yetta found that she could focus on their faces.

"Getting blood on your coat," Yetta murmured.

"That doesn't matter. It's ripped to ruins anyway. And we're in jail, so what good is a stupid coat?" Anna gave a laugh that turned midway into a near sob.

Yetta forced herself to sit up; she forced her eyes to keep a steady gaze on the other girls, not the iron bars.

"We'll be all right," she said. "We didn't do anything wrong. They can't keep us here."

"They kept my father in prison in Russia," another girl, Surka, said. "They didn't even tell him what he was charged with until he'd been there three years."

"That was Russia," Yetta said. "This is America."

At the other end of the jail cell, a ragged old woman began to laugh crazily, the sound pouring out of her mouth like a taunt. Or torture.

"She's been doing that since we got here," Anna whispered.

Yetta was noticing the other women in the cell now—scary women with gaunt, blank faces, sores where their mouths should be, ragged clothes that looked to be mostly held together with dirt. Or maybe they weren't actually wearing any clothes, just the filth.

And then she heard footsteps coming down the hallway outside the jail cell.

"Strikers!" a man's voice boomed out, echoing off the stone. "Your fines are paid!"

His key scraped in the lock. Yetta found she could scramble up with the others, though the wound on the side of her head throbbed and her whole body ached.

Rahel was waiting beside the jailer on the other side of the iron door.

"Oh, Yetta!" she cried, wrapping her arms around her sister. "I was so scared for you—"

"Tell your sister to stay off picket lines, then," the jailer growled.

Yetta wanted to fling back a retort: maybe "Tell the bosses to treat us fairly, and I will!"; maybe "Tell your policemen to arrest the right people next time!" But she could only bury her face in her sister's shoulder, let her sister guide her away from those iron bars and the rats and the crazy laughing woman and the women dressed in filth.

"How did . . . how could you pay the fine?" Yetta murmured when they were back out on the street.

"Union money," Rahel said. "And they gave me nickels for carfare, too, so we won't have to walk home. The trolley stop's right up there on the corner—can you make it that far?"

Around her, the other girls nodded wearily. Yetta was working something out in her head.

"The union doesn't have much money," she said. "If we spend it on carfare, we won't have any left for keeping the strike going. My legs aren't bad, just my head. I'll walk."

"But—" Rahel started.

"I'm walking too," Anna said.

"Me, too," Rosaria said.

"And me," Surka said.

In the end, they all did, one bedraggled, bloodied crew. Everyone on the sidewalk stared and whispered. Yetta wished they still had their picket signs.

"We're Triangle workers," she explained to some of the people who stared the most. "We're on strike. This is what happened."

The strike meant something different now. It wasn't just standing out in the sunshine carrying a sign, wearing a fine hat, looking pretty. It was more like . . .

Like a war.

Rahel kept her arm around Yetta's waist, holding her up, holding her steady.

"You still want the strike?" she whispered. "Even now?"

Yetta answered through split, bloodied lips.

"More than ever."

Rahel's face seemed especially pale, out here in the sunlight. She grimaced, then glanced over her shoulder to make sure no one else was listening.

"Yetta, those women who beat you up—they were . . . ladies of the evening. Women who . . . sell their bodies. If Papa knew . . ."

"Papa isn't here, is he?" Yetta said angrily. "Papa doesn't sit over a sewing machine ten, twelve hours a day. Papa doesn't have a contractor breathing down his neck. He doesn't have a man looking in his hair, patting down his clothes every day to make sure he hasn't stolen any shirtwaists. Papa doesn't have bosses who hire prostitutes to beat him up!"

Rahel slumped, and for a moment it seemed that it was Yetta holding Rahel up, not the other way around.

"You figured it out, then," Rahel said sadly. "That's what we thought down at union headquarters, too. The bosses hired those . . . those women. They bribed the police to arrest you."

Yetta nodded, not surprised.

"What I don't understand," Rahel said, "is, why *those* women? Why not just have the police beat you up and keep it simple?"

She attempted a wry smile, but it failed miserably.

"Because they're women," Yetta said. She remembered the police looking from her to the prostitutes, saying, *You're a striker, aren't you? . . . Then I can't see much difference.* "They want to say we're just as low as those women, just as unclean."

It was all of a piece, somehow, with the men back in her shtetl praying, "Thank you, God, for not making me a woman." Men thought women were worthless, stupid, easily cowed. Yetta narrowed her eyes, thinking thoughts she never would have dreamed of back in the shtetl. They weren't even thoughts that fit with her old socialist fervor. But they were what she believed now.

God made me, too, she thought. *And He made me to fight.*

Jane

*J*ane pulled the comforter up to her chin. There seemed no reason to get out of bed this morning. Ever since Eleanor and her friends had gone back to Vassar a few weeks ago, Jane's life had felt emptied out and pointless.

"Miss Wellington?" It was Miss Milhouse, sweeping the drapes back from the floor-to-ceiling windows, letting sunlight splash into the room. "You've slept quite late enough. You have a dress fitting at half past eleven, and you've not had breakfast yet. You're leaving yourself no time to prepare your toilette. . . ."

Jane sighed, barely listening. What did a dress fitting matter? The new dress had ruffles where many of her old dresses had bows, and it was a butter-cream color she'd not had in her wardrobe before. But it was really the same as every other dress she owned. Along with her corset, it would pinch in so much at the waist that she'd barely be able to breathe; it would seem not so much an article of clothing as a cage.

Ever since her father had forbidden her to go to college, everything seemed like a cage.

No, some nitpicky, precise part of her brain corrected.

He didn't forbid it. He just called women's colleges preposterous, and you were scared to say anything else.

Jane sighed again.

Miss Milhouse whirled around from the windows and marched directly toward the bed.

"Really, Miss Wellington," she said briskly. "You must expunge yourself of this . . . this torpor."

She came to the side of Jane's bed and reached out as though she were going to fluff the pillows. Instead, she grabbed Jane by the shoulders and began shaking them.

"You simply must—"

A look like horror crept over Miss Milhouse's expression. She dropped Jane's shoulders and turned away, plunging her face into her hands. Her whole body quivered, as if shaken by silent sobs.

Miss Milhouse—crying?

"I'm sorry," Jane said in a small voice, like a small child who doesn't quite understand what she's being scolded for.

Miss Milhouse spun back around, brushing tears away, pretending they'd never happened.

"You *will* be ready for the dress fitting on time," she said. "I insist on it. And then, this afternoon, perhaps . . . perhaps I can take you for a treat."

An ice cream sundae, probably, Jane thought. *Who cares?*

But Miss Milhouse was rushing out of the room. She quickly reappeared, carrying a newspaper. She waved it in front of Jane's eyes, so quickly Jane could only focus on a few words at a time: WILBUR WRIGHT, and then SURE TO FLY.

"He did it," Miss Milhouse said. "People are saying he flew his aeroplane twenty miles this morning, up the Hudson

River. In the city! Can you imagine? If the weather holds out, he'll be flying an exhibition this afternoon, for everyone to see, at the Hudson-Fulton Celebration. If you'd like, I could take you to watch."

Jane felt a flicker of interest. An aeroplane—a machine taking a man high into the sky. Incredible. She remembered how excited everyone had been when the news came out that the Wright brothers had flown the first plane. And now, for the first time, Wilbur Wright had brought his contraption to New York City. It was probably the most amazing thing she'd ever get the chance to see.

But her mind snagged on verbs. *To watch. To see.* It reminded her of the most recent letter she'd gotten from Eleanor at Vassar. The letter had begun with apologies for not writing sooner, because of all the classes Eleanor was taking, the Social Improvement Club meetings, the Hiking Club's outings. Then the letter had taken on a lecturing tone.

I am sorry that your father will not allow you to attend college. Perhaps you can eventually persuade him to take a more enlightened view. But, if that is not possible, then one must make the best of one's situation and set one's sights on achievable goals. Some of my friends are planning a grand tour of Europe next summer. I am certain that your father would allow you that; everyone's father allows that! If I were you, I would endeavor to show him a good faith effort that you are mature enough and responsible enough for this trip. Study your French, study your Italian, study the tour guides we poor college girls don't have the time to glance at. . . .

There was a postscript, too: *I am such a dunderhead with languages that you will have to be the one who translates. Study your Italian most especially!*

It was almost an invitation, almost a plan of action. At first, Jane had been excited, and she dove immediately into Italian grammar and vocabulary. She was good with languages; the French and Latin she'd learned at school had slipped into her brain with very little effort on her part. But the sentences in the Italian phrasebook seemed to taunt her: *Ho bisogno di un portabagagli per le miei valigie.* I need a porter to carry my bags. *Vorremmo pranzare adesso. Che cosa mi consiglia lei?* We'd like to have dinner now. What do you recommend? *Quando in comincia la gita? Vogliami vedere il museo.* When does the tour begin? We want to see the museum. *Vorremmo vedere un'opera. Quale opera presentano?* We would like to watch an opera. What opera are they performing? They made the European grand tour sound like her regular life, just in a different place. Seeing, watching—what if her whole life passed by and she never *did* anything?

Now she blinked up at Miss Milhouse.

"Will Mr. Wright be giving people rides in his aeroplane?" she asked.

Miss Milhouse gasped.

"I should say not!" she said, scandalized. "And even if he were, surely you realize that would be much too dangerous for a girl!"

Surely she did. Surely she realized exactly how many ways she was caged.

Miss Milhouse kept talking, but Jane closed her eyes and went back to sleep.

Bella

Bella heard the music as soon as her sewing machine stopped.

Give me your hand,
Turn out your toe,
All lovers know
The way to go. . . .

Curiously, she peered far down the row of tables. At the end of the room, between the cloakroom and the elevators, someone had set up a box with a disk and a horn. How could it be? The tinkly, delicate music seemed to be pouring out of the horn.

"Is that a phonograph?" a girl breathed incredulously behind Bella.

"Yes. We'll have dancing at lunchtime now. If you wish, of course," Signor Carlotti said.

Bella peered up at him, puzzled. He'd been so nice the past few weeks, she couldn't get used to it. Once, when a shirtwaist snagged, he said, "Don't worry about it. I'm sure you didn't do that on purpose." Once, when he saw that she had only a crust of bread for lunch, he said, "That's not much to live on. Here's a penny. Go buy something from a peddler." He hadn't yelled at her at all since that day he'd walked her home. It made her suspicious.

But music . . . With no more will than moths have near flame, she and the other girls drifted toward the phonograph.

The girl who sat at the sewing machine next to Bella, whose name Bella didn't even know, said something. She pointed to herself, then Bella, and pantomimed a swaying movement. Bella understood it to mean, *Want to dance?*

Bella nodded. She touched her rough, calloused hand to the other girl's rough, calloused hand, and they slipped out into the midst of other girls beginning tentative dance steps. Heel, toe, whirl . . . Bella hadn't danced since she'd left Calia. This wasn't a dance she knew, wasn't music she'd ever heard before. But she watched the other girls' feet, she let her partner lead, and she didn't do too badly. At the end of the song there was an extra, fancy step, and Bella's feet got twisted. She lost her balance and knocked her partner over, bumping into the first row of sewing machines. She looked around for Signor Carlotti, sure that he would be right there screaming at them any minute. She saw him at the edge of the dancers.

He was smiling.

Bella and the other girl collapsed into giggles.

"Frances," the other girl said, pointing at herself.

"Bella," Bella said, doing the same.

That was all they really understood of each other's languages, but it was enough. They danced for the rest of the half hour, stopping to swallow their meager lunches only while Signor Carlotti was changing the phonograph between songs. Everyone did. The dancing was a tonic after hours hunched over the machines; they didn't want to miss a minute of it.

"Last song," Signor Carlotti said, and even he sounded regretful.

This one was a livelier tune, and Bella and Frances spun over near the windows. Bella dipped so close to the glass that she could feel the cold seeping in through the pane. It was a chilly day, and she was glad to be inside, dancing. But in that one dip she could see straight down to the street—nine stories down, a frightening sight. She could see the girls holding signs, walking up and down the sidewalks so strangely. They were there every morning when Bella arrived and every evening when Bella left; she hadn't realized they were also there all day, while she worked.

"What are they doing?" she asked Frances. At first Frances didn't seem to understand, but then she released a frightened-sounding torrent of words. Was she that terrified of the girls with signs? Maybe she was just saying that she was afraid of heights.

"It's a strike, isn't it?" Bella asked. "Strike? What does that mean, anyway?"

Another torrent of words. This time Bella recognized one word, repeated several times. *Scab . . . scab . . . scab . . .*

"Do they call you a scab too?" Bella asked, for that was the word the girls with signs hurled at her every morning and every evening. Bella thought the word must mean something like "thief" or "criminal," because that was how they said it, as though Bella had stolen their last crust of bread directly from their mouths. But Bella hadn't done anything to these girls; she didn't understand why they were outside in the cold.

"Back to work now," Signor Carlotti said, before Frances had a chance to answer. A little of his old sternness had crept back into his voice. Bella wondered if it was because he knew they were talking about the strike.

The music ended and the machines whirred back to life. Guiding one shirtwaist after another under the darting needle, just like always, Bella began to wonder if she'd imagined the whole thing—the dancing, the music. Or not imagined it exactly: misunderstood. The more she thought about it, the more the gaiety reminded her of the time back home when they found their last goat dead.

"Well, *buono*," Mama had said, putting on a fake smile. "This just means we can have a feast! We'll have all the goat meat we want!"

But only little Guilia was fooled, her tears drying up at the prospect of a feast. All the others understood that the goat's death meant one good meal and then the end of goat's milk, goat's cheese, goat's fur and—most of all—the end of any chance, ever again, of more baby goats. And then, after they'd roasted the goat and pretended to enjoy their one last feast, they'd all gotten sick. Evidently whatever killed the goat wasn't very good for humans, either.

I am like Guilia here, Bella thought. *Something is happening and I don't understand.*

But it was too hard to figure out. It was easier to lose herself in a daydream of Pietro coming back, whisking her off into those dance steps she'd just done with Frances. In her daydreams, with Pietro, she never stumbled once.

. . .

It was quitting time, and Bella squeezed into the elevator with the other girls. Their merry chatter got quieter and quieter the closer they got to ground level; the little box was completely silent by the time the doors slid open. Someone clutched Bella's arm—Bella glanced over and saw that it was Frances.

"There's safety in numbers," Frances said. Bella was sure that was what she said. Bella clutched Frances's arm right back.

They stepped out of the elevator and pushed their way out of the main doors to the street. The strikers saw them immediately and ran over, screaming.

"Scabs!"

"Scabs!"

"How dare you!"

"You're taking our jobs!"

Was Bella understanding them right? Could that really be what they were saying?

Bella was glad of the burly policemen who pushed the strikers back. All the same, a girl broke through the police line and began pulling on Bella's arm. She jerked her away from Frances.

"No! Don't!" someone screamed. It was another striker, but someone Bella recognized this time: Yetta, the girl who'd walked Bella home.

Yetta dropped her sign and rushed over to help.

"You can't do that!" Yetta was screaming at the first striker, in words even Bella could clearly understand. "Don't hit anyone!"

A policeman saw the girls struggling. He smashed his club down squarely on Yetta's head and clamped his beefy hand around her arm, jerking her so hard that her feet left the ground.

"No!" Bella screamed. "Don't hurt her! She was trying to help me!"

But the policeman didn't understand. He shoved Bella away and pulled Yetta and the other striker toward a police wagon parked on the street.

Was Yetta being arrested? Just for helping Bella?

Bella stood alone in the midst of the scuffle. Frances was nowhere to be seen now. The other workers had scattered, and it was just the strikers and the policemen battling it out. Bella caught a glimpse of Rocco Luciano on the other side of the street and rushed toward him.

"Papa said I could walk you home," Rocco said shyly.

"We've got to find someone who speaks English!" Bella said, looking around frantically. "Someone who can understand me and then explain—"

"I can speak English," Rocco said. "Some."

Bella stared at him.

"Don't tell Mama and Papa," he said. "But sometimes, when they think I'm out shining shoes or selling newspapers, I go to school instead. I can even *read* English now. I practice on the newspapers."

Bella's answer was to grab Rocco's arm and drag him toward the nearest policeman, one who was just standing there watching the others shoving strikers into the police wagon.

"Tell him they arrested the wrong person!" Bella said. "Tell him that Yetta was really trying to help me, she didn't do anything wrong, she shouldn't be in that police wagon—"

"Are you crazy? I'm not going to talk to the police!" Rocco said.

But the policeman was already glaring down at them. He raised his club, like he was going to beat them just for standing there.

Rocco gulped, and said something that sounded like, "*Scusi*, sir-uh," and then he rattled off a fast string of words. In response, the policeman growled something and shoved them away. Rocco grabbed Bella's hand and they both took off running, dashing around peddlers' carts and shoppers' bundles and horses and cars and the whole crowded craziness that was New York City. It reminded Bella of a time back home when she and her brother Giovanni had seen a wolf in the mountains, and they'd run and run and run, all the way back to their house. Now, Rocco stopped as soon as they got back to Little Italy. He bent over, panting.

"Can't . . . believe . . . you made me . . . talk to . . . a cop," he said, grasping for air.

He was still holding her hand. Blushing, he dropped it.

"What did he say?" Bella asked. "Is he going to let Yetta go?"

"What do you think?" Rocco asked bitterly. "He said, 'So what? Stay out of it or I'll arrest you, too!'" Rocco kicked at the pavement, the sole of his boot slapping loudly where it'd come loose from the leather. "They'd never listen to me. I'm nobody and nothing. But someday . . . someday . . ."

He got a faraway look in his eye, like people back in Italy did when they talked about going to America. Bella and Rocco were already in America, and they still had to look far away for any hope.

Bella leaned over and gave him a light kiss on the forehead, the way she'd kiss Giovanni or Ricardo or Dominic, her brothers.

"Thank you for trying," she said.

But Rocco didn't respond the way Giovanni or Ricardo or Dominic would, pushing her away and muttering "Yuck!" Rocco touched the place on his forehead wonderingly.

"Oh," he said. "Oh. Wow."

Oh, no, Bella thought.

Yetta

This isn't working," Rahel said.

Yetta's answer was to lean down and pull off a thick icicle from the bottom of a drainpipe that didn't quite reach the street. It was late November now, and the strike was still going on. That meant it was awfully cold on the picket line—Yetta thought maybe her toes were frozen, and she hadn't been able to feel her fingers for the past hour. But at least now ice was readily available—and free—for bruises and black eyes. She held the icicle up to her throbbing cheek, then shifted it to the knot on her head.

"I'm not quitting," she said.

Rahel sighed.

"I didn't say we should," she said.

"At least tonight I got away from the policeman before he put me into the paddy wagon," Yetta said. "So the union won't have to pay bail again."

"Yours, anyway," Rahel said. "What about the other twenty girls who were arrested?"

Yetta shrugged, which made her back ache where the policeman's baton had hit her—had it been Wednesday? Thursday? Last week sometime. She had bruises on top of bruises; it was hard to tell them apart.

"We made the *New York Times*," she said. "Not just the *Forward*, not just the *Call*. The *New York Times*!"

She said this as though she knew all about the newspapers in New York City, how impressive it was to be noticed by a newspaper that rich people read, instead of just newspapers printed in Yiddish or newspapers read only by socialists. She knew this only because one of the other girls had explained it to her.

"But the *New York Times* mainly just wrote about Miss Dreier being arrested," Rahel said bitterly. "Poor girls being arrested don't count."

Miss Mary Dreier was the president of the Women's Trade Union League, an odd group that Yetta had never heard of before the strike. It was workers and rich women all in the same club, which Yetta had a hard time understanding. But Miss Dreier had left her limousine and her mansion and her furs and everything else she owned to come and walk the picket line with all the strikers.

"I like Miss Dreier," Yetta said.

"So do I," Rahel said. "But the police released *her* at the station right away."

"And Mr. Blanck told the *Times*, 'Oh, no, there's no strike going on. . . .'"

"And, 'Everyone in my factory makes at least eight dollars a week—most of them make sixteen.'"

Yetta was giggling now, even though it made her face hurt.

"He sounded like such a fool! Anyone reading that had to know that he was lying!" she said.

Rahel got serious again.

"Not the rich people," she said. "Not the other factory owners. But we don't need *them*. We need other people like us. Workers."

"The union meeting tonight better not be just a bunch of old men in fancy suits telling us how noble our cause is," Yetta said.

"No," Rahel said. "It can't be."

They had a quick, cold supper at home, because they didn't want to waste any coal or time heating up the stove. Soon they were back out on the streets.

"How far is it?" Yetta asked, hoping her voice didn't betray how tired she was, how much her feet ached already.

"Cooper Union?" Rahel asked. "Just four blocks from Triangle."

As they got closer, Yetta forgot her feet. There was such a tide of people moving toward the huge brownstone building: men, women, girls; Jews, Italians, Americans . . .

"There must be hundreds of people going to this meeting," Yetta marveled, as the crowd carried them into the building, down into the Great Hall in the cellar.

"Thousands," Rahel corrected, her eyes glowing with something like pride. "Shirtwaist workers from shops all over the city. They're going to need other meeting halls for the overflow crowd. We'll have to have messengers going back and forth, telling them what the speakers say. . . . Isn't it glorious?"

She left Yetta near a pillar in the huge hall, with a good view of the stage. Yetta studied the arches that flared out from the pillars, the crowd packing in tight. She heard a girl behind her say, in awed tones, "Abraham Lincoln spoke here once." Yetta didn't know who Abraham Lincoln was, but that whispering just added to the electric charge in the audience. *We're like tinder,* Yetta thought. *Just one spark, that's all we need . . .*

Rahel came back, her face flushed with excitement.

"They don't need me to run messages out to the overflow halls," she said. "They've already had dozens of people volunteer."

The speeches began. Except for Mary Dreier, it was, indeed, all men on the stage—well, really, what did Yetta expect? These were important men, famous men, Yetta knew that: Meyer Landon, the socialist lawyer; Abraham Cahan, editor of the *Forward*, Benjamin Feigenbaum, a union leader . . . And the most impressive speaker of all, Samuel Gompers, president of the American Federation of Labor.

But after two hours of speeches, Yetta felt less and less like tinder, and more and more like . . . sleeping.

"This is almost as bad as sitting at the sewing machine all day," Yetta leaned over to grumble to Rahel.

"Shh. Just wait. Mr. Gompers is next," Rahel said.

Mr. Feigenbaum introduced him, and the whole crowd sprang to its feet, clapping. Maybe they were just tired of sitting for so long; maybe they were convinced he would finally say what they wanted to hear.

Mr. Gompers stroked his bushy moustache, held his arm up to acknowledge the applause.

"A man would be less than human," he said, "if he were not impressed with your reception. I want you men and women not to give all your enthusiasm for a man, no matter who he may be. I would prefer that you put all of your enthusiasm into your union and your cause."

All right, sounds good to me, Yetta thought, clapping as she sat down again.

"I have never declared a strike in my life," he continued. "I have done my share to prevent strikes, but there comes a time when not to strike is but to rivet the chains of slavery upon our wrists."

Exactly! Yetta thought.

He went on. And on. Most of the other speakers had spoken in Yiddish, but Mr. Gompers was addressing the crowd in English. Yetta found she had to concentrate very hard to understand what he was saying. And then she found that she wasn't always able to concentrate that hard. She'd listen, let her attention wander, listen again.

She sat up straight and listened intently, though, when he began to talk about what the Triangle workers were already doing.

"This is the time and the opportunity, and I doubt if you let it pass whether it can be created again in five or ten years or a generation," he said.

Finally! Yetta thought. She had chills going up her spine, for she saw how it was going to happen. Mr. Gompers was about to tell the entire audience that all of them should go out on strike, all the shirtwaist workers throughout the entire city, in support of the Triangle workers and another factory that was already on strike, Leiserson's. A general strike, it was called, everyone unified in an entire industry, not just at one or two factories.

"I say, friends," Mr. Gompers continued. Yetta was hanging on to every word now. "I say, do not enter too hastily—"

What? How would this be hasty?

"But when you can't get the manufacturers to give you what you want, then strike," he said. "And when you strike, let the manufacturers know that you are on strike. . . . Have faith in yourselves, to be true to your comrades. . . . If you strike, be cool, calm, collected. . . ."

No, no, no, no, no! Yetta wanted to scream. *Not cool! Not calm! We're a tinderbox! We're explosive!*

Around her, people were standing up to clap again, but even the applause sounded puzzled. He hadn't called for a general strike. Not quite. He'd stepped to the edge, and then stepped back.

Mr. Feigenbaum was at the podium now, introducing the next speaker, another socialist, Jacob Panken. Yetta had heard him speak before. She groaned.

"He'll go on forever," she complained to Rahel. "What's the point of just listening to all this talk?" Talk was nothing compared with bruises and beatings and jail cells. Better that she should go home and get some sleep and be ready for picketing in the morning, rather than listening to all this hot air.

But somebody else was rushing toward the stage—a girl.

"I want to say a few words!" she called out in Yiddish.

"It's Clara Lemlich," Rahel whispered, sounding more awestruck than she'd been about Mr. Gompers. "The striker from Leiserson's."

Yetta had heard about Clara Lemlich. In the union, she was famous for her determination, her loyalty, her courage. She'd been in lots of strikes. But she was tiny—hurrying down the aisle, she looked no older than Yetta herself.

Mr. Feigenbaum and Mr. Panken looked down at her

from the podium, as if to say, *You're just a girl. How dare you interrupt us!* Rahel surprised Yetta by yelling out, "Get her on the platform!" Others in the audience took up the cry. "Let's hear what she has to say! Let her speak!"

The two men stood aside, as if they had no choice. Clara's curly hair bounced and her skirts swayed as she climbed up on the stage. Her head barely reached over the top of the podium.

"I have listened to all these speakers. I have no more patience for talk," she said, as if she knew exactly what Yetta had been thinking. "I am one of those who feels and suffers from the things described. I move that we go on a general strike! Now!"

The room exploded with cheers. Yetta screamed too, each "Hurrah!" speaking volumes. *I am sore, I am tired, I am battered and bruised, this is just the help I need!* And, *A girl called this strike. A girl! We can do it! All of us girls together . . .*

Mr. Feigenbaum moved back to the podium, waved his arms to silence the crowd.

"Uh," he said. "Is there a second to this motion?"

The crowd exploded again.

Mr. Feigenbaum wasn't satisfied.

"It won't be easy," he said. "Those who fear hunger and cold should not be ashamed to vote against the strike."

There was a grumbling in the crowd, a grumbling against Mr. Feigenbaum. A grumbling against hunger and cold and the bosses who made it worse. A grumbling against all the men who ruled the world.

"If you vote to strike," he said, "you've vowing to struggle till the end."

"We will! Just let us vote!" Yetta yelled, and she wasn't the only one.

Mr. Feigenbaum stared out at the crowd, his ancient, glittering eyes taking measure of their zeal.

"Do you mean faith?" he asked. "Will you take the old Jewish oath?"

Yetta knew the oath he was talking about, but she was surprised he'd brought it up. Girls didn't take old Jewish oaths. Oaths were the province of men. But she raised her right hand, as thousands of other arms lifted into the air around her, and she chanted, with thousands of other voices, "If I turn traitor to the cause I now pledge, may this hand wither from the arm I now raise."

There. It was done.

Jane

$\mathcal{E}$leanor Kensington's voice rushed at Jane, straight from the telephone receiver.

"A bunch of us are going to walk the picket line with the shirtwaist strikers today. Would you care to join us? It'll be such a lark!"

Jane pulled the receiver back from her ear, looked at it, then nestled it back under the giant puff of her hair. She leaned toward the mouthpiece.

"Are you calling from Vassar?" she asked.

In most of Jane's experience, invitations were issued by handwritten notes; the polite response was made in the same fashion. No one had ever forbidden her to use the phone, exactly, but she knew that Miss Milhouse, at least, viewed it as not quite proper. Jane was awed by the notion that Eleanor might be sitting up there at Vassar, and talking to Jane, here in New York City.

She was also awed that Eleanor cared enough to call her. Jane hadn't gotten even a letter from Eleanor in a long time.

Eleanor laughed, the sound amplified and echo-y over the phone.

"No, silly, I'm back in the city. We came down last night,

everyone from my social work class. The professor said she'd give us extra credit if we'd go to the strike and write a paper about it afterward. And between you and me, I really need that extra credit!"

"I—I'll have to check my calendar," Jane said, even though she knew what her calendar looked like for the day: blank.

Eleanor laughed again.

"Oh, whatever you're supposed to be doing today, send your regrets," she said. "The strike will probably end soon—lots of manufacturers have settled already. You may never get a chance to do something like this again!"

Indeed. Some mornings, lying in bed, Jane could just feel all sorts of chances slipping away.

"I'll go," Jane decided.

"How delightful!" Eleanor exclaimed. "I'll tell my chauffeur to pick you up at—oh, wait, Jefferson will already be taking me, Melissa, Agnes, Opal, Emma, Lydia . . . Any chance you could have *your* chauffeur take you and a few of my other friends?"

Had Eleanor called her just because her friends needed a ride?

Jane put aside this thought as disloyal.

"I'll have to check," she said. "Father may need Mr. Corrigan's services today."

"Well, call me back immediately," Eleanor said.

Jane hung the receiver back on the hook where it belonged and went off in search of Mr. Corrigan. She was surprised that his eyes swam with tears as soon as she explained what she wanted.

"Oh, Miss Wellington," he said, taking up her hands and, quite improperly, patting them. "That's such a kindness you'd be doing. Those poor, poor girls, out there in the cold. You've been following the strike, have you? The uprising of the twenty thousand, the papers have been calling it, though I'd wager there are thirty or forty thousand involved. Such brave girls . . . And with all the society women helping out, to try to protect the girls from the police . . . Miss Wellington, I'd be proud to take you and your friends down there!"

Jane was ashamed to admit that she hadn't heard of the strike until Eleanor called. What did he mean, society women were protecting girls from the police?

That afternoon, Mr. Corrigan had the car ready right on time, with plenty of lap blankets and hot chocolate in a thick jug.

"Can't have any of you freezing out there," he muttered, as the girls piled in.

"We'll be going to the Triangle Shirtwaist Factory, one of the biggest in the city," Eleanor directed him before climbing into her own car. "In the Asch Building, at the corner of Washington Place and Greene Street."

"Yes, miss," Mr. Corrigan said.

The talk in the car was of the extra credit paper the girls would have to write and of the heavy load of exams coming up at Vassar. Jane, who was facing neither papers nor exams, had nothing to contribute. When the conversation flagged, one girl squealed, "Oh, I just thought—I was going to put on my old boots today, but I forgot and wore my new ones. You don't think they'll be ruined, do you?"

She stuck out a shapely ankle covered in the latest style of boot, the leather so new, it sparkled.

"We'll just be walking around, talking to the strikers," another girl said. "What do you think is going to happen?"

"Don't you remember that suffrage rally where those awful men started booing and throwing rotten tomatoes? And the speakers just kept talking, so it would have been rude of us to get up and leave?"

Jane had missed that event. She started worrying a little about her own boots.

"Now, Celeste, you know your papa would buy you another pair," the other girl argued. "You should be thinking about the strikers."

"Oh, no—how are we going to understand them?" a third girl asked. "The professor said most of them are immigrants. Russians, Poles, Italians . . ."

"I know Italian," Jane offered, and for the first time the other girls looked at her with something like respect.

They pulled up in front of the factory, and Jane was surprised to see that it was the same building she'd mistaken for a school all those months ago, that time she was on her way to tea. But the girls walking in front of the building didn't look so happy now. They looked grim and cold. Jane wondered if she should give them the hot chocolate, but then what would she and Eleanor's friends have to warm themselves with on the way home?

"I'll be parked right around the corner," Mr. Corrigan said. "If you need anything, just let me know."

He looked a little worried now, but Jane wasn't sure what he thought would happen. There were just small clusters of girls walking around. What was dangerous about that?

Jane and the others piled out of the car.

"Thank you for coming," a tall woman in a lovely hat greeted them. "I'm Violet Pike—Vassar, class of oh-seven. I'm so glad Professor Trenton agreed that this would be educational for you. All of us must work together for the women's rights cause to succeed—"

"I thought this was a strike," Jane said.

"Oh, indeed, indeed," Miss Pike said. "But it's all one and the same in the final analysis, isn't it? The tragedy of the workers' condition threatens us all. And if women have the vote, then society as a whole will be enriched. *We* would not allow such abominations to occur, such as these girls being forced to work for pennies, for hours on end. These are our sisters!"

She gestured toward the strikers behind her. Up close, Jane could tell that Miss Milhouse's criticisms of the working girls' clothes had been all too accurate. Some of the girls' skirts were just one step up from rags. And if they worked in a shirtwaist factory, wouldn't you think they'd have decent shirtwaists—as advertising, if nothing else? Mostly, though, Jane noticed that not a one of them had an adequate coat. She pulled her own good wool tighter around her shoulders and shivered.

"Here are the rules for picketing," Miss Pike said, handing around flyers. Jane read one when it came her way:

DON'T WALK IN GROUPS OF MORE
THAN TWO OR THREE.
DON'T STAND IN FRONT OF THE SHOP;
WALK UP AND DOWN THE BLOCK.
DON'T STOP THE PERSON YOU WISH TO TALK TO;
WALK ALONGSIDE OF HIM.
DON'T GET EXCITED AND SHOUT

WHEN YOU ARE TALKING.
DON'T PUT YOUR HAND ON THE PERSON YOU ARE
SPEAKING TO. DON'T TOUCH HIS SLEEVE OR BUTTON.
THIS MAY BE CONSTRUED AS A "TECHNICAL ASSAULT."
DON'T CALL ANYONE "SCAB" OR USE ABUSIVE
LANGUAGE OF ANY KIND.
PLEAD, PERSUADE, APPEAL,
BUT DO NOT THREATEN.
IF A POLICEMAN ARRESTS YOU AND YOU ARE SURE
THAT YOU HAVE COMMITTED NO OFFENSES, TAKE
DOWN HIS NUMBER AND GIVE IT TO YOUR
UNION OFFICERS.

If a policeman arrests you . . . ? Jane thought. What had she gotten herself into? What would Father say if he knew she was here?

"Don't worry," Miss Pike said, because some of the other girls were looking a little pale as well. "The police have been very respectful of *us*. It's just those poor factory girls . . ."

Jane and all the Vassar girls turned and looked at the strikers again. This time Jane saw beyond their ragged clothes, their laughable attempts at fashionable hats, the poor quality of the "rats" holding up their pompadours. She saw the girls' faces now, the courage in their gaze, the intensity in their eyes. These girls didn't just look cold and grim. They looked determined.

"What are all these funny symbols below the rules for picketing?" one of the Vassar girls asked Miss Pike. "Some sort of code?"

"Oh, that's Yiddish," Miss Pike said. "Many of these girls

are of a Hebraic background, and they can't read English."

Hebraic? Hebrew? That made the girls seem even more foreign and exotic. Jane felt like she did at the Central Park Menagerie, watching completely different species. *Here are the bears, the swans, the Hebrews and the Italian girls . . .*

"But don't let me keep you," Miss Pike said. "I'm sure you've got so much you'll want to ask them!"

A bit timidly, Jane fell into step beside one of the strikers. The girl smiled at her and nodded, making an unbelievably battered hat sway on the tower of her thick, dark hair. Jane tried to think of something she could say in Italian.

"*Ti piace andare a l'opera?*" she finally asked, which she hoped was close to "Do you like to go to the opera?"

The girl looked at her blankly.

"I'm sorry," she said in accented but precise English. "I don't understand."

Embarrassed, Jane looked down at her feet.

"I thought maybe you were Italian," she said.

The girl looked like she wanted to say "Are you crazy?" but she only shrugged politely and said, "No, I came here from Russia. I'm Yetta."

"Jane Wellington," Jane said. "Can I hear you say something in Russian?"

"I don't know Russian, just Yiddish," the girl said. "And English of course."

Well, that was confusing! How could somebody be from a certain country and not even speak the language? Jane wondered if she'd misunderstood. She didn't know what to say next.

"Would you like to hear about our strike?" the girl offered.

"Oh, yes," Jane said, relieved that she wouldn't have to keep the conversation going.

"We—the Triangle workers—have been out on strike since September twenty-seventh," Yetta said quickly, as if she'd had to recite this many times. "That's two and a half months we've been without pay. The bosses locked us out. Then, on November twenty-second, our union, Local 25, voted for a general strike and shirtwaist workers all across the city walked out."

"But the strike's almost over, right?" Jane asked.

Yetta broke off her recitation, her mouth shaping into a round *O* of surprise. She brought both hands up to clutch her cheeks, which were suddenly flushed.

"Did you hear something new?" she asked excitedly. "Did Mr. Blanck and Mr. Harris agree to recognize the union? They agreed to a closed shop? How about limiting our hours—"

"I don't know," Jane said, strangely embarrassed to have sparked such excitement. She struggled to remember exactly what Eleanor had told her. "I just heard, lots of the manufacturers have settled already. . . ."

"Oh," Yetta said. Disappointment passed over her face, then was replaced once more by determination. "Yes, that's true. The smaller shops, they couldn't afford to have their workers out, so they agreed right away to the workers' demands. We've won in those shops. But the big manufacturers like Triangle, they're hiring scabs; they won't talk to us . . ." Her expression, so rosy a moment ago, seemed chiseled out of stone now. "The strike is *not* almost over."

Jane burrowed her hands deeper into the fur muff she usually wore only when she was ice skating. She was cold already, and she'd only been out here a few minutes.

"Why does it matter so much?" she asked.

"Do you know what it is like to work in a shirtwaist factory?" Yetta asked. "In the wintertime, I'm there before the sun comes up, and if the boss wants to make me work until midnight, he can do that. What could I do to stop him? I'm just a girl. Just one girl. I can work, day in and day out, hour after hour at the sewing machines, and then at the end of the week if he decides he doesn't want to pay me for all my work, what can I do? He can make all sorts of excuses—'Oh, I had to charge you for the use of the sewing machine—for the electricity to run it—for the needles that broke. . . .' He can make up any excuse he wants, but if he doesn't want to pay me what I'm owed, he doesn't have to. What can I do? I'm just one girl."

Jane had not supposed that it would be any different than that, working in a factory. But she hadn't really thought about it before.

So why don't you just find another job? she wanted to say, but feared it would sound insensitive. Or just plain ignorant. What did she know about jobs for factory girls?

"And," Yetta continued, "the bosses lock us in—"

"What?" Jane said.

"They. Lock. Us. In," Yetta said, very distinctly, as if she'd feared her English wasn't clear enough. "They lock the doors so we can't sneak out—not that we could, anyway, because they're always watching us, even when we have to use the . . . facilities. But they're so afraid that we'll steal the shirtwaists that they keep us under lock and key. It's like we're in prison just because they think we might commit a crime."

This was something Jane could relate to. Being locked in was like being caged.

What can I do? I'm just a girl. . . . The words Yetta had repeated were still echoing in Jane's head.

"You broke out," Jane said. "The strike is how you broke out of those locks."

Yetta gave her a look that Jane remembered from school—the same look that teachers used when Jane gave a correct response to a question the teachers thought was too hard for her.

"Yes," Yetta said. "I don't mind working. This strike"—she gestured at her sign, at the path ahead of her on the sidewalk—"this is harder than sitting at a sewing machine all day. It's harder than milking cows and baking bread and all the other work I've done in my life. But this strike is for something. It takes me somewhere. It helps us all. If the bosses at Triangle recognize the union, then . . ."

Jane was not really listening. She wanted to talk about breaking locks again. She started to say, "So you're an escape artist. Like Harry Houdini." She wanted to know how it worked. But before she could open her mouth, a pair of hands shoved at Yetta's shoulders. Yetta's head pitched forward, then back, the battered hat sliding precariously low.

"Ya dirty striker! Blocking the sidewalk!" a voice snarled.

Jane whirled around and saw a disgustingly filthy man with a scar zigzagging down his cheek and an eye that sagged in its socket. He reached into his pocket and waved a bottle high in the air, as if toasting his assault on Yetta. Then he lowered the bottle to his lips and gulped. He puckered his lips, as if contemplating what to do next. Slowly, almost elegantly, he spat his mouthful of whiskey full into Yetta's face, the liquid dripping down her eyebrows, her cheeks, her lace collar. He turned and leered at Jane, as if planning to attack her next.

"No!" Jane screamed. Terrified, she took off running. She didn't stop until she was safely back at the car. She scrambled in, pulled the lap robe over her legs, and cowered against the leather seat.

"Miss Wellington! What's wrong?" Mr. Corrigan asked.

"Take me home!" Jane begged. "Take me home and lock all the doors and please, please, protect me, somebody protect me . . ."

"There, there, miss. It's all right. Here come the police," Mr. Corrigan said soothingly.

The police rushed up in their wagons and scrambled out in waves. But they paid no attention to the filthy man. They paid little attention to the Vassar girls. They were too busy beating their clubs against the strikers' backs, grabbing the strikers and shoving them into the wagons. From the safety of her car and her fur-lined lap robe, Jane saw it all. She watched to the very end, when she got one last glimpse of Yetta in the police wagon, being carried off with her fellow strikers. Even then, behind bars, with blood and whiskey and spittle smeared across her face, Yetta held her head as high and proud as an Astor, as a Vanderbilt, as the loftiest society grande dame.

"She's that free," Jane whispered to herself. "That free, even on her way to jail . . ."

Bella

The Luciano baby was sick. Bella could hear it crying late into the night, its thin, high-pitched, unnatural-sounding wail interrupted only by spasms of coughing. The baby's crib—a drawer pulled out of a chest and laid haphazardly on the floor—was right on the other side of the wall from the bed where Bella slept with the two little Luciano girls, so each wail seemed to drill straight into Bella's head. Even with her hands over her ears, Bella couldn't block out the sound. She was so tired, so desperate to sleep. But she was torn—she also longed to storm into Signor and Signora Luciano's bedroom, snatch up the infant, and whisper the same soothing lullabies that she'd heard her mother croon to Guilia when Guilia was a baby.

What kind of mother was Signora Luciano, that she could let the baby cry like that and not do a thing?

Other tenants in the surrounding apartments began pounding on the walls.

"Make that baby shut up!"

"Can't a man get any sleep around here?"

Bella rolled away from the wall and leaned toward Serefina, the little Luciano girl lying right beside her.

"There's a poultice my mama used to make," Bella whispered. "For when we had coughs. But it uses flaxseed. Is there any flaxseed in New York City?"

Bella's relationship with the Luciano children had changed in the last few weeks. She still hated Signor and Signora Luciano, but Rocco must have said something to his younger brothers and sisters. Now, sometimes, when Bella fell asleep over her unfinished pile of flowers, one of the Luciano children would nudge her awake before Signora Luciano noticed and began screaming at her. When one of the Luciano girls scooped out macaroni for the boarders, Bella's bowl always seemed to contain extra noodles. And at night now, she and the girls huddled tightly together, uniting their body heat against the winter chill of the tenement. Sometimes, in the haziness of nearly falling asleep at night or nearly waking up in the morning, Bella could imagine that she was cuddled up again with her own siblings, children she loved. Coupled with Signor Carlotti's new, unexpected kindnesses at work, and the dancing every day at lunchtime, being friends with the Luciano children made Bella's life downright bearable. Maybe even happy.

Except for the wailing baby.

"You know how to make the baby better?" Serefina whispered back.

"It might work," Bella said.

Serefina slid out from under the thin cotton blanket, being careful not to disturb her younger sister, who had somehow, miraculously, managed to fall asleep despite the baby's crying. She climbed over the top end of the bed, her nightshirt dragging pitifully on the floor. She pushed open the door to her parents' bedroom.

"Bella says you need flaxseed," Serefina said. "For a poultice."

Bella heard Signor Luciano swearing, cursing "useless peasant remedies." She climbed over the top of the bed herself, suddenly full of righteous indignation on the baby's behalf. *You're going to let your own baby cough itself to death without trying to help at all?* she wanted to scream. But she stopped short when she reached the doorway. Signora Luciano wasn't lying in her bed, lounging around while her baby screamed. She had the baby in her arms and was pacing up and down the floor. She was pounding on the baby's back, bouncing it up and down, trying everything to soothe it.

And still the baby screamed.

Signora Luciano had her back turned to Bella; she couldn't have known Bella was standing right there.

"We have to go to a doctor," Signora Luciano was pleading with her husband. "We can use Bella's money to pay for medicine."

What? Surely Bella had misunderstood; surely Signora Luciano's voice was distorted by the strain of trying to make herself heard over the baby's wails. But Bella felt a chill go through her that had nothing to do with the cold wind rattling through the tenement or the iciness of the floor beneath her stockinged feet.

"What do you mean, 'use Bella's money'?" Bella demanded. "What money?"

Signora Luciano turned around, a motion that made the baby wail louder. It also made Signora Luciano's shadow loom larger in the dim light from the kerosene lamp.

"I mean, the money from you paying rent," Signora

Luciano snarled. "Now, leave us alone. Go back to bed. This is family business that doesn't concern you."

Bella hadn't paid any rent since the beginning of the month, almost three weeks ago. She was certain that the Lucianos had already spent that money long ago, on potatoes and flour and kerosene and the rent to their own landlord. All she could think about was the coins she'd placed in Signor Luciano's hand only the day before, Saturday afternoon. Coins he'd promised to wire to Bella's mama back in Calia, immediately.

"Why would you call the rent 'Bella's money'? Why not Nico's or Benito's or—" Bella couldn't even think of the names of all the male boarders. She was dizzy suddenly; she had to grip the door frame. "You sent my money to my family, didn't you? On Saturday, didn't you go right away to the Banco di Napoli and send the money for me? Didn't you?" She was screaming at Signor Luciano now, her voice mixing with the baby's wails.

She saw Signor Luciano exchange glances with his wife. She heard Nico's voice rumbling behind her. "You ought to tell her the truth, Luciano." And then other people in other tenements were banging on the walls, calling out, "What happened to the girl's money, Luciano?"

Signor Luciano glanced around frantically, like a man suddenly finding himself on trial for a crime he thought was secret. Signora Luciano stepped between her husband and Bella. Her bloodshot eyes gleamed red in the lamplight; her mouth was an ugly gash in her cruel face.

"What does it matter what he did with your money?" she asked, her voice filled with venom, with contempt. "Your family is dead."

. . .

"No!" Bella wailed, her voice as panicked and desperate and full of pain as the baby's cry. "My family—I've been sending them money since I got here. . . ." She was clutching at a twisted logic. Her thoughts flickered like the light from the kerosene lamp. Even if Signor Luciano weren't honest, even if he'd been stealing her money, even if he'd lied all along, her family had to be alive because she'd *wanted* to send them money, she'd tried, she'd hunched over the sewing machine for so many hours, so many days, so many weeks, always imagining her brothers eating grapes, her mama pouring out grains of wheat, her sister with a new ribbon in her hair . . .

"It's true," Signora Luciano hissed. "They died right after you left home. Some fever, I guess. Or the malaria. Pietro had a letter about it. He knew, but even he didn't tell you. He was enjoying it too much, you batting your eyes at him and giving him all your money. . . . He had a lot of money to go out drinking with, didn't he?"

"No!" Bella wailed again. "Pietro, he—"

But she was too choked up to say anything else. She couldn't stand another minute of being near this horrible woman, listening to these horrible words. She whirled around, grabbed the doorknob, stormed out of the apartment. The darkness of the landing enveloped her, but she could still hear the Luciano baby crying—louder now, as if he'd taken on her pain along with his own. She clutched the railing and raced down the stairs, out the front door. Out on the side-walk she stepped in snow, the crystals of ice crunching beneath her stockings, sliding up against the bare skin of her legs. For the first time, she stopped, seeing the danger in the icy glitter. She had no shoes on, no coat.

What does it matter . . . ? Your family is dead. Signora Luciano's cruel voice seemed to echo up and down the street, off the fire escapes, the pavement, the walls. Such a cold place, New York City, so cruel . . .

Bella didn't know that she'd pitched herself forward into the snow until she felt someone lifting her up. It was Serefina, placing Bella's boots on her feet, wrapping a blanket around her shoulders.

"Rocco sent me," the little girl said. "He says to come back."

"No," Bella said, the word coming out like a sob. "It isn't true, don't you see? I can't stay in a room with a lie like that."

Serefina stared up at her, old-lady wisdom in her little-girl eyes.

"Then keep moving," she said. "Keep moving or you'll freeze."

If I freeze to death and my family is dead, then we'll all be dead in heaven together, Bella thought. But she couldn't let herself believe that her family was dead; they needed her to stay alive and make money so they would stay alive too. She stumbled to her feet, because doing otherwise would be like admitting that Signora Luciano was right, that her family was dead.

"Leave me alone," she told Serefina, her words as slurred as a drunk's.

She lurched away down the street, frozen puddles cracking beneath her feet. She had no plans, no destination in mind. Nightmarish faces leered at her out of alleyways and she took off running, blindly, desperately, terrified. She remembered the stories she'd heard on the boat about girls captured and sold into white slavery, girls used by horrible men for horrible deeds.

"Mama wouldn't want that to happen to me," she sobbed, and she ran harder, faster. She'd stop and collapse against a building to catch her breath, and then something would frighten her again: a shadow on a wall, a cruel voice still echoing in her head. Your family is dead. . . .

That, she couldn't run away from. But she tried. All night long she tried, darting down alleys, stumbling over bricks, falling and struggling back up over and over and over again. She was surprised to see the first rays of daylight fall across the tall buildings, surprised that such a thing as daylight still existed.

"My job!" she gasped. She had to get to work, had to earn money for Mama and the little ones, because if Signor Luciano hadn't sent any of her money, surely they were terribly hungry now. She could picture them all huddling inside their one, bare room, the winter wind howling outside the door. They would be so hungry by now that maybe they were boiling plain water just to pretend to themselves that they had food, maybe they were even . . .

"No!" Bella screamed, and the people around her on the street stared at her as though she were a madwoman. She grabbed the coat of the person nearest her, a man with a long beard and long curls on either side of his face.

"I'm lost—how do I get to the Triangle Shirtwaist Factory?" she demanded.

The man stared at her blankly, uncomprehending and maybe a little afraid. She tried out the language she'd heard at work, words and rhythms she'd been absorbing for months but had never attempted herself.

"Triangle factory—where?" she asked.

"Ah," the man said, nodding, looking a little less frightened. "Where the girls are striking. Turn right here, then left. Go straight for five blocks? Six? Until you see the pickets . . ." He pointed, gestured, held up fingers for the five blocks, the six. "Are you a striker?" He was looking at her sympathetically now, as if that would excuse her odd behavior. "Here. Take this."

He pressed something into her hand, and then he slipped back into the crowd before Bella thought to look to see what it was: one thin, precious dime. She slid it into her pocket, thinking, *For Mama and the little ones. This could help until payday. . . .*

She struggled through the crowd toward the factory. It was hard walking alone in the clot of people, with no Pietro, no Nico, no Signor Luciano to lead the way. Bella pursed her lips and muttered to herself, "I don't need them. . . ."

The buildings around her began to look familiar. She'd reached the corner opposite the factory. But she still needed to fight her way through the strikers, fight her way all alone while they called out "Scab! Scab!" and pleaded "Don't go in there! Please don't!" She leaned against the wall, gasping for breath and gathering her strength and nerve.

"Bella," someone said beside her.

It was Rocco Luciano.

Bella narrowed her eyes, glared.

"Get away from me," she snarled, an entire night of anger and fear boiled down into four words.

Rocco grabbed her arm.

"I'm sorry about what my parents did," he said. "I didn't know. You have to believe—they were good people, back in Italy. But here, it's always the money, the money, there's never enough money."

Bella tore her arm away, out of his grasp.

"You think my family is rich?" she asked, her voice coming out in ragged gasps. "You don't think they needed the money more?"

Rocco looked down, as if ashamed to meet her eyes. Bella saw the cowlick at the back of his head, a little boy's cowlick.

"I have the letter," he said. "It was in Pietro's things when he left."

Bella grabbed at him, as desperate now to cling to him in the surging crowd as she'd been willing a moment before to shove him away forever.

"Where is it? What does it say?" she begged.

Rocco held out a thin, battered envelope. It looked as though it had traveled from far away, but Bella could make no sense of the scrawlings on the front, the arcs and loops of letters she'd never had a chance to learn.

"I can't really read Italian," Rocco said. "But this word here is "Calia"—he pointed to lines of official-looking ink near the stamp— "and the letter inside is signed by a priest. Father Guidani, I think?"

"Our priest," Bella breathed. "In my village."

She tightened her grip on Rocco's sleeve. He unfolded the letter and they both stared at it.

"Maybe it doesn't say they're dead," Bella said in a tight voice she barely recognized as her own. "Maybe it says they were delighted to receive the money Pietro sent for me, they have enough food to last the winter, they'll have Father Guidani write again in the spring. . . ."

Rocco was silent for a moment, then he said, "Bella, I don't think so. I think that word right there—"

Bella snatched the letter from his hand.

"I'll have someone else read it to me," she said. "Someone *educated*. Someone who wants my family to be alive, who doesn't want all my money for their own family. A priest . . ."

"The priests around here are Irish," Rocco said. "They only know English. But at the bank—"

"I'm not going to the bank!" Bella snapped. The bank was part of Pietro's world, Signor Luciano's world—how could she trust the men there? She thought of Signor Carlotti, her boss. He probably knew how to read and write. But he'd known Pietro, he'd cheated her himself, he'd lied to her— how could she believe anything he said?

Was there anyone in the entire city she could trust?

Bella's eyes fell on the strikers walking their path across the street, the strikers who'd yelled and jeered at her every day for the past three months. But there was one girl in that line-up of picketers who'd once shown Bella the best way to snip threads from shirtwaists, who'd walked her home when Pietro vanished, who'd stopped another striker from hitting her.

Clutching the letter against her chest, Bella dashed out into the street.

"Yetta!" she screamed.

Yetta

Yetta was sick of society women and college girls. They came down to the picket line in their fancy cars, cooing and simpering and wrinkling their noses in distaste if so much as a speck of mud attached itself to their fancy skirts or fancy boots. They moaned, "Oh, you poor thing," as if Yetta and the other strikers were the damsels in distress in some movie at the nickelodeon—as if the strike were being put on just for their entertainment.

Rahel said the society women's money was keeping the strike going.

"They've made so many donations, they're paying our bail and court fines when we're arrested, they're hiring our lawyers—and you heard that Mrs. Belmont put up her house as a guaranty to get girls out of jail, didn't you?" she asked, when Yetta complained. "Her house is worth four hundred thousand dollars. Four . . . hundred . . . thousand . . . dollars!"

Yetta had stared at her sister in disbelief.

"So now, because of their money, the judges are sentencing girls to the workhouse rather than just fining them," Yetta argued. "Thank you so much, that's so much better, going to the workhouse!"

She herself hadn't been sent to the workhouse yet, but she knew that she would, the next time she was arrested. She'd been arrested too many times.

"Anyhow," she told Rahel. "Their money isn't keeping the strike going. Our spirit is. Our spirit and—and God."

She wondered if Rahel would comment on the fact that Yetta was talking about God again. But Rahel was staring off into the distance once more, as if she'd forgotten Yetta, forgotten the strike.

There was, actually, one outside girl who'd shown up at the strike that Yetta liked: Jane Wellington. Jane came for the first time in early December. She didn't say "Oh, how awful!" or "How do you survive?" or "You're so brave!" She didn't say much of anything. But when Yetta was telling her about the strike, there had been one moment when it seemed as though she understood, as though a girl who had a fur muff and a gold ring and a hat with six ostrich feathers could actually know what it was like to be in Yetta's battered, holey-soled shoes. Then Jane got scared off by a common bum, and Yetta thought that was the last she'd see of her. But lately Jane had been coming back, mostly on her own, without any simpering, giggly friends. She'd walk alongside the strikers, not saying much, and once, when another girl said, "Thank you for coming," Jane had shrugged and said, "I'm not really doing anything. Just watching." And Yetta liked it that Jane knew that, that she understood that the strike was for the strikers, not society women who were just bored with trying on dresses and throwing parties and whatever else society women did.

Now Yetta shouldered her sign in the early winter dawn,

steeling herself against the cold that stole in through her
boots, her thin jacket, the tattered hat that had been through
more battles than most soldiers. She'd taken the early shift
on purpose, because it was the hardest and the coldest and
the worst, and she wanted to spare the other girls if she
could. But she couldn't ignore the cold herself. And her
stomach was growling because she'd eaten only once the day
before, and not at all yet this morning—she knew Rahel was
worried about being able to afford food. Which was worse,
to tap into the strikers' emergency relief fund, or to use up
the money they'd been saving to bring the rest of their family to America?

Yetta clutched her sign as if it were holding her up, not
the other way around. She needed food to be able to think
clearly enough to decide how to buy food. Yet another
dilemma worthy of Papa's Talmudic thinking. She shook her
head fiercely and glared at all the fancy cars in the street.
Maybe one of them belonged to Mr. Harris or Mr. Blanck,
and maybe she could go out and talk to them directly.

Please, you were once poor immigrants yourself . . .

She did not think that anything she could say would convince such heartless men, who would let their workers stand
out in the cold for three months.

"Yetta!" someone called—or maybe they didn't, maybe
Yetta was so tired and hungry that she was imagining things
now. But she turned her head just in time to see a flash of
color, cars slamming on their brakes, a girl collapsing before
a shiny bumper. And then horns were honking, their *ah-ooo-
gahs* sounding like despairing geese. A man jumped out of the
car that had hit the girl, crying out, "Saints preserve us! I
didn't even see her. . . ." But the girl was standing up again,

looking around, dazed. It was Bella, the Italian girl who'd started out as a finisher with Yetta all those months ago.

And the bosses drive their workers to throw themselves in front of cars, Yetta thought.

Bella didn't seem to notice that she'd just been hit by a car. She kept wading through the traffic, calling out, "Yetta! Yetta!"

She wants to join the strike now, Yetta thought. In spite of herself, she imagined how much the society women would love *this* story: *And one girl was so desperate to walk the picket line that she got up from being hit by a car and took up her sign right away. . . .*

But Bella was sobbing, waving a piece of paper over her head. She had never been one to show up at the factory in the latest fashions—in fact, Yetta suspected that Bella still wore the same clothes that she'd worn over from Italy, and *no one* did that. Even the poorest girl somehow managed to buy a shirtwaist and a skirt and a pair of high-button shoes. But now Bella looked worse than ever. Her hair was tangled and it stuck out all over the place, as if she'd purposely messed it up instead of pulling it back into a pompadour or knot. She clutched a dirty, tattered blanket around her shoulders—and was that just a nightshirt beneath the blanket?

"Per favore, per favore," Bella cried, and a bunch of other foreign words that Yetta didn't understand. Yetta shrugged helplessly, and Bella shook the paper in her face.

"What . . . say?" Bella tried again, this time in passable Yiddish. "These words here . . . what them?"

Yetta glanced at the paper, what she could see of it in Bella's quivering hands.

"It's in Italian," a boy said helpfully, suddenly appearing at Bella's elbow.

"I only know how to read Yiddish. And a little English," Yetta said apologetically. "Maybe Rosaria—" She looked around, but none of the Italian strikers were picketing that morning. She saw the man from the car that had hit Bella walking toward them, alongside Jane Wellington. "Jane knows how to speak Italian. Maybe she can read it too."

The man was apologizing and lamenting, "Jesus, Mary, and Joseph, you scared me! I thought I'd killed you! And then when you got back up and walked away, it was like a miracle from the Lord Himself. . . ."

Bella ignored him and thrust her paper at Jane, jabbering away.

"She wants you to read that," Yetta translated.

Jane looked overwhelmed, but she took the paper. She looked at it, looked up.

"It says people are dead," she said in a frightened whisper.

Bella stood there, looking from Yetta to Jane, uncomprehending.

"Tell her in Italian," Yetta commanded. She suddenly felt as though the cold seeping in through her clothes had finally reached her heart.

"'*Mi dispiace informavi che Angelina Rossetti, Dominic Rossetti, Giovanni Rossetti, Ricardo Rossetti e Guilia Rossetti anno perdutto la vita.*' I regret to inform you that Angelina Rossetti, Dominic Rossetti, Giovanni Rossetti, Ricardo Rossetti, and Guilia Rossetti have lost their lives," Jane read in a choked voice.

Bella's face was still uncomprehending. "They're dead," Yetta said in Yiddish.

Bella staggered back, like one hit by an unbearable blow.

"All of them?" she whimpered.

"Angelina, Dominic, Giovanni, Ricardo, Guilia—is that all of them?"

Bella threw herself to the ground.

"La mi famiglia e morta!" she wailed. *"La mi famiglia e morta!"* And even Yetta, who knew no Italian, could understand this: *My family is dead! My family is dead!* It was an unearthly sound, seeming to soar beyond the tenth floor of the factory, higher even than the skyscrapers.

The boy dashed forward and began tugging on Bella's arm, pleading, arguing—Yetta couldn't tell what he wanted. But Bella flung him away, unbelievably strong in her grief. The boy's head slammed into the wall of the Triangle building, but he sprang back up, tried again. "Stay away from me!" Bella seemed to be screaming. "I want nothing to do with you!" Yetta wondered if the boy had killed Bella's family.

Jane peered from Bella to Yetta.

"What should we do?" she asked.

Yetta held more tightly to her picket sign. She swayed a little, hungry, tired, cold. The sound of Bella's keening seemed to whirl around her. *I can walk the picket line for hours on end,* she wanted to tell Jane. *I can go without food. I can defy the bosses as long as they defy us. Or I can pick this girl up, soothe her in her grief, take care of her. Don't you see? I cannot do everything.*

It didn't matter. Yetta didn't have to say anything. Because Jane suddenly straightened up, suddenly decided.

"I'll take her home with me," she announced, sounding a little stunned, as if her conclusion surprised even her. "That's what I'll do. Mr. Corrigan, put this girl in the car. Now."

Jane

Mr. Corrigan just stood there.

"But your father—Miss Milhouse—"

"I said, put her in the car!" Jane commanded, and for the first time in her life, she thought she sounded a little bit like her father. He was always that forceful, ordering the servants around.

Mr. Corrigan gave Jane a puzzled glance, but he obediently bent over and scooped the wailing girl into his arms.

"Bella!" screamed the boy hovering nearby.

He clutched at the girl's hand, but she shoved him away.

"I don't think Bella wants you to come with her," Jane said, and she was just as glad. This boy looked like a complete ragamuffin, one of those urchins who stood on street corners hawking papers or picking pockets. His knickers were in tatters, and no one had bothered to patch any of the holes in his shirt. His thick hair straggled down into his eyes—was his family too poor even to own scissors? Or— just too lazy to use them?

Mr. Corrigan turned his back on the boy, shielding Bella from the boy's grasp. Bella's body must have been very light, because Mr. Corrigan only needed one arm to hold her while he tugged on the handle of the car door. Then he slid her onto the car seat.

"Miss—?" he said, offering Jane one last chance to come to her senses and cast the girl back out into the street.

"You ran into her!" Jane said fiercely. "She's in pain and in mourning and we can help!"

Mr. Corrigan shrugged, his head bowed—a servant's answer. *It is as you command,* that shrug said. *I will not pretend that I am capable of thinking for myself.*

"I will let you know how she is," Jane said to Yetta, as if Yetta had asked.

Yetta's face was unreadable, but she gave a small nod.

"Miss Wellington, shall I pull the car around for you?" Mr. Corrigan asked.

Jane saw what he meant. He'd put Bella on the side of the car closest to the curb; unless he turned the car around, Jane would have to step out into traffic to get to the door on the other side.

"No, no, I'll be fine," Jane said airily.

But it was frightening stepping out into the street. A car zigzagged past her, blaring its horn. She had to dodge horse droppings. And she'd moved so rapidly that Mr. Corrigan didn't have time to step out before her, hold the door for her. For the first time in her life, Jane grasped the handle of the car door herself, opening and shutting it without her driver's assistance.

"Home, please," she instructed Mr. Corrigan.

He pulled away from the curb. Jane turned her attention to Bella, who was no longer thrashing about and screaming but huddled on the seat, sobbing softly. She did not seem to realize that she'd been transferred from the sidewalk to the car. On the whole, she was not much cleaner or any better kempt than the ragamuffin boy. The hair hiding her face might as well have been tied in knots, and Jane wasn't sure if that was dirt or blood on her arm.

Jane suffered a pang of regret: *What have I done?* But her next thought was triumphant: *I did something! Finally! For once I'm not just standing around watching. . . .*

Jane couldn't have said why she'd begun haunting the picket line the past few weeks. Whenever she could escape Miss Milhouse's watchful eye, she'd sneaked out of Christmas brunches, Christmas luncheons, Christmas teas, just to have Mr. Corrigan drive her down to the Triangle factory to stand in the cold, her fingers getting frostbit, her elaborate hairstyles so often destroyed by the wind. She disgusted herself. It would be different if she were actually helping—bringing hampers of food, maybe, or joining her voice with the strikers' as they called out to passersby. Or even, as Eleanor Kensington had done, throwing herself at a police officer, begging, "Arrest me! Arrest me instead of touching even one of these poor, poor girls! They're not doing a thing wrong. So if you have to arrest someone, arrest me!" (The police officer had carefully dodged her and walked in the other direction. As did the next police officer. No one, it seemed, was willing to arrest Eleanor Kensington.) But Jane crept timidly away when the police came; she'd done nothing but watch.

Until now.

The girl on the seat beside her snuffled, one sob completely spent, the next just a whimper building in her chest. Jane pulled out her handkerchief and slid it under that veil of tangled hair, awkwardly wiping the girl's nose. She mostly ended up wiping the handkerchief on the hair, so it wasn't exactly a successful effort. But the girl didn't seem to notice, as the next sob grew from one little whimper to something truly frightening, racking her whole body.

Jane stared at the girl, wondering that she was capable of crying with such abandon. The way the girl had thrown herself to the ground, wailing—it had been so sad, but also so . . . pure. Jane remembered the moment she'd learned of her own mother's death. Miss Milhouse had told her: "She died in her sleep, completely at peace . . . you know she'd been sick for such a long time." Miss Milhouse's method of delivering the news had made it seem as though it would be selfish to cry. So Jane hadn't. She'd stood there, a little girl of nine, stoic and silent and pale, while Miss Milhouse began fussing about fittings for the mourning clothes and the proper dress for the funeral. Jane wished now that she'd been able to wail like this girl. She wished such mourning had been considered proper— or that she hadn't let herself care that it wasn't.

Mr. Corrigan pulled into their long, curving driveway.

"Shall I—?" he asked, still sounding doubtful that Jane really meant to be bringing this wailing girl home.

"Carry her up the stairs," Jane ordered briskly.

Miss Milhouse was waiting in the foyer.

"Where have you been?" she demanded. "The Aberfoyles' party—"

"I'm not going to the Aberfoyles' party," Jane said. "I'm busy."

"But all those eligible men home from college . . ." Miss Milhouse caught a glimpse of the wailing girl in Mr.

Corrigan's arms. She let out a shriek. "What is that?"

"It's a girl. Mr. Corrigan accidentally ran into her. She just lost her entire family," Jane said.

Miss Milhouse recoiled.

"Well, then, give her a few coins for pity and send her on her way," Miss Milhouse said, her face a mask of revulsion. "You shouldn't have brought her *here*. If she knows where we live she'll come around begging for money all the time. She might even know a lawyer. . . . And, ugh, she's so filthy—*down*stairs, Mr. Corrigan. I—"

"Put her in my room," Jane commanded. "You can lay her on my bed."

"But, your white coverlet, Jane! That's mud on her boots—mud or worse—"

Jane responded by tugging on the girl's boots, even as Mr. Corrigan carried her up the stairs. The boots came off to reveal filthy, patched stockings, with equally dirty skin peeking through the holes.

"Draw a bath," Jane said.

"Well, I never!—Jane Wellington, I am not touching this verminous creature, and I forbid you to have anything to do with her either!" Miss Milhouse said. "Now, Mr. Corrigan, I insist, take her back where she belongs."

Mr. Corrigan kept walking up the stairs.

So, there! Jane thought. *I am the mistress of the house! Miss Milhouse is just a servant!*

This was a new thought, a surprise.

Mr. Corrigan gently set the girl down on Jane's bed; he himself walked into Jane's private bathroom and turned on the faucets. And then he retired from Jane's room, pulling

Miss Milhouse along with him and gently shutting the doors behind them.

Jane was alone with the filthy, sobbing girl.

Some of the dirt and snot from her face, Jane saw, had already been transferred to the white coverlet. The sound of the water rushing into the bathtub caught Jane's attention. She went into the bathroom and turned the faucets off. She wet a cloth and brought it back to the bed, but the water dripped across the sheets. She tugged on the girl's arm.

"You'll have to come with me," she said.

Dazed, still crying, the girl stumbled to her feet and swayed her way toward the bathroom. Jane thought about summoning her newest Irish maid, Bridie, who'd replaced Sally—Bridie was especially good at washing hair. Bridie would know how to wash away all that filth. But Bridie might complain to Miss Milhouse, might decline to help because she'd been hired only to take care of Jane. And Bridie wasn't the gentlest of maids; Jane didn't want Bridie pulling on Bella's hair when Bella was already sobbing so tragically.

Jane touched Bella's dress, ready to lift it over the girl's shoulders. Jane had had maids dress and undress her many times, but she'd never once tried to help anyone else with her clothes. She couldn't figure out how it would work. Bella pulled away, murmuring something that sounded vaguely like an Italian version of "I can do it myself."

Dialect, Jane thought. She remembered a line from one of her Italian guidebooks: *In the countryside, and particularly in the* mezzogiorno, *in the southern part of Italy, the peasants have no knowledge of their own language, and instead speak only localized dialect. A peasant from one village may be completely incapable of conversing with a peasant from another village only scant miles away. It is recommended that travelers avoid these areas entirely. . . .*

Bella slipped into the tub as soon as she had her clothes off. Jane had never seen another girl without at least stays and petticoats on; she was stunned to see how badly Bella's ribs stuck out, how thin and wobbly her legs appeared. It was the fashion to pull one's corset very tight, to make a female's waist all but disappear. But Jane had never seen someone as skeletal as Bella, so clearly on the verge of starvation—on the verge of disappearing completely.

"I—I'll go tell the kitchen to send up a tray of food while you're bathing," Jane stammered. "Here's a towel for when you're done. And here, you can put on one of my night-gowns."

It was bright daylight outside, midmorning, but Jane had the sense that someone as emaciated as Bella—and as grief-stricken—should definitely be convalescing in bed. She scrambled down the stairs, so rattled that she forgot she could summon any servant she wanted just by ringing a bell. In the kitchen she spat out orders at the undercooks, then carried the tray of oatmeal and eggs and bacon up the stairs herself.

Bella was out of the tub now, wearing the nightgown and curled up under the coverlet. She was also sound asleep.

Jane leaned in close to make sure that Bella was still breathing. And then she sat down beside the bed and watched, because she didn't know what else to do. Only, it didn't feel like just watching anymore. It felt like keeping guard.

Bella

ella woke up warm—warm and cushioned and cozy. She was sure this was a dream because she hadn't been warm in weeks; she'd never in her life slept in a comfortable bed. She flailed about, reaching out for the Luciano children or her own siblings. She'd never in her life slept alone, either. But she was alone now, in this great expanse of white sheets and soft blankets.

Then she remembered. She remembered that she truly was alone, as alone as a girl could possibly be, and the sobs came back, wails pushing out once more from her raw throat, tears pouring out again from her swollen eyes.

"Ssh," someone said, hovering over her in the dim, twilit room. "Here. Have some soup. *Zuppa.*"

Bella swallowed hot broth, which was no consolation for the sorrow and grief, for her unbearable loss. But it slid down her throat comfortingly. She slid back into sleep, where she could dream of running through her village with her brothers and sister, all of them healthy and strong and little-child chubby, as they never had been in life. She could dream of baking with Mama, using flour from such overflowing bags that they could make loaf after loaf after loaf. She even dreamed of Papa, shouldering his hoe and singing as he went off to work, no longer bent over and work-worn and aged before his time.

When she woke again, the liquid the voice urged on her was bitter and molasses-thick, clogging her throat like tears.

"Medicine," the voice said. "Please. *Per favore.* You need it."

Bella swallowed it, just so the voice would leave her alone and she could fall back asleep.

She wasn't sure how many days passed before she woke for good, but sunlight splashed in through high, arched windows, illuminating roses painted on the wall. *No—rose wall-paper*, she told herself, pleased that she could identify such a foreign, American phenomenon. She must have heard one of the girls in the factory talking about wallpaper, describing the glories that were possible with paper and paste.

The factory . . . She waited for the panic to hit her—the panic, the sorrow, the fear—as she followed the trail of thoughts that began with sunshine on wallpaper roses. If the sun was up, she was supposed to be in the factory, unless it was Sunday, in which case she was supposed to be crowded around the Luciano table, twisting wire into fake roses. She hadn't been to the factory for so long that she'd probably lost her job, which meant that she wouldn't have any money to send home to Mama . . . though Signor Luciano hadn't sent any of the other money she'd made before, he'd just lied and kept it for himself.

And anyhow, Mama and the little ones were dead.

The panic and sorrow and fear that she had expected came slowly and was muffled. It was like all those times she and her brothers had thrown pebbles off the cliffs—the sound of the pebbles hitting the ground was so delayed and so far away, the noise seemed unrelated. Bella had moved beyond grief. She could close her eyes and *see* her family, happy, healthy, well fed. It was possible to hold that vision in her head, along with the knowledge that they had been all been dead for months.

"They're in heaven," she whispered. "Just like Father Guidani always promised . . ."

At those words, something stirred at the other end of the vast room, on an odd sort of couch that Bella had thought was covered with frills and lace and ruffles. The frills and lace and ruffles actually seemed to be covering a girl lying on the couch.

The girl sat up, and the frills and lace and ruffles floated into place on the most elaborate dress Bella had ever seen. Bella felt great sympathy for the sewing machine operator who'd had to concoct that monstrosity. She hoped that the operator's boss didn't stand over her screaming like Signor Carlotti always did, because sewing a dress like that would take a lot of concentration.

"Where am I?" Bella asked. "Who are you?"

The girl said something—maybe "Are you feeling better now?" or "Did you sleep well?"—some sort of soothing phrase. But Bella didn't understand any of the words.

The girl came closer. She was beautiful, with rosy cheeks, green eyes that sparkled like jewels, shining dark hair pulled back with a ribbon. But her face seemed nightmarish to Bella. This was the girl who'd read Pietro's letter.

"You!" Bella gasped. "What did you do with my letter? Did Rocco take it back? Please, I know it was full of bad news, it was cursed, but it was about my family. . . ."

She struggled to get out of bed, but the girl held her back. She was still talking—Bella knew these words must be "Calm down" or "Stay put," but they only upset Bella more.

"I don't understand!" she complained first in her own language, then in the language she'd learned in the factory.

The girl kept jabbering away. Finally she touched Bella's shoulder, pushing her back against the pillows. Then the girl ran to the door and called out. A tall, thin, unpleasant-looking woman appeared in the doorway, her mouth twisted as though she'd been sucking on lemons.

The girl and the woman seemed to be arguing, the woman's face contorting even more unpleasantly. Then the woman went away and the girl came back to Bella's side.

"Yetta," the girl said, with a bunch of other incomprehensible words. Bella knew she was saying "Yetta will come" or "Yetta will help."

Bella decided she could wait for that.

Yetta

Yetta straightened the sign on the side of the car:
THE WORKHOUSE IS NO ANSWER TO DEMANDS FOR JUSTICE.

"Stop that! You'll scratch the paint!" the man in the
chauffeur's uniform snapped at her.

"Paint be hanged! Our message is more important!"
scolded the owner of the car, a woman in a floral dress and
a towering hat held in place by no fewer than six jeweled hat
pins.

"She'll be growling at me to sand it down and repaint it
immediately if there's so much as a nick in that paint after this
parade," the man muttered to Yetta, almost apologetically.
"And it'll be my fault, no doubt. It always is, according to her."

Yetta was confused about whose side she should favor.
The chauffeur's—the poor, powerless worker scolded unfairly
by his unreasonable boss? Or the woman's—the charitable
socialite, nobly donating her car to the cause for the day, seeing beyond superficial details like paint to seek justice, sisterhood, unity?

Yetta had felt confused by many things in the past several days, ever since Bella collapsed at her feet. She felt
vaguely guilty, as if she'd done something wrong and didn't

even know what it was. Confiding in Rahel hadn't helped.

"Oh, that poor girl," Rahel had murmured. "You should have brought her home yourself."

"She's a gentile," Yetta said.

"She's your fellow worker!"

"No—she's a scab!"

"You said yourself you don't think she understands about the strike or the union," Rahel argued. "We can't know the troubles she's seen—imagine, if that were our family."

Yetta didn't want to imagine such horrible things. That was why she refused to read the news from Russia in the Yiddish newspapers. She didn't want to know about pogroms starting up again when she needed to devote all her mind, all her strength, all her spirit to the fight at hand, the fight she could win: the strike.

"Ride with us, Yetta!" someone hollered from the next car up.

"All right!" Yetta yelled back, but she took a few moments to survey the entire lineup of cars parked along the sidewalk. This is what everyone would see, the gleaming cars—millionaires' cars, millionairesses' cars—packed full of plump society women and scrawny, desperate, underfed shirtwaist workers. This was the newest way the rich women had decided to support the strike: with an automobile parade, an idea they'd taken from the suffrage movement in England. Each car carried a different sign on its side: THE POLICE ARE FOR OUR PROTECTION, NOT OUR ABUSE; STRIKERS SEEKING JUSTICE; VOTES FOR WOMEN. Yetta was starting to come around to the suffragists' point of view. If these women could vote, they would vote to help her. And if Yetta herself could vote . . .

Amazing, Yetta thought. *Back home I couldn't have chosen my own husband. And here I'm thinking about choosing presidents, governors, mayors, laws . . .*

She laughed, suddenly giddy, and scrambled into the car with her friends. The seat of the automobile was luxurious leather, and a delicate glass vase was mounted at the front, filled with fragrant roses. *It's December 21,* Yetta thought. *How could they have roses in December?* But the most surprising thing in the car was the person behind the wheel: a woman.

"That's Inez Milholland," Yetta's friend, Anna, whispered. "She drives her own car. All the other women have chauffeurs, but she drives herself."

"Ready, girls?" Inez asked merrily. Inez was young, perhaps only a few years older than Rahel. But she drove confidently, steering her car away from the curb, honking at the people they passed.

My first ride in an automobile, and the driver's a woman, Yetta thought. *And it's part of our strike!* She wished she could somehow go back in time and visit her old self back in Russia, sitting on her milking stool. *Just wait until you see what's going to happen to you in America!* Yetta wanted to tell her old self.

Beside her, Anna was talking about a strike fund-raiser she'd gone to at the Colony Club, an exclusive club for rich women. They'd invited a handful of strikers to tell about how the police and the bosses were treating them.

"There were seven forks stretched out beside each plate," Anna said, her voice deep and awed. "Seven! Every time the waiters brought out a new food, we had to use a different fork. Can you imagine?"

"How much money did you raise for the strike?" Yetta asked.

"One thousand three hundred dollars," Inez said from the front seat. "But it's not enough. We've got to do more."

Yetta decided she liked this Inez. The automobile was really only inching along, no faster than a horse and wagon, parading slowly through the streets of Lower Manhattan. But Yetta felt as though she could feel time speeding by, see the world changing before her eyes: walls falling down, bridges being built. Anna, who probably didn't even own a fork, had gotten to go through seven in one meal; Yetta, who hated rich people, had found one she actually admired. And she was riding in an automobile with a woman at the wheel!

On the sidewalks, people turned and stared, then cheered. Yetta didn't know if they were cheering for the strike or the signs or just the strange sight of carloads full of excited, giddy girls parading down the street. She hoped Mr. Blanck and Mr. Harris were watching through their office windows.

You cannot hide us away in your factory, cheating us in private, Yetta wanted to tell them. *We're telling the whole city what you do, how you treat us, how girls' lives and health are sacrificed so you can make your millions!*

"Did you hear?" Anna asked her, almost shouting over the noise of the car and the crowds. "They say Triangle's moved most of its manufacturing out to Yonkers."

"And other companies are going to Philadelphia," said another girl, Sadie.

That wasn't how it was supposed to work!

"Then we'll have to extend the general strike out to Yonkers and Philadelphia," Yetta said. "All shirtwaist workers everywhere will have to join us."

She spoke bravely, as confidently as ever. But what if that didn't happen? What if the strike failed? What if all they had to show for their bravery and hunger and frostbite and bruises was a single ride in a fancy car and a single meal with too many forks?

"Justice for shirtwaist workers!" Yetta screamed out the window, trying to outscream her own thoughts. "Support our strike!"

Men on the sidewalk waved their hats at her; women and children clapped. But one man seemed to be peering at her too closely, his eyes squinting together. He had the ruddy coloring of an Irishman, and Yetta didn't know any Irishmen, but he called out, "Yetta? Is that you? Please! I have to talk to you!"

Then Yetta recognized him: He was Jane Wellington's chauffeur.

"Stop the car!" she told Inez. "Let me out!"

Inez braked and Yetta scrambled out, wincing as the slush on the street soaked through the holes in her boots. On the sidewalk, the chauffeur bowed slightly, as if Yetta were one of the fancy society women herself.

"Miss Wellington sent me," he said. "The girls picketing at Triangle said you were in the automobile parade. It's about that poor Italian girl—"

"Bella? Is she all right?" Yetta asked.

"She's been sick for a week," the chauffeur said. "She's better now, but Miss Wellington can't understand a word she's saying, and Miss Wellington's father is coming back from his business trip tomorrow, and Miss Milhouse says the creature—pardon my language, I mean, the girl—has to be out of the house by nightfall, and Mrs. O'Malley, the housekeeper, she wants to fumigate the whole room, and Miss Wellington has been just like a little tiger, I didn't know she had it in her, she says she's not about to throw some poor, sick girl out in the streets when she's just lost her whole family and been hit by a car her own chauffeur was driving, but, you know, Mr. Wellington's a hard, hard man and—"

"What do you want me to do?" Yetta asked. She'd gotten lost somewhere between the first Miss This and the Mrs. That, and her English just wasn't up to keeping track of a mister, too.

"Come and help Miss Jane talk to the Italian girl," the chauffeur said.

Out of the corner of her eye, Yetta could see Inez Milholland's shiny car turning the corner, the parade going on without her. She could hear the other strikers calling out, "Yetta! Come on!" And yet she could see the pleading in this man's eyes, his desperation.

I wanted choices, she told herself. *How can I think of deciding on governors and mayors and laws if I can't even decide this?*

"Please," the man said.

Yetta turned on her heel.

"I'll meet you back at Triangle!" she called to her friends. "Tell Rahel I'm just . . ." *What? Atoning for my sins? Helping a fellow worker? Trying to win her approval?* The car was out of sight before Yetta could decide how to put it.

"My car—I mean, the Wellington car—is just around the corner," the chauffeur said. "I'm Mr. Corrigan, by the way. Miss Wellington will be very glad to see you. That Miss Milhouse her father hired to take care of her when her mother died is just a . . . well, she's a word I can't use in front of a young lady like yourself. You're one of those shirtwaist strikers, are you? We're all so proud of you, the whole city is—"

"Not our bosses," Yetta said dryly. "Not the police."

"Well, the rest of us are. Other workers. Did I tell you that my niece works in a coat factory?"

They had reached the Wellington car by then. Mr. Corrigan held the door open for Yetta, once again acting as though she were some fine high-society heiress.

Is it because he thinks of me as a friend of Jane's, and therefore practically her equal, not just another immigrant who still has the dust of Ellis Island on her shoes? Yetta wondered. *Or is it because he's so impressed by the strike?*

Yetta really wanted to know the answer, but it wasn't something she could ask. She slid onto the leather seat, which was every bit as fine as the leather seat in Inez Milholland's car.

Who would have thought I'd have my second automobile ride the same day as my first? Yetta marveled. *Who would have thought I'd become an expert on leather seats?*

Mr. Corrigan drove her into parts of the city she'd never seen before, where the mansions sprawled across entire blocks and elaborate gates and fences protected vast yards from the street. Yetta began to feel less and less like a proud shirtwaist striker; she became more and more aware of the holes in her boots. One house she saw seemed to have an entire forest contained in one wing. "That's the Vanderbilts' famous conservatory," Mr. Corrigan said, when he saw her staring at it. But Yetta was most puzzled by the wreaths and bows and greenery that seemed to be hung on every house.

"What are those for?" she finally asked.

"You mean the Christmas decorations?" Mr. Corrigan asked. "Haven't you ever seen . . . Oh. I don't suppose you have."

And then Yetta felt even more alien and out of place.

Even Mr. Corrigan had fallen silent by the time they pulled into a long, curving driveway in front of one of the huge mansions. *This is a mistake*, Yetta wanted to tell him. *I barely know Bella. I can't help Jane—not if she lives in a house like this*. . . . Still, Yetta held her head high as Mr. Corrigan opened the door for her and extended his hand to help her out of the car.

"The butler, Mr. Stiles, will show you up to Miss Wellington's room," Mr. Corrigan said.

"Thank you," Yetta said in her haughtiest voice, as though she'd never in her life crouched in cow manure pulling milk out of a cow's teat, as though she'd never had to live on four dollars a week, as though she didn't have a single hole in either boot.

Inside the mansion the ceilings were high and echoing, and the butler who came to the front door wore such fine clothes that Yetta was certain that he must be Jane's father, that "hard, hard man," back from his business trip early. Fortunately, before Yetta had a chance to say anything, the butler said, "Miss Wellington has been awaiting your arrival." He whisked Yetta across acres of marble floor and up a grand staircase that seemed to stretch into the heavens; it was that far between the first and second floor.

Jane's room could have held three or four of the tenement apartments like those Yetta and Rahel lived in. But Jane surprised Yetta by clutching her hands as soon as Yetta walked in the door.

"I'm so glad you came," Jane said. "I haven't been able to talk to her at all. Her letter was in Italian, real Italian that

I could read, but I guess she only speaks a dialect. And I don't think she knows any English at all. . . ."

Bella was in a bed the size of a boat, her head propped up against a pile of pure-white pillows. Her face was nearly as pale as the pillows, and her tragic eyes burned like embers. Yetta found that she didn't know what to say to her in any language.

"My letter," Bella said in Yiddish that was a bit garbled, but perfectly understandable. "I want my letter back and she won't give it to me. Why doesn't she understand my English?"

"That's Yiddish you're speaking," Yetta said.

"No, it's not," Bella said irritably. "It's the English I learned in the factory."

"It's Yiddish! You must have learned Yiddish because there were so many of us Jews in the factory. Listen"—Yetta switched languages—"English sounds like this."

Bella stared up at Yetta, her eyes seeming to grow in her pale face.

"I don't even know what Yiddish is," she said, in Yiddish.

Yetta started laughing first. She wasn't even sure what she was laughing at: the Yiddish that Bella thought was English or the fact that Yetta had thought that Jane's butler was her father or the fact that she was standing in this incredible mansion with holes in her boots. But after a split second, Bella started laughing too, and together they laughed and laughed and laughed, until somehow it made sense for Yetta to throw her arms around Bella's shoulders and whisper, "I'm sorry about your family." Bella nodded then, with tears threatening in her eyes, but the laughter was still there too.

"What's so funny?" Jane asked, her voice a little prickly, sounding like Yetta had back in the shtetl when Rahel went off with the older girls and left Yetta behind.

She has this huge house, Yetta thought. *She has this huge room. And she feels left out and jealous just because she doesn't understand two immigrant girls speaking Yiddish?*

Suddenly Yetta didn't feel so bad about the holes in her boots.

"Bella learned Yiddish by mistake," Yetta said. "She thought she was speaking English."

"Wish I could learn a new language just by mistake," Jane said. "I've been studying Italian for weeks, and it's totally useless."

"You were able to translate Bella's letter, weren't you?" Yetta said comfortingly.

"Yes. It's right over there on my desk. I went back through it with the phrase book and wrote out the translation word by word, just in case I was wrong," Jane said. She gestured helplessly. "I was hoping I was wrong."

"But you weren't?" Yetta asked.

Frowning, Jane shook her head.

Yetta walked over to the desk—another grand affair, painted white with gold trim—and picked up two sheets of paper and brought them back to Bella. The tears swam even more deeply in Bella's dark eyes. She clutched the original Italian letter to her chest.

"When?" she asked. "When did it happen?"

Yetta translated. Jane came over to the bed and peered down at the second sheet of paper.

"It says Guilia—Gull-ia? Gui-uh-lia?—I'm not sure I'm

saying that right. She succumbed to a fever on July 2, Giovanni and Dominic on July 3, Ricardo and Angelina on July 6," Jane said grimly.

"July," Yetta told Bella. "The first week of July."

Bella gasped. She said something rapidly in Italian—something that sounded like swear words. She was sitting straight up in bed now.

"If Signor Carlotti paid me, first week," she said, switching back to Yiddish, "Mama and the little ones would have had food, they would have been strong enough to fight off any fever—the blood of my family's deaths is on Signor Carlotti's hands!"

"Signor Carlotti didn't pay you for your first week?" Yetta asked.

"No. He said I was a"—Bella searched for the right word—"learner."

"That's why we're on strike," Yetta said. "We're trying to stop Signor Carlotti and the other bosses from doing things like that, cheating us, not paying us what they owe."

"I strike too, then!" Bella said. "I—" Her Yiddish failed her. *"Vendichero la mia famiglia!"*

"Avenge my family," Jane said. "That I understood."

Yetta had not even been trying to persuade Bella to join the strike. But Bella was already shoving the bed covers back, struggling to climb from the heap of pillows as if she intended to join the picket line right that moment, in her frilly nightgown.

"Wait! Where are you going?" Jane asked. "You've been sick—you had a fever yourself. You can't—"

At that moment a tall woman pushed her way into the room. She wore a lovely gown of pearl gray silk, and her silvery hair swept regally away from her face, but there was something ugly about her, an angry set to her mouth, a coldness in her eyes.

"Miss Wellington, *really!*" she snapped. "This is simply scandalous! It's bad enough that you're associating with that Italian girl, but now, entertaining *another* vagrant in your own private quarters—it simply isn't done!"

"Bella and Yetta aren't vagrants," Jane said stoutly. "They're working girls."

Yetta heard the admiration in Jane's voice, and suddenly even the holes in Yetta's shoes seemed like badges of honor.

The woman fixed Yetta with a glare that seemed to scorn holey shoes, Jews, Italians, immigrants, and anyone else without marble foyers.

"And you!" the woman practically spat at Yetta. "Even if Miss Wellington has temporarily taken leave of her senses, then I would think a working girl would know her place! What if I rang up your employer and had a little discussion about *your* behavior—invading our home, taking advantage of Miss Wellington's innocence and naiveté? How much of the Wellington family silver have you managed to slip into those pockets of yours?"

The woman couldn't have hurt Yetta more if she'd slapped her.

"I haven't touched your silver! And anyhow—I'm on strike! The bosses don't *own* me, they don't have any control at all over what I do outside of work! I can go anywhere I want!" Yetta argued hotly, just as Jane hissed, "Miss Milhouse! You must apologize this instant! Yetta is my guest! I invited her into my home!"

From the bed, Bella cried, "Stop it! I'll just go!" She spoke in Yiddish, so only Yetta understood. But Jane and Miss Milhouse stopped screaming at each other as Bella threw back the covers and struggled to free her legs from the bedding. And then Bella slipped down to the floor and stood on her own two bare feet. She took a tentative step forward, only a little wobbly.

"No! You're still sick!" Jane pleaded.

"Oh, please," Miss Milhouse said scornfully. "Did you think she was some stray puppy I'd let you keep? We're just lucky she was too sick to stab us all to death in the middle of the night and steal your best jewelry."

Yetta was glad that Bella didn't understand English. Yetta reached out to steady Bella, to hold her up. She intended to get Bella out of here safely even if she had to carry her out in her own arms.

"Miss Milhouse!" Jane said, in such a cold, hard voice that it sounded almost like an imitation of the older woman's. It was like a whip cracking in the room. "You will leave my room this instant. You will pack up your things and leave this house as soon as you can. You will not take any family silver or jewelry. You are no longer employed here. And—no, you will not get any references. You . . . are . . . fired!"

Everyone froze. For a moment Yetta thought they must all look like one of those tableaux she'd seen at the Yiddish theater: Yetta clutching Bella's arm, holding Bella mid-sway; Miss Milhouse squinting her mean old eyes at Jane; Jane standing tall with her clenched fists and her pursed lips and her barely contained fury.

Then Miss Milhouse began to laugh.

"Oh, that was very amusing," she said, her voice rippling with mirth. "You're even more foolish than I thought! You can't fire me! You're just a girl. You're *nothing*. Just a bit of fluff your father's going to use to marry off, to enhance his business. That's all you're worth. That's all any girl is worth. That's why these girls"—she gestured condescendingly at Yetta and Bella—"these girls are worthless."

Jane sagged against the wall, as if the air had gone out of her lungs.

"I'll tell my father to fire you!" she said, but her voice was thin and reedy now. Even Yetta could tell this was a hollow threat.

"And whom do you think he'll believe?" Miss Milhouse scoffed. "*Moi*, his longtime, faithful servant? Or you, his useless, troublesome daughter, who wants to consort with guttersnipes?"

Yetta saw no point in listening to any more of this.

"Could you please tell me where you put Bella's clothes?" she asked, as haughtily as she could. "Bella and I shall be leaving now." She thought her English teacher would be particularly proud of that "shall," even though her accent was as thick as ever.

"Oh, please, you don't have to!" Jane protested.

"We need to get back to the strike," Yetta said firmly, and that sounded so wonderful all of a sudden, to be out in the bracing wind, carrying a sign, telling the whole world the truth, instead of standing in this overheated, overdecorated room, being falsely polite.

Jane's mouth and cheeks quivered, as if she was trying very hard not to cry. But she whirled around and dashed toward a large wardrobe at the opposite side of the room.

"The clothes are right in—" she began.

"I had them burned," Miss Milhouse interrupted. "They were filthy and probably crawling with vermin. I couldn't allow them to be kept in this house."

"What?" Jane said.

Yetta swallowed hard.

"You could have just washed them," she said. "Those were probably the only clothes Bella owned."

Something made her want to cup her hands over Bella's ears so she didn't have to hear any of this, even if she didn't understand.

Jane swung open the doors of the wardrobe and began pulling out armloads of dresses.

"She can have some of my clothes, then," Jane said, her voice swooping dangerously toward sobs. "She can have anything she wants, because Miss Milhouse stole her clothes— yes, that's right, it *was* stealing, taking another person's belongings—and maybe Bella's clothes weren't worth as much as jewels or silver, but if that was all she had . . ."

Jane had practically buried herself in ruffles and frills and lace, and layers and layers of shiny taffetas, silk-embroidered net, heavy velveteen. Yetta had never seen so many dresses in one place, even in a store.

"None of your clothes would fit, and besides, why would a working girl need a party dress or a day gown?" Miss Milhouse asked, putting a particularly scornful emphasis on the words "working girl." "Just give her a penny or two. I'm sure that's more than her clothes cost."

"I won't send her away in a nightgown and bare feet!" Jane

said. She pulled out the plainest dress in the stack, a dark blue wool serge, and shook it at Miss Milhouse. "I haven't worn this all season, and it's a little small, so it could probably be cut down to fit. And she can have a pair of my boots—Yetta, do you want a pair too? Yours look a little . . . worn."

Yetta could feel the holes in her boots, the sore, blistered places on her feet where the holes rubbed, even through her stockings and the cardboard she'd used to try to block the holes. She could feel the slush that had invaded her boots, so that her stockings squished a little every time she took a step and her feet were always wet and cold. She tossed her head.

"My boots are fine," she said. "I bought them with money I earned myself. I don't need charity."

"See?" Miss Milhouse said. "Girls like that don't ever appreciate what you do for them."

Yetta regretted her pride the minute she saw Jane bend her head down, hiding her tears in velvet and silk. But Yetta couldn't back down now, not with Miss Milhouse staring so disdainfully.

It took an unbearably long time to bundle Bella into the blue serge dress, which hung on her small frame in an almost comical way. She kept having to tug the neckline back into place, because the dress threatened to slip off her shoulders entirely. The too-large boots were no better: They flapped on her feet and almost tripped her going down the stairs.

"A coat!" Jane cried. "You can't go out in this weather without a coat!"

"You are not giving that girl one of your coats!" Miss Milhouse snapped. "She didn't have a coat to begin with!"

"Then Mr. Corrigan will drive Yetta and Bella back to

their homes," Jane insisted. "And here, take some money—"

She crammed dollar bills into Bella's hands, which neither Bella nor Yetta bothered to count until they were both sitting in the car, Yetta getting her third automobile ride of the day.

"Twenty dollars," Bella said. "It's a fortune. I'd have to work a month for that much money."

Yetta looked back at the Wellington mansion. She thought she could make out Jane's sad face in one of the windows. And then Jane ducked her head down, as though she were sobbing.

"You couldn't pay me any amount of money to live in that house, with that woman," Yetta said. "A million dollars wouldn't be enough!"

Bella shrugged, the dress slipping sideways off her shoulders once again.

"Jane took good care of me," she said. "And now . . ." Her voice was very soft. Yetta had to lean in close to hear. "Now I have nowhere to go."

Yetta didn't even know the whole of Bella's story, didn't know how she'd ended up in America all by herself, how she'd come to be sobbing in front of the Triangle factory over a letter from Italy. But she immediately put her arm around Bella's shoulders, and the two of them huddled together against the cold of the Wellingtons' car.

"You can come and live with Rahel and me," Yetta said. "Girls like us, we stick together."

Jane

ane stood with her face pressed against the glass, watching Bella and Yetta leave. Tears streamed down her cheeks.

"It goes without saying that you will be confined to your room until your father returns home," Miss Milhouse said behind her. Her voice was as cold and hard as the icy windowpane. "And you can rest assured that he will receive a full report of your indiscretions. Such impertinence! Such behavior! I am simply appalled!"

Miss Milhouse whirled on her heel and left the room, jerking the door shut behind her.

Jane threw herself across her bed, ready to sob into her pillows. And then she experienced something odd. It was like she could see herself from above: a girl in a crumpled dress lying on a messy coverlet and scrambled sheets, her shoulders shaking helplessly, her pompadour trembling.

Fluff, she thought. *Useless. Only worth marrying off, not even worth that if I can't stop sobbing and act normal . . .*

Another scene came into her mind: the last time she'd visited her mother's sickroom. Mother was always so fragile, too sick for Jane to hug. That day, she'd been like a shadow in her bed, a wisp in a lacy nightgown. Mother had weakly clasped Jane's hand and murmured, "Ladies like us, we're too delicate for this world. . . ."

But she'd been sick. Jane wasn't. Jane knew about other kinds of women now: women who stood up and spoke out for suffrage, even when men threw rotten tomatoes and tried to boo them off the stage. Women—and girls!—who walked on picket lines, demanding their rights, even when bums spit at them and police beat them. Miss Milhouse would call those women unladylike or shameful or lower-class; she'd think they deserved the rotten tomatoes, the spit, the beatings. She'd expect Jane to agree.

Willfully, Jane shoved against the pillows, pushing herself back up.

"No," she said aloud, and it was a denial of so many things.

She grabbed the paper she'd written Bella's translation on. She flipped it over, held it against the nightstand, and began making notes on the back:

1. Buy coats for Bella and Yetta.
2. Have Mr. Corrigan deliver them along with hampers of food. He'll know where they live because of dropping them off today.
3. Go down to picket line and join in. Carry a picket sign. Get arrested if I must.
4. Convince Father to make strike donation. . . .

Bella

Bella had never been part of anything before except her family. Even in Calia, her family had had to struggle so hard to survive that they existed only on the outskirts of village life; in church, they sat at the back, not quite able to believe that they belonged in such a holy place, in the same room as something as grand as the gilded cross. Since she'd left Calia, Bella had always been an outsider: among the families on the ship, in the factory, at the Lucianos', on the street. She spoke the wrong language, wore the wrong clothes, trusted the wrong people.

But now . . . Bella had not known it was possible to stand shoulder to shoulder with another girl, one from Poland or Lithuania or some other place Bella had never heard of, both of them holding signs high over their heads, both of them longing just as strongly for exactly the same thing. Both of them completely connected. It did not make up for losing her family—that was a pain that still weighed her heart down, would never stop weighing her heart down—or for the anguish of losing Pietro, of being cheated by the Lucianos. But the strike was something to hold on to, something to hope for and dream about.

It was a reason to live.

Bella became one of the best strikers. She struggled through snowdrifts up to her knees to get to the picket line, she held her sign high even when the winter winds gusted so strongly they threatened to carry it away—and threatened to carry her away. Bella had never known such a fearsome winter, but she set her face against the icy wind, let the snow fall on her hair, and called out again and again and again, in three different languages, until her voice was hoarse, "Justice for shirtwaist workers! Justice for shirtwaist workers!" Even when she didn't completely understand everything, she cheered as loudly as anyone else when there was good news about the strike: Twenty thousand shirtwaist workers walked out on strike in Philadelphia, in support of their fellow workers in New York. The union and the rich women threw a reception and dance in the strikers' honor. The *New York Call* began planning a special strike edition that the strikers could sell to raise more money for the union. Bella begged to be one of the strikers who got to sell the papers.

"I didn't think anyone could be more *farbrente* than Yetta," Rahel said, one morning as the three of them shivered over breakfast. "But you might be."

"What's *farbrente*?" Bella asked.

"It means you're a fervent girl," Rahel said. "Someone who'll do anything for her cause."

"Hurray for the *farbrente*!" Yetta cheered. "Hurray for us all!"

Rahel abruptly turned back to the cupboard, as if intending to search for more food on the bare shelves. Or as if she didn't think she herself was *farbrente*, and didn't think she deserved the cheer.

It was interesting living with the two sisters, who looked so much alike and yet were so different. Rahel was quiet and self-assured; Yetta was excitable, always very happy or very disappointed or just very loud. She was very everything.

Three other girls lived in the tenement with them, but they were gone early in the morning and came back late at night, so Bella barely saw them. But Bella knew that they were Jewish too. She noticed that no one else in the tenement crossed herself when she prayed, no one mentioned a single saint, nobody worried that they didn't have a horned lucky charm hanging by the door to ward off evil spirits.

"What's 'Jewish' mean, anyhow?" she asked Yetta once as they were trudging toward the union hall.

"We're God's chosen people," Yetta said. "And . . . we're still waiting for our messiah. You have Jesus, but we're still waiting."

"I'd share," Bella said.

Yetta laughed, though not in a cruel way.

"My father could tell you a million reasons why that wouldn't work," she said. "I just can't explain it. Back home, girls weren't supposed to learn much about religion. We were just supposed to keep the house and fix the food and earn the money so the men could be holy enough for all of us. But I think . . . I think there are different ways to wait for the Messiah, different ways to be holy. I don't think anyone understands God well enough. I think I want to live a million years so I have time to think about all of it!"

"Good luck with that," Bella said. She tried to step over

a particularly high snow bank blocking the sidewalk. The snow flowed over the top of her boots—she'd stuffed cardboard in the toes, just so they'd stay on, but the boots were still too loose around her ankles. "Sometimes," she said, "sometimes I pray that God will let me die young."

Yetta stopped in her tracks.

"Don't say that."

"Oh, I wouldn't kill myself," Bella said. "That'd be a mortal sin. But if God let me die, I'd be in heaven with my family." Running through the village with my brothers and sister . . . baking with Mama . . . hoeing the beans with Papa . . .

"But you'd have to wait a million years before you got to see me again," Yetta said. "And I don't know how it works, if Jews and Italians go to the same place after they die. We might never see each other again!" She peered earnestly up at the sky, a thin gray strip barely visible between the towering buildings. "Please! I beg of you! Don't let Bella die young! We need her for the strike!" she yelled up at the heavens. Then she glanced back at Bella and punched her in the arm. "There. I canceled you out."

Bella was glad that the streets were virtually empty, that everyone else had been driven away by the snow. She clutched Yetta's arm, because, without coats, they had to huddle together for warmth.

"I think I'm forgetting them," she said softly. "My family, I mean. It's been so long since I've seen them—sometimes I forget they're dead. I forget to grieve, because I think they're still there, back home in Calia. Is that . . . is that . . . *evil?*"

Yetta bit her lip, already so pale and chapped from the cold.

"Rahel would know what to tell you," she said. "She'd have the exact right words to say to make you feel better, to tell you what to do."

"I want to know what you think," Bella said.

Yetta tilted her head close to Bella's.

"I don't think it's evil, how you're forgetting. Sometimes I think I'm forgetting my family, too, and I know they're still alive. I hope. It's natural, when they're so far away, to forget, to mostly just think about life here."

"If I'd stayed in Calia, I probably would have died too. With my family," Bella said.

Yetta took her by the shoulders and shook her so hard her teeth rattled.

"But you *didn't*," she said. "You didn't stay there, you didn't die—you were saved! Isn't that worth something? Isn't that worth living for, here and now?"

Christmas was not a holiday for Jews. Bella probably should have figured that out, but it was still odd, waking up December twenty-fifth to nothing. The union hall and the picket lines were closed for the day, but there were no songs, no rejoicing, no giggling little brothers running around banging on pots and pans. And, missing that, Bella knew that she would never truly forget her family.

"If you want," Yetta said over their measly, cold breakfast, "you could go to your synagogue—er, temple, er—"

"*Chiesa*," Bella said. "Church. But, no." She couldn't bear the thought of sitting in a pew alone.

Just then there was a knock at the door. Rahel sprang up to get it quickly before it woke the other girls.

Rocco Luciano stood out in the hallway, a mashed, poorly wrapped package under his arm.

"*Buon Natale,*" he said.

Bella wanted to hug him. But she didn't—she reminded herself that she was still angry with the entire Luciano family.

Rocco held out the package.

"Signor Carlotti told me you were living here now," he said. "I got you your very own shirtwaist and skirt. So you can look American like all the other girls. . . ." His eyes got big then, as if he'd just noticed that Bella was wearing the blue serge dress. She and Yetta and Rahel had ripped out some of the seams and resewn them; it fit quite well now, and looked very elegant, Bella thought.

"Oh," Rocco said sadly. "You already look American."

Bella unwrapped the package and held up the clothes. They were the cheapest shirtwaist and skirt possible, undoubtedly bought second- or third-hand from a peddler's cart. A month ago, Bella would have considered them an incredible gift. But now she refolded them and started to hand them back.

"Rocco," she said, "you should give this to your mother."

"Wouldn't fit," he said.

Bella tried not to giggle at that.

"Then sell them and give her the money for your family," she said. "For your brothers and sisters and the baby—"

"The baby died," Rocco said.

Bella saw the effort he made to keep his face still while he said that, not to let any sorrow break through his expression.

"I'm sorry," she said softly.

Rocco shrugged.

"It was just a baby. Babies die all the time. Just about all the babies on the whole block died. The nurse said it was whooping cough."

"I'm sorry," Bella said again. There was nothing more she could say about the Luciano baby, because she'd never once taken it in her arms and cradled it against her chest. She'd never loved it. She'd just listened to the baby cry and resented it, resented the way its misery mirrored her own.

"But our baby—I thought he was going to grow up," Rocco said. "I thought I'd get to teach him how to shine shoes, and show him the best corner for selling newspapers. . . ."

Bella remembered that she'd sometimes seen Rocco lean over the baby, letting the baby suck his finger. She remembered that Signora Luciano yelled at him when he did that, because he was wasting time he was supposed to be spending making flowers.

Rocco seemed to shake himself, shaking off his old hopes.

"I'm sorry about your family, too," he said. "And I promise, for my family, I will repay all the money my father owes you. Here's the first part."

He held out one penny. Bella hesitated, then took it. She placed the shirtwaist and skirt neatly on the table. She patted Rocco's head.

"Thank you," she said, quite formally. "Thank you for the gift and the repayment. I accept your promise. But, Rocco—if your own family is hungry, spend the money on them. Or if they need medicine, that comes first. I can wait. I'm fine."

"You're out on strike," Rocco said.

"And that's why I'm fine, don't you see? I'm standing up for myself."

Rocco squinted, as if this was a new concept, a girl standing up for herself.

"Oh," he said. "I wanted to tell you, too . . . I found out what Pietro did with your money, that he said he was sending to your family. He was using it to pay off the padrone for your ticket to America. He told his friends he wanted to wait to tell you about your family until the debt was all paid, because he wanted some good news to give you with the bad."

Bella blinked.

"Then . . . then *he* didn't cheat me," she said. Tears stung at Bella's eyes—this changed everything. Pietro had hidden the letter to protect Bella, not to take advantage of her. All that time Bella had been daydreaming about Pietro, maybe he'd been daydreaming about her, too.

"Oh, Rocco," Bella said. "This is even a better present than the clothing." Rocco recoiled a little, and she hurried to add, "Though the clothing is *magnifico*, it's so kind of you to bring me a present at all."

Rocco nodded stiffly, but he soon slipped back out the door.

"What was that all about?" Yetta burst out as soon as he was gone. Of course, she'd understood nothing, because Rocco and Bella had been speaking Italian.

Bella started to explain, but the story shifted in the telling. She couldn't make Pietro's secrecy sound noble and kind. *Just because I am a girl, I don't have to be protected that much,* she thought. *That just made things worse when I did find out, that my family had been dead for so long and I didn't even know it.*

"If Pietro ever comes back and we get married," she told Yetta and Rahel, "he's going to have to promise not to keep any more secrets like that."

And this was something different about Bella, maybe from being on strike and standing up for herself. She wasn't the terrified girl she'd been when she'd first come to America. She wasn't as easily fooled or as desperate as she'd been when Signor Luciano was stealing her money.

But she was glad that she'd be able to daydream about Pietro again.

Yetta

Yetta crowded into a rented hall with Rahel and Bella and hundreds of other workers, to listen to the union officials talk. A new proposal had come in from the manufacturers who hadn't settled yet—even Triangle.

"It's really quite generous," the union man said from behind his podium. "Shorter hours, fairer wages, four holidays a year with full pay, no more petty fines and charges for thread, for needles . . . It's almost everything you've been asking for."

"What about the union?" Yetta yelled out. "Are they going to recognize the union?"

After all the time she'd spent picketing and trampling around in the snow, her voice was too hoarse to carry to the front of the room. But others picked up her cry: "Can we keep our union? Will they give us a closed shop?"

"What's a closed shop?" Bella whispered.

"It means that the factories will only hire union members. If they can hire anyone they want, why would they bother negotiating with us?" Yetta said. "Why would they bother following any of the rules they agree to if they can just hire nonunion workers and treat them however they want?"

The man at the podium held up his hand, trying to silence the questions.

"Now, now," he said. "You have to be willing to compromise. You can't expect to win everything. That's, uh"—he looked down at his notes, as if he needed extra help—"that's the one concession the manufacturers weren't willing to make. No closed shops, no union recognition. So we'll just have to make the best of the circumstances. Now, if you're ready to vote on this fine proposal—"

"Voting's no good without the union!" Yetta shouted. "What do you think we've been fighting for?"

This was almost as bad as when the Triangle owners started a fake union. Yetta had to remind herself that this man was supposed to be representing her and the other workers, not the owners.

At least she wasn't alone in her outrage. Around her, others began shouting, "That's a terrible proposal!" "Send it back!" "I won't vote on that!"

Girls who were standing on tables, just so they could see, began stomping their feet; other girls leaned over the banisters, calling out, "For this I've been starving for three months?" "For this I went to the workhouse?"

"Now, calm down," the man behind the podium said. "We have to be reasonable—"

That's all Yetta could hear before his voice was drowned out by a chant flowing through the hall: "Union! Union! Union!"

The man gathered up his papers and scurried away.

The chanting girls spilled out into the streets, too riled up to notice the cold. Yetta thought it would be great to have another automobile parade now, while everyone was so excited, or to march to City Hall again, as strikers had done in early December. But it was night now, and dark; there was nowhere to go but home. By the time they reached their own tenement, the cold had seeped through their clothes again. Bella's face was almost blue in the light from the street lamps, and Yetta's teeth were chattering.

"I wonder if that was wise," Rahel said, as the three of them stood warming themselves over the feeble heat of the stove.

"You mean, rejecting that ridiculous offer?" Yetta asked. "Of course it was wise! That offer was *nothing*."

"Maybe it was the best we could get," Rahel said.

"Without union recognition?" Yetta said incredulously. "They'd have us back at our machines, and five minutes later some boss would be whispering into some girl's ear, 'Yes, I know you're supposed to work only ten hours today, but I'll need you to stay late.' Or, 'I know there were not supposed to be any more fines, but I saw you break that needle. That's five cents off your pay this week. . . .' Without the union, without a closed shop, what could she do?"

"And did you see how excited everyone was?" Bella asked, her eyes shining.

Rahel looked sadly at the two younger girls.

"Excited, yes," she said. "But it was like a riot of skeletons. Did you see how feeble everyone is becoming? I wager, not a single girl there had a decent meal today. And there was as much coughing and sneezing as cheering. The girl beside me was burning up with fever, and so weak, her friends had to hold her up. And, Bella, you're not completely well yet yourself—"

"I'm fine," Bella insisted, but she couldn't help coughing. Her face still looked blue, even indoors.

"The rich women are still helping us out," Yetta argued. "Why, the three of us still have the money Jane gave us—"

"Except for the part we gave to the union," Rahel said. "And what we spent on rent. And everything we spent on food. We can't live on that money much longer."

Yetta stamped her feet with impatience.

"There's still a rally with the rich women next week," she said. "At Carnegie Hall . . ."

But when the night of the rally arrived, January 2, 1910, a brand-new year, Yetta could feel a difference in the air. Maybe it was because of Rahel, who sat staring off into space, her face blank, even as the speakers up on the stage praised the strikers' courage, their perseverance, their cause. Maybe it was because Yetta heard so many of the rich people grumbling as they left: "A little too radical for my tastes, frankly," and "Isn't it appalling, how those socialists are deluding those poor little girls?"

One man in a tuxedo, pushing his way out the door near Yetta, complained, "I hear the union turned down a perfectly good offer. The girls who are still striking are just lazy. They don't want to work."

"That's not true!" Yetta yelled, and began fighting through the crowd to get to the man, to make him understand.

"Yetta, no," Rahel said, and pulled on her arm to hold her back.

"But—" Yetta protested. It was too late—the man had already disappeared into the crowd. Yetta turned around to complain to Rahel, and bumped directly into Jane Wellington.

Jane was beaming at her.

"I saw you from across the hall," Jane panted, tugging at her corset as if desperate for air. "I thought I'd never catch up—how *are* you? How's the strike going?"

"Fine," Yetta said.

"I've been so worried about you and Bella," Jane said. "I've wanted to come down to the picket line, but Miss Milhouse practically has me under lock and key. I had to sneak out tonight. But I want to help so much. I think soon . . ."

The crowd surged forward, separating Yetta and Jane. Yetta made no effort to get back to her. It was too depressing. Jane had so much money. She lived in a mansion, she owned more dresses than stores did, she had servants waiting on her hand and foot. If a girl like Jane could be kept under lock and key, what hope was there for a girl like Yetta?

"It's over," Rahel said.

Yetta blinked up at her sister. Normally Yetta wasn't much for sleeping late, but it was February now. Yetta had had six more weeks of picketing through snowdrifts and screaming herself hoarse and being beaten up and arrested. Earlier this morning, Yetta had crawled out of bed and immediately fallen to the floor. Rahel had insisted on tucking her back into the blankets.

"Bella and I can take your picketing slots today," Rahel told her then. "One day in bed will do you a world of good, and it won't hurt the strike at all."

Yetta had fallen directly back to sleep. She wondered if she was still dreaming, imagining that Rahel had returned.

"Got to . . . get back . . . to striking," she murmured, struggling to lift her head from the pillow.

"No, Yetta. Didn't you hear me?" Rahel said, her voice firm and all too real. "The strike is over. They sent us home."

Yetta gasped, fully awake now. She sat up straight, drawing on some reserve of energy she hadn't known she had.

"You voted?" she asked. "Without me?"

Rahel shook her head.

"The union leaders settled," she said. "They want us to go back to work."

"No vote?" Yetta croaked out. She squinted into the dim light coming from the next room. "Did we—did we win?"

"Triangle said they'd give us higher wages and shorter hours," Rahel said.

"But not a closed shop," Bella added.

"Then—that's not good enough!" Yetta said. "That's just what we turned down in December! What we refused to vote on!"

"Everyone's tired, Yetta," Rahel said. She sounded tired herself, like some old crone who'd lived a long, hard life.

"But the strike was going so well!" Yetta said. "The college girls are still donating money, the Yiddish theaters had those benefit plays . . . George Bernard Shaw himself sent a telegram about the strike!" Never mind that she hadn't heard of George Bernard Shaw until the telegram—he was some famous playwright in England. In England!

Rahel sat down on the edge of the bed and stroked Yetta's hair, just like she had when Yetta was a little child.

"So much spirit," she murmured sadly. "Yetta, can't you see? It had to end. The society women are arguing with the socialists, the union leaders want to be done with us so they can get started with the cloakmakers' strike—"

"They just think they can win that one because it's all men," Yetta said bitterly.

Rahel didn't disagree.

"Our people have been waiting thousands of years for the Messiah," Rahel said. "You can't expect to change the world in a few short months."

"Five months," Yetta corrected her angrily. "Five months of freezing and starving and all but killing ourselves to say, 'Look, world, we *matter*. So what if we're poor? So what if we're girls? So what if our English isn't so great? The bosses owe us some common decency. We deserve to be treated like human beings.' And now—now you're just going to go sit down at your machine again, quiet as a mouse, and sew when the bosses say sew, and stop when the bosses say stop, and let them tell you when you're allowed to use the facilities, and when you get only an apple turnover for working late, and—"

"No," Rahel said quietly. "I'm not going to do that."

Yetta was surprised to see that Rahel was shaking.

"What other choice do we have?" Yetta demanded.

Rahel looked down. She was twisting her hands in her lap, nervously.

"Maybe now isn't the best time to tell you."

"What?"

Rahel looked back up. Maybe her eyes were blazing passionately; maybe they were dull and glazed. Yetta just couldn't tell in the dim light.

"I'm going to marry Mr. Cohen," Rahel said, and her voice was as firm as a slamming door, revealing nothing else.

For a minute, Yetta just stared at her sister, speechless. She felt suddenly that she didn't know her sister very well, had never known her very well. Then she gulped and asked, "Who's Mr. Cohen?"

"From my English class," Rahel said. "You met him on the sidewalk that one night, after we walked Bella home. He's been . . . courting me. If it hadn't been for the strike, he would have been taking me to movies and dances, bringing me flowers. But as it is . . . he's asked me to marry him."

Yetta leaned back against the iron frame of the bed, trying to make sense of this, trying to make sense of her sister.

"Do you love him?" Yetta asked, her voice strangely shy and husky.

Rahel shrugged.

"I think so. But what do I know about love? How can I be sure?" she asked. "He's very handsome. His English is good. And he owns his own grocery. I can help him in the store, so he doesn't have to hire anyone else. And maybe later, when there's more business or when we have babies, he could hire you, too, so you wouldn't have to work in the factory either. You can live with us, of course. . . ."

Yetta tried to picture this life Rahel was describing: Rahel as a storekeeper's wife, Yetta as the spinster aunt/servant, juggling a crying baby as she stands on a ladder reaching for cans of food, trying to calm customers who grumble about broken crackers, rotting potatoes, spoiled bologna. That wasn't Yetta! Yetta was a shirtwaist striker!

Not anymore . . .

Yetta glared at Rahel.

"If you wanted Mama's life, why did you bother leaving the shtetl?" Yetta asked coldly. "Are you a revolutionary or not?"

"Oh, Yetta," Rahel said despairingly. "I was always a better revolutionary in your mind than in reality."

"But in Russia . . ."

"I was just an ignorant girl from the shtetl. Everyone in the movement was so sophisticated and they knew everything—and the boys were so handsome—so of course I joined. The leaders didn't even know my name. I didn't know anything about the plot to kill the *Czar*."

"But you had to run for your life—"

"Mostly because I was Jewish," Rahel said. She shifted positions, and now Yetta could see that her eyes were fierce and blazing. "There was a horrible pogrom in Bialystok—houses burning, Jews beaten to death, tossed out of windows and killed . . ."

Yetta had known this—known it without wanting to. But she'd tried not to remember it.

"And, Yetta, it's not safe for Mother and Father even in the shtetl," Rahel continued. "I've been reading the papers, and it's just a matter of time until the Russians pick our shtetl, pick our family for the next pogrom."

"That's why we're saving money to bring them here," Yetta said, as if she were the older sister and Rahel was some small child who needed everything spelled out for her.

Rahel gave a harsh laugh.

"Yes, and do you know how long that would take on our wages? Years and years and years . . . Unless there's a bad season when we're out of work, or there's another strike, and it will take even longer."

Yetta hated the way Rahel made it sound like it was selfish to have a strike, like it had been selfish of Yetta to take the first ticket to America that Rahel could afford.

"Why did you go out on strike at all?" Yetta demanded in a choked voice.

"Because I thought it would last a week," Rahel said. "I thought we'd get a little more money out of it. I thought . . . I thought having the union would help. But I'm not like you. I don't need the world to know that I matter."

Yetta jerked back, as if she'd been slapped.

"Then why didn't you quit?" she asked cruelly. "That second week, why didn't you say, 'Oh, well, this isn't working, back to my machine'?"

"They'd beaten you up by then," Rahel said. "Everything changed. And then I took the oath."

If I turn traitor to this cause I now pledge, may this hand wither. . . . Yetta looked down at her right hand, unwithered but badly chapped, cracked along the fingertips because of the cold, bruised where she'd hit the pavement once when a policeman knocked her down.

"So it's all right to quit now?" Yetta asked. "You can break the oath if you're getting married?"

"The union settled," Rahel said. "I'm not breaking the oath. I'm going on with my life. And Yetta—with Mr. Cohen, we'll keep kosher. He closes his grocery for the Sabbath. He's a good Jew."

"Father would be so proud," Yetta said, but she wasn't praising Rahel. She wondered how Rahel could do it—

willingly plunge back into a world where the men made all the decisions, where only their opinions mattered, where women just worked to help their husbands.

"Yetta—"

"I won't work in Mr. Cohen's store," Yetta said. "I won't live with you."

"But you're my sister!" It was a strangled cry, like something ripped from Rahel's throat. Rahel's face twisted, painfully, as if holding back her sobs hurt worse than letting them out.

"I'll stay with Bella," Yetta said. She looked around for her Italian friend—her fellow fervent striker—but Bella had tactfully slipped away, to let the sisters talk by themselves. Yetta knew how Bella respected family, how she grieved and longed for the sister she lost, the brothers, the mother, the father. *And I just shoved my own sister away,* Yetta thought with a sudden pang. *My sister, my only sister, my only family in America . . .*

But she couldn't take anything back. *Rahel is the one who's leaving,* Yetta reminded herself.

"Bella and me, we'll be fine," Yetta said. Somehow she managed to keep the heartache out of her voice. She forged on with false cheer, fake certainty. "Everything will work out. We'll go back to the factory. Just not quietly. Not meek as mice. And don't worry—I'll still give you money for bringing our family over."

Rahel reached out for Yetta, then drew her arms back when Yetta flinched. Yetta wondered which argument Rahel was about to throw at her: maybe "But Bella's not family! She's not even Jewish!" or, "They'll fire you if you're not meek as mice!" or even, "Mr. Cohen and I won't need your money! We'll bring the family over all by ourselves!" But Rahel surprised her by clutching her hand and saying, "Don't go back to Triangle. Go to one of the other shops, one that settled early, that agreed to recognize the union."

Yetta pulled her hand away.

"I *will* go back to Triangle," she said, and it was like taking another vow. "I'm not done fighting there. I don't know how I'll do it, but I'm sure—I can still do *something* to change that place."

Maybe it was easy for Rahel to give up on the strike, to just walk away. Rahel hadn't been beaten as many times as Yetta had; she hadn't spent as much time on the picket line. She'd mostly sat in the union office, shuffling papers. She hadn't been spat at; she hadn't had a policeman tell her she was the same as a streetwalker. Hadn't the strike made any difference to her at all?

"I can't stop you," Rahel said, and it was almost like she was saying Yetta wasn't her sister anymore, that she was letting her go. She was agreeing that they would take completely different paths for the rest of their lives.

"Good," Yetta said, and she turned her face to the wall, away from Rahel, so her sister wouldn't see her cry.

Jane

Jane's father hadn't come home in December. He sent a telegram saying that his business trip had to be extended unexpectedly; he had to miss Christmas. The letter that followed the telegram said he was sure Jane was too busy going to parties to care about his absence.

Jane wasn't going to parties. That was the only rebellion she was capable of: to refuse to put on sparkling dresses, to refuse to make polite chatter, to refuse to mince across a dance floor. But in her battle of wills with Miss Milhouse, that also meant she wasn't allowed to go to the picket line, wasn't allowed to give any money to the strike fund, wasn't allowed to buy coats or food for Bella and Yetta.

Jane had made an unpleasant discovery: She was a very rich girl, but she had no money.

Money she could control, anyway, and wasn't that what really mattered? The twenty dollars she'd crammed into Bella's hands as Miss Milhouse shoved her out the door had been the last of the birthday money Jane's father had given her, when he thought she'd spend it on a new hat or a necklace or ring. Jane had plenty of silks and furs; she ate oranges that came up by railroad from Florida, oysters from Cape Cod, caviar imported from Russia. But Miss Milhouse controlled Jane's clothing budget; the cook and the housekeeper ordered everything else. And her father went over every bill with a gimlet eye.

As soon as Jane could manage to escape Miss Milhouse's attention even for a minute, she sneaked down to the garage to talk to Mr. Corrigan.

"Please, if you could just take some food to those girl strikers—take some from the pantry. Cook will never miss it," Jane said.

Mr. Corrigan had his head under the hood of the car. He was very slow about leaning back from the engine, looking over at Jane.

"Cook," he said, "has counted every bag of flour, every carton of salt, every pound of potatoes. Aye, she'd miss it if we took so much as a dried pea."

Jane had not bothered putting on a coat when she sneaked out of the house; she'd thought that might look suspicious. She shivered in the cold garage, and wondered why it was fashionable to wear such a thin, gauzy dress in the wintertime. Was it just to show off the fact that Jane's father could afford a fine furnace, strong enough to heat their entire house?

"Then *buy* some food for them, and I'll pay you back when my father gets home," Jane said. "If you could buy Bella and Yetta each a coat, too—I know you probably don't know much about women's fashions, but I'm sure anything warm would be marvelous. . . . Maybe your wife would be willing to help you?"

Mr. Corrigan took off his chauffeur's cap and ran grease-rimmed fingers through his thick hair.

"Miss Jane," he said, and Jane knew that she should scold him for being so familiar, but she didn't. "Your father pays me twenty-five dollars a week. I have seven children. I'm all for supporting the girl strikers, but I don't have the money to go buying any of them new coats, not when my own children are wearing last year's, with the hems let down. And I'm not taking food out of my own children's mouths just on the promise that you'll pay me back when your father gets home!"

Jane had not known that Mr. Corrigan had seven children. She didn't know that her father paid him only twenty-five dollars a week. Why, she had hats that cost twice that amount!

"I *would* pay you back," Jane said.

Mr. Corrigan ducked back under the hood of the car, attacking some part of the engine with a wrench. He twisted and turned: he grunted and his face turned red with the exertion. He lifted out some metal contraption that, for all Jane knew, might be the entire engine. The metal was covered with grease and grime and it scared Jane, somehow, to see what filth and ugliness lay beneath the gleaming, polished exterior of her car.

Mr. Corrigan looked over at Jane.

"I can't lose my job," he said. "I can't, not with seven children to support. Miss Milhouse says I'm not allowed to drive you anyplace now without her permission. But some night, if Miss Milhouse is sleeping—and you're sure she's asleep!—and you want to go to one of those strike meetings . . . I'll take you."

Jane saw that this was the best he could offer—that as far as he was concerned, it was a lot to offer. So that was how she got to go to the meeting at Carnegie Hall. But the rally was a big frustration. She couldn't really listen to any of the speakers because she was so busy looking around trying to make sure that no one who might know Miss

Milhouse would see her, and trying to see if Yetta and Bella were anywhere in the crowd. She did spot Yetta at the last moment, and she felt such a ridiculous surge of hope: Maybe Yetta could tell her what to do to fight Miss Milhouse, how to survive without any money in her control. Wasn't that sort of like what Yetta was doing in the strike?

Jane elbowed and edged and—once—actually kicked her way through the crowd, fighting her way over to Yetta. But Yetta only stood there with her face like a vault, closed and locked tight.

"How's the strike going?" Jane said.

"Fine."

And then Jane babbled on while the crowd swept Yetta away: Yetta moving forward, making history, changing the world, while Jane's life was so small that she'd had to put laudanum in Miss Milhouse's tea just to get out of the house.

Do I want to help Yetta, or do I want her to help me? Jane wondered, standing alone in the swirling crowd.

Either way, Jane had failed.

Jane's father finally came home in February. Jane heard him at the door, and she rushed down the stairs immediately. She knew she had to get to him first, before Miss Milhouse had a chance to poison his mind against her.

"Father!" Jane cried, and threw her arms around his shoulders.

"Eh? What's this?" Father said, turning abruptly, the way he would if he thought someone was picking his pocket.

Jane gave him a peck on the cheek, though she couldn't remember ever kissing him before. He always kept her at such a distance, with his cloud of cigar smoke and his gruffness. And his grief. Surely it was mostly his grief over losing Mother that made him so unapproachable.

"Yes, of course I want the luggage sent up to my room!" Father growled at the butler, ignoring Jane. "Did everyone forget their jobs while I was away?"

Jane clutched at her father's arm. He shook her away.

"What are you doing?" he asked. "Why are you acting like a strumpet?"

Jane looked up at him and made a feeble attempt at batting her eyes. She'd seen other girls manipulate their fathers—"Oh, Papa, please, it's just a pair of kid gloves. . . . They're so darling, don't you agree?" She knew she should start with the sweet talk, the declarations of how she'd missed him, how Christmas had been so empty without him. But now, faced with her own real glaring, growling father— a hundred times more irritable than she'd remembered— everything she'd planned to say died on her tongue.

Father frowned suspiciously.

"You want something, don't you?"

"Th-there's a strike," Jane stammered. "Of shirtwaist girls. Girls who make shirtwaists. And the bosses are really mean to them, and I just want to help, by giving them food and warm coats, so they don't get too sick to walk the picket line—"

"Humph," Father said. "If they go back to work, they can buy their own food and coats."

"But they can't afford it, don't you see?" Jane said. "They don't make enough money."

Father lifted his cigar from his mouth, looked around, yelled: "Mrs. O'Malley! Did you move my ashtray?"

The housekeeper bustled in, apologizing, "Sorry, sir, I'm so sorry, one of the maids was just cleaning it—"

Father stalked into his study, flicked the ash into the fireplace. He turned back to Jane.

"Miss Milhouse was right. You have fallen in with a dangerous, socialist crowd. She was very wise to nip this in the bud," he said.

Jane saw that she'd made a huge mistake. Miss Milhouse had obviously written to Father while he was away. Jane should have done that too. She'd been counting entirely too much on the power of batted eyelashes, the effect of a daughter lovingly kissing her father's cheek.

Father sat down at his desk, as if he expected Jane to know that she'd been dismissed. She stood on the threshold of his study. She'd been trained practically since birth to know what she was supposed to do now: slink back to her room. Fluff her hair and freshen her face and come down to dinner to make polite conversation as if nothing had ever happened. She'd been trained to know her place just as surely as the servants had. Whether her father was away for a day or three months or a year, she was still supposed to jump back into proper position the minute he returned. Just as, someday, she'd be expected to play that role for a husband. She was supposed to be as easily controlled as an ashtray.

Jane stood on the threshold and looked back and forth—foyer or study, white marble or dark wood . . . She felt like she was making a momentous decision. The other time she'd felt this way, deciding to bring Bella home, she'd been impulsive, like someone tossing a coin into the air, letting chance determine her fate. That decision could have gone either way. This time, Jane wanted to be sure she knew what she was doing.

She swallowed hard and stepped forward, into her father's study.

"I have *not* fallen in with a dangerous, socialist crowd," she said. "What they say is true. Those girls don't make enough money. And their bosses have paid off the police and other . . . other *thugs* to beat them up. It isn't right."

Father blew out a thin stream of smoke.

"Girls shouldn't be walking the picket line," he said. "For that matter, they shouldn't be working in factories."

"What would you have them do to survive?" Jane asked.

Father was rifling through papers, lifting them from one stack into another.

"Their fathers or brothers or husbands should take care of them," he said, without even looking up.

"What if they don't have fathers or brothers or husbands?" Jane asked. She was thinking of the Italian girl, Bella. But something caught in her throat, a cry twisted. "What if that was me?"

Father slammed his hand down on his stack of papers.

"For heaven's sake, Jane, this is ridiculous!" he fumed. "*You* would never be in a situation like those girls. They're not like you. I'm not sure what stories they've told you to get your sympathy, but I can assure you, it's really none of your business and probably mostly lies, besides. They're very calculating, those Jews."

"They're not all Jewish," Jane said. "They're Italian, Irish—"

"Immigrants," Father said, biting down on his cigar. His lip curled up in disgust.

"Some are Americans!" Jane said. "And anyhow, I've seen the police beating them, it's not just stories I've heard—I've seen it with my own eyes! The girls are doing nothing more than walk around, and they get punched and kicked . . . and they're *girls!*"

Father smashed his cigar down into the ashtray Mrs. O'Malley slipped onto his desk before tiptoeing back out.

"It's unfortunate that there are girls involved," Father said. "But that's how it is in business. It's not some polite little game of croquet. Why, I've hired strikebreakers myself."

Strikebreakers, Jane thought dizzily. *The people beating up the strikers.* In her mind she could see fists hitting faces, heads jerking back, bodies crumbling to the ground. *My own father would hire such cretins, arrange such attacks?*

"When?" she asked, through lips that felt strangely numb.

Father waved his cigar at her impatiently.

"You were a baby," he said, in a tone that implied she was a baby still, in terms of what she knew about the world.

"Did . . . did Mother know?"

"What does it matter?" Father said. "It had to be done. If I'd let the union in, let the workers take control of my factory, I'd have been ruined. It's a battlefield out there, and only the strong can survive. You better be glad I hired strikebreakers, young lady, because otherwise we wouldn't have any of this." His gesture took in the dark wood paneling of his study, the marble floor of the foyer, the servants waiting outside the door. "I can assure you, you wouldn't have such nice dresses."

Jane looked down at her frothy dress, a sea of ruffles and frills.

"Then I don't want them," Jane said. She tore at the collar of the dress, but that was ridiculous—this dress was so complicated it usually took both a maid and Miss Milhouse to get her in and out of it. And would she really want to be standing there in front of her father in her under-things?

His money paid for my under-things, too. . . .

"I don't want anything your money buys, if that's how you got it!" Jane yelled. "Hiring strikebreakers, hurting people, probably starving them too—"

"Oh, please, Jane," Father huffed. "That's how the world works! Some people are rich and some are poor, and by God, if I can be on the rich side, that's where I'm going to stand! Would you have us all living in hovels, wearing sackcloth and ashes, eating gruel? That's what the socialists want. They'd pull everyone down to their level if they could—"

But Jane had already whirled away from him. Blindly, she darted out the study door, out the front door . . . Mr. Corrigan was standing in the driveway by the car, brushing snow from the windshield.

"Please!" Jane shouted at him, sliding into the backseat. "You have to take me to . . ." Where could she go? Somewhere away from this house, away from her father.

Mr. Corrigan glanced nervously back at the house, at the huge windows staring out at them, where anyone could be watching.

"I'm sorry, miss," he said. "I'm not allowed."

"Fine!" Jane shouted. "Be that way!" Her father's tainted money had bought the car, too, and bought Mr. Corrigan's services. She slipped back out into the snow, slamming the car door behind her. She began stomping off down the snowy driveway.

"Wait!" Mr. Corrigan called. "You don't have your coat!"
Jane shrugged, and kept going.

"Then"—Mr. Corrigan chased after her and placed one of
the lap blankets from the car around her shoulders— "at
least wear this!"

Jane knew she should shove it down in the snow, because
her father's money had bought the lap blanket, just like
everything else. But it was warm around her shoulders, and
it made her feel a solidarity with Bella, who'd also huddled
in a blanket in her moment of tragedy: Bella had lost her
entire family, and now Jane had to break away from her
father, because he was an evil, evil man.

Jane tramped through the snow, past mansions and monstrous estates. Some of them were houses she'd always
admired and secretly envied, but now when she glanced
toward the twists of wrought-iron gates she thought she saw
the twisted faces of workers who'd toiled and starved just so
the industrialists could have a fine gate. It was like seeing
the grimy engine beneath the car's gleaming exterior:
Suddenly she could see how all the glitter and elegance, all the
excess and opulence, had been built on the backs of workers
like Bella and Yetta, workers calling out for justice.

*And workers like Mr. Corrigan trying to support seven children
on twenty-five dollars a week, because that's all my father pays him.*

Jane walked all the way to Eleanor Kensington's house,
blocks and blocks away.

She pounded the knocker of the front door, and it wasn't
until the butler came to the door and fixed her with a dis-
dainful stare that she realized how disheveled she must look,
how many rules of polite society she was breaking. It was

late afternoon, maybe even early evening by now; the Kensington family would be preparing to sit down to their dinner. The time for social calls had ended hours ago.

"I must see Miss Kensington. Eleanor," Jane said. "It's an emergency."

And then she realized that Eleanor probably wasn't even there; she'd be back at Vassar. And Jane didn't have train fare with her. She didn't have any money at all.

But the butler was stepping aside, letting her in.

"Your card?" he asked.

Jane had forgotten about the whole rigmarole of presenting an engraved name card, of waiting to find out whether a friend was "at home" to receive guests—it all seemed so unbearably ridiculous that Jane didn't even feel embarrassed.

"I said, this is an emergency! I didn't have time to bring my cards with me. Just tell Eleanor that Jane Wellington has to see her!"

The butler retreated. Jane watched the snow from her boots melt onto the Kensingtons' Persian rug. What money bought that rug?

Shipping interests . . . Are there strikebreakers for shipping interests?

Miraculously, the butler reappeared quickly, and silently led Jane up to Eleanor's room. Eleanor was sitting there in a deep-red ball gown, while three maids fussed over her hair.

"You're lucky you caught me," Eleanor said. "I just came back from Vassar for the Van Renssalaers' Valentine dance. I'm going back to school tomorrow morning—and won't I be tired!" Her eyes took in the gray blanket around Jane's shoulders, the slush-stained ring around the bottom of Jane's dress. "I assume you've decided not to go to the ball?"

Jane had not been invited. Perhaps she would have been if she'd gone to all the Christmas social events, if she'd been nicer to Lilly Aberfoyle all those months ago when they were having tea.

"I don't care about any stupid dance," Jane said savagely. "This is about the shirtwaist strike. I found out that my own *father* has hired strikebreakers before. He's just as bad as the shirtwaist bosses! Everything we have is tainted!"

"Hmm. That's an interesting perspective," Eleanor said. She watched in her huge dressing-table mirror as one of the maids pulled a ringlet down to its full length, each hair gleaming like gold.

"I-interesting?" Jane sputtered. "It's appalling! Horrifying! Devastating!"

Eleanor looked at the maids hovering around her.

"Girls, Jane and I need some privacy," she said. "You can come back and do my hair later. That way I can be fashionably late and make a big entrance." The maids froze around her, as if they feared being fired if they didn't finish Eleanor's hair immediately. "I said, go!" Eleanor commanded. The girls scattered.

When they were gone, Jane demanded, "Has *your* father ever hired strikebreakers?"

"Oh, probably," Eleanor said, toying with a ringlet. "Dockworkers are a pretty rough crowd. So are shipowners."

"But, then—did your father get upset about your helping out with the shirtwaist strike?"

"He thought it was sweet that I was concerned about the less fortunate girls. But he didn't really take much notice of it." Eleanor shrugged. "He doesn't think girls and women matter much."

"But that's not what you think," Jane argued. "You think women should vote. You think we should have rights. You think the shirtwaist girls deserve justice. You think strike-breakers are wrong. You think—"

"Yes, yes, of course," Eleanor said impatiently. "You know what I think. I don't agree with Father about much of anything."

Jane stared at Eleanor's elegant red ball gown, the perfect flow of silk.

"But you take his money," Jane said. "You eat his food, you wear dresses bought with his money, you let him pay for you to go to Vassar. . . ."

"What's my choice?" Eleanor said. "Working in some factory as a shirtwaist girl? No, thank you."

Jane narrowed her eyes. "Sometimes, maybe, to get what you want, I bet you even let him think that you agree with him." Jane remembered the kiss she'd given her own father, and blushed.

"You want me to apologize for being nice to my own father?" Eleanor asked. She sprang to her feet in a flurry of rustling silk. "I've done nothing wrong. I'm working for all sorts of worthy causes. Some people just use different strategies than others. It's like . . . Here. Feel this." She tapped her tiny waist.

"I beg your pardon?" Jane gasped.

"All right, feel your own waist," Eleanor said. "Feel your corset under your dress, those rigid spines that won't let you breathe—you hate your corset, don't you?"

"Who doesn't?" Jane whispered.

"My point exactly," Eleanor said. "If I ripped it off now, I'd split all the seams in my dress, my mother would faint, my father would have an apoplectic fit—it'd be quite the faux pas if I went to the ball tonight without my corset. Almost as bad as if I wore that blanket of yours!"

She grinned, trying to make a joke, but Jane didn't laugh.

"So?" Jane said icily.

"So, instead, I've been letting my corset out gradually. My friends and I took a vow at school. Now, every time I go to a dress fitting, I make sure the corset is a little looser, a little less confining. . . ."

"You're still wearing a corset," Jane said.

"But eventually I won't be," Eleanor said. "Don't you see? It's a matter of doing things gradually, changing the world one corset string at a time."

"That's easy for you to say," Jane retorted. "But you can't tell the shirtwaist girls, 'Eventually you'll have fair wages, eventually we'll stop having the strikebreakers beat you up, eventually maybe you'll be able to afford a coat.' They're freezing *now*! They're starving *now*!"

Eleanor sighed.

"Jane," she said. "Go home. Tell your father you love him no matter what. Tell him you just feel sorry for the poor girls who don't have wonderful, rich fathers like him. You play your cards right, I'm sure he'll come around!"

Jane felt betrayed. Eleanor was the one person she thought would understand.

"I walked all the way over here," Jane said. "I thought—"

"I'll have my chauffeur take you home," Eleanor said

briskly, as if all that mattered was Jane's transportation.

Jane let herself be led out to the Kensingtons' car. What else could she do? She slumped in her seat. She couldn't face the thought of walking back into her own marble foyer: defeated, humbled, lost. Couldn't, couldn't, couldn't. She leaned forward.

"Excuse me, sir?" she called out to the Kensingtons' chauffeur, over the rumble of the motor. "I gave you the wrong address. I actually need to go to another location. I'm not sure of the exact street number, but it's the Asch Building, near Washington Square."

She would go back to Triangle.

Bella

ella and Yetta were walking home from work. They'd been back at Triangle for a week now, and Bella was still rediscovering the twinges and aches that went along with hunching over a sewing machine all day. She stretched, twisting her head this way and that, raising and lowering her shoulders. This brought a puff of air up her skirt, but for once it didn't seem unbearably cold.

"I think spring is coming," Bella said. "Can you feel it?"

She held out her hand, experimentally. A snowflake immediately landed on her outstretched palm.

"I think spring's still a long way off," Yetta said, kicking at the slush on the sidewalk.

Yetta had been in a bad mood ever since the strike ended, ever since Rahel's wedding, ever since she'd started back to work. Bella had tried again and again and again to cheer her up, and failed each time.

Suddenly Bella heard a screech of brakes out in the street. The sound reminded her of the worst morning of her life, so she didn't bother looking until she heard someone screaming, "Bella! Yetta! Wait for me!"

It was Jane, the rich girl who'd rescued Bella that awful

morning. She came rushing toward them through the traffic, prompting honking horns and more screeching brakes. She was wearing one of her usual fancy, frilly dresses, and her beautiful gold ring gleamed even in the weak winter light. But she looked crazy: wild-eyed, wild-haired, coatless, hatless, and dragging a gray blanket behind her through the snow.

"Where are your picket signs?" she yelled. "I came to help you with your strike. I'll stand with you every day on the picket line. I will! If I can't give money, I'll do what I can. And if I'm arrested—well, fine! That would serve my father right!"

She was sobbing or gasping for air—Bella couldn't really tell which. In New York, Bella had discovered, people rarely moved out of the way for anyone else. But the crowd on the sidewalk moved out of the way for Jane, as if they were all glad that she wasn't yelling at them.

When Jane was right in front of Bella and Yetta, blocking their path, Yetta finally replied in a flat voice: "The strike's over. Go home."

Jane froze in her tracks.

"What? It can't be! I've been watching the *Times* every day—"

"The *Times* didn't even bother writing about us when the strike ended," Yetta said, and Bella could hear the barely suppressed rage in her voice. "The *Call* did, the *Forward* did—do you want to know what the Forward wrote about Triangle? 'With blood this name will be written in the history of the American workers' movement, and with feeling will this history recall the names of the strikers of this shop—of the crusaders.' And yet the factory can reopen, just like the strike never happened, and do business with stores all over the country—who would do business with criminals like that?"

"My father would," Jane whispered. "My father is an evil man, and I never knew it until your strike. It's all wrong—everything I have was bought with blood—I can't go back, I can't. How can your strike be over?" The last part was a wail. For a moment Bella feared that Jane would just fall over, right there in the snow. She reached out a hand to steady the other girl.

"You ran away from home?" Yetta asked. "For our strike?" Something like surprise crept over Jane's face.

"Why, yes, I suppose I did," she said. "That's what it's called. Running away from home."

"Where will you go?" Bella asked.

Jane turned to Bella in amazement.

"Bella? You speak English now?" she marveled.

"I learned it in the strike," Bella said. "Some. But you—go where?"

Jane slumped against the building behind her.

"I don't know," she admitted.

For a moment, Bella forgot that Jane was a rich girl. She forgot that Jane lived in a huge mansion with marble floors and puffy beds and servants waiting on her hand and foot. She only remembered what it was like to be alone and afraid, cut off from family, betrayed.

"You come home with us," she told Jane.

Yetta

Yetta pulled the last shirtwaist from her machine and slid it into the trough that ran the length of the table, ready to go to the next girl. Sewing was boring—there was no other word for it. Somehow it seemed worse since the strike, because her thoughts darted back and forth with each thrust of the needle: *Maybe I shouldn't have been so mean to Rahel, maybe we shouldn't have come back to Triangle, maybe I could have tried harder during the strike to keep it going, if only I'd been out picketing that last day . . . what if this is all there is to the rest of my life, watching a needle go up and down?*

She felt every bit as restless as she had back in the shtetl, milking cows. Only weaker. She still wasn't fully recovered from the illness she'd had at the end of the strike, and the filmy dust that hung in the air of the factory only made her cough worse. Bella had told her about the babies who'd died from a cough—what if something like that happened to Yetta?

When Yetta began thinking like that, she wanted to hop a train and head west, she wanted to jump up on the table and call out for another strike, she wanted to hurl her sewing machine out the window and laugh to see it smash against the sidewalk. She wanted extravagance, drama, revenge. Life.

But she had no money—no money to take a train, no money to survive a strike, no money to repay the bosses for a smashed sewing machine. *Don't you know? In America, money is God*, the painted woman had told her, after beating her up during the strike. Yetta still didn't want to believe that, but it was hard not to.

Yetta stood up from her machine, turned around, and almost ran into one of the cutters.

One of the many bad things about coming back to Triangle was that Yetta now worked on the eighth floor, where the cutters had their tables. They took up half the room, strutting around with their sharp knives drawn, smoking endlessly even though there were signs on the walls forbidding it. Once Yetta had even seen a cutter drop his cigarette on a pile of shirtwaist collars, and all he did was laugh when his assistant had to throw the collars to the ground and stomp out the flame. He didn't even get in trouble. Those cutters! So what if they could slice through layers and layers of fabric with a single stroke? So what if they held the entire company's fortune in their hand every time they made a cut with their knife through the expensive material? They reminded Yetta all too much of the men back in her shtetl who thought they were holier than everyone else. Besides, she hadn't forgiven any of the cutters for the way two of them had beaten up the contractors who'd first called for a strike, way back in the summertime.

This cutter seemed younger than the others, maybe not so cocky. He had brown hair curling at his temples, and honey-colored eyes—in another mood, Yetta might have called him handsome. Now she regarded him sourly.

"Excuse me," she said briskly, trying to step past him.

He touched her arm, stopping her.

"You're Yetta, aren't you?" he asked. "The one who has a rich girl staying with her?"

Yetta pulled her arm away.

"More like a poor girl," she said, snorting in a most unladylike way. "Jane didn't bring a penny with her when she ran away from home."

At least Jane had provided a bit of a distraction. She was fascinated by everything in the tenement: the bed improvised from a board laid across two chairs, the bathroom shared with three other apartments, the gas heat that could be purchased by placing a penny in the meter on the wall. And she wanted to talk endlessly about how it might be possible that bosses and workers could get along, that factories could be run to respect everyone. Still, she didn't seem to understand that the potatoes she ate cost money. And Bella and Yetta were too timid to mention it, too afraid of appearing inhospitable.

"We don't want to sound as greedy as Mr. Harris and Mr. Blanck," Bella had argued, when Yetta suggested hinting to Jane about the rent due at the end of the week.

Sometimes, Yetta thought she and Bella should just kick Jane out, send her back to her pretty clothes and her show-offy mansion, where she belonged. But then Yetta would hear Jane sobbing at night, sobbing the way Yetta wanted to sob, because the strike was over and the world wasn't fair and Rahel had moved away, moved apart from Yetta. . . .

"Maybe you should tell the rich girl to get a job," the cutter said.

That made Yetta laugh out loud.

"I can just see her, sitting at one of these machines. . . . She thinks it's awful that we don't get a break for tea every afternoon," Yetta said.

"Does the rich girl have fancy manners?" the cutter asked.

Yetta shrugged. "Of course. She's rich. She holds her pinky like this even when she's just drinking water." Yetta extended her pinky, curled her other fingers in, and pretended to drink from a teacup. Secretly, Yetta wondered if she should copy Jane, but that would probably look silly, an immigrant shtetl girl putting on airs.

"Does she speak any foreign languages?" the cutter asked.

"French, Italian, and—what's it called?—Latin. She went to some big finishing school."

The cutter leaned closer.

"I heard Mr. Bernstein talking—you know, he's Mr. Blanck's brother-in-law. He says Mr. Blanck's wife is looking for a governess for their daughters. Someone who could help them get along in society. Learn how to socialize with the goyim."

Yetta had never thought before about Mr. Blanck having a wife or daughters. It was like trying to imagine the devil's family.

"Well, maybe I'll tell Jane to apply for that job," Yetta said, shrugging. "Thanks, I guess."

The cutter smiled.

"I'm Jacob, by the way."

Yetta tilted her head.

"Where were you during the strike?"

"I—I just started here," Jacob said. "After the strike. After it was over."

His eyes darted left, then right. Yetta thought he was lying.

"But *during* the strike—where were you then?" she challenged.

He looked too healthy to have walked any picket lines or skipped any meals to save money for the strike. He actually had rosy cheeks.

"I was in another shop," Jacob said. "One that settled right away."

Yetta shrugged.

"If you say so," she muttered, brushing past him.

"I wasn't a scab!" Jacob yelled after her. "I wasn't! Ask anyone!"

Yetta wasn't in the mood to listen.

Jane

Jane lay in bed long after Bella and Yetta left for work. She could hear echoes of what Miss Milhouse had told her back in the fall when she wouldn't get up in the morning: *Really, Miss Wellington, you must expunge yourself of this torpor.* But that bed had had crisp white sheets and an elegant white coverlet; this bed had a rusted frame, a single worn, grayish sheet, and a stained, tattered quilt that Yetta's grandmother had made back in Russia. Jane could hear what Miss Milhouse would say if she could see Jane now: *Really, Miss Wellington! Such squalor! Such degradation! Such foolishness! You'll be ruined in society if anyone finds out where you are!* She could hear her father's words echoing in her mind: *Would you have us all living in hovels, wearing sackcloth and ashes, eating gruel?*

She knew exactly how her father and Miss Milhouse would view the tenement, with its cracked walls, its chipped sink, its hovering stench of rotted food and unwashed bodies. It had taken great effort for Jane herself not to wrinkle her nose in disgust the first time she'd stepped in here. But then Bella had said, "See our vase of flowers?"—pointing to a cheap glass on the table with two crumbled roses sticking up. "That's all that's left from Rahel's beautiful hat, after the strike," Yetta muttered. The flowers were fake, of course, but somehow they transformed the entire tenement for Jane. Suddenly she saw past the cracks and the chips and the cheapness. She saw the beauty of two battered cloth roses, the ingenuity of beds rigged from chairs, the cleverness and courage and triumph of two girls living on their own. And now, even hearing the echoes of Miss Milhouse's criticisms and her father's taunts, she could see the triumph and courage and nobility of Jane Wellington, lying on a rusty, tattered bed in a tenement instead of amid perfect, fluffy pillows in a mansion.

But what was she supposed to do next?

Just to prove that she could get out of bed, Jane sat up and eased away from the tattered quilt. She slid her feet into her boots right away, because the floor was bare wood and full of splinters, as well as icy cold. She did not have to bother about changing clothes because she'd been sleeping in her dress—it was all she had.

"Could I possibly borrow a nightgown from one of you?" she'd asked the first night, and both Yetta and Bella had looked at her blankly. It appeared that neither of them had an extra. One nightshirt, one dress, one shirtwaist, one skirt—Jane had a hard time understanding such limitations. But now she had just one dress herself.

She made a feeble attempt to comb and pin up her hair, but she had no skill at that. Without maids, she was as helpless as a five-year-old. She dealt with that problem by turning away from the small sliver of broken mirror that hung on the wall. She slipped out the door and out to the street— some fresh air would do her good.

But the air in the street was bitterly cold and hardly fresh. There was a rancid smell of some foreign food cooking; an organ grinder's monkey bent down and defecated in the street; strangers' bodies pressed against hers disgracefully. The crowd parted, and Jane found herself on the curb. Someone pushed at her and she lost her balance, falling forward onto horsehide. Oh—a horse was lying in the street, ready to break her fall. How fortunate. The horsehair was soft, and Jane stroked it in relief. Then she realized that the hair was strangely cold and still to be attached to a living horse. The ribs below the horsehair moved neither up nor down.

The horse was dead, its rump half rotted.

Shrieking, Jane scrambled up. A gang of filthy-faced, snotty-nosed ragamuffins laughed uproariously to see her screaming. One laughed so hard he rolled in the street, right on top of the monkey's droppings. A little girl with tangled curls stared stupidly at Jane, her eyes seeping with some unknown infection.

Does no one have money to take away the dead horse from the street? Jane wondered. *To put those ragamuffins in school? To fix that girl's eyes?*

When Jane was little, she'd been fascinated with a stereoscope her mother kept in the parlor. You looked through two eyeholes at two separate pictures, and somehow the pictures merged into one that was three-dimensional and looked so real you felt you could reach out and touch it. With the stereoscope, the two pictures, separately, always looked somewhat alike: two views of Half Dome in Yosemite National Park, say, or two views of the Grand Canyon. But Jane's mind was working now like a different kind of stereoscope. In her mind, she held the view of the dead horse, the ragamuffins and the seepy-eyed girl alongside her memories of seeing the shirtwaist strikers calling fervently for justice, seeing her dozens of dresses strewn across the floor the day she'd offered one to Bella, and seeing an image of herself, lying in bed. With the stereoscope back home, Jane had always had trouble focusing, bringing the pictures together exactly. She was having the same trouble now.

One of the ragamuffins stopped laughing and appeared to be patting her hand comfortingly. No—he was trying to worm the ring from her finger.

"Oh, no, you don't!" Jane roared. "My mother gave me that ring!"

The ragamuffin had the ring off her finger and was about to slip it into his own pocket. Jane grabbed for it desperately, and succeeded only in swatting it away. It flew through the air, sparkling, and landed in the smashed monkey dung.

Jane did not hesitate. She snatched up the ring and raced away through the crowd—shoving, elbowing, kicking with all her might—until she was back in the tenement.

She slammed the door as hard as she could.

When Yetta and Bella got home, Jane was sitting at the kitchen table, staring at the vase of artificial flowers and turning her ring over and over in her hands. She'd scrubbed the ring in soapy water—scrubbed it and rinsed it and scrubbed it and rinsed it, again and again and again—but still she stopped and examined it every few minutes to make sure there was no filth caught in the engraved *J* on the ring's surface. As soon as Yetta and Bella opened the door, Jane said, "I need money. Money of my own."

Both of the other girls stopped in surprise, and then Bella rushed over to hug Jane while Yetta quietly closed the door.

"See? She understands," Bella said, flashing a glance at Yetta.

"It's not that we mind sharing," Yetta said apologetically. "It's just that the rent works out to two dollars a week, and we still owe the landlord extra from when we were on strike. And potatoes are five cents a pound, and with the three of us, it'd be ninety cents a week for milk, and—"

"And Yetta and me, we're only making six dollars a week, each," Bella said. "If we're lucky and the bosses pay it all."

Jane had been thinking, *Those are such small amounts of money; what are they talking about?* Until Bella chimed in with their salaries, which were small too.

I'm a burden, she realized.

"Oh!" she laughed, uncomfortably. "I didn't—you should have told me. But it's not just that. It's—I mean, it takes money for everything, and I didn't know that. It's not just for buying your way into society or for winning a proper husband. That dead horse and the girl's eyes and the raga-muffins—if I had money, my own money, I could have helped them, even the boy who tried to steal my ring. Maybe he was starving, maybe that was why he had no morals. Maybe no one ever taught him that stealing was wrong." Jane saw that Yetta and Bella had no idea what she was talking about. They looked totally confused. "I just want to *do* something, like you did with the strike."

"Not that that worked out so great," Yetta muttered.

Jane clutched at her head, knocking out hairpins and destroying the last vestige of her attempt at a hairstyle.

"I'm just so confused!" she moaned. "Maybe I'm just trying to justify going back to my father, if he'll even let me come back. Maybe I want you to say, 'It's all right to go home. It's—'"

"It is all right to go home," Bella said. "I miss my family too. If I could go back to them—"

"But I don't miss my father," Jane said. "I miss his money. It's not the same. His money is evil. But I still miss my flowered wallpaper and my clean glass windows and the orange juice from Florida and—and—and—you probably think I'm a horrible person. Maybe I don't really want to help the boy who tried to steal my ring. Maybe I don't even care. Maybe it's all about me. I want to go to college and I want to take a grand tour of Europe and I want to have real roses on my table—"

Yetta leaned in close.

"So earn the money yourself," she said fiercely. "Earn your own money and save it. And then use it however you want."

Jane blinked back tears.

"I'm not like you," she said. "I'm not brave and courageous and strong. I couldn't sit there all day at the sewing machine. I don't even know how to sew!" She remembered what Eleanor had said, the scorn in her voice when she hissed, *"What's my choice? Working in some factory as a shirtwaist girl?* No, thank you." Jane didn't want Yetta and Bella to think that she was similarly scornful. "Don't you see?" she wailed. "I'm useless. I was raised to be totally dependent on others." She shoved a tangled strand of hair out of her eyes. "I can't even do my own hair! Just a few nights away from home and I stink and I'm filthy and my hair's a wreck and I don't understand how you can do it, staying so clean and tidy and—and *cheerful*—living in these circumstances." She waved her hand wildly, the gesture taking in every chip and crack in the room, every belch of smoke from the stovepipe that layered filth and ash on every surface, every ice crystal creeping up the insides of the windows.

"We're not *saints*," Bella said, at the same time that Yetta muttered, "I'm not cheerful." The two girls exchanged glances, and then Bella ventured, "Yetta heard of a job you could do. Not sewing. Something that uses what you know. How you were raised."

Yetta sat down at the table.

"The Blancks need a governess for their daughters," she said. "Someone who can teach them to get along in society."

Jane gaped at her.

"Oh, my heavens," she said. "You want me to be Miss Milhouse."

It was funny, actually, in a cruel way. Having escaped her jailer, Jane was now expected to become a jailer.

"You want me to teach other girls to pull their corset strings so tight they can't breathe," Jane said. "To speak only when spoken to. To lower their eyes and simper and say 'Oh, you beast,' when boys flirt, whether they like it or not. To always let men think that they are smarter and stronger and better. . . ."

"Maybe you could be a subversive governess," Yetta suggested. "*Pretend* that you're telling them all those things but secretly tell them the truth. 'Unions are good.' 'Women should vote.' 'Girls are as smart as boys.' Maybe you could even spy on Mr. Blanck for us, let us know what he's planning for Triangle."

This appealed to Jane. The thought of being a servant

was horrifying, but espionage—that was glamorous. She remembered hearing rumors about one of the other girls at her finishing school, that the girl's grandmother had been a spy during the Civil War. The notion seemed too incredible to be believed, but Jane had not been able to stop herself from staring when the old woman came to an end-of-term singing concert. Jane was disappointed in the woman's steel-gray hair, her wrinkles, and her prim black dress with the cameo pinned at the neck. She looked entirely ordinary. But maybe that was the secret of being a good spy.

"Begging your pardon," Bella said, pulling up her own chair at the table. "I think what's wrong with Miss Milhouse is that she doesn't love you. I'm sorry!—I'm sorry if that's hurtful. But listen to me. I had brothers and a sister who had runny noses all the time and were rough and tumble and never left me alone for a minute. And I loved them. I loved them with a love that was so deep and so true that I crossed the ocean, I came to America, trying to save their lives. And then I lived with the Lucianos, and their children had runny noses and they were dirty and the baby cried all the time, and I hated them because they weren't Giovanni and Ricardo and Dominic and Guilia. I don't think I would have crossed the street to save any of *their* lives, so—"

"Not even Rocco's?" Yetta asked.

"That came later," Bella said, with stiff dignity. "Later I liked Serefina, too, and I'm sorry that the baby died. But when I hated them, at first, that wasn't good, and if I had been their—what's it called?—their governess, I would have been very mean to them. So, spying or no, whatever you tell them, what you should decide on, is whether or not you think these are children you can care about. Because children should have people who love them."

This was the most Jane had ever heard Bella say, in her lilting accent that made even English words sound foreign. But Jane understood what she meant. She twisted the ring on her finger, traced the clean swoop of the engraved *J* with her thumbnail.

"My mother loved me," she said. "My father—I don't know. It never really seemed like it." That was hard to admit, that her own father might not love her. Even if he was a horrible, evil, strikebreaking man. She went on. "And Miss Milhouse—you're right. She's never loved me."

Jane thought how easy that had made it for her to run away. Other girls had living, loving mothers telling them to tighten their corsets and to marry the wealthiest man who made an offer—or the man with the most impressive European title. And of course they listened, because their mothers loved them, and they loved their mothers.

Maybe love could be a trap, too.

Jane felt dazed, and no less confused. But she nodded solemnly at Bella, at Yetta.

"Thank you for your advice," she said. "I will remember it. I don't know if anyone would hire me as a governess. But I will try. I will try."

Yetta and Bella worked hard getting Jane ready to meet the Blancks. They decided she should wear the serge dress she'd given Bella, back in December.

"You mean, you can let out the seams again?" Jane marveled. "Just like that? You didn't cut the dress down to fit?"

"Cut in haste, repent at leisure," Yetta said, waving scissors at her reprovingly.

"Oh, is that a proverb in Russia, too?" Jane asked.

"No, I learned it in my English class," Yetta said. "But I don't really understand it—isn't leisure good? Isn't it something you want? Like time to have fun? Why would you repent while you were having fun?"

"Leisure can also be just, time to stop and think," Jane said. "What the proverb means is that if you do something in a hurry, without thinking about it, then when you do stop and think, you'll regret it."

Like running away from home? Jane wondered.

She pushed that thought aside, because Bella and Yetta were so merry, fitting the dress back together, trying out new styles for Jane's hair, showing her how to polish her boots until they gleamed.

"What will we do about a hat?" Bella moaned.

Jane thought of the rows and rows of hats sitting on shelves back at her own house. Hats with feathers, hats with flowers, even one with a little stuffed dove tucked along the brim . . .

Bella seemed to be thinking along the same lines.

"If you'd just remembered to wear one when you came here," she scolded.

"You always had such beautiful hats when you came to the picket line," Yetta said dreamily.

"But they're tainted, remember?" Jane said. "Bought with my evil father's evil money . . ."

"So was your dress and your boots and that blanket, and you brought those!"

"I do like that warm blanket," Bella said. "I'm glad you brought it." She was the one who'd been sleeping with it at night, because she was the one who had to sleep on the bed improvised from chairs. Worst bed, best blanket—it seemed only fair.

"Wish you'd bought a blanket for me, too," Yetta joked.

"And maybe one of those soft pillows . . ." Bella said.

"And I've always wanted to try orange juice. I wouldn't have complained if you'd brought some of that," Yetta added.

"*I* had some at Jane's house," Bella bragged. "Isn't that what you gave me, in the mornings? And those sausages—I wouldn't have minded if you'd brought us some of those sausages!"

They were teasing her, and that was all right. She hadn't known: They craved luxuries too. They were poor girls, but they were still girls; they wanted the frilly dresses and ruffly skirts and glorious hats that Jane had always taken for granted.

"Since I'm taking the serge dress back from you, Bella, you should have my day gown," Jane said, holding out the stained lace dress she'd been wearing for days. "I think it will come clean."

"Oh, I've got the shirtwaist and skirt that Rocco gave me for Christmas," Bella said, reaching out and touching the lace edging on one sleeve. "Where would I ever wear a dress like that? We should hang it on the wall, to show people that we've got more clothes than we need." Tears glistened in her eyes. "I never thought, back in Calia, that I'd ever have so much in America."

It was strange: What was poverty to Jane was untold riches to Bella.

"I know!" Yetta said, bolting upright. She rushed out the door, and came back a few minutes later holding a hat out in front of her, like someone proudly displaying a trophy.

"Sadie across the hall said you could borrow it, just for tomorrow," Yetta said. "Prettiest hat in the building, don't you think? Try it on!"

The Miss Milhouse voice that seemed to have taken up residence in Jane's head hissed, *Absolutely not! It's undoubtedly crawling with vermin, a hat borrowed from a strange girl in a tenement. And, anyhow, see how the velvet's worn thin at the crown and the fake chrysanthemums don't begin to cover it? And you know chrysanthemums are dreadfully out of style this season. . . .* But another voice in Jane's head, the one that was getting stronger, said that it was incredibly kind of Sadie-across-the-hall to loan her best hat to a stranger. Jane reached forward, took the hat, and placed it on her head.

"Perfect!" Yetta said.

"Lovely!" Bella agreed.

So Jane was in borrowed and resewn finery when she stood on the front step of the Blanck home. *It's much smaller than my house,* she told herself, to make herself feel better about the borrowed hat and the made-over dress. Except— was her "house" the Wellington mansion or the tenement she shared with Bella and Yetta?

A butler opened the door. He looked appropriately scornful, as if he knew about the tenement, knew that chrysanthemums were out of style on hats.

"Yes?" he said.

"I understand that Mrs. Blanck is looking for a governess," Jane said.

"Servants' entrance is at the back," the butler said, beginning to shut the door.

Jane stuck her foot in the door.

"I want Mrs. Blanck to understand that I know how young ladies should behave," she said. "That I can *show* them how to act. And which door to use."

The butler looked chagrined and let her in.

"Don't tell Mrs. Blanck I don't know proper butlering," he said. "I'm such a greenhorn, I keep thinking they're going to fire me. At least you have the accent right."

"I don't have an accent," Jane said.

"Exactly," the butler said. "You sound like a proper American."

Jane decided it wasn't worth protesting that she *was* a proper American.

The butler led her to a gaudy, overstuffed parlor and went to alert Mrs. Blanck. Jane wondered if the servants at her own house had kept secrets from her and her father. *Of course they did*, she thought, remembering how Mr. Corrigan had kept the secret about taking Jane to the strike rally. But this made her see things differently, once again. Maybe being a servant wouldn't be so bad. She'd have allies.

A short, heavyset woman in an overly frilled gown appeared in the doorway of the parlor. Jane remembered to rise, respectfully.

"Mrs. Blanck," she said. *"Je m'appelle Mademoiselle Michaud.* I am Mademoiselle Michaud." She and Yetta and Bella had agreed that she shouldn't use her own name. Using French— and then translating—seemed deliciously pretentious.

"How very nice to meet you," Mrs. Blanck said, looking

sufficiently impressed. "Please, sit down."

Her words were heavily accented, in a way that seemed oddly familiar. Where else have I heard . . . Oh. Yetta. Everyone in our tenement building except Bella and me. Mrs. Blanck must be from Russia.

At least now Jane knew better than to ask her to say something in Russian.

Mrs. Blanck was twisting her hands in her lap.

"I want the best for my daughters," she said.

"Of course you do," Jane said, and she was surprised that her voice came out sounding so warm and supportive. She couldn't help liking someone who had her daughters' best interest at heart.

"My husband and I . . ." Mrs. Blanck seemed to be deciding how much she could say. She leaned forward, as if prepared to confide news of a delicate nature. "We were not born to money. Most of our lives have been struggle, struggle, struggle."

Jane longed to ask questions. *Were you starving back in Russia, like Bella was in Italy? Did you live in fear of being killed because you were Jewish, like Rahel and Yetta? Were you a shirtwaist girl when you first came to America? Did you work in a sweatshop? Did you live in a tenement?* It seemed, suddenly, as though that could all be true. Jane looked around the crowded parlor, with its stuffed birds under glass and carved Egyptian statues and clashing striped and flowered wallpaper. Miss Milhouse would have sniffed, "A bit overdone, wouldn't you say? Ostentation by the nouveau riche is never appealing." But it seemed only sad to Jane, that Mrs. Blanck was trying so hard.

"My husband is a business genius," Mrs. Blanck said. "Now we are able to provide better lives for our children. We want their lives to be easy, full of wealth and accomplishment."

This was Jane's cue to say, "I can speak four languages. I can play the piano. I know which fork to use during each course of a formal dinner. I could be very useful to you." But she remembered Bella's advice: *What you should decide on is whether or not you think these are children you can care about. . . .*

"I should like to meet your daughters," Jane said.

"Now?"

Jane nodded.

Mrs. Blanck looked a bit uncertain, but she hollered over to the butler, "Brodsky! Tell Millicent and Harriet to come down here!"

If Jane got this job, she could teach Mrs. Blanck that a bell was a much more appropriate way to summon a servant than yelling. Maybe it was too late for Mrs. Blanck, but Jane could teach the girls, at least, that the Victorian era of parlor design was long past, and that stripes and flowers didn't go together on wallpaper. This was a family longing for her knowledge; they wanted what she'd had and taken for granted.

And had run away from.

The girls appeared at the entryway to the parlor. Millicent, the older one, was about eleven or twelve, a shy-looking girl with a giant ribbon in her hair. Harriet, the younger one, was four or five, and had a look of mischief about her.

"Stand up straight now, girls," Mrs. Blanck said.

They seemed to be trying to, but Harriet kept wriggling

sideways to scratch furtively at a place on her arm along the seam of the sleeve.

Lace sleeves, Jane thought. *Itchiest clothing on the entire planet. Especially where the seams meet.*

Unexpectedly, Jane remembered something about herself at four or five: the time she'd hidden under her father's desk during the birthday party. Like Harriet, she'd had lacy sleeves on her dress then. And the reason she'd thought the desk would be such a great hiding place was because no one would tell her to stop scratching if she hid there.

"Say hello to Mademoiselle Michaud, girls," Mrs. Blanck instructed. "If you are polite enough—and keep your hands down, Harriet!—she might become your next governess."

Mrs. Blanck turned back to Jane expectantly, her eyes begging, *Please, don't find fault with my daughters.* Jane saw that she had the advantage here. Mrs. Blanck was impressed with—even cowed by—Jane's unaccented English and her upper-class bearing and her lack of bragging or babbling. Mrs. Blanck admired everything that Jane's father's money had bought. There would be an interview, and Jane would have to lie a little about how a girl like herself had reached such reduced circumstances that she was applying to be a governess for immigrants' daughters. Jane would only have to imply some unfortunate tragedy, too delicate a matter to divulge—and really, was that such a lie? Jane would have no problems convincing Mrs. Blanck to offer her this job. The question was, did Jane want it?

Jane thought about all the reasons on each side: the degradation of being a servant versus the value of earning her own money. The chance to be a subversive influence versus the possibility of turning into Miss Milhouse. The opportunity to spy and help Yetta and Bella's union versus the dangers of working for an evil man. But it really came down to watching Harriet scratch her arm.

These girls are a lot like me, Jane thought. *Like I was.*

Someday they would grow up and learn where their money had come from. They'd learn that their father had hired prostitutes and policemen to beat up innocent girls, his own employees. If Jane ever figured out how to deal with the revelations about her own father, maybe she could help Millicent and Harriet.

There's more to life than ease and wealth and accomplishment, she could tell them. *There's . . .*

Well. Surely she could figure it all out in time to teach it to Millicent and Harriet.

Bella

Spring came, just as Bella had predicted. The best part of every day now was walking to and from work, in the soft spring breeze. It wasn't hot enough yet that the garbage in the street stank, but the snowdrifts and the ice chunks and the cruel winter winds were long gone. Sometimes, walking home, Bella linked her elbows with her friends' and skipped down the sidewalk, pulling them along.

"Aren't you tired from working?" Yetta asked, one sunny Saturday afternoon.

"Yes," Bella said. "Too tired to walk like this." For the next few steps she imitated Yetta's walk: trudging along with her head down, sliding her feet against the pavement as if they were much too heavy to lift.

Jane laughed.

"That's a science experiment I should have Millicent and Harriet do," she said. "Which takes more energy, trudging or skipping? At the very least, it might wear Harriet out before she completely exhausts me!"

Jane had been working as the Blanck girls' governess for a month now. Early on, she'd worked out an arrangement with Mr. Blanck's chauffeur: Each morning, Jane walked to the Triangle factory with Yetta and Bella, and then the chauffeur, who'd just dropped off Mr. Blanck, would take her back to the Blancks' house. They reversed the process each evening when they could. If Mr. Blanck needed the chauffeur for some other purpose, Jane took a trolley.

Bella loved having Jane walk along with them. She loved hearing Jane's stories of Millicent and Harriet and their lives: their trips to Macy's, their trips to Florida, their picnics and museum outings and walks in the park.

"You said Mrs. Blanck wanted you to take Millicent and Harriet shopping today," Bella prompted now. "Did Millicent get the pink gloves she wanted? Were they as soft as a feather, like the advertisement said?"

Yetta jerked her arm away and stopped on the sidewalk.

"How can you?" Yetta fumed. "How can you want to hear about Millicent buying her thirteenth pair of gloves at Macy's when her father cheats you out of being able to afford any? There's a direct connection—our underpaid labor paid for those gloves!"

"Well, if I paid for those gloves, shouldn't I want to know what they look like?" Bella joked, trying to jolly Yetta into a better mood. Yetta only glowered more. Bella tugged on her arm, pulling her forward again.

"You have to understand," Bella continued, speaking seriously now. "I am so much richer in America than I ever was in Italy. I have food now. Why should I worry about not having gloves?"

"Don't you want more out of life than potatoes and bread?" Yetta asked.

Bella considered this. Jane was waiting for her answer too.

"I want to see my family again, but no amount of money could bring them back to life," Bella said slowly. "I want Pietro to come back from South Carolina and marry me and whisk me off to the castle that he deserves because he's as handsome as a prince—" This drew a reluctant giggle from Yetta and an outright chuckle from Jane.

"But that's not going to happen," Bella admitted. "I didn't ever really know Pietro, so it's more like he's just a dream to me. A fantasy."

"Besides, if he came back and asked for your hand in marriage, Rocco Luciano would challenge him to a duel," Jane teased. "He'd scream in his pipsqueak voice, 'Unhand the lady! Bella Rossetti is the love of *my* life!'"

"Oh, please," Bella protested. "Rocco Luciano is a little boy." But she blushed. She did look forward to seeing Rocco every Sunday when he came with his penny or two to pay off his family's debt. He'd even showed her the calculations he'd made, that he'd have the whole debt paid off in twenty years.

"What else do you want?" Yetta asked quietly.

Bella looked around to make sure no one else on the sidewalk was listening to their conversation.

"I—I want to know how to read," she said. "If I'd been able to read the letter from back home, the one about my family . . . It wouldn't have changed what it said, but I wouldn't have felt so helpless, so stupid. Back in Calia, it didn't matter. I didn't know five people who could read. But here—I can't read that street sign." She pointed high over her head, to a green sign filled with squirmy letters. "I can't read the advertisements. At the factory, I can't read the signs on the walls. There could be a sign saying 'All Italian girls get a five-dollar raise' and I wouldn't even know it. Signor Carlotti could go on cheating me forever!"

"I'd tell you about that sign," Yetta said. "But then I'd complain because the Jewish girls weren't getting the five dollars too!"

"I can teach you how to read," Jane said, squeezing her arm. "I didn't know you wanted that."

"I'd help too," Yetta said. "But I'm not very good at reading much besides Yiddish."

"Then I'll teach you both to read English," Jane said quickly.

Bella made a face. "Here you are, wanting to go to college," she said. "And I'd just be learning my ABC's, like Harriet Blanck."

"At least you know there are ABC's," Jane said comfortingly. "So you've made a start."

Bella was glad that her friends hadn't made fun of her. She was surprised when Yetta stepped forward and linked arms with Jane as well as Bella, so they made a closed circle on the sidewalk.

"We should make a pact," Yetta said. "I haven't been back to English class since the strike. But we should all keep learning things—Jane, at her college level, and Bella and me at our beginner level—"

"Oh, you're so far ahead of me!" Bella protested.

Yetta shrugged that off.

"And I will try not to be so grumpy all the time, because if I'm learning I will feel like I'm getting *somewhere*," Yetta continued.

"Hear, hear to that!" Jane cheered.

"So we will not be stupid girls," Bella said.

"And we will not be useless girls," Jane added.

"And we will not be powerless girls," Yetta finished.

Somehow it had become a serious vow they were making, standing there in the middle of the sidewalk with the crowds streaming around them. They kept their arms linked, a protection against the rest of the world.

"And someday we will vote, just like men," Jane said.

"And we will stay not stupid and not useless and not powerless—and, and we will stay friends!—even after I marry Pietro and Yetta marries that cutter who's always hanging around her machine—" Bella began.

"What? I would never marry Jacob!"

Bella ignored Yetta's protests.

"And after Jane elopes with Mr. Blanck's chauffeur!" Bella finished.

Jane went pale at those words. Too late, Bella remembered that Jane really was a rich girl who still probably expected to marry a millionaire, not an immigrant chauffeur.

"I'm sorry!" she gasped. "You won't marry a servant! You'll marry . . ." Bella hesitated. Then she thought of something Yetta had told her. "You'll marry one of those New York University law students next door to the factory!"

"That's okay," Jane said, shrugging. "Who knows whom I will marry? Or if I ever will? It's just—have you ever *seen* Mr. Blanck's chauffeur? He's fifty years old and bald as a post. He's as old as my father!" She winced, as if even mentioning her father was painful.

Bella wanted to recapture the feeling of unity they'd had, just a moment ago.

"In my village," she said, "on midsummer's night, June twenty-third, men can pledge to become *compari di San Giovanni*, friends that can be even closer than family. We are not men, and it is not June, but—I think that is what we just did."

The other two nodded solemnly.

"We're—wait, don't tell me—because we're females, it'd be . . . *comari*. *Comari di* 'triangle,' Jane said.

"Triangle? But only two of us work there," Bella protested.

"No, no, not Triangle like the factory. Triangle like the shape," Jane said. "With three sides? What we are making, standing here now?"

Bella had thought they were in a circle, but suddenly she understood.

"You mean, like on the sign for the factory? That shape? The name means something? It's not just a word?" She began to laugh at herself. "I can't believe that I've been working there for more than a year and I didn't even know that! I will be a very hard student to teach!"

"No, don't worry—you've learned it now. Your first lesson!" Jane grinned. "There's something in geometry about a triangle being the strongest shape. And that's us. The three of us are a much better triangle than the factory!"

Comari di triangle, Bella thought. They were only words, but they warmed her heart. As she and Yetta and Jane turned and continued walking home, she felt almost as though she'd gotten one of her wishes. Her family had not come back to life, but it was like she had a family again. She had Yetta and Jane. Her *comari*.

Yetta

It happened again: The cutter's assistant, Jacob, was standing behind Yetta when she scraped her chair back at the end of the day.

"Do you like to dance?" he asked.

"Do I look like the kind of girl who has time to dance?" Yetta snapped back, unfolding herself from the chair. She crossed her arms self-consciously, covering the worn spots on her skirt. Then she changed her mind and put her hands on her hips, her fingers all but pointing to the threadbare places. "Do I look like I have the money for the kind of dresses girls need for dancing? I send all my money back to my family in Russia. Anyhow, I'm busy taking English lessons at night."

"I take English lessons too," Jacob said.

"You do?"

"Yes, but mine don't meet on Saturday nights. I thought . . . maybe you would go dancing with me then."

Yetta looked across the factory floor to the row of windows that lined the walls, facing Greene Street. The windows were open, letting in a gentle April breeze. Even in New York City, April smelled of flowers budding and leaves unfurling and green things springing back to life. The breeze had been teasing Yetta all day, calling her away from her machine, calling her to something that she desperately longed for but couldn't have defined or described.

Maybe it *was* dancing.

"We could practice our English together," Jacob said.

Yetta jerked her attention back to Jacob, just another arrogant cutter even if he did have those maddeningly handsome curls and honey-colored eyes. The thought of practicing English while dancing made Yetta think of Rahel helping her husband in his store. It made her think of their mother selling eggs and cheese to supply their father's religious texts, but never buying anything for herself.

It made her think that Jacob wanted to dance with her for all the wrong reasons.

"No, thank you," Yetta said, with great dignity. She held her head high as she walked past him. She deliberately went to the Washington Place door, the nearest one, forgetting that it was locked. *Something else the strike should have changed,* she thought. She had to thread her way back through the maze of tables and baskets and stacked shirtwaist parts, and then wait in line for the elevator. Although she was very careful not to watch—or, not to watch in a way that anyone could tell—she was aware of how Jacob walked back to his table, how he scraped scraps of fabric into the huge bin underneath, how he kicked the bin and slapped his hand against the table.

What is wrong with me? Yetta wondered. *Would it have killed me to say yes?*

When she got down to Greene Street, Bella and Jane were waiting for her, giggling.

"We're picking out a law student for Jane to marry some-day," Bella said, laughing. "How about that one?"

The boy she pointed to had chestnut hair—Yetta thought he might be the same one who'd asked her about the strike, way back in October.

"Better that you should be picking out law students to help us with the union," Yetta snapped.

The chestnut-haired boy was brushing past her.

"Excuse me, sir," she said boldly, tugging on his sleeve. "Are you a law student?"

"Uh, y-yes," he said, startled. This was not the same student Yetta had talked to before. This one didn't seem nearly so sure of himself, and he was walking alone, not with a pack of friends. He looked from Yetta to Bella to Jane, and back to Yetta. "Charles Livingston, at your service."

"Charmed, I'm sure," Jane said, automatically, as if that response was required.

"I'm Yetta, and this is Bella and Jane," Yetta said. "Are you aware that there is a great injustice going on right next door to your law school? At the Triangle Shirtwaist Factory, the owners agreed to certain conditions at the end of our strike, and I believe every single one of those conditions has now been violated. It's as if the strike never happened. Aren't there any laws to help us?"

"I—I don't know," Charles said. "I'm just a first-year. I'd have to ask my professors." He hesitated. "I do know, when your strike was going on, they said American laws were designed to protect business owners, not workers." He recited the last part as though from memory. "They asked us if we thought that was fair."

"And do you?" Yetta asked.

Charles shrugged.

"What do I know? I'm only a first-year. I'm only eighteen years old."

"I'm only sixteen," Yetta said, "and *I* know. I know because I've lived it. It's *not* fair. It's not right."

"Well, then you could vote—oops, sorry. Forgot I was talking to a girl. You could tell your husband or boyfriend to vote—"

"Forget it!" Yetta said, stalking away.

Bella and Jane caught up with her a few moments later.

"I can't believe you did that!" Bella said, giggling. "Just going up to a man like that, a total stranger, and talking to him—"

"Talking? That was haranguing! That was lecturing! That was incredible!" Jane snorted. "Though I must say, you probably just ruined my chances of ever marrying *that* law student!"

Yetta whirled on her friends.

"Why would you want to marry somebody who doesn't even know what he thinks about injustice?" she asked.

"I suppose he'd be awfully malleable," Jane said thoughtfully. "You could just convince him to think the way you do. You probably could tell him how to vote."

"But what if I want to vote all by myself? Cast my own ballot?" Yetta asked. "Stand on my own two feet? It's like . . . dancing. Why does the man always get to lead?" She stamped her feet, because that wasn't what she was trying to say. "Why is the whole world stacked in favor of rich Christian men when God made me a poor Jewish girl?"

"Maybe God thinks you're up to the challenge," Jane said quietly.

"Mr. Harris and Mr. Blanck are Jewish too," Bella pointed out. "So that's not—ooh, wait. Dancing. Don't tell me . . . that cutter actually asked you to a dance, didn't he? You're going, aren't you? You can borrow a hat from Sadie across the hall, and—"

"Never mind!" Yetta said, stomping away from them.

"I thought you promised not to be grumpy anymore!" Jane called after her.

Yetta pretended not to notice.

Fueled by indignation, she got back to the tenement building far ahead of Bella and Jane. The sidewalks were crowded, as usual, so Yetta was practically inside the front door before she noticed the woman standing nearby.

"Yetta!" a familiar voice called out.

It was Rahel, leaning against the railing. She reached out and gathered Yetta into her arms. Yetta almost gave in, almost let herself relax into her older sister's hug. Rahel had gained weight as a grocer's wife; she was very solid now. It would be such a relief for Yetta to spill everything to Rahel, to tell her about Jacob inviting her to dance and about feeling confused and about the way the April breeze seemed so determined to lure her away from her machine. Maybe Rahel would even quote something their mother used to say: *Men ken nisht tantsn af tsvey khasenes af eyn mol.* You cannot dance at two weddings at the same time. Meaning, maybe Yetta was right to turn Jacob down. He was a distraction. Except, that saying was about weddings, and weddings were a sore subject between Yetta and Rahel. Yetta had barely danced at all at Rahel's wedding. She'd mostly sat there, in stony silence.

Now Yetta held herself stiff and pulled away.

"It's been so long since you came to the store," Rahel complained.

"There's another store, closer," Yetta said, deliberately misunderstanding. She knew Rahel wasn't just trying to drum up business. "You remember what it's like. When you work all day at the sewing machine, you don't want to walk an extra block or two to get groceries."

Rahel frowned and tilted her head to the side, regarding her sister sadly.

"Let's go sit on the fire escape," she said. "Just you and me. I've got something to tell you."

Did you hear me invite you in? Yetta wanted to say, but that would have been too rude. Rahel led the way up the stairs and through the apartment. She pulled a mattress out onto the fire escape to sit on, and soon they were both outside again, three stories above the street, their backs propped against the wall, the breeze teasing at their hair.

Rahel turned to Yetta, her eyes gleaming, and said, "I'm going to have a baby. *We're* going to have a baby. Samuel and me. You're going to be an aunt."

Of course. That was how these things happened. First the wedding, then a baby. Still, Yetta felt like she'd had the wind knocked out of her. A baby. Another way for Rahel to be different from Yetta.

"*Mazel tov,*" Yetta said, weakly.

Rahel stared out over the street.

"Please tell me you're happy for me," she said quietly.

"Didn't I say *mazel tov*?" Yetta asked. "Didn't you hear me?"

"You didn't sound like you meant it."

Yetta shrugged.

"It's just . . . this happened fast, didn't it?" She picked at the threadbare patch on her skirt. "I thought you wanted to save money to bring our family over from Russia."

"The baby won't be here until January," Rahel said. "We're still saving money."

"But babies are expensive," Yetta said. "They need clothes and food, and more clothes because they grow so fast. . . . You'll have this whole new family and maybe you won't care anymore about Mother and Father." *Or me*, she wanted to say, but that would sound so childish and selfish.

"Yetta, I already have a whole new family, ever since I married Samuel," Rahel said. "That doesn't change anything about Mother and Father." She brushed hair back from her eyes and squinted out over the street, with its peddlers hawking wares and women buying food and children squeezing in one last moment of playtime before they went home to do their chores. One huge mass of living, breathing, teeming humanity. "I—I never told you," she said. "In the pogrom, in Bialystok . . . I saw people burned alive. I saw people lighting other people on fire. This one girl—she might have been you or me. One minute, she was just standing there, in the window of her house. The next minute, she was covered in flames. A human torch. Gone in a flash."

This was the wrong story for a lovely April afternoon when Yetta had been invited to dance. Yetta clenched her teeth together and squeezed her eyes shut, shutting out the street scenes and the fire escape and the sight of Rahel's intense eyes. But she could still feel Rahel gripping her hand. She could still hear Rahel's voice.

"After I saw that, I thought I would never have a normal life again," Rahel whispered. "I had nightmares. Remember when that tenement building burned in the next block? That brought all the nightmares back again. I never thought I could get married and have a baby and—and be happy . . ."

Yetta pulled her hand from Rahel's grasp. She opened her eyes again.

"How could you want to have a normal life in a world where people set other people on fire?" Yetta murmured. "In a world where policemen beat up shirtwaist girls? How can that not make you want to change the world?"

Rahel leaned her head close to Yetta's.

"What was I supposed to do?" she asked. "Complain to the Czar? Go to Washington and yell at President Taft? I'm a girl. Maybe having a baby is the best thing I can do. To bring some happiness into this sad world . . ."

Yetta jerked away from Rahel, because she didn't want Rahel to see that she was shaking. She slid back in through the window. The tenement seemed so dim after the fire escape. The door opened, Bella and Jane bursting into the kitchen and crying out, "Yetta? Where are you? Are you all right?"

"I'm in here," Yetta called, trying to hold her voice steady. "Rahel's going to have a baby."

And then Bella and Jane were clustering around, saying all the things Yetta should have said: "Such good news!"

"How wonderful!" Bella's eyes shone with joy and she hugged Rahel the way Yetta should have.

These are my friends, Yetta wanted to tell Rahel. *Closer than family. Can you give me credit for their congratulations, for their happiness on your behalf? Can you see that I wish I could react the way they do—so kindly, so unselfishly? It is just that I myself have too many wishes, all tangled together like long hair in a spring breeze . . .*

She saw the sorrow and regret in her sister's eyes. She saw it, and did nothing.

Yetta, Bella, and Jane had become very skilled at digging newspapers and magazines out of the trash, so they could bring them home for reading lessons. Jane always read them first, to see what would work best for Bella, who could now pick out small words like "cat" and "rat," or for Yetta, who could puzzle out how to pronounce just about any word but had no idea what sentences like "A commission has been formed to make a recommendation regarding these circumstances" could possibly mean.

Sometimes, if Jane found an interesting story, she'd read it out loud for all of them. They'd been captivated for several nights by a romance tale in a *Ladies' Home Journal,* only to discover that the last page was missing.

"That's it?" Jane cried, staring in dismay at the ragged edges of the torn-out page. "That's all we get?"

"Oh, you know what was going to happen," Bella said comfortingly. "Serena was going to marry Mr. Godfrey, and they were going to live happily ever after." Her eyes glowed in the lamplight. "I love stories like that, don't you?"

"Maybe Serena convinced Mr. Godfrey to use part of his fortune to set up a union shirtwaist shop," Yetta said. "And everyone bought his shirtwaists and all the evil shirtwaist factory owners who abused their workers went out of business and—"

Bella hit Yetta in the face with a pillow.

"Not now," she said. "I'm trying to imagine how they would have described the final kiss. Maybe, 'He turned his smoldering eyes to her and . . .'"

Yetta had pretended all along that she wasn't really *that* interested in the story, but she took the magazine from Jane and flipped through it, just to make sure that the missing page wasn't in there somewhere.

"Nobody's eyes smolder in real life," she complained.

"Yours do when you talk about the union," Jane pointed out.

"Really?" Yetta stood up and looked in their sliver of mirror, but it was too dark to see anything but shadows. She sat back down on the bed. "It doesn't do any good. Any time I bring up the union at work, the other girls say, 'Yes, and I've still got debts from the strike,' or 'What use is it?' And there are so many new girls straight off the boat who don't even know what a union is."

"That was us, not so long ago, and *we* went out on strike. *We* fought for the union," Bella said.

"We lost," Yetta said.

"Next time, you'll win," Jane said. "People are still recovering. These things take time."

But Yetta was already recovered. Her cough was gone. Her greatest affliction now was the restless longing that so often threatened to overwhelm her. Sometimes, sitting at her sewing machine, the feeling of wanting to hop a train west or stand up on a table or throw a sewing machine out the window came over her so strongly that she was afraid she'd actually do it. Any one of those things, or all three in succession, one after the other.

Bella gave her friend a hug, as if she could sense Yetta's distress. Jane turned her attention to a newspaper, one only slightly stained with pickle juice.

"Maybe I can find a good story in—oh, wait! Take a look at this!" She pointed to a small story at the bottom of a page. Yetta squinted at it in the dim light.

"S-suff-rage puh-rad-de," she began, sounding out the words.

"Very good. There's going to be a suffrage parade here in New York City, just like the ones they've had in London. . . . Oh, we should go! May twenty-first—that's Saturday!"

"Saturday," Bella said. "Work. Remember?"

"Oh, right," Jane said, collapsing the newspaper in her lap. "I forgot."

Yetta sprang up from the bed and paced in the narrow space between it and the chairs.

"No, no—we should be able to do this," she said. "It's the slow season, remember? Lots of times they send us home with no work, anyhow. So you just tell Mr. Carlotti and I'll tell Mr. Kline, we can only work a half day Saturday."

"They'll dock our pay," Bella said.

"They'll probably dock our pay anyway," Yetta said. "We haven't gotten full wages in weeks."

"They'll fire us."

Yetta stumbled a little in her pacing. She righted herself, planted her feet firmly.

"Then we'll get another job," she said. "Listen, it's not so much to ask, to go to a parade on a Saturday afternoon just once in our lives, to call out our support for suffrage. In Yiddish, there's a saying, *'Beser tsu shtarbn shteyendik vi tsu lebn af di kni.'* It means, uh, 'Better to die on one's feet than to live on one's knees.' I don't know about you, but I *can't* live on my knees, always hunkered down, always worried about everything. And that's why I'm going to that parade, whether anyone else goes or not."

She expected Bella and Jane to make some sort of joke to lighten the mood, to give themselves a way out—maybe something like, "You think we could die at this suffrage parade? Then, no thanks!"

But they both nodded solemnly.

"I'm going," Bella said.

Yetta turned to Jane. She shrugged.

"I don't always know when Mrs. Blanck wants me to take the girls, but—I'll do my best."

Saturday afternoon, sneaking out at lunchtime, Yetta and Bella felt like prison escapees. Mr. Kline and Mr. Carlotti had lectured them about taking their jobs seriously, about how many other girls would be happy for the work, about how they were lucky to have jobs at all, this time of year. But they never actually forbade them to go.

"We could do this anytime we wanted," Yetta said, as the elevator zoomed down to the ground.

Bella was counting her pay for the week. It didn't take her very long.

"Not if we want to keep eating," she said grimly.

But when they stepped out into the sunshine, she was grinning too. It was hard not to. Yetta felt so free and happy. Jane was waiting for them at the corner.

And beside her, dressed in as much lace and as many frills as a china doll, was a little girl.

"I had to bring Harriet," Jane said, frowning apologetically.

Bella instantly bent down to Harriet's level.

"Hello, Harriet. I'm Bella. How old are you?"

"I'm this many," Harriet said, holding up five fingers. She placed her other hand on her head. "And I'm this tall!"

While the little girl was distracted, Yetta leaned in close and whispered in Jane's ear, "Won't you get in trouble if Mrs. Blanck finds out where you're taking her?"

"Oh, no," Jane laughed. "Mrs. Blanck wants her daughters to be modern American girls. I've convinced her that suffrage is part of that. I just don't think she'll tell her husband."

"She should tell him to treat his workers better, too," Yetta said.

A shadow crossed Jane's face. Yetta wasn't sure if Jane was thinking about her own parents, how her own father had hired strikebreakers and said it didn't matter if her mother knew or not. Or if Jane was thinking about how it'd been impossible, even working in the Blancks' house, to find out any information about Triangle that would help the union. Jane's sleuthing efforts had completely failed.

"Mr. Blanck wouldn't listen to anything his wife said about his business," Jane said. "They're totally different worlds, his work and his home." She grimaced. "He's actually a really good father. A lot better than mine ever was."

Yetta didn't want to think about Mr. Blanck or Jane's father today. She was actually glad when Harriet piped up self-importantly, "Millicent got to go to a birthday party, but I get to go to a parade."

"That's right," Jane said, patting Harriet's shoulder. "But first, I need to introduce you to my other friend. Yetta, this is Harriet. Harriet, this is Yetta."

"I'm very pleased to meet you," Harriet said carefully, looking to Jane for approval.

"Uh, yeah. Me, too," Yetta said. Then, to prove that socialist, suffragist immigrants could also have manners, she added, "Jane's told us a lot about you."

"That's Mademoiselle Michaud to her," Jane corrected.

But Harriet was already clapping her hands, crying out, "Bella and Yetta and Jane! Bella and Yetta and Jane!"

Yetta leaned close again and whispered to Jane, "Will she do this all the way to Fifth Avenue?"

"We'll take the trolley," Jane whispered back, "so we get there faster."

Harriet was actually still chanting when they climbed down from the trolley, into the throngs of people milling around on the sidewalks of Fifth Avenue. But Yetta could easily tune out the little girl's singsong in all the noise of the crowd.

"Can you believe all these people want women to vote?" she marveled to Bella. "This is for us! They want us to have a voice!"

Policemen cleared the street, and then the parade began. Row after row of women dressed in white carried huge signs:

VOTES FOR WOMEN; NEW YORKERS FOR SUFFRAGE; POLITICS MAY BE DIRTY, BUT WOMEN ARE GOOD AT CLEANING UP AFTER MEN!

Between the rows of marchers, cars full of even more suffragists glided along, draped in yellow bunting and decorated with jonquils and daisies. The cars made Yetta think of the strikers' automobile parade, her own moment of glory.

"I was in a parade like this once," Yetta told Harriet, because Jane and Bella already knew. "I rode in one of the cars."

Harriet blinked up at her.

"You must be really 'portant," she said.

"When we can vote, we'll all be important," Jane said.

Across the street, a small group of men were jeering, "Go home and wash the dishes!" "Does your husband know where you are?" "I'd just as soon let my dog vote!" Yetta wanted to rush across the street and tell them off: Why don't you wash your own dishes? Does your wife know where you are? I bet your dog could vote better than you do!

Then she noticed that there was another group on the sidelines, a group of women, holding up signs that said, NO VOTES FOR WOMEN!; NO TO SUFFRAGE; KEEP THE FAIRER SEX ABOVE THE FRAY! She nudged Jane and muttered, "Do those signs say what I think they say?" She was hoping that her reading skills had just failed her. "Why would any woman *not* want to vote?"

Jane winced.

"There's a whole club, the New York Association Opposed to Woman Suffrage," she said. "I read about it in the newspaper. They say women voting would destroy family life, or just be unnecessary, because women would always vote exactly like their husbands or fathers. But really"—she was carefully not looking at Bella or Yetta or Harriet—"they don't want their servants to have a vote. They don't want female immigrants voting."

Yetta felt her face burning. She watched a woman passing through the crowd, handing out fliers that said SUFFRAGE NOW! in big print at the top. Yetta shoved her way through the crowd and grabbed the woman's wrist.

"How can I join your cause?" Yetta begged. "How can I help?"

The woman jerked back a little in surprise, but she spoke firmly as she moved on through the crowd.

"We meet the second and fourth Thursday afternoons of every month at—"

"I can't meet on a Thursday afternoon," Yetta said. "I work. I'm a shirtwaist girl."

The woman stopped.

"A shirtwaist girl? Were you in the strike?"

"Yes. Till the very end."

The woman was looking at her with respect now—respect and sympathy.

"Then—here. Help me pass out these flyers," the woman said, handing her a stack. "And next year—if we don't have the vote by then—next year, come back and we'll put you *in* the parade!"

Yetta gave out the flyers until they were all gone. Then she found her way back to her friends.

"When women have the vote, fathers will want to send their daughters to college, just like boys," Jane was saying as the last of the parade went by.

"And girls won't feel like they can't go into banks, like they have to hand over all their money to the men in their family," Bella said.

"And we'll vote to make work fair," Yetta added.

Jane glanced warningly down at Harriet, clearly trying to remind Yetta that she couldn't say too much in front of the little girl.

"What do you think will happen when women can vote?" Jane asked the girl, to distract her. Harriet tilted her head to the side, considering.

"I'll get a pony for my birthday," she said, as if "women getting to vote" was just another way of saying "wishing." "And the pony will have wings, and I'll ride that pony right up to the sun, and the sun will give me flowers. . . ."

"It's fun to daydream, isn't it?" Bella said, smiling.

But we're not just daydreaming, telling ourselves fairy tales, playing little-girl let's-pretend, Yetta reminded herself. *Please, God, let it someday be true! Someday we really will be able to vote. Someday Triangle will be a closed union shop. And someday I won't be so restless. Someday I'll be able to sit back and say, "Yes, everything worked out. . . ."* Hope surged in Yetta for all those somedays, which seemed so far off. At least she knew a date for one hope: Next year, she *would* march in the suffrage parade.

Jane

$\mathcal{J}$ane leaned against the side of the Asch Building waiting for Yetta and Bella to come out after work. It was November now: The summer had melted away in a blur of trips to the beach with Millicent and Harriet, reading lessons and hot nights lying on the tenement fire escape with Yetta and Bella, ice cream cones shared three ways because they only had enough money for one. Autumn blew in with a flurry of falling leaves, and Jane had begun playing a memory game with herself: A year ago at this time, I refused to get out of bed to go watch Wilbur Wright's aeroplane. *A year ago, I hadn't even met Yetta. A year ago, Eleanor Kensington asked me if I wanted to join the picket line with the strikers. . . .* She knew Yetta and Bella played a similar type of game, but Bella's anniversaries were about death and disappearance, and Yetta's only reminded her of disappointment.

"Y-you're Yetta's friend, aren't you?" someone stuttered nearby. Jane turned and recognized the chestnut hair: It was Charles Livingston, the law student Yetta had harassed back in the spring. "Tell Yetta I have an answer now."

"An answer?"

He nodded impatiently.

"She asked about whether the strikers had any legal recourse if the company violated the terms of the strike agreement."

Jane didn't remember Yetta asking the question in quite those words.

"And?" she prompted.

"It was just a verbal agreement, as far as I can tell. Nothing was put in writing. So—there's nothing the strikers can do. Except go out on strike again of course." He started to turn away again, such an odd boy. Then, as if remembering something else, he turned back. "But one of my professors did write to the city building department complaining about the safety conditions he'd seen at Triangle. So that's something at least."

Safety conditions? Jane couldn't imagine the city building department caring. In the tenements she'd seen rusty pipes hanging out from the wall, children falling from half-demolished buildings, peddlers who scooped out food with the same hand they coughed into. And of course, the dead horse in the street. By comparison, Triangle was a marvel, a modern factory—that was something Bella and Yetta bragged about.

"What took you so long to answer Yetta's question?" she asked Charles.

"Well, last year I was just a first-year, so I was too scared of my professors to ask anything. And then I went to Europe over the summer—London, Paris, Rome, all the usual places. And then when I got back, they gave us so much homework right away that I was barely keeping up. But I'm a second-year now, so I'm getting better at figuring out what I really need to know."

Jane barely listened after he said the word "Europe," because it made her remember the trip Eleanor Kensington had been planning. If Jane hadn't run away from home, maybe right now she, too, would be slipping mention of the Eiffel Tower or the Coliseum or the Elgin Marbles into casual conversation. For a moment she felt a pang, but then she noticed the reediness in Charles Livingston's voice.

Such a callow, inexperienced youth, she thought. *And last November I was even worse. . . .*

"Thank you for your help," Jane said. "Yetta will appreciate your efforts."

Though that probably wasn't true, Jane reflected. It was more likely that Yetta would storm and fret and fume that there must be something the Triangle workers could do. Maybe if they all wrote letters to the city . . . ?

Jane smiled with fondness for her fervent friend as Charles Livingston nodded and reluctantly moved away. She leaned back against the building and idly watched the traffic. A year ago, she would have been thinking, *Is that car grander than ours? Is that chauffeur's uniform smarter than Mr. Corrigan's? How about that lady's hat —oh, dear, is that the latest fashion? Something new that I didn't know about? I must get a hat like that!* Now she didn't care about cars or chauffeur's uniforms, and she was wearing a hat that she and her friends had put together from bits and scraps and other women's cast-offs.

One of the cars in the street slowed down and pulled up to the curb. The chauffeur stepped out, shielding his eyes against the sunset. His car was unfamiliar, his uniform was unfamiliar, but there was something about the way he stood . . . He turned, and Jane caught a glimpse of a bushy gray moustache.

It was Mr. Corrigan, her father's chauffeur.

Ever since she'd run away, ever since she'd taken the job as the Blancks' governess, Jane had feared that someone from her old life would spot her, report her, drag her back home. But even wealthy Jewish immigrants like the Blancks patronized few of the same stores and restaurants and ice cream parlors as Jane's former friends; they didn't go to any of the same resorts or tourist hotels or beaches. And Jane knew her old friends' routines. She didn't take Harriet and Millicent to Macy's in the mornings when her old friends did their shopping; she didn't go to Central Park in the afternoon when they might be out bicycling. She watched the newspapers and made sure she wasn't anywhere near the theater or the opera house when there were big performances. Even at the suffrage parade she'd kept an eye out, ready to duck behind a street light or a sign post if she saw Eleanor Kensington or any of that crowd.

She'd never thought to worry about being spotted near Triangle by her father's chauffeur.

Instantly she whipped around, hiding her face from the street. Had he seen her? She decided to slip inside the Triangle factory doors just in case, but the crowd was thick on the sidewalk around her. Maybe the other direction would work better. . . . She turned around, and came face to face with Mr. Corrigan.

"Miss Wellington," he whispered.

He put his hands on her shoulders, stopping just short of pulling her into a hug. He had tears in his eyes.

"Faith and begorra, miss! I've been looking for you for months!"

"Really?" Jane said. "My father told you to—"

She saw the truth in Mr. Corrigan's eyes: Her father had had nothing to do with it. Jane started to turn away, but Mr. Corrigan tightened his grip on her shoulders.

"Now, don't be like that! Don't get lost again!"

"I haven't been lost," Jane said coldly. "I know exactly where I am."

Mr. Corrigan didn't even flinch. Ever the obedient servant, he wouldn't have flinched if she'd slapped him.

"I know your father's worried about you, because he has bags under his eyes and he's grumpier than ever," he said apologetically. "But, see, he told everyone that you're off visiting your aunt in Chicago. So that when you came home, your reputation wouldn't be ruined, you know? But, having said that, he couldn't go around inquiring about where you were."

Jane saw how it was, the intricacy of the lies that her father and society would consider necessary. That would *be* necessary. A girl who ran away from home would be ruined no matter where she went or what she did; everyone would assume that she'd surrendered her virtue, whether she actually had or not. So Jane's father had chosen to protect her reputation above all else.

Oh, yes—better to protect my reputation than to protect me, she thought bitterly. *I was lying in the street on rotting horseflesh, set upon by pickpockets who might have killed me just for the ring on my finger! And my father wasn't even trying to find me!*

Jane remembered that she hadn't needed protection. She'd escaped from the pickpockets all by herself. With Bella and Yetta's help, she'd managed to live on her own for the past nine months. She tossed her head haughtily.

"I've been quite all right without my father's concern," she said.

Mr. Corrigan's eyes seemed to be taking in the cheap quality of her hat, the threadbare fingertips of her gloves. She wouldn't have suspected that he was a man who knew about fashion, but she wondered if he could see that the blue serge she was wearing again was last season's dress. She even wondered if he could tell that, like Yetta, she now had holes in the soles of her boots.

"I'm sure your father thought that you'd come back home quickly," Mr. Corrigan said. "That a day or two would have been enough to—"

"What? Break my spirit?" Jane asked.

"Bring you to your senses," Mr. Corrigan finished in an even tone. "And maybe he *did* hire detectives, privately, that I don't know about."

"Not very good ones, obviously," Jane sneered. Though, she reflected, who would have been able to predict that she'd go live in the slums? That she'd work as a servant for immigrants? That she'd be happy?

"Come home," Mr. Corrigan said. "I'm sure your father will find it in his heart to forgive you."

He bowed his head humbly, a servant presuming to speak for his master.

"Forgive me? Forgive *me*?" Jane felt a sudden surge of outrage, as powerful as the indignation that Yetta seemed to carry around all the time. "He's the one who should be begging my forgiveness, for using me and my well-being as an excuse for exploiting his workers, for hiring strikebreakers to beat up his own employees, for . . . for exploiting *you*, Mr.

Corrigan. Haven't you noticed that he's exploiting *you*? My father owes an apology to all of society, for what he is and what he does—"

"Now, listen here, young lady." Mr. Corrigan's eyes flashed. "I would give my eyeteeth to get my daughters even a fraction of the advantages that you've had. Just to let them go to one of those fancy balls . . . They could live on that the rest of their lives. Maybe I would have even sold my soul to the devil to have them trade places with you, had the devil given me the opportunity, God protect my poor, weak soul from such temptation." He crossed himself, as if he were afraid the devil was listening. "You don't know what it's like for your father, and you his only child . . ."

Jane broke her gaze away from Mr. Corrigan's and stared out into the street. She was beginning to feel just the slightest twinge of doubt. What if her father weren't quite as bad as she thought? What if she were wrong?

Her eyes fell on the shiny car Mr. Corrigan had left parked by the curb.

"My father couldn't be too heartbroken if he had time to go out and buy a new car," Jane said, "and to outfit you in a new uniform . . . I'll warrant, he hasn't missed a single party since I've been gone, hasn't turned down a single social engagement!"

"He had to keep up appearances," Mr. Corrigan said, but it was like he was begging again, like Jane had the upper hand despite her ragged clothes.

"You know how it is to be a father," Jane said. "I'll tell you how it is to be a girl. I'm a servant now—me! A servant! All day long, I'm subject to the whims of a five-year-old and a twelve-year-old and a woman who can barely speak English. I look at a bun in a bakery window and I think, 'Can I afford to buy that? What else would I have to give up if I buy that bun?' But it's my decision whether I buy that bun or a piece of lace for my dress or a book that I can stay up all night to read, if I want to. It's my own money, and I'm beholden to nobody! I'm freer now than I was when I was going to all those fancy parties, and Miss Milhouse was telling me what to wear and how to do my hair and whom to be nice to and how to act and how to think—"

"Your father fired Miss Milhouse," Mr. Corrigan said.

Jane felt a spurt of spiteful glee—*At least I accomplished something by running away!* But that was followed quickly by something like sympathy. It mattered so much to Miss Milhouse to serve a prominent family; she'd always managed to imply that the Wellingtons weren't quite up to her standards. Now, cast out like this, she'd be forced several rungs down on the social ladder. She had no family—maybe she was even destitute now.

"She'd been pining after your father for years," Mr. Corrigan said quietly. "Though she knew he'd never actually marry someone in her position. And she found out that when your father was away last winter there was another woman. He proposed and . . . the woman turned him down. So they were both so unhappy last winter, neither of them could deal with you. . . ."

Jane took a step back. She didn't want to know any of this about the adults who'd ruled her life, that beneath their veneer of propriety they might have been concealing a turmoil of emotions too. Miss Milhouse—in love? Her father—spurned and rejected and lovelorn? It was too much to comprehend.

"No matter what you tell me, I'm not coming home," she said firmly.

"Can I at least tell your father that you're safe?" Mr. Corrigan said. "That I found you and you're still alive and healthy and as stubborn as ever?"

Jane considered this. She considered what a gift he was giving her, that he hadn't grabbed her and thrown her in the car and forced her to go home. That he was offering her a choice.

"No," she said. "He'd make you tell him where I am—where I'm living, where I'm working."

"I don't know any of that," Mr. Corrigan said. "I just saw you when I happened to be driving by, on a whim, just because you used to come down here during the strike."

Jane saw that Mr. Corrigan was as skilled as anyone at constructing intricate lies. Maybe she'd underestimated him all along.

"You've driven past here before, haven't you?" she asked.

"Many times," he said. "Whenever I could without arousing suspicion. It was the only clue I had. Because the Kensingtons' chauffeur told me where he dropped you off."

Tears stung at Jane's eyes, unexpectedly. Who would have guessed that the chauffeur would show more concern for her than her own father?

"I'll write my father a letter," she decided. "So it won't make any problems for you. And I'll post it from a mailbox he could never trace."

Already, she was having fun imagining which postal box she would choose. She should have written a letter months ago. She should have thought of it on her own.

"Miss Jane," Mr. Corrigan said. "Winter's coming. Maybe . . . maybe you think it's a lark being poor when it's warm out. But when it's cold . . . poor people freeze. They die. They die of influenza, of consumption, of fevers that no one even bothers to name."

"You don't have to worry about me," Jane said, prickly again. "I'll be fine."

"Let me bring you your winter clothes from last year," Mr. Corrigan said. "They're just sitting in your room; nobody's touched them. There's a maid who would help me smuggle them out—nobody would ever know."

So he had noticed the sad shape of her clothing. The Jane who'd stalked out of her father's house nine months ago would have sniffed and sneered and lectured him about tainted money and tainted clothes. But she was wearing the serge dress her father's money had purchased. Now it was something more like pride that prompted her to shake her head no.

"If nobody would know," she said slowly, "take the clothes for your daughters. Give them just that fraction of the advantages that I've had. You wouldn't have to trade your eyeteeth—or your soul."

"Oh, Miss Wellington, I couldn't do that," Mr. Corrigan said. "That'd be stealing."

It was amazing, Jane thought, the way rules tied people in knots. How people trying to do something right could end up causing harm. As if there weren't already enough harm done in the world by people who didn't care. And by people who wanted to do evil.

Impulsively, she threw her arms around Mr. Corrigan's shoulders, hugging him as she'd once tried to hug her own father, as she'd never been able to hug her mother. There were rules against such things, rules prohibiting a rich girl from hugging a servant, rules prohibiting a governess from hugging a chauffeur. But suddenly she didn't care.

Mr. Corrigan hugged her back.

"Come back and find me again sometime," Jane whispered. "Maybe sometime in the spring. I'll be fine, you'll see. Come back and tell me about your daughters. . . ." She would have said "and my father, too," but her throat had closed up.

"Aye, I will," Mr. Corrigan whispered back. "That I will."

Bella

It was another long winter. One night, after slogging through icy slush all the way home, after peeling off wet boots and trying to warm numb fingers over a stove that seemed incapable of putting out any heat, Bella mumbled, "It's worse this year, isn't it?"

"What is?" Jane said, replacing the blanket they always stuffed under the door now, to cut down on drafts.

"The cold," Bella said. "It doesn't make sense. Last year, there was more snow, and we were outside picketing. This year, I'm inside the factory all day, but my fingers seem stiffer, my feet ache more, I can't stop shivering. . . ."

"It's because last year we had hope," Yetta said. "Because of the strike. What's there to hope for now?"

"Spring," Bella said. "Rahel's baby to come. You to save enough money to bring your family over from Russia. Jane to save enough money for college. Pietro to come back. Rocco to finally finish paying off his debt. Jacob to try again to ask you out dancing. The union to be strong again . . ."

"Oh, Bella, those things are all so far off," Yetta said. "Or impossible. Or things I don't even care about." She slammed a pot down onto the stovetop. "Don't you ever want to have everything right now? Not to spend your whole life wishing for someday?"

Bella looked from Yetta to Jane, really peering at them, as if she wanted to memorize every detail: Jane's pale porcelain skin, Yetta's wind-chapped cheeks, their wind-whipped hair, their eyes rimmed with red from the icy, sooty air of winter. Her dear, dear friends, so cold and beaten down.

"You're right," she said. She backed away from the stove. She'd hadn't bothered removing her coat when she'd come in, so she didn't have to put it back on now. She did have to shove her feet back into her wet shoes. "I'm just—I'll be right back."

The wintry blast almost knocked her over as she struggled out the front door. She lifted the collar of her coat against the wind, thinking, *Isn't that something we can be grateful for now, Yetta—that this winter we actually have coats?* But coats were like food, a basic need. *Don't you want more out of life than potatoes and bread?* Yetta had asked her, all those months ago. And Bella did. The longer she was in America, the more Bella longed for.

She passed peddlers hunched against the wind, selling hot chestnuts and hot rolls straight from the bakery and hot potatoes wrapped and kept warm in ashes. The smells swirled around her and her stomach growled, but she kept walking. She needed to go where the rich people shopped, so she slipped onto a trolley. She felt so extravagant placing her nickel into the slot—extravagant and scared, because she wasn't used to getting around in the city by herself. Before, she'd always had Yetta and Jane, and before that, Signor Luciano or Nico or Pietro. But she sat up straight in her seat, and fixed the people around her with a determined stare, and nobody bothered her.

She waited until the conductor called out "Fifth Avenue," and then she stepped back down to the frozen street. She was glad she hadn't had to rely on reading signs—she was getting better at puzzling out letters and words, but she still had a long, long way to go. Now she ignored the signs and just looked in shop windows until she came to one displaying a huge bouquet of daisies and carnations and all sorts of other glorious blooms that had no right to exist in the wintertime. Bella wasn't used to shopping in stores, only at peddlers' carts. But she boldly pushed her way through the door.

"Yes?" the woman behind the counter asked, raising her eyebrows disdainfully.

"Roses," Bella said. "Do you have any roses?"

The woman pointed, as if words would be wasted on someone as poor as Bella.

There was only one rose left, in a vase off to the side that had obviously contained many more roses earlier in the day. The rose leaned out from the vase a little sadly, its petals just beginning to droop.

Bella caught her breath.

"How much?" she said.

"Fifty cents," the woman said.

That was a fortune, worth hours of work to Bella, earned from dozens and dozens of shirtwaists shoved through her machine. It was too much, but Bella wasn't ready to give up yet.

"That rose will be dead tomorrow," she said. "It's almost closing time. Nobody else will buy that—you'll just throw it out in the trash."

The woman gasped, offended.

"So you think I should give it to you, just like that? This isn't a *charity*! We're a fine establishment, not meant for riffraff like you." She gave a short, cruel laugh. "If you want the rose so much, come back tomorrow and get it out of the trash!"

Bella kept her head held high, though her cheeks burned.

"Ten cents," she said. She had to concentrate very hard to come up with understandable English. "I buy it for ten cents."

Another woman came out from the back of the store, an older lady with a willowy frame and elegant gray hair. The store clerk complained to the older lady, "Can you believe someone like *that* has come into our store? And she's trying to *barter* for our flowers! Shall I call the police?"

The gray-haired lady looked at Bella. Bella stood frozen, poised to run if the clerk picked up the phone to call the police.

"Sell her the rose," the gray-haired lady said. "Five cents."

Bella couldn't believe her good fortune. She would have been content to plunk her nickel down on the counter, grab the rose, and run away. But the gray-haired lady insisted on wetting a cloth and gently wrapping it around the stem, instructing Bella, "Now, place this in water as soon as you get home. . . ."

Bella nodded dumbly, her English abandoning her entirely.

Bella sheltered the rose inside her coat all the way down the street, on the trolley, back to her tenement. When she reached the apartment, Yetta and Jane sprang at her, crying out, "Where have you been!" and "We were so worried!" Bella fended them off.

"Just wait to see," she said, opening her coat slowly, drawing out the rose.

Yetta and Jane fell silent.

Bella placed the rose in the same glass they'd once used for storing the artificial roses from Rahel's destroyed hat. The other two clustered around, as awed and respectful as if she were lighting a candle in church. For a moment, all three of them just stared at the flower, admiring its deep, dusky red petals, the graceful arc of the leaves. Then Yetta broke the silence.

"You went out in a snowstorm to buy a flower?" she asked. "You spent money on a rose?"

"You wanted something to happen *now*," Bella said. "And you"—she turned toward Jane— "you wanted real flowers, not fake. So I . . ." She gestured at the rose, as if its beauty could speak for itself.

"Well, thank you, but—" Jane cleared her throat. "I can live without fresh flowers in December. I've discovered there are lots of things I can live without. You should have kept your money for yourself. Do you want me to pay you back—?"

"And me?" Yetta offered.

"No, no," Bella said. She wanted her friends to understand. "Yetta, you are saving for your family and, Jane, you are saving for college and Europe, and me, there is nothing for me to save for. So I can pay for our 'nows,' because we are not so poor that we cannot have anything. I cannot buy roses every night, but, sometimes. Roses and maybe tickets to the nickelodeon and maybe, next summer, that Coney Island place I keep hearing about . . ."

It was like she'd conjured up a spell in the icy room, like

the rose was a magic wand. Both her friends had dazed, slightly dreamy expressions on their faces. Even Yetta was speechless for once.

"So, tonight we are *comari di* Triangle *e rosa!*" Bella finished.

For the rest of the evening, they gathered around the rose as if it were a roaring fire. They stared at the rose while they ate their potatoes and pickled herring; while Jane read to them from the newspaper they'd found frozen onto the sidewalk and carefully thawed out over the stove; while Bella told the story, again and again, of going in search of the rose and standing up to the surly sales clerk. In her retelling, the clerk practically grew fangs and horns, the gray-haired lady all but swooped in with wings and a halo. And her friends laughed and laughed and laughed and told her again and again how brave she'd been.

In the morning, the rose was frozen, its stem caught in ice. Bella spread the petals across the kitchen table to dry out, and all three of them tucked petals into their pillowcases. Just that one rose carried them the rest of the way through the winter.

It made everything else they hoped for seem so much closer.

Yetta

Yetta was listening for the bell on the time clock, waiting to finish her day. It was a Saturday afternoon in March, and the spring breezes were back. She'd heard them rattling the windows when the machines were shut down for lunch; she knew that as soon as she stepped outside, they'd tease at her hair and tug at her hat. This year, the breezes seemed to carry a slightly different message: *Another year past and what do you have to show for yourself? So you can read English a little bit better, so you handed out a few suffrage fliers—do you think that that's enough?*

What would ever be enough for Yetta?

"I think they set the clocks back again," the girl beside her muttered. "It's got to be past quitting time!"

"And that's why we need a strong union, why we need a closed shop," Yetta muttered back.

The girl rolled her eyes at Yetta.

"Don't you ever give up?" she asked over the clatter of the machine.

"No," Yetta said, but she grinned at the girl, and the girl grinned back, and Yetta thought maybe, just maybe, they'd inched just a little closer to the solidarity Yetta longed for. This girl's name was Jennie, and she was new.

The bell finally rang, and Yetta and Jennie both stood up and stretched, reviving cramped muscles, unhunching rounded shoulders, stamping feet that had gone numb on the sewing machine pedal.

"I'm going dancing tonight," Jennie said, mischievously tapping out a rhythm on the floor. "What are you doing?"

"Um . . . I don't know," Yetta said. "I haven't decided yet."

Bella and Jane had been nagging her to go visit Rahel and the new baby, a little boy they'd named Benjamin. Bella and Jane had already gone once, but Yetta had had a cold then and only sent her regrets.

Well, really, I wouldn't want the baby getting sick because of me, Yetta told herself. *Maybe I'm not well enough, even yet. . . .*

"I bet that cutter who watches you all the time would take you dancing," Jennie said. "All you have to do is just . . ." She pantomimed cozying up to an invisible man, gazing up adoringly at the invisible man's face, fluttering her eyelashes.

Yetta blushed.

"There's not a cutter who watches me all the time," she said, but she couldn't help glancing toward Jacob's table. Jacob hadn't said a word to her about dancing since she'd turned down his invitation, all those months ago. But he did seem to find lots of reasons to walk past her sewing machine, to ride in the same elevator with her, morning and evening. Even halfway across the room, she could instantly pick out his figure in the cluster of cutters standing around laughing and talking and smoking. Jacob was bent over the table, smoothing out the layers of lawn fabric ready to be cut first thing Monday morning. There had to be at least a hundred and twenty layers of the gauzy fabric spread across the table, each one separated from the others by sheer tissue paper. Jacob handled it all so gently, almost lovingly. Above his head, the tissue-paper patterns dangled from wires, so when he stood up it was like watching someone across a forest, half hidden by hanging moss and low branches.

Suddenly Jacob and the other cutters jumped back. One of the men sprinted over to a shelf on the wall and seized a red fire pail. Jerkily, he raced back and threw the pail of water under one of the tables, at the huge bin of fabric scraps left over from days and days of cutting out shirtwaists.

"Not again! Those cutters and their cigarettes," Yetta said scornfully. It was clear what had happened: One of them had dropped a match or a cigarette butt or a still-burning ember into the scrap bin. At least someone was smart enough to keep buckets of water around, if the cutters couldn't be stopped from smoking.

But then there was a flash, and Yetta saw the flame jump, from under the table to the top of it. More men grabbed buckets, desperately pouring water onto the flames, but there'd been only three buckets on that shelf, so they had to run across the room for more.

The water was nothing to the fire. The flames raced the length of the lawn fabric; they sprang up to the dangling paper patterns and danced from one to the next, the patterns writhing down to ash and spitting off more flames. In seconds the fire had gone from being something to scoff at under a table to a voracious beast ready to engulf the entire room.

Beside Yetta, Jennie began to scream.

"Stop it! This is a fireproof building!" Yetta yelled at Jennie. *But we're tinder*, she remembered.

Yetta slammed her hands against Jennie's shoulders and screamed, "Go!"

The aisle between the sewing machine tables was narrow, and the wicker baskets where they stacked the shirtwaists kept snagging their skirts. And other girls were blocking the aisle, some screaming and hysterical like Jennie'd been. One girl fainted right at Yetta's feet. Yetta reached down and slapped her, jerked her up.

"No time for that!" Yetta screamed. "You'll die!"

Across the room, Yetta saw a spark land in a woman's hair. In seconds, the woman's whole pompadour was aflame. Everyone was screaming, but Yetta thought she could hear this woman's screams above all the others. The woman lurched across the room, slammed into one of the windows. No—slammed through. She'd thrown herself out the window.

We're on the eighth floor, Yetta thought numbly, and now it was her turn to freeze in panic and fear. Sparks were flying throughout the room now, landing everywhere. Anyone could be next.

Hands grabbed Yetta from behind.

"Yetta, come on!"

It was Jacob.

Jacob and Yetta shoved forward, toward the Washington Place stairs, pulling along Jennie and the girl who'd fainted. Yetta glanced back once more and was relieved to see that Mr. Bernstein, the factory manager, had had some of the men pull a fire hose out of the Greene Street stairwell. He stood over the worst of the flames, pointing the hose confidently.

No water came out.

"Turn it on! Turn it on!" Mr. Bernstein was screaming. Yetta wasn't sure if she could hear him or if she was just reading his lips. "Where is the water?" he screamed again.

Not a drop. He flung down the hose and ran.

Now Mr. Bernstein was rushing through the crowds of girls, some still heading toward the cloakroom to get their hats.

"Don't worry about your hats!" he screamed. "Just get out!"

He was slapping and punching the girls, beating them as though he blamed them for the fire. No—he was goading them toward the doors, toward the elevators and the fire escape. He was only slapping the hysterical girls, like Yetta had done with the girl who'd fainted. He was trying to save their lives.

We are on the same side now, Mr. Bernstein and me, Yetta marveled.

She shoved against a girl who'd dropped her purse, who'd seen her coins roll under the table.

"Don't stop for that!" Yetta screamed. "It's not worth it! Save your life!"

She and Jacob together pulled the girl up, lifting her past the table, toward the door. There were already dozens of other girls crowded around the door, screaming in Yiddish and English and what Yetta now recognized as Italian. "Open it! Open it!" "Oh, please, for the love of God!" *"Madonna mia, aiutami!"*

But it was locked.

Some of the girls were pounding on the elevator door, too, screaming for the elevator operator to come to them. Miraculously, the elevator door opened, and the crowd surged forward, sobbing and praying and screaming.

"Just wait—just wait—I'll come right back!" the operator hollered.

The doors were closing, but Yetta shoved Jennie forward, shoving her on top of the girls already in the elevator. Saving her, at least.

"*Will* he come back?" Yetta asked Jacob, and Jacob shrugged.

Yetta couldn't just stand there and wait. She wasn't going to stand still while the flames raced toward her, while others pressed their faces against a door that might never open. She grabbed Jacob's hand and pulled him along, circling around the fire. She looked back once and saw that someone had managed to open the door to the Washington Place stairs; the door opened in, toward the crowd. Maybe it hadn't been locked after all. Maybe it was just the weight of the crowd pushing forward, pinning it shut.

But it was too late to go back now. Flames were shooting across the path they'd just crossed, speeding across the oiled floor, licking up shirtwaists and fabric scraps and wicker baskets. The air itself seemed to be on fire, the flames living on fabric dust.

"Fire escape," Yetta moaned to Jacob, and it was so hot now that her words felt like flames themselves, painful on her tongue.

"No good," Jacob mumbled back. "Doesn't go all the way to the ground."

So they didn't head for the window near the airshaft, where people were climbing out one at a time, onto the rickety metal railing. What was left?

"Greene Street stairs," Jacob whispered.

Those were back by the table where the fire had started, where it now burned the fiercest. But there was a partition wall blocking off the stairs and the elevator from the rest of the room. On a normal workday that was where the guard sat, inspecting purses and glaring at the girls as if he thought they were all thieves. Today, maybe that partition was enough to keep the fire away from the stairs.

Yetta and Jacob raced on, skirting the flames, still

pulling along hysterical, senseless workers who didn't seem to know where to go. They passed a desk where the book-keeper, Miss Lipshutz, was shouting into the mouthpiece of a telephone, "Please! Somebody listen! Somebody's got to tell the ninth floor! Hello? Somebody—please!"

A spark landed on the sleeve of Yetta's shirtwaist, and she watched in horror as it sputtered and shimmered and burned straight through. She could feel it singeing her skin.

Jacob slapped his bare hand onto Yetta's sleeve, starving the flame.

"*A dank,*" Yetta whispered, but there was no time for him to say, "You're welcome," because they were at the doorway to the partition now, shoving their way behind it.

No flames here.

Girls were still standing by the freight elevator door, the only elevator they were normally allowed to use. They were pounding on the closed door like they thought that was their only chance. It was so hot behind the partition that Yetta could barely breathe.

Can people melt? she wondered. In her mind she saw wax dripping down from Sabbath candles. *My life, melting away . . .*

"Stairs!" Jacob screamed at the girls by the elevator door.

He jerked open the stairway door and it opened out, making another obstacle in the tiny vestibule. Yetta and Jacob shoved the girls through the doorway and scrambled in behind them. The stairway was airless and close and still hot, but there were no sparks flying through the air. Through the window in the stairwell, Yetta could see the workers scrambling down the fire escape, teetering precariously on the metal railings, struggling past the metal shutters.

"Hurry!" Yetta screamed at the girls around her. They

were sobbing hysterically, clutching the railing, clutching each other. They were yammering away in some language Yetta didn't recognize, or maybe it wasn't a language at all, just witless jabbering.

"The fire!" one of them managed to say. "What if it's everywhere?"

"There's no smoke coming from down there!" Yetta screamed at them, pointing at the landings below them. "Go down to the ground! You'll be safe! The flames are going up, not down!"

Up.

Yetta glanced up to the landing above her, remembering what the bookkeeper had been screaming into the phone: *Somebody listen! Somebody's got to tell the ninth floor!*

They didn't know. One flight up, on the ninth floor, where two hundred and fifty girls worked, where Yetta had worked before the strike, where Bella worked now—up there, they had no idea there was an inferno raging beneath them, eating up the air, climbing higher and higher and higher.

Almost on their own, Yetta's feet had already started slapping down the stairs, once she finally got the jabbering girls moving. But now she stopped.

Bella, she thought. My other friends. *My sisters. My comrades. My union.*

"What are you doing?" Jacob screamed, already three steps down.

"Somebody has to tell the ninth floor!" she screamed back. "I have to!"

She turned around and began clattering up the stairs.

Jane

"Papa's taking us shopping! Papa's taking us shopping!" Harriet chanted, bouncing up and down joyously in the elevator on the way to Mr. Blanck's office at the Triangle factory.

"Hush. Everybody knows that," Millicent said scornfully.

"She's just excited," Jane said mildly. She patted Harriet's shoulder, trying to calm her down, and gave Millicent and the elevator operator a sympathetic smile. Harriet's chanting was a bit maddening. But, as always, it was hard to know the best way to handle the girls. Miss Milhouse would have scolded Harriet soundly; she would have taken it as her personal mission to stifle the little girl's exuberant personality. And she would have praised Millicent to the skies for her tidiness, her aversion to noise and mess, her ability to sit or stand still practically forever without squirming or exclaiming.

Personally, Jane thought Millicent was in danger of becoming a priggish bore. And she worried that someday somebody *would* stifle Harriet's exuberance.

"Make it be like a stream," Bella had advised her, when Jane had asked for help. "You don't want to chop her off—*bam!*" She'd slammed the side of her right hand against her left palm. "But make it go a good way."

"You mean, I should try to channel her enthusiasm into positive outlets?" Jane asked.

After Jane explained what "channel," "enthusiasm," "positive," and "outlets" meant, Bella grinned and nodded: "Yes, yes, exactly! You say what is in my heart for that girl!"

Now, as the elevator zoomed upward, Harriet began tugging on the elevator operator's jacket.

"Mister, you didn't know we were going shopping, did you? Papa's taking us as a treat, because our mama went to Florida for the—what's it called?—social season. And she took the car with her, on the train, so we had to take a taxi cab to get here, and the taxi cab's still waiting outside, for us to come back. Except Madam'selle Michaud's not going shopping with us, just Papa, and—"

"Harriet," Jane said warningly.

"She's okay," the elevator operator said. "You're the Blanck girls, right? The boss's daughters?"

"Our papa and Uncle Isaac own the whole factory," Millicent bragged. "They employ more than seven hundred people."

"Millicent!" Jane shot the girl a reproving look. *Remember what I've told you about bragging?* she wanted to scold. But she'd always hated Miss Milhouse correcting her in front of other people, so she'd vowed not to do that to Millicent or Harriet. It was just really tempting at times like this. *First thing Monday morning, I need to have a little talk with both girls. . . .*

The elevator was gathering speed. Harriet clutched Jane's hand.

"What if the elevator goes all the way through the roof?" she asked.

"Silly, that would never happen," Millicent scoffed.

"Why not?"

"Because—because it wouldn't be proper," Millicent said. She lowered her voice, as if that would keep the elevator operator from hearing. "If we went through the roof, the people below us could see up our skirts."

The elevator operator's face turned red, he was trying so hard not to laugh.

Jane sighed.

"There are scientific reasons the elevator would never go through the roof," she said. "Because of how the elevator's made, how it works."

"How does it work?" Harriet asked.

Oops. Jane had been afraid she'd ask that. Somehow elevator mechanics had not been in the curriculum at Jane's finishing school.

"Next week we can go to the bookstore and find a book that explains it all," Jane said. "Or maybe you can find one with your papa."

"The elevator runs on a cable," the operator said. "The cable goes up to gears, and those are on the roof. Maybe sometime you can ask your papa to show you the gearbox. But if you want to go to the roof, you have to use the Greene Street stairs. That's the only way to get there."

"Thank you," Jane said, smiling gratefully at the operator. He was a pimply boy, maybe a little younger than her. A year ago, he would have been completely invisible to her, but now she wondered about his life. Which country had he come from? Did he bring his family with him, or was he all alone? Was he supporting a widowed mother and a younger brother and sister or two on his salary as an elevator operator? Did Mr. Blanck and Mr. Harris pay him more or less than they paid their sewing machine operators?

"Tenth floor," the operator announced, bringing the elevator to a halt and sweeping open the barred door. "Where your papa the boss works."

He had the slightest hint of mockery in his voice, just enough for Jane to hear. He even gave her a conspiratorial wink, which was much too forward, but somehow Jane didn't mind. She winked back, and stepped out onto the polished wood floor of a spacious reception area.

"Miss Mary! Miss Mary!" Harriet cried, running over to one of the desks.

"Oh, sweetie, Miss Mary's busy right now," said the short, frazzled-looking woman behind the desk. "The switchboard operator didn't come in today, so Miss Mary has to do all her typing *and* connect every call that comes in. The eighth floor can't even call the ninth floor without my help."

Harriet inspected the telephone switchboard behind the woman's desk, the wires hanging slack.

"So if you plug in this wire here, then—"

"Oh, sweetie, don't touch," Miss Mary said, gently pushing Harriet's hand away. "I really don't have time—I'll explain it to you some other day." She looked up at Jane. "You're the governess, right? You can just take them into Mr. Blanck's office, and then go tell him they're here."

"Where is Mr. Blanck?" Jane asked.

"Oh, he was just down on the ninth floor—no, wait, back

in the storeroom? I'm sorry, I'd look for him myself, but—"
The harried secretary gestured at the papers strewn across
her desk, the bill poking out from her typewriter.

A contraption beside the typewriter buzzed, and Miss
Mary looked over at it expectantly.

"What's that?" Harriet whispered.

"Oh, it's the new telautograph," Miss Mary said. "'The
latest in business machinery,' is how it's advertised. Looks
like there's a message coming from the eighth floor. They
write something on a pad of paper downstairs, and this pen
is supposed to write the same thing on this pad right here."

"Like magic," Harriet breathed.

The pen didn't move.

"It'd be magic if it ever worked right," Miss Mary snorted.
"Probably isn't anything anyhow, just the girls downstairs
playing with it on their way out the door."

Miss Mary turned back to her typing, and Jane shooed
the girls toward Mr. Blanck's office.

"I want to go see the showroom!" Harriet said, skipping
down the hall. "Madam'selle Michaud, you'll love it! You can
see all the latest fashions before Paris!"

"That's because even Paris doesn't know as much about
fashion as our papa," Millicent said, agreeing with her
younger sister for once.

"Some other time," Jane said. "Miss Mary said to wait in
his office, remember?"

They turned in at a doorway, but the sign on the door
said ISAAC HARRIS, not MAX BLANCK.

"Uncle Isaac!" Harriet called.

A man behind a desk waved, but there was another man

with him, a dapper-looking gentleman holding up samples of delicate embroidery. Jane flashed an apologetic look at Mr. Harris and pulled the girls away.

"Look, you can see into the pressing department from here," Harriet said, pointing past a break in the wall into a vast open space, where rows and rows of weary-looking workers stood over ironing boards. Each one of the irons was connected to the ceiling by an odd array of tubes.

"Is Papa afraid those workers are going to steal his irons?" Harriet asked. "Is that why the irons are tied up?"

Jane didn't have the slightest idea, so she was glad that Millicent answered first.

"No, silly. The gas comes down those tubes and heats the irons," Millicent said. "Papa says we must never ever go in there, because one of those irons could blister our skin in an instant."

And does he care at all about the workers operating the irons? Jane wondered bitterly. *Some of them look no older than Millicent!*

"Quick, now," she told the girls. "Into the office. Wait right there."

She was infected suddenly with some of Miss Mary's franticness, or maybe she was just tired of hearing the admiring tone in the girls' voices every time they mentioned their papa. Or maybe it was the sight of the haggard workers hunched over their irons, girls who looked entirely too young, who would probably look entirely too old after just a year or two on the job. Regardless, Jane was ready to be done working for the day, ready to be out in the fresh air, arm in arm with Bella and Yetta. She was pretty sure that she and Bella had finally convinced Yetta to go with them to visit Rahel and Rahel's new baby. It would probably be a touching family reunion.

Yes, Yetta will be so much happier if she'll just forgive her sister for getting married, Jane thought. *My father and I, on the other hand . . .*

She hadn't forgotten her promise to Mr. Corrigan to write her father a letter. She'd written him many, many letters, actually—she'd just torn them all up.

What is there to say?

Jane pulled the door shut on Millicent and Harriet, catching barely a glimpse of Mr. Blanck's imposing mahogany desk, of the lovely arched windows behind the desk. Harriet was scrambling into the huge leather chair.

"Harriet! A young lady would never put her feet up on the desk!" she heard Millicent cry out, in scandalized horror.

Jane decided to let Millicent wage that battle on her own. Secretly, she was thinking, *Oh, Harriet, maybe you should go on being the kind of girl who puts her feet on desks. Better that, than hiding under them . . .*

She scurried down the hall, back to the double elevator doors. She decided to look for Mr. Blanck on the ninth floor first. She knew that was where Bella worked, and it'd be good if she could warn Bella that she'd be a few minutes late getting out to the street, especially if it took her a long time to find Mr. Blanck.

Passing Miss Mary's desk, Jane was surprised to notice that the woman had vanished, leaving the telephone receiver hanging off the hook.

That's odd. She seemed like such a conscientious sort. . . .

A different elevator operator came up this time, a swarthily handsome Italian man.

If Bella's precious Pietro looks anything like that, no wonder she can't forget him! Jane thought. Then she had to hide her face so he didn't see her giggling at her own wickedness.

The elevator buzzed annoyingly. Again and again and again.

"Eighth floor's going crazy," the elevator operator growled. He scowled at the panel of lights that kept flashing at him as he shut the door behind Jane and the elevator began its descent. "Hold on a minute! I'm coming! I'm coming!"

"They've probably all got spring fever," Jane said. "And it's Saturday."

"Yeah, yeah," the operator grumbled, letting her out on the ninth floor. "But do they gotta take it out on me?"

The ninth floor was not what Jane expected. After the cleanliness and elegance of the tenth floor, she wasn't prepared for this dim, dirty space with the tables and the machines and the girls packed in so tightly together. The room was huge, but the tables stretched from one side of the building to the other. By the windows, there wasn't even space to walk around the tables. And shirtwaists and shirtwaist parts were piled everywhere, mountains of fabric by each machine.

No wonder Bella felt so overwhelmed, coming here from her tiny little village in Italy, Jane thought.

Jane herself felt a little overwhelmed.

"Excuse me. Do you know where I could find Mr. Blanck or Bella Rossetti?" she asked the girl at the nearest sewing machine.

The girl looked up blankly, and said something that might have been "I don't speak English" in some other language. Just then a bell sounded, and the machines stopped and hundreds of girls sprang up from their machines all at once. It spooked Jane a little, the darkness of the room and the foreign jabbering and the girls moving like machines, themselves. But then one of the girls stepping out of the cloakroom began to sing, "Ev'ry little movement has a meaning of its own"—one of those popular songs that you heard everywhere, nowadays. Some of the other girls joined in, and they all seemed so light-hearted suddenly. Saturday afternoon and the sun was shining and work was over; these girls looked happier than anyone Jane had ever seen at a formal ball.

Then, two tables away, Jane spotted Bella heading down the aisle between the tables and laughing and talking to the girls around her.

"Jane! What are you doing here?" Bella shouted over to her.

"Looking for you and Mr. Blanck," Jane said.

"Well, we wouldn't be together!" Bella called back merrily.

Jane worked her way through the crowd toward her friend. She explained about Millicent and Harriet and the shopping, and how long it would take her to get down to the sidewalk. Then Bella said, "Oh, wait, you have to meet my friends—this is Annie and Dora and Josie and Essie and Ida. And come here—" She pulled her back down the aisle between the tables. "This is my boss, Signor Carlotti. This is my friend, Jane Wellington, Signor Carlotti, and she knows proper Italian *and* proper English."

"Hello," Signor Carlotti said.

"I am a factory inspector," Jane said, suddenly inspired to lie. "If I were to interview the girls in this factory, would they tell me that you treat them with respect? Are you fair to all your workers?"

At the first word out of her mouth, Signor Carlotti's face changed—first, to awe at her upper-class accent, then to fear.

"Oh, er—yes! Yes! Of course!" Signor Carlotti exclaimed.

It was all Jane and Bella could do, not to double over giggling as they walked away.

"Maybe he really will change how he treats you, Monday morning!" Jane whispered.

"Oh, do you think so?" Bella asked wistfully.

Across the room, strangely, Jane heard Yetta's voice now. She couldn't make out the words, but Yetta seemed to be calling out in great excitement, from the midst of the crowd of girls getting ready to leave. Maybe she was talking them into another strike. Maybe this one would work— maybe Yetta would get her dearest wish.

"Doesn't Yetta work on the eighth floor?" Jane asked.

Before Bella could answer, screams came suddenly from the back of the room. Screams—and a great burst of light.

Bella

Bella couldn't tell what had happened. It was just like her first day of work, when everyone else was yelling and running and knocking over baskets and trampling shirtwaists they didn't bother to stop and pick up. And, for a moment, just like on that first day, Bella couldn't understand the words everyone else kept saying. The English part of her brain shut off, the Yiddish words in her brain evaporated, even the Italian she heard around her sounded garbled and foreign.

Then she smelled smoke, and the words made sense.

"Fire!"

"*S'brent!*"

"*Fuoco!*"

Jane clutched her shoulders.

"Where do we go? What do we do?" Jane asked. "We always had fire drills at school—where have they told you to go in the event of a fire?"

Bella didn't know what a fire drill was. People were crowded in all around her, shoving and pushing from behind, blocking the way in front of her. The tables on either side of the aisle seemed to be closing in on her. She was penned in, just like a goat or a pig.

No better than an animal, Bella thought, and somehow this seemed all of piece with not being able to read and wanting only food and Signor Carlotti spitting on her and Signor Luciano cheating her. *I bet back home your family slept with goats and chickens in the house*, Signora Luciano had sneered at her once, and Bella hadn't even understood that that was an insult. But now she'd seen how other people lived; she'd seen what Jane and Yetta expected out of life. She refused to think of herself as a hog in a pen waiting to be slaughtered.

"This way!" she said, grabbing Jane's hand and scrambling up on top of the nearest table.

From there, she could see the fire. It was blowing in the back window, one huge ball of flame rolling across the examining tables stacked with shirtwaists. The flames kept dividing, devouring stack after stack of shirtwaists, racing each other down the tables.

Where are they trying to get to? Bella wondered.

The first flame leaped from the examining table to the first row of sewing tables.

"It's coming toward us!" Jane screamed behind her. "Where do we go?"

Bella looked around frantically. Girls were packed in around the doors and elevators. Only a handful seemed to remember that there was another way out.

"The fire escape!" Bella screamed back, grateful for that day so long ago, before the strike, when she'd actually seen where the fire escape was.

The aisles were still crowded. Bella leaped from one table to the next, and somehow Jane managed to follow. Bella leaped again, suddenly surefooted. Except for the smoke burning her eyes and throat, she could have been back in the mountains near Calia, jumping from rock to rock.

"I've got to—make sure—Harriet and Millicent—are—all—right," Jane panted behind her, as they cleared another table. She began coughing, choking on the smoke.

Bella bent down and snatched up a pile of shirtwaist sleeves. She held two over her mouth and handed the others to Jane.

"Here. So you can breathe."

They kept racing across the tables. And it really was a race, because the flames were speeding toward the fire escape window too. Through the smoke, Bella could barely make out the progress of the fire. *The flames are going to get there first—no, we are!—no, look how fast the fire's moving. . . .*

They reached the end of the tables and jumped down to the floor. The flames were reaching for Bella's skirt, so she lifted it up as she ran for the fire escape. She had one leg out the window, balanced on the metal railing, when Jane grabbed for her arm.

"Wait—is that safe?" Jane asked.

She'd actually stopped to peer down at the rickety stairs, at the flames shooting out the eighth-floor window, at the eighth-floor shutters that seemed to be blocking the path of all the other girls already easing their way down.

"Safe?" Bella repeated numbly. Anything seemed safer than where they were now. But she pulled back a little, reconsidering. She shifted her weight back from the foot that was on the fire escape to the knee perched on the windowsill. And in that moment, the fire escape just . . . fell away.

"Madonna mia!" Bella cried. Jane grabbed her, pulling her back in through the window. "The other girls—"

Jane shook her head, maybe meaning, *Don't ask,* maybe meaning, *I saw it all, them falling, I can't even begin to tell you how awful it was. . . .* Bella tried to remember who'd been ahead of her on the fire escape—Dora? Essie? Ida? All of them? The boot of the girl immediately in front of Bella had had a fancy silver buckle, the kind of thing a girl would have been proud of, the kind of thing she would have gone around showing off, making sure her skirt flounced up to display it as much as possible. Had Bella seen that buckle before?

"Bella! Where's another exit?" Jane cried out.

But Bella couldn't think about anything but a fancy silver buckle.

Suddenly Yetta was there.

"Greene Street stairs!" Yetta was screaming. "Go!"

Bella grabbed her friends' hands and took off running again. But Yetta pulled her hand back.

"You go on!" she screamed. "I still have to—"

The rest of Yetta's words were lost in the crackle of advancing flames.

The smoke rose and fell and shifted. One minute, Bella could see ahead of her, a straight path to the partition by the door. The next minute, she was groping blindly forward, tripping over people who had fallen. She'd dropped the shirt-waist sleeves she'd been using to cover her mouth and nose. She grabbed up another stack, but just before she pressed it to her face she noticed that these shirtwaist sleeves were already burning. She dropped them to the floor, and began to sag toward the floor herself.

But she was still holding Jane's hand. Jane yanked her back up.

"The stairs—" Jane gasped.

They stumbled forward. Bella pulled her wool skirt up over her head, blocking out the smoke and the flames. *Immodest,* she thought, an English word she'd just learned. She didn't care.

Jane grabbed a bucket of water from a nearby shelf and flung it toward the fire, and some of it splashed back onto Bella. None of it seemed to reach the fire. Or, if it did, it didn't make any difference. The flames kept shooting forward. There were no more buckets left on the shelf, only some tipped over empty on the floor.

"The girls will be so scared," Jane breathed, and Bella knew she meant Harriet and Millicent, waiting in their father's office upstairs. "I've got to—"

She stopped, looking down.

"My skirt," she said.

A ring of flames was dancing along the bottom of her skirt. She stepped forward and the flames flared.

"We'll put it out," Bella said.

Jane began rushing toward a vat by the stairs.

"Water—"

"No, no! That's machine oil, sewing machine oil!" Bella screamed, pulling her back. The dark oil was bubbling over, running down the sides of the vat. The fire was beginning to race along the streams of oil. Bella had to jump past it. And then Jane was on one side of the flames, Bella on the other.

"Jane!" Bella screamed.

"Go on!" Jane screamed back. "Go get the girls! Make sure they're safe up there!"

"But you—"

"I'll go another way!" Jane said. "I'll meet you later!"

Bella whirled around. The pathway to the stairs was closing in. In a second it would be gone.

Bella ran forward.

Yetta

Yetta had burst onto the ninth floor shouting, "There's a fire on the eighth floor! Get out!" But there was so much Saturday-afternoon chatter, so many people crowded in between the tables and machines and towering stacks of shirtwaists. She doubted if anyone heard her.

The fire arrived only seconds later.

"Get out! Go!" Yetta screamed, grabbing shocked girls and shoving them toward the stairs. Having just seen the fire fly through the eighth floor, she could look at a stack of shirtwaist parts and know exactly how quickly that would turn to flame. "Go now!" she screamed. "You've only got a few minutes!"

Yetta didn't know when a second voice joined her own, a deeper voice urging just as loudly, "Don't stop to get your hat! Don't stop to get your gloves! Go!"

She looked around, and it was Jacob. He must have followed her up the stairs.

"What are you doing?" she screamed at him.

"The same thing as you!" he screamed back, then kept hollering, "Go! Go!"

Together they shoved girls into the elevator, lifted numb

women to their feet. Yetta took great joy in slapping a dazed Mr. Carlotti.

"Snap out of it!" she screamed at him. "Get out of here!"

When the smoke cleared a little with the breeze, Yetta saw Bella and Jane—Jane? *What's she doing here? No time to find out* . . . They were standing practically in the fire, so close to the fire escape that Yetta couldn't understand why they weren't climbing out. Yetta rushed toward them, ready to scream, "Just go out that window! Now!" So what if the fire escape didn't go down all the way to the ground? If it got them past the eighth floor they could climb in the windows on a lower floor, escape that way.

But when Yetta got over to the window, the fire escape seemed to have vanished.

There was no time to ask why or how. No time even to wonder.

"Greene Street stairs!" Yetta screamed. "Go!"

That seemed to be enough to bring them back to life, get them moving. But then Bella grabbed Yetta's hand, pulling her along too. Yetta wanted to go with her friends. In a matter of moments they could be down on the street, walking home. They could walk away from Triangle, this nightmarish place. They'd never have to come back again. They could get other jobs. They could all three hop a train west, live somewhere else. Yetta didn't have to be a shirtwaist girl anymore.

But people were dying *here*. Yetta could help *now*.

Yetta pulled her hand back.

"You go on!" she screamed. "I still have to help the others!"

Bella and Jane disappeared into the smoke. The smoke shifted a little, and for one instant Yetta could see clear across the room to the Washington Place door. Workers were clumped up against that door, just like they'd been on the eighth floor.

"They must think it's locked!" Yetta screamed at Jacob, who'd suddenly appeared beside her. "They don't know it opens in!"

How would they know? How many of them had ever used the Washington Place door? Yetta started racing across the room, gasping for breath. She had such a clear image in her head: She would push the panicky girls aside, turn the knob, jerk the door in toward the factory . . . And then everyone would stream out, safe.

"Pull it toward yourselves!" she started screaming as soon as she got close to the door.

Nobody seemed to be listening.

"I'll try it!" Jacob yelled.

Together they fought their way through the crowd. They took turns grasping the doorknob, yanking it, turning it, twisting it. But their hands slid off the knob; the knob didn't budge.

"This one *is* locked!" Yetta yelled in Jacob's ear. "It's locked!" she screamed at all the other workers clustered around. "Go another way!" She started pushing the other girls back from the door, yelling, "Take the other stairs! Take the other stairs!"

Jacob slid his hands down around Yetta's shoulders, pinning her arms to her side.

"Yetta," he whispered, his mouth right against her ear. "They can't."

Then Yetta looked back.

She'd seen the fire take over the eighth floor, starting

from one small spark in a scrap bin and advancing throughout the entire room. That hadn't prepared her at all for the ninth floor, where flames spilled in through the windows on every side. In the brief moments that Yetta had spent tugging on a locked door, the flames had taken over. The route that Yetta and Jacob had used just a minute before was blocked by a wall of fire now—a wall of fire sweeping ever closer.

Yetta and Jacob couldn't get back to the other stairs, either.

"Jacob," Yetta said, and she was ashamed that the word came out as a whimper. "I don't want to burn."

She remembered what Rahel had said about the pogrom in Bialystok: *This one girl—she might have been you or me. One minute, she was just standing there. . . . The next minute she was covered in flames. A human torch. Gone in a flash.*

"Not me. Not my life. Please. I don't want to go that way," she whispered. She wasn't sure if she was talking to Jacob or to God or just to herself.

"You won't burn," Jacob said

It seemed like an impossible promise. What else could happen, with the door locked, the flames beating mercilessly nearer? But Jacob was lifting her up—higher, higher, higher—into unbelievably fresh air.

He was lifting her toward the window.

Yetta remembered the woman with the burning hair who'd jumped out the window on the eighth floor. She squirmed in Jacob's arms.

"No! Not that either!"

"There's a ledge," Jacob said.

And then, somehow, they were both standing on the

ledge, just outside the window. The fire still raged behind them, but the cool breezes soothed their faces—the same breezes that had seemed to call and tease her earlier. Odd, how they were a comfort now. Yetta looked straight up into blue sky, into puffy white clouds sailing leisurely toward the horizon. Down below there were fire trucks and firemen and crowds screaming, but Yetta couldn't hear any of the voices. Her world had shrunk, for the moment, to blue sky and the feel of Jacob's arms around her.

"Why did you follow me?" she asked him, choking out the words. "You were safe on the stairs. You could be down there right now."

Jacob brushed a lock of hair away from her eyes.

"I was a scab during the strike," he said. Even now, there was such shame clotting his voice. "But I saw you picketing. I *saw* you. You were . . . incredible. I wanted to be on your side."

If there'd been time, Yetta could have joked, "Then join a strike, already. Don't go running into fires." But words were too precious, on this ledge, to make jokes. It was enough to hold on to Jacob, while he held on to her. She saw that she'd misjudged him, thinking he wanted to go dancing only to practice his English.

Right now she couldn't even think whether they were talking to each other in Yiddish or English.

"Yetta—we can't stay here," Jacob said.

She knew that. The flames were lapping at their heels, eager to escape the factory, to ruin the blue-sky world, too. The ledge was so narrow, they could only inch along. It was impossible to move far enough away from the window with its flames and smoke. But Yetta wanted one more moment of staring out into the blue sky.

It's Saturday, she thought. *Still the Sabbath.* Yetta knew it wouldn't be long before devout Jews—her father, Rahel's husband—would begin the havdalah prayers, dividing the sacredness of the Sabbath from ordinary, everyday life. But Yetta had not had a sacred day. She faced a different kind of divide.

"They're coming to rescue us," Jacob said.

And it was true—the fire truck down below had begun unfurling a ladder, reaching higher and higher, in a race with the flames at Yetta's heels. The ladder was four stories high, five stories high, six stories high . . .

The ladder stopped.

"Don't they have a longer ladder?" Yetta asked. "Don't they? Don't they?"

It was a useless question. The ladder had stopped growing. The flames were going to win.

"We could jump for the end of the ladder," Jacob said. "Or for the nets on the ground."

The firemen—impossibly tiny, down there on the ground—were indeed holding out nets, standing there so hopefully. Yetta could have laughed at their hopes. It was not exactly a plan Jacob was offering her, not exactly a chance, in the nets and the ladder. But it was something besides flame.

Jacob bowed to Yetta, as elegantly as if they were about to launch themselves onto a dance floor instead of into thin air. *He would have been a good dance partner,* Yetta thought with an ache. He wrapped his arms around Yetta; she wrapped her arms around him.

And then they jumped.

It does not take a long time to fall to the ground, even from nine stories up. But it felt like a lifetime to Yetta—she felt like she passed through years worth of Rosh Hashanahs, Yom Kippurs, Hanukkahs, Purims, Passovers. She had her regrets: *Oh, Rahel, I am so sorry I was mean to you. I never met your baby, never gave your husband a chance . . . I shouldn't have expected you to be like me, shouldn't have thought we had to be the same . . . And, oh, Jacob, what if I'd gone dancing with you sooner?* She saw now that so much more was possible than she'd ever believed. She could have danced at a thousand weddings, all at once.

They missed the ladder. Both of them stretched out a hand but the ladder rung slipped past them.

"There's still the net!" Jacob shouted. Or maybe there wasn't time for him to shout it; maybe she could only feel him thinking it. She was glad that he had his arms around her, glad that he'd helped her in the fire, glad that she wasn't alone.

Oh, Bella, you were smart to go looking for love. And, Jane, you were looking for all the right things, too. But oh, God, I tried so hard, I wanted so much to change the world. . . .

The net was right beneath them. Yetta felt a surge of gratitude for the firemen who angled the net so carefully, who ran to the exact right spot to catch two immigrant workers falling from the sky. These men were trying so hard to save her life. She and Jacob landed on the net, exactly in the center.

And then the net broke and they plunged on through.

It does not take a long time to fall to the ground, even from nine stories up. But it took a lifetime for Yetta. It took every single one of the last moments of her life.

Jane

*J*ane stamped out the fire licking at the bottom of her skirt.

And then she was so proud of herself: *Look!* she wanted to tell someone. *I did this! I didn't fall into a dead faint at the horror of it all! I didn't scream hysterically for a servant or a man to help me! I put out the fire all on my own!*

But there was no one to tell. And there were flames all around her. She could see Bella disappearing into the stairwell, and she almost called out, "No! Wait! Stay with me!"

But Bella, loyal to the end, would probably turn around and come back if Jane called to her. Jane couldn't do that to Bella, couldn't endanger her when she was only seconds away from safety.

And I'll be fine on my own, Jane told herself. *I'm not some ignorant immigrant shirtwaist girl, frightened out of her wits. I can think about this logically and reasonably.*

A towering wall of flames now stood between Jane and the stairs that Bella had used.

So I'll go back to the elevator I took before. Wonder which operator I'll get—the swarthy man or the pimply boy who winked at me? Jane was forcing herself to stay calm, to think about things that didn't matter. Because if she had time to think of things that didn't matter, she wasn't really in danger here; she didn't have to worry.

Around her, people were panicking, screaming, and scrambling away from the flames.

"Into the cloakroom! We'll be safe in the cloakroom!" one boy yelled, and there were actually people who followed him into the cramped, small room. Jane wanted to tell them that they needed to find another sanctuary; that anyone in the cloakroom was doomed. But the flames were already climbing the cloakroom walls. She couldn't get close enough to tell the people inside anything.

And anyhow, her feet were carrying her across the room, in a frantic dash for the elevator. She didn't have the breath to say anything to anyone.

Should have left my corset behind when I ran away from home.

She couldn't pretend anymore that her thoughts were logical and reasonable. They were disjointed, chaotic, haunted. The flames around her twisted and intertwined and multiplied just as randomly. For a second Jane could see Miss Milhouse's scornful countenance looming ahead of her in the fire. She could hear Miss Milhouse's voice in her head, scolding her, telling her it was her own fault she'd gotten caught in this fire: *Whatever did you expect, associating with shirtwaist girls?*

Jane spat into the fire, the most uncouth, ill-mannered act of her life.

"I will not think your thoughts anymore, Miss Milhouse!" she screamed, her voice miraculously back again.

Through the smoke now, she could see the elevator right in front of her, the doors open, the pimply elevator operator helping workers in.

"Wait for me! Wait for me!" Jane sobbed. "Oh, please, wait for me!"

A huge crowd stood between Jane and the elevator, all screaming and shoving their way in.

"Oh, but you have to save me," Jane yelled. "Don't you know who I am? I'm—"

She stopped. What was she going to say? *I'm Jane Wellington. I'm from a rich family. I'm the Blanck girls' governess. I'm planning to go to college. I'm due a grand tour of Europe.* What did any of that matter? Why was her life worth any more than anyone else's?

The elevator doors were closing.

The workers nearest the doors jammed their arms and legs between the doors. They leaped onto the top of the elevator, they slid down the elevator cables, they jumped down the elevator shaft. Jane wasn't close enough to do any of that.

"He'll come back, won't he?" Jane asked. "Won't he?"

Nobody answered.

Jane looked behind her. The flames were so close now. To keep away from them, she had to cram in tightly against the other people: scrawny boys and dazed-looking girls and women with a world's weight of sorrow in their eyes.

"Oh," Jane breathed, a catch in her throat. "I don't want to die."

"None of us do, darling," an old woman said. She was a crone in a tattered shawl, clutching beads and murmuring, "Hail, Mary, full of grace . . ." But she stopped her prayers for a moment and drew Jane into a hug.

She's probably somebody's mother, Jane thought. *There will be children who cry when she's gone. Children and maybe grandchildren, too, all sobbing, missing her . . .*

"Mama," Jane whispered into this strange women's smoky shawl. She stayed in the woman's embrace, packed in with all the other workers. The elevator didn't come back.

The elevator didn't come back.

The elevator didn't come back.

So this is how it ends, Jane thought.

She'd banished Miss Milhouse's thoughts from her mind, but she knew how her father and Miss Milhouse and all of society would view this, Jane dying with the shirtwaist workers, in the embrace of a crone with a shawl and a rosary. Her death would be seen as a defeat, a disgrace, a sign that girls who run away from home always come to a bad end.

No, Jane thought. *No.*

She saw that she'd expected to go back, someday. Sending the letter to her father would have been her first step. When she got tired of living on pickled herring and pasta, she might have compromised her principles, might have let Mr. Corrigan stage a "prodigal daughter" reunion with her father. Her father probably would have taken her back.

Or she might have saved her money, worked her way up to teaching at a school, worked her way into college and married one of her classmates' brothers, someone like that unformed, uninformed law student, Charles Livingston. And, back in high society, she would be That Daring Girl Who Spent a Year Slumming It in the Tenements. She'd be like that matronly grandmother who'd once worked as a spy in the war—the picture of propriety with a shocking past.

No, Jane thought again. None of that would happen now.

She would die pure, her principles intact, society shunned.

This, too, can be seen as a triumph, Jane thought.

Jane and the crone in the shawl and all the other workers had slumped down to the floor because there wasn't any air left anywhere else. They were all lying together, but Jane made sure that she moved her hand to the top of the pile, so that anyone who found them would see her signet ring, would see that it wasn't just poor people who died.

The tragedy of the workers' condition threatens us all. Jane had heard the Vassar suffragist say that during the shirtwaist strike, back when Jane was just a foolish rich girl in a frilly dress. She hadn't understood the words then, any more than she understood the fire now. But she felt connected to the crone in the shawl, the pimply elevator operator, the boy who thought the cloakroom was a safe haven. And Bella and Yetta and Millicent and Harriet Blanck . . . All of them were threatened by the fire escape that fell away from the building, by the blocked stairway, by the tiny elevators that served the entire ten-story building. All of them were threatened by this fire.

Around her the workers were screaming out prayers and curses. Screaming, then murmuring, then just moving their lips, their words known only to God. Jane discovered that she herself was sobbing tearlessly, or maybe her tears were evaporating in the heat the moment her eyes produced them. Her only prayer was still, "I don't want to die."

Oh, please, God, don't let me die, she thought. *I've never even had a chance to live.*

Or had she?

Jane remembered that day so long ago, when she'd been on her way to tea in Washington Square just as the Triangle workers were spilling out of their factory. She'd been so taken with the sight of them; she'd envied them, without understanding why. She believed now that she'd probably witnessed their first attempt at a strike—their first heady moment of standing up for themselves, of challenging the men in power. They'd looked so alive that day, so full of life.

Everything she'd done since then had been a quest—a quest to fill her own life with meaning. She'd gone from lying uselessly in bed, to standing on the picket line watching, to taking in Bella. And then she'd stood up for herself, she'd taught Harriet and Millicent—oh, *Lord, I hope I taught them something*—she'd learned to appreciate a single red rose with Yetta and Bella.

But I'm not finished yet. I'm not finished.

The fire was inches from her skirt and there was nowhere left to go. The air was nothing but smoke. The elevator wasn't coming back.

I am *finished*, Jane thought, but it wasn't like she was giving up. Giving up would have been marrying whatever boy her father picked out for her, drinking tepid tea the rest of her life with women she didn't even like. This was more like a blaze of glory, seeing all her choices tallied up, seeing what her life had meant.

I was alive, she thought. *I lived. I mattered.*

She squeezed in tighter against the old woman in the shawl, hugging the crone as she'd always wanted to hug her own mother. The crone and the other workers had also lived, had also mattered.

And now they were also dying. All of them were dying together.

Bella

Bella was crying and gasping for air in the smoky stair-well. Flames glowed on the landing below, but that didn't matter; she wasn't supposed to go that way. *Go get the girls*, Jane had said. *Make sure they're safe up there. . . .*

Up there. Up. Blinded by smoke and tears, Bella inched forward until her feet struck the first step leading to the tenth floor. *The girls will be so scared*, Jane had said, and Bella could picture them, standing alone in smoke and flame, clutching each other, their faces pale and terrified beneath the perky bows in their hair. Then the smoke did something to Bella's eyes, and it wasn't the prim, proper little Blanck girls she was seeing. It was other children: scruffy, barefoot, half-starved, runny-nosed Italian peasant children—three boys and a girl, wearing only rags.

"Guilia," Bella whispered. "Dominic. Ricardo. Giovanni."

They may have looked half starved and ragged, but they were grinning from ear to ear; they were jumping up and down and cheering. They were beckoning to her.

"My family," Bella whispered. "I'm coming. . . ."

But then she saw her mother with her brothers and

sister, and Mama wasn't grinning and cheering. She was shaking her head.

No. Not yet, she said.

"But I wanted to die young, Mama," Bella sobbed. "It's all right. I'll be with you."

No. Mama kept shaking her head, even as she faded back into the smoke, only her voice remaining. *You're alive. Live. Save the living.*

The words flickered in Bella's mind like flames, but stronger than flames. Choking on her sobs and the smoke and her sorrow that her family had disappeared, Bella stumbled up the stairs. She didn't care that flames lashed in through the broken window and sizzled on the wet skirt she held over her head. She couldn't die now. Mama had said she should live.

She burst onto the tenth floor and dropped her skirt down to its proper position. People were running and screaming here, too, but the smoke and the flames had only begun to roll in the windows. Across the room, Bella could see the bows on two little girls' heads bobbing up and down, like they were skipping. No—like they were hopping over flames in their path, or jumping up and down in terror.

Bella took off running for those bows.

Just as she neared the other side of the room, the Washington Place elevator doors sprang open. A whole crowd of people crammed onto the elevator, sweeping one of the bow-girls along with them. It was little Harriet, her pretty face twisted in fear.

"Papa!" she screamed. "Papa!"

And then a man in a dark suit reached into the elevator and pulled her out. As the elevator lurched away, plunging down through the fire below, Mr. Blanck hugged his daughter close to his chest, wrapping his suit coat around her shoulders. Harriet nestled her head against his neck, sobbing into his collar. Millicent clutched onto the bottom of his coat.

They don't need me, Bella thought. *They've got their father. Their big, strong, rich father.*

But Mr. Blanck was only standing there, with a dazed look on his stout face.

"Sir!" Bella cried. She'd never spoken to Mr. Blanck before. He was her boss. He was a man. But she had to yell at him now. "Sir! You can't stay here! You've got to get out!"

Mr. Blanck turned, startled, his eyes unfocused.

"There you are, Mademoiselle Michaud," he said, vaguely. "I couldn't think where you might have gotten to."

He slid Harriet into Bella's arms.

He thinks I'm Jane, Bella thought. *Can't he tell the difference? Didn't he hear my accent? Is one girl just the same as another to him?*

Bella remembered that her face was covered in soot, her hair was in total disarray, her shirtwaist was stained ash gray. And with everyone screaming, it was hard to hear anything. She leaned her face close to Harriet's and asked, "Do you know who I am?"

"Bella and Yetta and Jane," Harriet whispered back. "You're Bella, the one who talks funny."

Encircled in the safety of Bella's arms, Harriet seemed calmer and more reasonable than her father. Of course, with her face pressed against Bella's shirtwaist, she couldn't see the flames climbing through the Greene Street windows, streaming across the ironing boards.

"Harriet," Bella whispered. "We need to get away from here. Don't be scared if we have to start running."

"But I wanted to go to the roof. Papa was 'sposed to take us to the roof."

The roof. It wasn't a bad idea. Especially when the elevator was silent and shut and the ninth floor was an inferno and the fire kept pouring in the windows. Bella turned toward the nearest stairway, carrying Harriet and pulling on Mr. Blanck's sleeve.

Harriet squirmed in Bella's arms.

"No!" she said. "Those are the wrong stairs. The 'vator operator said only the Greene Street stairs go up to the roof. Only the Greene Street stairs!"

"That's true," Mr. Blanck said vacantly. "She's right."

Bella turned him around so they were facing the other stairway. Those were the stairs Bella had used only moments before, to climb to the tenth floor. But now the door was hidden by the billows of smoke, and the flames were thickest on that side of the room.

"Hurry up!" she snapped at Mr. Blanck.

They made it halfway across the room before Mr. Blanck stopped again. A man was standing on a table, pounding on a piece of glass in the ceiling. Bella could tell this was ridiculous: He was using his bare hands, and the glass was thick. But Mr. Blanck blinked up at the man.

"Mr. Silk?" he called. "Do you think the skylight's the best way out?"

Mr. Silk didn't hear or didn't bother answering, but Mr. Blanck kept standing there, waiting.

Bella put Harriet down on the ground—"Just for a second,"

she whispered to the girl—and ran over to the table.

"Sir!" she hollered. "Sir! Come down from there! Use the stairs!"

While Bella was standing by the table, another man emerged from the smoke and picked up Harriet Blanck, took Mr. Blanck's arm, and led the whole group of them toward the stairs.

"Don't worry. I'll take you to safety," the man said, and Mr. Blanck said, "Thank you, Markowitz. I knew I could count on you."

What about me? Bella wanted to yell after him. But it didn't matter. Somebody was taking care of the girls, and Bella didn't have to worry about them anymore.

The smoke was thicker now. Bella could barely see the stupid man still pounding on the skylight. Dimly, she could hear voices around her, other people rushing toward the stairs. A girl slumped against Bella's back, then slid down to the floor. Bella crouched down beside the girl.

"What are you doing?" Bella screamed at her.

The girl was still breathing, so she wasn't dead; she'd just fainted.

"Wake up!" Bella screamed, shaking the girl's shoulders. The girl's head rolled from side to side; her eyes lolled in their sockets.

Live, Bella's mama had told her. *Save the living.* But it didn't seem as though Bella could do both. Was Bella supposed to save the fainting girl and the stupid man? Or was she supposed to save herself?

Another man appeared in the smoke—Mr. Bernstein, the factory manager.

"Lucy Wesselofsky, get off that floor!" he screamed. "Mr. Silk, come down from that table!"

And then Bella and Mr. Bernstein were working together, lifting the girl, pulling down the man, shoving them both toward the stairs. Bella felt as though she were walking through fire, breathing flames. Or maybe it was only the heat, pressing in on all sides of them. They reached the stairwell, and there were flames there, too, reaching in through the broken window.

"I can't . . . ," the girl, Lucy, moaned.

"You will!" Bella shouted at her.

Lucy had a jacket on, and Bella pulled it up over both their heads, shielding their faces as they ran blindly up the stairs. Bella stopped running only when she felt fresh air in her lungs. As soon as they stumbled out onto the roof, she lowered the jacket and discovered that it was burning now too, lines of flame shooting along the collar, along the seams and cuffs.

Bella dropped the jacket. She patted out the sparks on her skirt.

"It's no better up here," Lucy sobbed.

That wasn't exactly true. There was a serene blue sky overhead, and pure white clouds that seemed a million miles away from flames and smoke. But the smoke was blowing out into the sky, and the flames were beginning to crawl up from the tenth floor.

"Then we keep going," Bella said.

She realized that that was what she'd been doing her entire life. Her father died, and Bella went to America. Pietro vanished, and she started working two jobs. Her mother and siblings died, and she joined the strike. The strike ended, and she and Yetta helped Jane. On and on and on it went; she'd had to climb back from one tragedy or setback after another. That was life.

But life was also three girls skipping down the street, their arms entwined; Rocco Luciano paying his penny back faithfully, every single week; Rahel's new baby. It was bread and potatoes and roses, velvet and real.

Lucy had begun to stumble over toward the edge of the roof.

"No!" Bella screamed at her. "You'll fall!"

It was a sheer drop down to Greene Street, ten stories below. Bella couldn't even see clear to the ground, through all the smoke and flames and floating ash. Bella tugged Lucy over to the side of the roof facing Washington Place, but there was no safe way down from there, either. Frantically, she looked around. The other two sides of the roof ran into towering brick walls, walls two or three times Bella's height.

"You brought me here to die!" Lucy spat at her. "You ruined my jacket for nothing!"

"No, wait—"

Through the smoke, Bella saw a man beginning to climb one of the walls, digging his fingers into the mortar, balancing his toes between the bricks. At the top, he disappeared over the edge—onto the roof of the building next door, Bella realized. It was just taller than the Asch Building; that was why it looked like nothing but a wall.

Moments later, the man came back to the edge of the other building's roof and lowered a ladder down toward the factory.

"We'll go that way," Bella said. "That building's not on fire."

They rushed over with dozens of others who'd escaped from the tenth floor. Mr. Blanck was already handing Harriet up the ladder, then Millicent climbed up behind her, almost falling because she was trying so hard to hold her skirt in close around her legs. Men were shoving Mr. Blanck up the ladder.

"Bella! Come up here! There's no fire on this roof!" Harriet cried out, leaning over the edge. Now that she was safe, she seemed to regard the whole experience as an adventure. Millicent was retching and trembling and Mr. Blanck was sweating and moaning, "My factory . . . my factory . . . ," but Harriet sounded as if she'd done nothing more dangerous than riding a Ferris wheel at Coney Island.

"Thanks, but I'm going to wait for Jane," Bella called back to her.

She made sure that Lucy climbed up to safety, without fainting again or falling. Then Bella backed away from the ladder, peering into the faces around her. Only thirty or forty people had found their way to the roof, but it was hard to tell if Jane was among them. Everyone was soot-covered and singed, and the smoke swirled around them. Bella kept walking backward, staring.

Somebody grabbed her arm.

"Careful, there, miss."

It was Mr. Bernstein, the factory manager again. He pointed at the ground. She'd been one step away from falling down into a huge hole, a gaping pit of flames. Why was there a hole in the roof? Bella squinted, puzzled, her mind flashing back to a man standing on a table, pounding on seemingly unbreakable glass. The skylight. This was where the skylight had been—the man's attempt to break it had been pitiful, but the fire had shattered the glass almost effortlessly.

Bella stared down into the flames, hypnotized.

"It's not safe here," Mr. Bernstein said. "Go over to the ladders."

"I'm looking for my friend," Bella said. "What if she's still down there?"

She pointed down into the fire, where the flames bubbled across the remains of a table.

"There was nobody left on the tenth floor," Mr. Bernstein said impatiently. "Or the eighth. I don't think. I was on the eighth floor too."

"What about the ninth?" Bella asked.

Mr. Bernstein turned his head, avoiding smoke. Avoiding her question.

"Somebody!" he yelled. "Get this girl out of here!"

A figure appeared out of the smoke, a young man.

"Yes, sir," he said.

He tugged on Bella's arm, pulling her toward another set of ladders rigged up alongside the other building.

"They said the NYU library was in danger of burning," the young man said. "I said, 'So are those girls on that roof. Let the law books burn. I'm going to save the girls.'"

Bella liked the sound of his voice, so firm and certain in the shifting smoke.

"Yetta and Jane were both on the ninth floor," she said. The words were pounding in her head now that she herself was being saved. She barely realized that she'd spoken aloud until the young man startled at the names.

"Yetta and Jane—?" For the first time, he peered at Bella closely, as if trying to discern her features under the soot and ash. "You were with that crowd?"

Then Bella recognized the young man: It was Charles Livingston, the law student Yetta had badgered with her questions about union rights.

"We thought you'd marry Jane someday," Bella said, with a giggle that twisted in her throat. Maybe it wasn't a giggle at all. Maybe it was a sob.

"Really?" Charles said. "Not until we get you to safety."

He handed her up the ladder, to other law students. But then he climbed up behind her and led her down stairs crowded with boys carrying books. They made it to an elevator, then out to the sidewalk.

"I always meet Yetta and Jane by the Greene Street door," Bella told Charles. "They'll be waiting for me. They'll be worried."

But the sidewalk was blocked off by fire trucks and firemen and policemen shooing the crowds away. The policemen were completely different from how they'd been during the strike: They weren't slamming heads together and beating people with their nightsticks. They were patting the backs of sobbing girls. They were—could it be?—sobbing themselves.

"Yetta and Jane have to see this," Bella told Charles. "We can wait right across the street. They'll find me. They will."

Bella couldn't have said when she knew that they wouldn't. It felt like hours that she and Charles stood there. It felt like an eternity. She could see the sheets covering the lumps on the sidewalk—sheets dropped so hurriedly that a hand stuck out here, a boot with a shiny buckle stuck out there. She could see the firemen carrying out more lumps draped with sheets. These lumps seemed too small some-how, burned down to their essence. Bella didn't need to see underneath the sheet on the Washington Place sidewalk that covered two bodies, not one. She didn't need to hear the fireman who muttered, as he carried out yet another corpse: "At least this one had a nice ring before she died." She knew without evidence, without proof, without actually knowing.

Bella began keening. She stood on her own two feet, leaning on no one, but Charles stood beside her, his arm around her shoulders as she wailed. And then Rocco was there and Rahel, hugging her and sobbing and wailing, too. When Bella's family had died, she'd felt so alone; she'd been frantic in her grief because she was the only one left to mourn them. But now she was surrounded by mothers and fathers, brothers and sisters, husbands and wives, boyfriends and girlfriends and fiancés, all mourning for their own dead. And it seemed to Bella that she could feel the sorrow spread-ing, to millionaires in their mansions and to women in fur coats who'd walked a picket line beside a hungry girl they now wondered about, to college girls who'd gone to jail for an immigrant girl's job, to young, dreamy-eyed men who'd bought a strike-edition newspaper from a pretty girl they now remembered as if she were their first, true, lost love. And, to Bella, at a moment when everything else seemed so tragically wrong, this, at least, seemed right: that all of New York City was grieving with her.

Mrs. Livingston

Harriet is crying now, wailing in the same broken-hearted way Mrs. Livingston had wailed, all those years ago. It is a messy sort of crying, for Harriet seems to be past caring about wiping away snot or tears, past even thinking about propriety or appearances.

Mrs. Livingston does not hand the girl a handkerchief. She lets her cry.

"Papa told us Jane survived," Harriet finally sobs out. "He said—he said he fired her and forbade her to ever see us again, because she left us alone during the fire."

Even after all these years, that stings.

"Jane didn't know about the fire," Mrs. Livingston protests. "Not when she left you. And when she couldn't get back to the stairs, she told me to look for you."

As she has done so many times, Mrs. Livingston thinks about how that day could have gone differently. She still wants to rewrite history. What if Jane had heard an alarm before she got to the ninth floor? What if she'd carried Harriet and Millicent up to the roof before the flames came? What if she'd ridden the elevator straight down to the street? And what if Yetta had realized that the ninth floor was nearly hopeless—what if she and Jacob had run down the stairs, not up? What if they hadn't been so noble? But changing even one of her friends' actions meant that Mrs. Livingston's life might have been forfeited, in place of Yetta's or Jane's. Failing to save their own lives, they'd saved hers instead.

For the longest time, Mrs. Livingston wished that she could have traded fates with them.

"When you came and got us from beside the elevator," Harriet says slowly. "It was Jane who sent you to us?"

Mrs. Livingston nods, her throat suddenly too swollen to speak.

"Then, you saved our lives," Harriet says. "You got Papa to start walking toward the stairs."

"Lots of people helped you," Mrs. Livingston says. It is a delicate thing, saving somebody's life. That's why, when she tries to rewrite history, she gets so paralyzed. If only the fire escape had worked, if only the elevators had been bigger, if only the door hadn't been locked, if only the fire department had had better nets, bigger ladders . . . Just to save Yetta's life, just to save Jane's, even in hindsight, would have required such stitching-over of history, so much changing of the world as it had actually been.

Harriet is sniffling now. She pulls a lace-trimmed handkerchief out of her pocket—evidently she had one all along, but was too overwrought to use it before. She dabs at her eyes, wipes her nose.

"The fire was a terrible thing. A disaster," she says. "I wish it had never happened. But it was an *accident.* My father and Uncle Isaac didn't want anyone to die."

"They could have enforced the rules about smoking," Mrs. Livingston says. "They could have had fire drills. They could have told us the fire had started. They could have—"

Harriet whips up out of her chair.

"Lots of factories were like Triangle!" she hisses, right in Mrs. Livingston's face. "That's what factories *were*, back then— they were crowded and noisy and busy, and there wasn't any money for extras, because the factory owners had to compete with every other factory owner. A few pennies here and there could be the difference between staying in business and starving on the streets."

"Extras?" Mrs. Livingston asks. "Something that could have saved one hundred and forty-six lives is an extra?"

Harriet collapses back into her chair.

"No," she whispers. White-faced, she stares past Mrs. Livingston's shoulder. "In March 1908, a furnace overheated in a primary school in Collinwood, Ohio. The exits were defective and people panicked. More than one hundred and seventy children burned, suffocated, or were crushed to death. February 1909, a wooden theater in Acalpulco, Mexico, caught fire during a film, and three hundred people were killed. November 1909, in Cherry, Illinois, there was a mine explosion and fire, and over two hundred and fifty miners died. Shall I go on?"

"No," Mrs. Livingston says.

"Why is my father the worst criminal?" Harriet asks. "Why is the Triangle fire the one that everyone remembers?"

Mrs. Livingston wants to say, *We should remember them all, everyone who's lost.* But the numbers are overwhelming. Harriet has clearly selected these tragedies—*memorized* these tragedies—because of their death counts. Mrs. Livingston cannot think about one hundred seventy dead children. She cannot think about three hundred people going out for a night on the town, excited about seeing a moving picture, then meeting the end of their lives. She cannot think about being trapped under the ground, dying there. She can only remember Yetta and Jane, can only miss and mourn them.

"I think . . . I think people remember the Triangle fire because of the strike," she tells Harriet. "People had cheered us on. They'd donated money to our cause, they'd bailed us out of jail, they'd marveled at our courage. We weren't faceless and anonymous and easily forgotten after the strike. And then so many of us died so young, so tragically, so soon after. People felt like they knew us. They took our deaths personally."

Harriet absorbs this. She's slumped over in her chair now, utterly defeated.

"Come here," Mrs. Livingston says.

She leads Harriet up the stairs, pushes open a door.

"Ssh," she warns.

Inside the dim room, in two beds, there are two little girls sound asleep, deep into their afternoon naps.

"My daughters," Mrs. Livingston whispers. "Yetta is four and Jane is two."

Harriet nods, her eyes brimming with tears. She seems to see the beauty of the sleep-tangled dark curls, the peaceful rise and fall of each little chest, the fierceness in the way Yetta hugs her favorite doll, the soothing rhythm of Jane sucking her thumb. She stands there watching the little girls until Mrs. Livingston beckons to her and they tiptoe back down the stairs.

"You have to understand," Mrs. Livingston says, settling back into her chair. "They can't ever replace my friends. They don't make up for anyone I lost. But they are . . . a way to carry on. A way to remember that isn't sorrow and grief." She pauses. "Rahel has a daughter named Yetta too."

Harriet stares down at her lap.

"I went to college because of Jane," she says. "Over my parents' objections. They said it wasn't necessary for a girl. Pah! Did my father need a college education to become the Shirtwaist King?"

Mrs. Livingston smiles at the inflections in Harriet's voice, so reminiscent of Yetta's accent, so clearly an imitation of Mr. and Mrs. Blanck. Harriet looks up, her eyes blazing.

"But I remembered Jane talking about girls going to college, about how they should get an education, just as much as boys. I think I remember it better because of how she disappeared, after the fire."

Mrs. Livingston nods, accepting this. Agreeing. "There were all those laws passed because of the fire, to improve working conditions," she says. "Yetta would have been so proud of those. And the Red Cross fire relief committee helped Rahel bring their family over after the fire, just before a pogrom destroyed their village. It's so wrong, it shouldn't have worked this way, but . . . Yetta's death accomplished so many of the things that she'd wanted to accomplish with her life."

"It's a shame she didn't live to see what happened," Harriet says. "And I wish Jane had seen me graduate from college."

Mrs. Livingston tilts her head thoughtfully.

"The fire led to a few other good things—Charles

Livingston became a labor lawyer, a passionate one. He's done so much good in his field, although I wish he wouldn't tell his story quite so often, about how he was inspired by his experiences rescuing dozens and dozens of shirtwaist girls. . . ." Her eyes twinkle—mocking and forgiving, all at once.

"Is *that* who you married?" Harriet asks. "The detectives didn't tell me, but I assumed—"

"Oh, no!" Mrs. Livingston laughs. "Me and Charles? No, no, no. My husband is Italian. He just changed his name because—"

Harriet gasps.

"So Pietro did come back for you? How romantic!"

"Not Pietro," Mrs. Livingston says. "Although he did send a letter after the fire, asking if I was all right—and inviting me to his wedding in South Carolina." She shrugs. "I got a much better husband than Pietro. I married Rocco."

Harriet almost falls off her chair in surprise.

"The little boy?" she asks. "The one who kept paying you pennies for his family's debt?"

Mrs. Livingston smiles.

"He grew up," she says. "Rather nicely."

Harriet still appears scandalized.

"He's only two years younger than me," Mrs. Livingston adds. "I just always thought of him as a little boy. Until I . . . started thinking of him differently."

"And I guess this way he didn't have to worry about paying you any more pennies," Harriet muses. She looks around, her eyes taking in each detail of the spacious parlor: the new sofa, the paintings hung over the fireplace, the gleaming crystals encircling the lamps. Mrs. Livingston's house is not extravagantly furnished, but it's clear that she's come a long way from being a poor shirtwaist girl who thought a single red rose was the ultimate in luxury.

"But how . . . ?" Harriet begins, and hesitates, because it's impossible to phrase her question politely.

"After the fire, the Livingston family was so helpful," Mrs. Livingston says. "Charles's parents were just as appalled and horrified as he was, and they wanted to *do* something. They asked me for advice about how to make a difference for 'those poor people on the Lower East Side.' And that just happened to be the same day that Rocco's parents kicked him out because they'd found out that he was going to school instead of shining shoes and selling newspapers all day long. So I suggested that the Livingstons take him in and pay for his education. They adopted him, and now he's a doctor." She grins mischievously, in a way that makes her look like a teenaged shirtwaist girl again. "People are always a little confused by the name Rocco Livingston."

"I guess this way you don't have to worry about dealing with Signora Luciano as your mother-in-law," Harriet muses.

"Oh, no," Mrs. Livingston says. "The Lucianos forgave Rocco when he set Papa Luciano up with his own grocery store a few years ago. They're so different now. We go over there every Sunday, and Mama Luciano is always nice to me, unless I suggest that my mother would have used more oregano in the pasta sauce. . . ." She knows she cannot explain to this American girl what it is like to go to the Lucianos' each Sunday. It is a little bit like going back to Italy, except an Italy where there is always enough to eat. Some weeks, Mrs. Livingston lives for those Sunday visits.

And some weeks, she can only see the people who aren't sitting around that table, the ones who weren't as lucky as the Livingstons and the Lucianos.

"What did you do right after the fire?" Harriet asks. "When you didn't have your friends to live with, when you didn't even have a job anymore . . ."

"Rahel and her husband took me in," Mrs. Livingston says. "I was their baby nurse, their store clerk. I did what they'd wanted Yetta to do, except that because of me their children speak Yiddish and English with an Italian accent. And I began mixing in Hebrew with the Latin prayers at church." She rolls her eyes, to let Harriet know that nobody minded this. She can make the stories of that time in her life sound so light and funny, a comical mishmash of Italian and Jewish culture. What she remembers most is crying on Rahel's shoulder, and Rahel crying on hers. But they always ended up laughing afterward, wiping away tears and agreeing, "Yetta would think we are fools and *schmendriks*, crying like this." So maybe the funny stories aren't lies.

"Then," Mrs. Livingston continued, "I helped Rahel take care of her parents when they got here, sick and old and baffled by America. And I went to school. It sounds like nothing to a college graduate, I know, but I did earn my eighth-grade diploma."

"Jane and Yetta should have been here to see that, too," Harriet says.

Mrs. Livingston nods.

"I think they know," she says.

Harriet squints at her doubtfully.

"You act like you can know what their last moments

were like," she says. "How do you know they weren't cursing God's name, cursing my father's name, screaming in
misery and pain and terror the entire time?"

Her voice cracks. Mrs. Livingston can tell this is a
question she's been longing to ask ever since Mrs.
Livingston finished her story.

"I can't *know*," Mrs. Livingston says. "But I feel it. I am
certain. Just as certain as I am that I saw my mother in the
flames and smoke. After the fire I had dreams, Yetta and Jane
each coming to talk to me, to tell me not to be sad anymore.
And Rahel had some of the same dreams. We were finishing
each other's sentences, describing what Yetta had said, how
she apologized for never seeing the baby. And . . ."

"Yes?" Harriet says.

"Remember all those letters Jane had tried to write to
her father?" Mrs. Livingston asks. "She didn't know this, but
I kept all the letters she tore up and threw away. I pulled
them out of the trash. I had such respect for the written
word then—it seemed like a sin not to keep each and every
one. I glued them back together. When I could read them, I
learned . . ." She swallowed hard. "Every one of them began
with some variation of, 'Don't worry about me, Father, for I
am alive and well and happier than I've ever been. . . .'"

Harriet winces.

"Those letters were all written before the fire," she says
brusquely. "How could they give you any idea what she went
through that last day?"

"I put the letters in a big packet and I got Jane's signet
ring from the morgue and I took them all to her father.
And . . . he had had dreams too. He knew, somehow."

Mrs. Livingston can tell that Harriet—a modern, bobbed-hair girl, a college graduate—is not convinced by dreams and coincidences. She probably thinks that Mrs. Livingston imagined her mother in the smoke, too.

"Did Mr. Wellington regret driving Jane away?" Harriet asks. "Did he regret hiring strikebreakers, making his fortune over the top of dead bodies?"

Her voice is still harsh and angry, judging Jane's father.

"When Mr. Wellington died," Mrs. Livingston says, "he left most of his fortune to the suffrage movement."

Harriet raises one eyebrow, in surprise.

"Was that enough?" she asks. "Did he earn his atonement?"

Mrs. Livingston frowns.

"Why are you asking me? I'm not a priest. I'm not a rabbi. Who am I to decide?"

Harriet toys with the fringe of the antimacassar on her chair.

"My father," she says, "was defiant on the witness stand. He was acquitted of any responsibility for the Triangle fire because he could afford to hire Max Steuer, the best lawyer in the city. And Mr. Steuer tricked the shirtwaist girls on the witness stand into sounding like liars. My father and Uncle Isaac collected more than sixty thousand dollars in insurance money, even above the costs of the fire, money they didn't have to share with anyone else. Two years later—" Her voice grows thick. She tries again. "Two years later my father was fined for once again locking his employees into his factory during the workday. He's lucky there was not another fire."

Mrs. Livingston feels a blast of fury sweep over her, as

if, with Yetta gone, she has to experience the indignation on her friend's behalf as well as her own. How could someone learn so little from his worst mistakes?

"He was fined only twenty dollars," Harriet says. "And the judge apologized for fining him at all."

She sounds so forlorn and sorrowful that Mrs. Livingston cannot hold on to her fury.

"The world," she says dryly, "is not a perfect place even yet."

"Bella," Harriet says, and Mrs. Livingston recognizes the same pleading tone that Harriet had had in her voice as a five-year-old. "What should I do? When I come into my inheritance, should I give it up like Jane did? I—I'm not that brave or that good. I wouldn't know how to survive being poor. But how can I keep taking money earned from . . . from evil?"

This, Mrs. Livingston realizes, is what Harriet has really comes to ask her. The details of leaping flames and screaming, terrified girls were only previews to what really matters: now. What can any of us do now?

Mrs. Livingston is tempted to repeat her earlier answer: *I'm not a priest. I'm not a rabbi. Who am I to decide?* She has only an eighth-grade diploma, earned at night school, not a college degree. She was illiterate until she was sixteen; she grew up in a one-room hut and slept with goats and chickens. She is, still, nobody.

But she has stared directly into the face of Mr. Blanck's evil. Into the flames. She lost her two best friends, her *comari*, to his carelessness, to his devotion to the accumulation of money above all other goals, even the goal of keeping his own workers alive. Even now, she sometimes has nightmares where she has a thousand shirtwaists to sew, and Signor Carlotti is breathing down her neck, and then the shirtwaists are on fire and the sewing machine is made out of skeletons and Signor Carlotti's face is burning, melting like a candle, and he's still screaming, "Faster! Sew faster! There are a hundred girls coming into Ellis Island right now who'll take your job if you can't do it right! They'd be willing to die for this job—why aren't you?"

Mrs. Livingston always wakes from those nightmares sobbing.

"Harriet," she says in a ragged voice. "If you are asking me for forgiveness, or absolution—" She has forgotten that absolution is a Catholic concept, not a Jewish one.

"It would kill Papa if I spurned him," Harriet says. "If I even told him that I disapprove of him . . . He's always been such a wonderful father, so loving and kind. He's always given us everything we ever wanted."

Mrs. Livingston thinks of the landowners back in Italy who let the peasants die—their children probably thought they were wonderful too. But she keeps her mouth shut and waits for Harriet to go on.

"Anyhow," Harriet says. "Nothing I can do could ever bring back Yetta and Jane."

"That's not true," Mrs. Livingston argues. "How you live, how you spend your money, the ways you honor their memory—all of that can bring them back. Their spirit, anyway."

"That's not enough," Harriet says.

It's not. Sometimes Mrs. Livingston feels like Yetta, with her perpetual yearning. It's not enough to have two lovely daughters, to have a handsome, loving husband, to have charitable work and new friends and in-laws. Nothing can ever be enough when Mrs. Livingston has such gaping holes in her heart. But Mrs. Livingston has learned to live with that.

She sighs.

"Jane did not plan on dying when she was only seventeen," she says. "She was like a work-in-progress, still figuring out what she believed, what that meant about how she wanted to live her life. For what it's worth, I think she would have forgiven her father eventually. Somehow."

"And she would have gone to college," Harriet says. "She would have become a famous teacher—she was really good at teaching, did you know that? And Yetta would have married Jacob; she would have become a famous union organizer. My father took all that away from both of them."

"You can't give it back," Mrs. Livingston says. "But there are other girls out there now, girls who are hungry and confused, eager and hopeful, but nobody's giving them a chance. . . ."

"So you're saying if I take my father's money, I have to be a do-gooder instead of a flapper?" Harriet asks. "Help others instead of just having fun?"

"You asked me," Mrs. Livingston says.

Harriet sits there. Mrs. Livingston knows what others would see: a pretty girl with bobbed hair and a fringed dress. A surface kind of person, someone who's been groomed her whole life to look good entering a party on the arm of a wealthy man. But Mrs. Livingston sees a soul in turmoil, a young girl looking for the right answers, not just the easy ones.

"Mama?" It is little Yetta, standing at the top of the

stairs. "I woke up and you didn't come and get me."

She pushes tangled curls out of her eyes and stares accusingly down at her mother.

"That's because I didn't know you were awake," Mrs. Livingston says lightly. She pats the space beside her on the couch. "Come down here, Yetta, there's someone I'd like you to meet. A—a friend of mine."

Harriet stiffens at the word "friend," as if she understands what Mrs. Livingston is offering, what she is asking. This is like lions lying down with lambs, like swords being hammered into plowshares, like fires of bitterness and sorrow and grief finally being extinguished.

"I'm not really your mother's friend," Harriet says. "Not yet. But I would like to be."

She looks over at Mrs. Livingston hopefully. *This is why money is not God in America,* Mrs. Livingston thinks. *This is why, when they said on the boat, 'Anythingis possible in America,' they were not just talking about striking it rich. This is how I finally escape the fire, by becoming friends with Harriet Blanck, who is trying to escape too.*

Mrs. Livingston spreads her arms, and her daughter, little Yetta, races down the stairs and throws herself into her mother's embrace, so trustingly. *She'll never know,* Mrs. Livingston thinks. But no—she will someday. Someday Mrs. Livingston will tell her daughter the story of the Triangle fire, and she dares to hope that by then it will be hard for her daughter to believe, hard for her to even imagine a time when life meant so little, when tragedy came so easily, when the whole world needed to wake up. She dares to hope that she and her daughters and Harriet Blanck can play a role in moving the world further and further away from that time.

Mrs. Livingston hugs little Yetta close and whispers into her daughter's hair, "We will not be stupid girls. We will not be powerless girls. We will not be useless girls." And, for just a moment, she believes she can hear two other voices whispering along with her.

AUTHOR'S NOTE

The shirtwaist strike of 1909-10 really happened.

The Triangle Shirtwaist Factory fire of March 25, 1911, really happened.

Personally, when I've just read a historical novel that seemed completely real to me—as I hope this book seemed completely real to you—I hate to then read an author's note explaining, "Well, this was real, but this wasn't; this event didn't actually occur, but it could have; this character I completely made up." Because then the story recedes back into distant history, and what seemed so alive and immediate and tangible is gone. So I won't tell you which parts of this book didn't really happen. Suffice it to say that I tried to stick to the historical facts as much as possible, unless I felt I had a really, really good reason not to. And if you feel you must distill the history from the fiction, then you are welcome to do research of your own. I'll even suggest ways to do that. (More about that later.)

If you just want to know more about the early 1900s and the strike and the fire and what they meant to history, read on.

In many ways, the early 1900s were not such a different time period from our own. Americans then were fascinated with the latest technology—although their "new" technology was airplanes and automobiles and up-to-date sewing machines, not computers and iPods and video cell phones. There were stunning disparities between the rich and the poor, and reformers were calling out for change. And, at a time when huge numbers of foreigners were pouring into the United States looking for economic opportunity or religious freedom—or just a better chance of staying alive—Americans had mixed feelings about welcoming these newcomers.

For many Italians and Russian Jews, even a half-hearted welcome was far better than what they faced in their homelands. In southern Italy, peasants were starving. Without land of their own, with economic and governmental and agricultural systems that seemed to guarantee their starvation, many of them felt they had no choice but to leave for America or Argentina or some other country—anywhere they might have a chance. In most cases, the Italian immigrants intended to return home as soon as they'd saved up enough money. That often didn't go as planned. A common witticism was that Italians came to America expecting to see streets paved with gold—but when they got here, they discovered that not only were the streets not paved with gold, they weren't paved at all. And furthermore, the Italians were expected to do the paving!

The Russian Jews who came to America were fleeing not just poverty, but religious persecution as well. In Russia they faced severe limits on where they could live and what jobs they could hold. And repeatedly during the late 1800s and early 1900s, mobs of Russian peasants slaughtered whole communities of Jews, in pogroms that the government did little to stop and sometimes actively encouraged.

Girls like Bella and Yetta who came to America faced additional challenges because of their gender. Among those welcoming them to the United States were factory owners eager to exploit their desperation, ignorance, and subservience. As one factory owner bluntly put it, "I want no experienced girl, but only those greenhorns (new immigrants) . . . just come from the old country. And I let them work hard, like the devil, for less wages." Girls weren't supposed to complain, they weren't supposed to speak out, they weren't supposed to think that they might have rights of their own.

Those attitudes make the story of the shirtwaist strike all

the more amazing. Although both males and females participated in the strike, it quickly became known as an uprising of girls. The Triangle workers were among the first shirtwaist makers to go on strike in the fall of 1909, after the owners resorted to locking out their own employees in an attempt to kill the fledgling union. Like Rahel, some of their workers had had union experience in the old country, but most of the strikers were leaping into the unknown when they picked up their first picket sign. The broader union the Triangle workers were part of Local 25 of the International Ladies' Garment Workers' Union, had just been formed in 1906 and had only one hundred members by 1909. So male labor leaders could perhaps be excused for thinking that girls wouldn't make good strikers.

How wrong they were.

At the huge Local 25 union meeting at the Cooper Union on November 22, 1909, it was indeed a female, Clara Lemlich, who made the call for a general strike. At least twenty thousand workers—perhaps even more than forty thousand—from hundreds of New York City shops walked off the job within the next week. Most of the smaller manufacturers were forced to settle quickly, agreeing to closed shops, better hours, higher wages, and similar demands. But the Triangle owners and several other large manufacturers dug in their heels. At several times during the strike, they hired thugs and prostitutes to beat the strikers. They also bribed the police to look the other way, join in the beatings, and/or to arrest the strikers whether they'd broken any laws or not. (I found it a bizarre juxtaposition that the date of Wilbur Wright's historic flight up the Hudson River—October 4, 1909—was also apparently the date of the first beatings of the Triangle strikers. The two events give such opposite perspectives on human progress.)

Meanwhile, the new hires and the other employees who crossed the picket line and continued working—the "scabs," as the strikers called them—found a much more pleasant environment than usual. Besides special foods, music, and dancing at lunchtime, some workers even got taxi service, and were picked up and dropped off each day by automobile. For poor immigrant girls in 1909, that must have seemed like the ultimate in luxury.

At the other extreme, workers at some factories told of priests coming in during their lunch hour, and telling them that they would go to hell if they joined the strike. Similarly, one judge told a worker, "You are on strike against God."

Still, the strikers persisted, even as weeks passed and the arrests and beatings continued and autumn faded into a brutally cold winter. But they weren't alone. The manufacturers must have been horrified to hear about the suffragists, society women, and college girls rallying to the cause. (And I have to believe that there must have been many wealthy businessmen, like Jane's father, who were shocked by their wives' and daughters' latest charitable endeavor.)

The *New York Times* of December 19, 1909, mocked the wealthy females' interest in the strike as springing from a "'you-a-girl-and-me-a-girl' spirit . . . The factory girl makes shirtwaists and the college girl wears them." But the wealthy women and girls really did seem to feel a bond of sisterhood that crossed economic lines. And suffragists saw the call for female workers' rights as being very closely related to their own longing for the right to vote.

The American suffrage movement was at a low point in its history before the shirtwaist strike. Women in a few other countries—New Zealand, Australia, Finland—had already won the right to vote; in England, militant suffragettes such as Emmeline Pankhurst were constantly making headlines by smashing windows, chaining themselves to railings, and staging hunger strikes in jail. But the American movement was floundering after its strongest leaders, Elizabeth Cady Stanton and Susan B. Anthony, died in 1902 and 1906, respectively.

Still, the suffrage movement had recently gained the support of the wealthy but controversial Alva Belmont, and she quickly latched on to the shirtwaist strike as one of her pet causes. If you wanted publicity, money, or daring ideas in 1909, Alva Belmont was a good person to have on your side. A consummate social climber, she'd married a Vanderbilt, married off her daughter to the ninth Duke of Marlborough, divorced her husband, and married another wealthy man who seemed to be the true love of her life. In 1909 she was a new widow, emerging from mourning and eager to find an outlet for her money, energies, and skill. She sat for hours at night court and put up her own house to bail out shirtwaist girls (its $400,000 value then being equivalent to about $8.6 million today). She rented the Hippodrome amphitheater in early December, drawing seven thousand people to listen to strikers, socialists, suffragists, and assorted other speakers. She organized the automobile parade in mid-December that brought even greater attention to the strike.

Meanwhile, Anne Morgan, daughter of financier John Pierpont Morgan—who was so wealthy and powerful, he'd once saved the United States government from bankruptcy—got involved in the strike too, through the Women's Trade Union League. Anne Morgan organized a fund-raiser at the exclusive Colony Club, bringing strikers who barely had enough money to eat, to tell their stories to the wives and daughters of millionaires. With college girls and new college graduates like Violet Pike and Inez Milholland donating their time and money as well, the strikers had some very fervent, wealthy, and powerful allies.

Unfortunately, the alliance with the so-called "Mink Brigade" began falling apart almost as quickly as it formed. Anne Morgan and many other wealthy strike supporters were horrified by the Carnegie Hall rally on January 2; it was as if they'd suddenly discovered that they'd been—gasp!—associating with socialists. Morgan patronizingly chose to believe that the socialists were taking advantage of the poor, innocent, ignorant shirtwaist girls; socialists responded that the shirtwaist girls were in greater danger from the "pretended friendship" of the rich. Some of the shirtwaist strikers did come to resent the wealthy women, particularly when they seemed to be getting all of the attention. They also wondered if the suffragists really cared about them at all, or if they were just using the strike to further their own cause.

AUTHOR'S NOTE

By January, only a small number of workers were still on strike—estimates range from five hundred to about three thousand. Some wealthy women and college girls continued their support to the very end, along with many on the Lower East Side who'd helped all along: landlords who stopped collecting rent and even provided bail money; grocery store owners who extended credit; theater owners who gave benefit plays; even strikers from settled shops who donated part of their wages back to the cause. But resources were strained. No matter how brave and fervent they were, the shirtwaist strikers could not continue forever living on two dollars a week from the strike fund.

The strike limped to an end in February. Labor leaders tried to portray the final outcome as a victory—and included Triangle on their published list of settled shops—but the Triangle workers saw few improvements, and never received their longed-for union recognition. Even some of the shops that had settled early were already breaking their promises. Still, the strike did show very dramatically that the female garment workers could organize and strike, and it paved the way for later union victories and workplace reforms. The strike is also often credited with reviving the suffrage movement (though it took another decade, until 1920, for women to win the vote nationwide).

The Triangle fire occurred just thirteen months after the strike ended. Eyewitnesses immediately made the connection between the burning, falling workers and the brave strikers. As William Gunn Shepherd, a news reporter who happened to be walking through Washington Square just as the fire broke out, put it:

"I looked upon the heap of dead bodies and I remembered these girls were the shirtwaist makers. I remembered their great strike of last year in which these same girls had demanded more sanitary conditions and more safety precautions in the shops. These dead bodies were the answer."

A total of one hundred forty-six workers—one hundred twenty-three females and twenty-three males—were killed in the Triangle fire. Workplace deaths were all too common in the early 1900s; worker safety was a priority for very few factory owners at the time. But so many died in the Triangle fire that it stood as the worst workplace disaster in New York City for the next ninety years, until September 11, 2001.

The fire is believed to have started with a match or cigarette butt in the overflowing scrap bin under a cutter's table on the eighth floor. Smokers had caused fires at Triangle before, so even though no one enforced the posted signs forbidding smoking, they did keep water buckets on shelves along the walls. (That caution didn't extend to making sure that the firehoses in the stairwells worked.) All the other smoking-related fires had been quickly doused; on March 25, 1911, the workers weren't so lucky.

The conditions on the eighth floor of the Triangle factory that day could hardly have been more ideal for helping a fire spread quickly. The wind blew up the elevator shaft and sped the flames along, drawing them from the scrap bin full of thin, highly flammable fabric, to the cutters' tables spread with layers and layers of the same fabric, to the flimsy paper patterns hanging overhead. And then the flames leaped to the rows of sewing machines, with all their piles of shirtwaists and shirtwaist pieces, their crowds of terrified workers.

The Triangle workers had never had a fire drill. It's likely that many of them didn't realize there was a fire escape, didn't even know that there was any exit except the elevators behind the Greene Street partition—close to where the ever-growing fire was now burning. The conditions at Triangle were ideal for panic as well as fire.

But as bad as the situation was on the eighth floor, workers there had a big advantage over their fellow employees on the ninth and tenth floors: on the eighth floor, they knew right away that the fire had started.

Bookkeeper Dinah Lipschitz, the factory manager's cousin, did try to send a message from her desk on the eighth floor to the tenth floor. Oddly, the first method she tried was the telautograph, which was sort of a bad, early-1900s version of a fax machine. It didn't work right, and Mary Alter, sitting at her desk on the tenth floor, decided to ignore it. When Lipschitz finally thought to use the telephone instead—a few, dangerously wasted moments later—Alter left her desk to notify others on the tenth floor rather than calling anyone on the ninth. So the ninth-floor workers had no warning until the waves of flame and smoke began rolling in through their windows.

It's no surprise that most of the dead came from the ninth floor. Maybe the biggest surprise is that so many of them survived.

Some did manage to scramble down the substandard, inadequate fire escape—at least down to a lower floor the flames hadn't reached. But the fire escape was quickly blocked by the warped eighth-floor shutters, causing a logjam of panicked workers pushing and shoving and desperate to get out. Under their weight, the whole fire escape collapsed, sending about two dozen people plunging to their death at the bottom of the smoky airshaft.

Other ninth-floor workers managed to make it to the Greene Street stairs before the flames cut off that exit. If they knew to go up to the roof with the tenth-floor workers, they had a good chance of surviving. But the ones who staked their fate on the Washington Place stairs were doomed. At the eighth-floor door onto that stairway, workers told of a machinist named Louis Brown turning a key in the lock, pulling the door open, and letting them escape. No one showed up with a key at the ninth-floor door.

Oddly, many of the workers who survived took an escape route that should have seemed insanely risky: the elevators. Two elevator operators, Joseph Zito and Gaspar Mortillalo, showed immense bravery, returning again and again to the scene of the fire, carrying down a dozen or more workers with each trip. Descending from the ninth and tenth floors meant passing the eighth-floor flames, already licking into the elevator shaft. Still, many workers who couldn't fit into the elevators threw themselves onto the roofs of the elevator cars or tried to slide down the elevator cables. Some of them survived too, although nineteen bodies were recovered from the elevator shaft after the fire. Altogether, Zito and Mortillalo are credited with rescuing more than one hundred fifty workers, about half of all the survivors.

Once the elevators stopped running, the Greene Street stairs were blocked, and the fire escape had collapsed, the ninth-floor workers who hadn't escaped were down to two choices: jump or burn.

The fire department received the first report of the fire at 4:45 p.m., and had people on the scene by 4:47 p.m. New York City prided itself on its up-to-date, modern fire department. Even the immigrants knew this: Eastern European Jews assured newcomers who'd witnessed pogroms in the old country, "In America, they don't let you burn." But in a city already packed with skyscrapers, the fire department had no ladders that reached above the level of about a sixth or seventh floor. The firemen did have nets, and that must have given some small sense of hope to the workers shoving their way out the windows, desperate to escape the flames. But it was false hope. Even, say, a hundred-pound teenaged girl tumbling down from a ninth-floor window would have hit the net with a force of more than a ton. The firemen put their nets away after a few moments, but the bodies kept falling. News reporter William Gunn Shepherd counted sixty-two people who died hitting the ground.

The firemen had the fire under control by 5:15 p.m., barely a half an hour after it started. That was when they began discovering the charred bodies on the ninth floor: some fifty corpses crammed near the Washington Place door, huddled in the cloakroom, or scattered elsewhere in the room.

The Triangle fire was horrific and appalling, with a few moments of heroic bravery and miraculous rescue. The workers and executives who escaped to the roof were fortunate that the building next door was being painted, so New York University law students were easily able to find ladders to lower down to the Triangle building roof. One student reportedly carried an unconscious worker up the ladder by her hair—which must have been terrifying ten stories above the ground, in the midst of smoke and flames. On the other side of the roof, Triangle co-owner Isaac Harris managed to climb up the brick wall of another adjoining building, break a skylight with his bare hands, and find a janitor to get a ladder to lower down there, as well. Factory manager Samuel Bernstein—who was anything but a beloved boss under normal circumstances—seems to have been practically an action-movie hero during the fire, saving lives on both the eighth and tenth floors, and on the roof.

Harris's and Bernstein's courage made co-owner Max Blanck look even more cowardly. Blanck had his two daughters there to worry about, and he did manage to snatch his screaming, terrified five-year-old out of the elevator when the panicked crowd swept her out of his reach. But after that, he mostly just let others guide him and his daughters to safety.

The most incredible thing about the Triangle fire, though, is not the fire itself, or the deaths or the amazing rescues. It is what followed: The fire changed history. By twenty-first-century standards, the conditions that led to so many of the deaths at Triangle are hard to believe. But the Triangle fire is a big part of the reason that we have a lot of those twenty-first-century standards.

The outcry against the fire and the factory owners was practically instantaneous, even in a world without CNN and internet updates and twenty-four-hour news. Many who'd united in support of the strike came together again to mourn and protest. An estimated four hundred thousand people showed up for the funeral parade for seven victims of the fire who were never identified or claimed.

New York City newspapers were relentless in their coverage of the tragedy. Politically ambitious publisher William Randolph Hearst used his paper, *The American*, to blame city officials; he set up his own commission to suggest new laws for safer factories. Others weren't so sure about who deserved the blame. The *Evening Journal* published a drawing of a gallows on its front page, labeled, "This Ought to Fit Somebody; Who Is He?"

AUTHOR'S NOTE

In mid-April, Max Blanck and Isaac Harris were arrested and charged with manslaughter. By the time of the trial eight months later, the district attorney's office had narrowed the case to focus on only one death: that of a worker, Margaret Schwartz, who'd died near the Washington Place door on the ninth floor. The plan was to show a direct link between Schwartz's death and the Triangle owners' policy of keeping that door locked.

But the defense attorney, Max Steuer, skillfully managed to throw doubt on workers' testimony about the locked door, on Schwartz's chances of survival even if she'd made it through the door, and on the authenticity of the lock itself, when the prosecution produced it. Both men were acquitted.

Yet several suspicious details weren't fully explored in the trial. Two years later, a series of articles in *Collier's* magazine looked at a different aspect of the Triangle owners' potential guilt: their previously cozy relationship with fire. Harris and Blanck had collected hefty insurance payments for fires at Triangle and another of their factories, the Diamond Waist Company, five times in the decade leading up to 1911. Conveniently, all those fires occurred outside of work hours, at the end of busy seasons (usually in April), when the companies were saddled with a potentially crippling amount of extra inventory. From two fires in 1902 alone, Harris and Blanck collected more than $32,000, equivalent today to about $726,000. At the time of the 1911 fire, the two men were carrying $200,000 in insurance on their factory, estimated to be about $80,000 more than the factory was worth.

The *Collier's* articles were careful to point out that neither man was ever charged with arson, and certainly no one was implying that they would have purposely started the 1911 fire with the factory full of workers—and with Blanck's own daughters visiting on the tenth floor. But the insurance system was designed to reward big purchasers even if they were rotten risks. So factory owners in the fickle fashion business had economic incentives to make their factories *more*, not less, likely to catch fire. The ragman who normally carried off the fabric scraps from Triangle testified at the trial that he hadn't been there since mid-January. So by the end of March there were two-and-a-half months' worth of highly flammable scraps lying around; the factory was ready, perhaps, for another off-hours fire if the owners decided they could make more in insurance money than from selling their shirtwaists. If Harris and Blanck had installed sprinklers or any other fire-safety apparatus, that might have stopped their useful fires, as well as the potentially fatal ones. The *Collier's* articles made it clear that the insurance system encouraged business owners to play with fire—and workers were the ones who got burned.

Because Harris and Blanck faced no direct punishment, the public clamored all the more for government action. Activists worried that politics as usual would kill the reform movement, as had happened so often before. But, under pressure, New York's governor appointed a Factory Investigating Commission with unprecedented powers. Within two years there were laws about automatic sprinklers in high-rise buildings, mandatory fire drills in large businesses, requirements for doors being unlocked and swinging outward. And there were other protections for workers, especially women and children. The entire state Department of Labor was changed to enforce those protections.

One of the people involved in the Factory Investigating Commission was a young woman named Frances Perkins. Coincidentally, on the afternoon of March 25, 1911, she had been having tea at a friend's home on Washington Square. Hearing fire alarms, they went to investigate. So Perkins saw everything firsthand: the smoke and flames, the falling bodies, the grieving families. Two decades later, when President Franklin Delano Roosevelt chose her as his Secretary of Labor—making her the first female cabinet officer in American history—she carried the memories with her and made many of the reforms nationwide. As she put it, "The Triangle fire was the first day of the New Deal."

From the distance of nearly a century, it is easy to feel

smug, to believe that tragedies like the Triangle fire are safely in the past. We have other things to worry about now. But people forget. They still break laws and, weighing their risks, come down in favor of profits rather than lives. As recently as 1991, twenty-five people were killed in a fire at a chicken-processing plant in Hamlet, North Carolina—killed, because their factory doors were locked. With recent political focus on illegal immigration, more and more stories are coming out about immigrants working in the United States in unbelievable circumstances, living like virtual slaves. And with increasing globalization, many of the products we use come from factories in countries without many worker protections. In 1993, at least one hundred eighty-eight workers were killed in a fire at a toy factory in Thailand; the exact death toll was never known, because many of the bodies were never found. In just one of a series of factory tragedies in Bangladesh, more than fifty people were killed in February 2006 in a textile mill fire where locked doors were once again an issue. Both the Thai and Bangladeshi factories were making products intended for the American market. Like the shirtwaist-wearing college girls in 1909, we have to ask ourselves what responsibility we bear for the people who make our clothes and other possessions.

The Triangle fire may have happened nearly a century ago, but its ghosts have reason to haunt us still.

If you are interested in learning more about the Triangle strike and/or fire, I would recommend reading three books in particular:

Von Drehle, David. Triangle: *The Fire that Changed America.* New York: Atlantic Monthly Press, 2003.
Stein, Leon. *The Triangle Fire.* Ithaca, N.Y.: Cornell University Press, 1962.
Dash, Joan. *We Shall Not Be Moved: The Women's Factory Strike of 1909.* New York: Scholastic, Inc., 1996.

I found all of those books to be very useful while I was

writing this one, and they, along with newspaper articles of the time, were the source of much of the information in this author's note.

Many of the websites I found concerning the Triangle strike and fire were less useful, and often inaccurate. But an excellent site is http://www.ilr.cornell.edu/trianglefire/.

I won't list all the other resources I used to write this book (it's long enough already), but some of the other books I found especially helpful, and would recommend to anyone who's really, really interested, include:

Cohen, Rose. *Out of the Shadow: A Russian Jewish Girlhood on the Lower East Side*. Ithaca, N.Y.: Cornell University Press, 1995.

Ewen, Elizabeth. *Immigrant Women in the Land of Dollars: Life and Culture on the Lower East Side, 1890-1925*. New York: Monthly Review Press, 1985.

Flexner, Eleanor, and Fitzgerald, Ellen. *Century of Struggle: The Woman's Rights Movement in the United States*. Cambridge, Mass.: Belknap Press of Harvard University Press, 1975.

Glenn, Susan. *Daughters of the Shtetl: Life and Labor in the Immigrant Generation*. Ithaca, N.Y.: Cornell University Press, 1990.

Homberger, Eric. Mrs. *Astor's New York: Money and Social Power in a Gilded Age*. New Haven, Conn.: Yale University Press, 2002.

Hoobler, Dorothy. *The Italian American Family Album*. New York: Oxford University Press, 1994.

How We Lived: a Documentary History of Immigrant Jews in America, 1880-1930. Irving Howe and Kenneth Libo, ed. New York: R. Marek Publishers, 1979.

Howe, Irving. *World of Our Fathers: The Journey of the Eastern European Jews to America and the Life They Found and Made*. New York: Harcourt Brace Jovanovich, 1976.

Iorizzo, Luciano, and Mondello, Salvatore. *The Italian Americans*. Boston: G. K. Hall, 1980.

Levi, Carlo. *Christ Stopped at Eboli: the Story of a Year.* New York: Farrar, Straus & Giroux, 1963.

Malkiel, Theresa S. *The Diary of a Shirtwaist Striker.* Ithaca, N.Y.: Cornell University Press, 1910.

McClymer, John F. *The Triangle Strike and Fire.* Fort Worth: Harcourt Brace College Publishers, 1998.

A Bintel Brief: Sixty Years of Letters from the Lower East Side to the Jewish Daily Forward, Isaac Metzker, ed. New York: Schocken Books, 1971.

Out of the Sweatshop: The Struggle for Industrial Democracy. Leon Stein, ed. New York: Quadrangle/The New York Times Book Co., 1977.

Stuart, Amanda Mackenzie. *Consuelo and Alva Vanderbilt: The Story of a Daughter and a Mother in the Gilded Age.* New York: HarperCollins Publishers, 2005.

I am very grateful to live in a community with an excellent library system; that gratitude multiplied exponentially while I was researching this book. At one point I came across a mention of a book published in 1919 called *The Italian Emigration of Our Times.* I thought it sounded exactly like what I needed, but assumed it'd be hard to locate. And then I found it on the shelf at the Columbus Metropolitan Library. So was another helpful gem, *Women's Suffrage, Arguments, and Results, 1910-1911,* a collection of brochures actually *from* 1910-11. Perfect!

I also plagued the librarians at the Worthington Libraries for pesky details, and they were always gracious and helpful and patient. I particularly appreciated Ann Badger, of the Northwest Library, calling upon her physics expert brother, Chris, to solve a rather grisly science problem for me to make sure that what I was writing was accurate. And the library's virtual reference room was invaluable.

I owe thanks to many people for this book. I'm very grateful to my editor, David Gale, for suggesting that I write about the Triangle fire in the first place. He, associate editor Alexandra Cooper, and my agent, Tracey Adams, all gave me

AUTHOR'S NOTE

insightful advice on early drafts. I'm also grateful to my family for putting up with me while I was mentally living in another century, and particularly to my children for serving as research assistants on a couple occasions. Dr. Paul Glasser, associate dean of the Max Weinreich Center of the YIVO Institute, very kindly helped me with Yiddish translations. My friend Rosie Azzaro helped me with the Italian and told me about her own family emigrating from Italy to Canada. I owe additional thanks to Christopher James, public affairs officer at New York University, for giving me a tour of the building where the Triangle fire occurred. (It is still standing and is now part of NYU—structurally, it actually was fireproof.) Though the building has been renovated and is very different from the Asch Building of 1911, I was able to look out the windows where the Triangle workers jumped or fell, and see exactly how far down it was to the street. Then it was very eerie to climb to the roof and hear about how NYU employees had stood in that same spot on September 11, 2001, watching as people fell from the World Trade Center. At that moment, the Triangle fire didn't seem very long ago at all.